SUCH A PRETTY, PRETTY GIRL

A Novel by

WINSTON GROOM

Published by Random House Large Print
in association with Random House, Inc.
New York

All rights reserved under International and
Pan-American Copyright Conventions.
Published in the United States of America
by Random House Large Print
in association with Random House, Inc.,
New York, and simultaneously in Canada
by Random House of Canada Limited, Toronto.
Distributed by Random House, Inc., New York.

Library of Congress Cataloging-in-Publication Data
Groom, Winston, 1944–
Such a pretty, pretty girl : a novel / Winston Groom.
p.   cm.
ISBN 0-375-70570-8
1. Large type books.   I. Title.
[PS3557.R56S83   1999b]
813'.54—dc21   98-53876
CIP

Random House Web Address: http://www.randomhouse.com/
Printed in the United States of America
FIRST LARGE PRINT EDITION

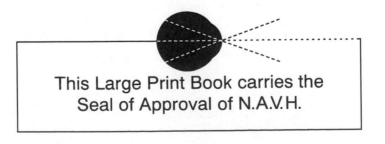

This Large Print Book carries the
Seal of Approval of N.A.V.H.

To Elaine Kaufman,
guardian angel of writers, great and small

SUCH A

PRETTY,

PRETTY

GIRL

CHAPTER 1

IT WAS RAINING in Los Angeles that evening, an omen of some magnitude out here. Sort of like Friday the thirteenth, I imagine, in other places. I saw her as soon as I walked into the bar of the Peninsula Hotel, long strands of lustrous auburn hair barely touching her shoulders, looking fashionable as ever in a navy blue suit. That sudden flush feeling rushed to my cheeks and then down to a pang in my stomach. In some ways it was like stumbling across a snake in the woods. Of course, I'd never exactly thought of Delia that way, although she sure had me snakebit once. She was in deep conversation at a table with two guys and another woman and didn't notice me. I made my way to my table to meet Toby Burr, the movie producer, wondering if one of those two guys was Delia's new husband.

I could tell that this was going to be a power night at the Peninsula, which had in many ways replaced the old bar at the Beverly Hills Hotel after it closed two years for renovations. Groups of producers, directors, actors, and even a genuine movie star or two sat leaning over mahogany tables sipping drinks in the dimly lit room, deep in conspiratorial-looking powwows. The bar itself was loaded two-deep with the usual assortment of Zsa Zsa Gabor look-alikes, and other wannabes or wanna-meets occasionally turning around to scope out the table crowd and decide how to position themselves when a good-looking girl or guy got up to go to the restrooms. It was a ratfuck, but at least some of the right rats were here. Burr was at his usual table in the back by the gas-log fireplace, which flickered invitingly even in summer. As usual, he didn't rise, just stuck out his hand.

"Why, old Johnny, you look a little pale. See a ghost?"

"Maybe I did," I said, sitting down. "See that girl over there?" I nodded discreetly as possible to Delia's table.

"Why," Burr said, peering, as usual, very indiscreetly, "that's Delia Jamison, the TV news babe. What about it?"

I don't know why, but Burr reminded me of Erich von Stroheim in *Sunset Blvd.*

"Old flame," I said. "Haven't seen her in person in maybe fifteen years."

"What, no—still carrying a torch?" Burr asked with great insensitivity, but he was still a good enough friend to get away with it.

"A candle, maybe. She still looks terrific, doesn't she?"

In fact, I hadn't really thought about Delia much during all this time, but some people always affect you no matter what. I'd known Delia in another life almost, but obviously she'd been lurking in the shadows of my "lizard brain," that dark primordial thing at the base of your neck.

"Better even in person," Burr remarked coarsely. "It's refreshing at my time of life to see a truly beautiful woman of, shall we say, 'a certain age.' "

But Burr was right. Delia seemed to get better looking as the years went on. Nearly two decades earlier in New York, when we'd been an item, I remember thinking she was one of those women who would probably "wear well." But then it was over between us and she was gone—until one day, about a year ago when I arrived back out here to start writing another movie, she suddenly resurfaced as lead anchor on a big L.A. network affiliate. Flipping around the dial one night, I was flabbergasted to see her face, looking right at me, as if she were speaking to me, personally, with those deep green eyes twinkling and her wide lush Deborah Norville lips mouthing out some local news story. I didn't catch a word of what she said; just sat there, shocked.

"By the way, Johnny, looks like you could use a drink," Burr offered. He summoned a waitress.

"Thanks," I said. "Just a white wine, please."

"You're not off the scotch, are you?" Burr asked.

"Yep."

"Wonderful. Open a bottle of Sonoma Chardonnay Reserve, ninety-five," Burr told her.

"Must have been quite an affair," Burr observed. "Why didn't I ever hear about it?"

"It was over before your time," I lied. A half lie. By the time I met Burr, the thing had fallen apart, the really passionate part of it, but there had still been some hollerin' left to do.

"You seem a little distracted," Burr said. "Want to go someplace else?"

"No, Toby," I told him. "What's on your mind?"

AN HOUR LATER Toby Burr still wasn't finished with his spiel. I sort of knew what he wanted before this meeting. I was already doing a doctoring job on one of his scripts, but now, as I suspected, he wanted me to do an adaptation of a book he'd bought about some guy who almost loses his wife over a horse race bet. I'd seen in the trades that Toby had acquired the property, a big best-seller by some million-dollar typist. It was the sort of movie I did with Toby years earlier, when I'd just left the newspaper business to come out to Hollywood and make my mark as a screenwriter. Now I'd done that beyond my wildest expectations and I didn't need anymore to do some script about any goddamn horseplayer and his flaky wife. But Toby had given me my start twenty years ago and while I have a lot of faults, ingratitude isn't one of them. I told him to send me the book. It would have been a hell of a lot easier for me to just go to the bookstore near my hotel and buy one, but producers and directors like the idea of having such things delivered over by liveried limo drivers. To motion picture moguls, I suppose they somehow think such gestures make it all more real.

Still sipping on the first glass of wine, I turned slightly to see if Delia was still there. Not only was she, but she was staring directly at *me* with the loveliest expression of astonishment and joy on her face. At least that's what I thought I saw. We locked eyes for a moment and I finally gave a little wave. Not much, barely lifted my hand off the table in recognition, but she picked up on it with a big toothy grin that gave me another stomach pang.

Burr said something and I turned back to listen, but my heart really wasn't in it. For me, seeing Delia again brought to mind old Rick, in *Casablanca,* encountering Ilsa in his establishment for the first time since, well . . .

"Why don't you come up to Santa Barbara with Sarah and me this weekend?" Burr asked. "We could sail up the coast for a bit and talk about the screenplay—that is, after you've read the book."

"I don't think so this weekend, Toby. I've got some cleaning up to do on another project and I have to get back to New York by the end of the month. My doorman's getting tired of walking my dog." I glanced slightly again toward Delia's table and was wrenched to find she suddenly wasn't there, though the others still were.

"You don't want to be in L.A. this weekend, you idiot! It's Labor Day. Nobody stays in town on Labor Day."

"Only us laborers," I said. I had an urge to turn again to see if Delia might have returned. Maybe she had just gone to the ladies' room. . . ."

"I've got a great girl up there I'd like you to meet," Burr was saying. "She's a producer at Warner's. Smart, young, pretty. She just moved in a couple of doors down. Graduated from Smith too," he added gratuitously.

"Does she talk like thihihiss?" I said sarcastically.

I was expecting some equally innocuous retort from Burr; instead his eyes were riveted above and behind me and his mouth was sort of dropped open. At the same time I felt a touch on my shoulder.

I turned a final time and there she was. The great Delia Jamison, in all her five-foot-ten-inch glory. I felt my heart race a little but tried not to show it. Despite what should have been my better judgment, I was genuinely glad to see her.

"Johnny, Johnny," she said in a firm, studied, mid-Atlantic accent I didn't remember as being natural to her. "I can't believe it's really you!"

"You were expecting Al Pacino?" I said stupidly.

"Well," she breathed happily, "I can see you haven't changed a bit." But she smiled broadly and bent down to give me a hug as I tried to rise up politely, and this time I thought she meant it. I honestly did.

"Listen," Delia whispered in my ear, "I have to get back to my table now, but they'll be leaving in a bit. I just can't get over it that you're really here! Can we have a drink when you're finished?"

"Absolutely," I said. "Let's just keep an eye out on one another."

When she had gone, I said to Toby, "Pal, I'm going to need a little privacy in a few minutes. That okay with you?"

"Of course," he said, "although my feelings are quite hurt," and then he leaned across the table and said in a hush, "Look, Johnny, it's probably none of my business, but I can sort of feel this gal is eating at you a little. Trust me like a father. I don't need my screenwriters distracted. Keep your guard up, huh?"

"Sure, Toby," I said, "but it wasn't necessary for you to tell me that." In fact, it was, and afterward I wished he'd put it more strongly.

"So," SHE SAID, "tell me all about you."

Delia had settled into Toby's leather-seated *banc* opposite me and was leaning across with her breasts resting on the tabletop. Even in her conservative suit she was as inviting as I ever remembered. For a moment I thought she was going to reach out and take my hand, but she didn't. Instead she ordered a scotch on the rocks.

"Well, it's been a long time. I wouldn't even know where to start." And that was true. What was it, fourteen, fifteen years now?

"Oh, I know a lot about you already," she said. "I followed you in the papers and television and everywhere. I watched the Academy Awards last year. I was so proud of you, Johnny. I cried when you won."

Another pang. Here was somebody who had once hurt me as bad as I've ever been hurt, and now she's crying when I win some tinhorn statue? But Delia could be that way. There were times, when she wanted to, that she could make you feel like the only man in the world. I reminded myself of that, and also that she was a married woman.

"That was an aberration," I told her disingenuously. Actually, winning that silly little prize was the highlight of my career—at least as a movie writer.

"No, it wasn't," she said. "It was wonderful. Don't say that."

Well, she had my number there again. It seemed like Delia always had my number. She hated bullshit, and she knew it when she saw it. In fact, she had one of the best built-in shit detectors I've ever known, although sometimes it needed to be retuned.

"Well, it didn't hurt my career," I told her, trying to wriggle off the bullshit hook, "or my pocketbook." In fact, on that movie I'd managed against all odds—or at least my talent agency had—to wangle a contract for gross points in the show. Few as they were, I wound up with nearly eight million dollars in royalties. Of course, the IRS stepped in and took their half, but it still left me pretty comfortable.

"Otherwise," I said, "I've been doing okay. Lots of work thrown my way nowadays, but I can pretty much pick and choose now. I'd still like to get into another novel, though. No matter how great it appears on screen, script writing is still hackwork. It's the actors who make it real."

"But what else?" she asked. "It's been how long now—ten years?"

"Fifteen, I think." I wished I hadn't said that the moment it rolled off my tongue.

"So what have you been doing besides working?" Delia asked.

She had a way of always being able to smile when she spoke and it made her quite beautiful and appealing. The smile was sort of downturned, but it was one of the loveliest smiles I can remember. She had a rather long, angular face with high cheekbones and peaches-and-cream skin through which, in sunlight, you could barely see tiny blue veins. A patrician face, even though she came from good, and I'd always assumed, rich, Midwestern stock.

"Not much," I answered.

"What about women?" she said. "Are you . . . ?"

"I was for a while. It lasted about three years. She was a decorator in New York, but, well, I guess I could blame it on business, but that's probably not it. I guess it was my fault. Too much social life, I suppose."

"Well, as I remember, you were always pretty social," Delia said.

She was, or at least she had been, paradoxical about all that herself. Even though she had grown up in Kansas City, I'd understood she came from a pretty social background, private schools and so on; from that old-line stock whose principal activities always seemed to revolve around money, horses, and an expertise in ballroom dancing—even if it was Midwest style. But Delia wasn't always into that. She was a product of an era when, even among those hometown girls I knew, shunning a formal debut became the "in" thing to do. Sure, she could dress up and go to cocktail parties and dances with the best of them, and half the guys at the New York Racquet Club, or the Brooke or the Century, slathered over her. But she often blew all that off. It was my impression in those days that with the kind of dough her family had, she could have ridden in limousines, but, in New York, when I knew her, she'd usually take the bus or subway, and not even cabs except at night. Good old Midwestern practicality maybe. And intriguing.

"I don't do much social stuff anymore," I told her. And at least that was true. I'd sort of had my fill of it. I kept a place in New York—sometimes I wondered why—but I preferred my other home up in the mountains of Virginia, a private and beautiful spot where the trout fishing and grouse shooting were superb. As a southerner, I certainly felt more at home there than in L.A. or New York and would parole myself as much as possible to go south again.

"Do you still have your place in New York?" Delia asked, as if she was reading my mind.

"Not the one you'd remember."

"So where do you live there now?"

"At the Carlyle," I told her.

"Oh no," she laughed. "You've become so fashionable!" I couldn't tell if she was kidding or not.

"And so what kind of car are you driving now?" she asked.

I knew she'd asked that because when we'd been seeing each other in the old days I drove a gigantic red Cadillac sedan that my friends referred to as the Pimpmobile—this while everyone else our age had the politically correct small cars that became popular after the gas crisis of the late 1970s.

"A Mercedes," I told her.

"Oh, Johnny," she said, laughing again. "I'm disappointed in you. I thought you'd always be kind of different."

"Well," I said, "if it's any consolation, this Mercedes is special and, for what it's worth, it's *bigger* than the Cadillac."

Delia kept laughing about how I was a Mercedes man now and it was still the great laugh I remembered. Somehow I was getting more comfortable with the conversation. She had put me at ease, and I had already forgotten what Toby had told me, as if we had simply picked up where we left off all those years ago.

"So now, tell me about yourself. I'm tired of talking about me," I said.

"Why don't we save 'me' for another time," Delia said. "I've got to get back to the studio for the eleven o'clock news."

Just then one of the white-jacketed bellmen passed by our table carrying a brass pole with a white cardboard sign on which was written, DELIA JAMISON.

"Oops," she said, "I guess I'd better find out what this is." She got up and headed for the phone at the end of the bar.

Whoever it was, the conversation was quick, but when Delia returned she was ashen and glanced around nervously as she sat down, as though she expected something or someone she didn't want to see.

"I have to go," she said.

"Is something wrong?"

"No."

"Are you sure? You look a little upset."

"No, no . . . well, yes, in a way, but I can't talk about it."

"Hey, Delia, are you—"

"I just have to go, Johnny. Maybe we can talk about it later. Maybe dinner or something—give me a call at the station, okay?"

"Sure," I replied, "but uh, what about your husband? I mean, I read that little story on you last year in *Los Angeles* magazine. It said you'd been recently married." The notion of that gave me another pang— the wrong kind.

"Brad? Oh, he's in San Francisco. He—I mean we—live there. That's where we met, when I was working for WQSF. He owns a company that builds computer software. But then this TV anchor job opened here and I just couldn't turn it down. We commute one place or the other on weekends, but my weeknights are usually free." She smiled, and yet I thought there was a wistful tone in her voice. But she still seemed overwrought, and kept glancing uneasily around the room.

"Delia, are you sure nothing's wrong?"

She took a breath and said to me in a steely way, "It's something a little scary, but I honestly can't talk about it right now. Give me a call," she said, rising majestically. "If you want to."

I got up also. "Can I see you to your car?"

"No, they'll bring it around to the front. Thanks, Johnny. I'll talk to you later." She kissed me on the cheek and gave me a little society hug and then made her way across the lounge. A few heads turned, but Delia was oblivious.

CHAPTER 2

MY NAME IS John Drayton Lightfoot. I was raised in a small town on the coast of North Carolina, where they used to call me Lightning, but nobody ever does anymore except old childhood pals. My family is in the rice business. We buy it, package it, and sell it under the Lightfoot label and have made a pretty good living out of it for four generations. I, however, am the black sheep of the family, or was until recently, when the Academy Awards were announced.

After college at Chapel Hill, and a two-year stint in the army, I got into the newspaper business, which to my father and grandfather and uncles was not a re-spectable occupation. Often I felt that way myself. Who wants to go around at daybreak to the grieving family of a strangled child and beat on their door for a newspaper quote? But after serving that apprentice-ship, I found myself covering more august subjects in Washington and then New York and I finally wound up with a column in a fairly respectable paper. Still, that wasn't enough. I wanted to become a novelist, which in those days I ignorantly thought was an exalted profession. It is not, at least no more than most professions performed honestly and with diligence.

In any case, I got into the screen-writing business on a fluke. A fellow I met in New York at Elaine's Restaurant was a very well known television screenwriter. He was an older guy and one night under the influence of strong spirits asked if I'd help him with a series he was doing, a fictionalized account of the mob. I said sure. It was an eight-part thing and he gave me a couple of segments to research and write and he was as good and stern a mentor for script writing as I've ever known. And then, right in the middle of it all, he died.

Nobody at the network knew what to do. The project was half finished and there was a lot of money already tied up. The network people asked what I had written. I showed them and they were impressed and agreed I had a grasp of the story and a knack for dialogue and drama and so they hired me on to finish it. It won three Emmys and I was off and rolling.

Other projects came along and finally a movie, which got a lot of praise and turned me into a veritable movie nut. I'd stay up all night for a good old movie or rent them on video. Over the years I've probably seen every decent film ever made and I guarantee you, they don't make 'em like they used to. Meantime, I was still trying to write my novel and when it was finally published it got generally good notice, including one from *The New York Times,* and became what they called a critical success, which is a publishing euphemism for commercial flop, and so I went back to script writing.

That's how I met Delia.

At a New Year's Eve party that a very famous screenwriter throws every year in his Central Park West apartment—there were dozens of bigwigs there. The actors and actresses were all stars and the producers and directors were top-drawer. If a bomb had gone off in the place, it would have taken Hollywood five years to recover.

I was standing by the bar waiting for a scotch and soda, my drink of choice in those days, when she came up to me.

"Hi," she said, "aren't you the writer?"

"Guilty as charged," I said.

"I saw your picture in a *Times* review of your book a few months ago. I've been meaning to get it."

Now that seemed a pretty straightforward come-on, and this girl was a lot more than just "not hard to look at." Drop-dead gorgeous. I'm tall, but she was too—I'd have guessed nearly six feet in high heels. And she was slender, with incredibly long legs. "Good wheels," we used to say in those days. She had dark green eyes, almost like jade, and long auburn hair done up in a kind of queue around her head and was wearing red pants and a white silk blouse that didn't quite contain her. A nice package. Those were the times before the boob jobs everybody in L.A.'s got now, and so I never questioned their veracity as I would these days.

But what impressed me most was the boldness in

her poise. Most girls in those days, at least the ones I met, didn't have much of it, by which I mean they'd never think of going right up to a guy and making a pass. They might have positioned themselves to be passed at, but Delia wasn't shy, which later figured big in what eventually happened between us. And then there were her smarts. She'd read the ringing review of my book in the *Times* but chose instead to bring up the criticism of it in the *New York Review of Books,* where as usual they took it apart and tried to resurrect it again, without success. I hate talking about reviews, but somehow she made me, and we wound up in a discussion about it.

"Do you think they were right to say you 'glorified' the war in Vietnam?" she asked.

"No, but everybody's entitled to his opinion. It wasn't particularly glorified when I was there." I was only five or six years older than her, but she almost made me feel I was talking with a far more sophisticated woman.

"But they complained you'd chosen the 'traditional' way to write about it," Delia said, "like all the other novels on wars, World War One, World War Two."

"Yeah, well, I didn't have a pipeline into nouveau writing then. Still don't. I took a hundred seventy-two boys over there and brought back a hundred fifty-nine alive. I suppose that's the best I could do and I wrote it the way I saw it."

She looked at me for a long moment and then smiled. "Book reviewers can be pissy, can't they?"

"I suppose so," I said, "especially when they all think they're Edmund Wilsons."

I think in that moment it was cinched. There was an immediate connection that seemed unbreakable. I noticed what I took to be her date craning his neck in a doorway, trying to figure out whether to come over and break this up. Delia saw that coming too and said to me quickly, "It's D. H. Jamison on East Seventieth. Only one in the book." And then she was gone.

I waited the obligatory couple of days, then phoned her. By this time New York was gripped in the depths of winter. The streets were a soggy mush of ice and slush, and stepping off a curbing often as not sank you ankle-deep in ice water. A rotten city. I fixed myself a scotch and dialed Delia's number. A machine answered, so I left a message, laid a fire in the fireplace, and got into the shower. I was toweling off when the phone rang.

"Johnny," said a commanding feminine voice. "It's Delia Jamison." I was in heaven.

NEXT EVENING THE two of us were having dinner at P. J. Clarke's, which was a pretty interesting place in those days. I wasn't sure Delia was ready for Elaine's yet. Too many distractions, including, I figured, wolves who might have been pals of mine but who, I knew, would be circling around her in case nothing worked out. P.J.'s was more a sports figures restaurant and they served up the best hamburgers in town. Besides, for at least this first night, I wanted her all to myself.

Turned out she wanted to become an editor and was taking a few journalism courses in college. That evening I think I fell in love, but of course that's impossible on such short notice. There were no dents or chinks or missing parts, so far as I could tell that night. She was quick to pick up on everything and seemed supremely fascinated with me and my life and, for that matter, life in general. Toward the end of the evening, with some trepidation, I told her: "Listen, this is a miserable town this time of year. I'm thinking about going out to Bermuda for a few days. Want to come along?"

Her eyes looked puzzled for a moment; she was obviously studying the proposition. She certainly knew what it probably would entail.

"Look," I added hastily, "if you're thinking what I think you're thinking, don't worry. I don't chase girls around couches. The studio heads do that better. You can do what you want to do and have a separate room."

"When?" she asked.

"Soon as I can make the arrangements."

WHEN I WALKED up to my suite in the Peninsula that night I was both tired and energized. I didn't know quite what to make of Delia's sudden reappearance in my life, or her seemingly inviting demeanor. On the one hand, she was a former lover sitting in a cozy bar with me, living five hundred miles apart from her husband, and when I'd asked how married life was treating her, she'd not replied, "Oh, it's so wonderful, I am so blissfully happy," but instead merely, "Well it's different than I expected." Nor did I know what to make of the mysterious phone call that seemed to get her so upset. Was it something from work? From past experience I knew Delia was subject to over-reaction, but in this case she'd seemed clearly anx-ious, almost frightened. Anyway, she'd indicated that she might tell me about it later and this certainly gave me an excuse to call her.

The rain still pattered outside. My balcony doors were open and the rain had slickened its tile floor. A freak Pacific storm. I turned on the tube and there she was, looking right at me. I bet she knew I was watch-ing. It was a pretty masterful performance, as such things go on local television. She had a firm and im-posing presence that was to be believed and her voice was pleasant, but clipped with an impression of ur-gency. Just the right mix for drawing and holding the millions of viewers her affiliate had in Los Angeles.

After the broadcast I lay down on my bed and tried reading a magazine. I barely got started when the phone rang.

"Johnny, it's me," she said. "I just got off the air."

"Yes," I said. "I know. I just watched you."

"Did you?" she said, as though that revelation touched her deeply.

"You're very good."

"I was wondering," she said, "would you like to have dinner or something next Tuesday?"

"Well, sure," I answered. Like I said, Delia was anything but shy. I told her I'd call her at the studio Tuesday afternoon after Labor Day. I went to bed wondering what the "or something" might be.

I SPENT LABOR Day weekend in kind of a daze. I was trying to fix up Toby Burr's script for Fox that somebody else had botched. I could see all sorts of things wrong with it, but my instructions from Burr were to "write up the girl," meaning that they needed more strong scenes and dialogue for the female lead so they could get a higher-class actress interested in taking the part. That's Hollywood for you.

Burr was right, of course. L.A. was stone-cold dead on the holiday, but I enjoyed walking around in what had finally become the interminable sunshine again. I walked down to Rodeo Drive, which is right around the corner. The stores were mostly closed and I had a sandwich at an outdoor café and walked some more. There were all sorts of extravagant display windows to look in. I came to one toward the end of the street that contained some antique jewelry I found exquisite. I've never liked new jewelry. The old stuff has character and workmanship.

It all of a sudden reminded me of Delia and the time that I'd bought her a gold bracelet years ago when we were still an item. From her reaction, looking back on it now, I think that was the beginning of the end for us—at least in her mind. It had been near Delia's birthday in early May and on impulse I'd stopped at the window of a fashionable jeweler on New York's Madison Avenue where I saw the bracelet on display. It wasn't exorbitant. I didn't give exorbitant gifts to women then. Don't now, for that matter. But it was lavish enough, an antique with elegant engraving. She opened the little gift-wrapped box over dinner at Le Cirque, where I'd taken her for her birthday.

"Oh, Johnny, I can't accept this," she said.

I thought she was kidding, but she wasn't.

"It's much too much."

"No, it isn't," I told her. "It'll look fabulous on you."

"You're sweet, but I just don't take expensive presents," she said, putting the bracelet back in its box and gently pushing it across the table to my side.

"But why?" I asked, bewildered. "Besides, it isn't that expensive."

"It's expensive enough. I've found expensive presents always come with a price."

"What price?"

"I just can't take it," she said firmly.

The rest of dinner was strained, at least for me. Ironically, Delia had somehow managed to make me feel cheap, even though the cost of the bracelet wasn't much more than the price of the meal I would be paying for in a few minutes. It wasn't until months later that I realized the gesture might actually have initiated our breakup, which was soon to come. Apparently, in her way of thinking, I'd crossed the line.

I stood there awhile under the brilliant California sun, pondering all these memories in front of the jewelry store on Rodeo Drive, then marched straight back to the Peninsula and got to work "writing up the girl."

Tuesday rolled around all too slowly. In the afternoon I dialed her TV station and Delia was on the line shortly.

"Would you like to come to me," I asked, "or meet someplace?"

"Whatever you want," she said. "Where're we going?"

"Tell you the truth, I haven't really thought about it," I said. "Why don't you come to me." That wasn't the truth. I'd thought about it all right; I just hadn't decided. I didn't want to take her to Spago or Morton's or the Ivy or someplace where I'd be sure to be recognized. In New York, almost nobody recognizes me, except maybe at Elaine's, but out here, after the Academy thing, I was pretty well known and people would be dropping by the table all evening and maybe even the gossip columnists would get into the act. In my monumental stupidity it had not occurred to me that Delia herself was one of the most well known faces in the entire Los Angeles area and if anyone was going to be recognized, it would probably be her.

"About seven-thirty?" she asked.

"Fine. Just ring my room and I'll meet you downstairs."

"Okeey-dokeey," she said, tantalizingly drawing the words out.

AT SEVEN-THIRTY ON the dot my phone rang. The desk said she was here. That surprised me a little because in the old days Delia was habitually late. Perhaps the news business had finally made her punctual. She was standing in the lobby when I got off the elevator, wearing an attractively conservative white skirt with a gray blouse and green jacket. She had an Hermes scarf around her neck. At least I think it was Hermes because that's what everybody out here wears. Wouldn't be caught dead in an Armani scarf.

"You don't have a car out here, do you?" she asked.

"Yes, I rent one. It's in the garage. I'll get them to bring it around."

"Why don't we go in mine?" she said. "It's right out here." She pointed to a dark green BMW convertible parked on the brick pavement next to the hotel's Rolls.

"Sure," I said, and we got in. It occurred to me I'd never ridden in a car Delia drove before. When I knew her, she hadn't even owned one, and now I understood why. Closest comparison I could make would be with a stoned cyclo driver in Bangkok. I directed her to a little Italian bistro I knew off Santa

Monica Boulevard. It was dark inside and as they led us to a table in the back, only a few people seemed to recognize Delia and they didn't seem like the sort to come up to our table. I ordered a bottle of red wine and Delia ordered a Manhattan on the rocks. Then I pulled out a cigarette and lit it—another filthy habit I'd been unable to kick entirely over the years. Mostly I smoke cigars, but the authorities, with their sanctimonious desire to control everybody's lives, forbid them in restaurants, preferring instead that patrons smell the stink of tobacco floor-sweepings over the aroma of an eight-dollar, aged Cuban broadleaf.

"May I have one?" Delia asked.

"Of course, I'm sorry," I said. "Do you still smoke?"

"Every once in a while."

"So," I said, "you were going to tell me about yourself tonight." I had decided to let her bring up the subject of the mysterious phone call in her own good time.

"Wellll," she began, again drawing out her words as though she was trying to think of where to begin. "After, ah, well, after we stopped seeing each other, I got a job at a fashion magazine—as an assistant to one of the editors. Actually, it was a nowhere job. All it meant was that I was dressing up the models, and then—"

"Oh, I remember that," I interrupted. "We were still seeing a little of each other then, I think. I remember you telling me about that."

Indeed she had. After our third or fourth breakup,

Delia would come back into my life from time to time. I still recall it as a painful memory that lasted several years.

But our little winter fling in Bermuda had turned out to be a treasured time, I thought, in both our lives. My family owns a house there and has for generations. It's on a windswept cliff on the ocean near the Coral Beach Club. Bermuda is not far off the coast of the Carolinas and before the days of planes you could leave by ship from Wilmington or Charleston and be there in a day. At that time of year Bermuda, at its longitude, can still be chilly—and it was, but nothing to compare with New York. The days were sunny and the highs in the sixties and nights were cool and we built fires and looked out over the sea.

That first night we just stayed up and talked and I found out a little of her background and she mine. At one point she mentioned almost casually that she didn't really like dating southern men.

"You never can tell what they're thinking," she said.

At the time I didn't think much of it, but later I discovered that Delia was a fairly suspicious person and the remark was telling.

Another thing was that she hadn't gotten along with her father, though he had died some years earlier. The reasons for the break were never made clear, but it was a little perturbing because in the past I'd dated several girls who had relationship problems with their fathers and to a one they were very unstable people. But otherwise she seemed so sweet and smart and forthright, I simply forgot about it as we sat by the fire and got to know each other.

In the morning she came out of her bedroom as I was squeezing orange juice. We had a local cook we used when the family was there, but I hadn't called her. I had the makings of breakfast on the counter, bread for toast, eggs for frying, sausage, and so on. I thought she would help, but she didn't offer. Somehow I'd liked the idea of us fixing breakfast together. It would have given it a sort of homey touch.

Finally, as she was relaxing in a lounge chair and I went about the cooking, Delia said, "Oh, by the way, I'd help you, but I don't cook."

"No?" I asked.

"Never learned. I've tried a few times and always make a mess. You're better off without me."

First woman I'd ever met who not only admitted she couldn't cook, but wouldn't even try. Somehow I found this intriguing. She wasn't entirely undomesticated, however. At one point she noticed I had a button missing from my shirt and sewed one back on for me.

That afternoon we went for a walk along the beach and presently some riders on horseback appeared ahead of us.

"If you'd like to ride," I said, "Coral Beach has stables."

"I'd love it," she said. "I grew up on horses."

We walked on. The sun was warm and Delia took

off her blue pullover and wrapped it around her waist. In a while we came to a little cove in the cliffs that was out of the wind.

"I'd like to lie down and get some sun," she said. "Is that okay?"

We found a spot in the sand and Delia lay back with her head resting on a big rock, her eyes closed, facing up at the bright sun. I lay beside her for a long while. She might have been asleep, but I don't think so. I watched her face, serene as a child's. At one point she yawned and stretched and I turned over so that I was right beside her and kissed her lightly on the cheek.

"You know," I said, "I'd like to make love to you tonight."

There was a moment of silence. She never opened her eyes but gave a little murmur that was definitely not a no and had all the appearances of being a yes.

CHAPTER 3

A WAITER HAD TAKEN our order as Delia and I continued our catching up. I got the veal piccata, which I knew to be quite good, and she went for the beef tenderloin, which seemed odd in an Italian place, but Delia was always a little different. Maybe more than a little. Anyway, we were still talking about her career at the fashion magazine.

"Actually, I hated it," she said.

Turns out that her duties were pretty mundane, helping out on fashion shoots, getting the models ready, and, besides, it was kind of a sexist place. Always a little shy about her looks in public, Delia had taken to wearing sort of baggy clothes to disguise her figure, and one day the woman she worked for remarked about this.

"She said, 'You know, you ought to dress more, well, in "style".' That's what she told me," Delia said.

Now, knowing Delia as I do—at least as I did—I could have guessed what her reaction would have been, and I was right. She had been furious. But judging from the way she seemed now, she'd probably just have ignored it these days. There was a lot more poise I saw, and balance, and I didn't see any of the old uncertainty. What the hell did I expect, though— that time stood still for nearly twenty years?

The magazine experience was about the time of my last fling with Delia. By that time we had long since ceased being a couple, but during those years she would waltz into my life every six months or so; we'd have a day or two of fun and sex and then she'd disappear again. When I asked her on some of those occasions if she was involved with anybody, she'd sometimes answer, "Well, actually I am, sort of." This, for me, of course, was the equivalent to a sharp blow to the stomach, but Delia always prided herself on being completely honest. Those were the times when I figured that if they gave out prizes for brutal honesty, she'd take first place every time. Experiences like this later made me realize Delia had a kind of emotional detachment I hadn't credited her with when we were seriously involved. But things are often not what they seem and, as it turned out, neither was she.

After the fashion magazine she'd drifted into free-lance jobs and then one day decided to take some advice I had given her years earlier. I always thought she'd be perfect for the broadcast business. She had the smarts for journalism, I knew—because it was a structured thing. She sometimes talked about writing fiction, but I never believed she'd make it there. Delia was one of those people who accept the rules dispassionately and play by them, but you can't write good novels like that. You have to break the rules—all of them, if necessary, and her strident honesty would get in the way with all that. Newspapers were of course an option, but why waste those looks on newspapers—and, for that matter, her voice—I told her. It was perfectly seductive and commanding at the same time. Television was groaning for bright, beautiful talent, but she'd never seemed interested, even though I'd offered to make some introductions.

Eventually, though, that's what she did. First she got a job on a local radio affiliate part-time; then they hired her on staff after a few months and within a year she was on air as a reporter. I was in California much of this time and never knew any of this. One thing led to another and after a few years she somehow got on with a television station in Chicago, where she was an instant success. Finally she made it to the evening anchor desk in San Francisco. And now she was sitting across from me in Los Angeles, the top market in the nation.

"My steak is chewy," she said, poking her fork at the piece of beef as if it was a dead rat.

I called the maître d' over and she repeated the complaint. He was sympathetic, asking if she wanted another steak.

"No, no," she said. "I think I'll have the chicken." He shrugged and headed toward the kitchen. I didn't say anything. Delia could be difficult that way. Most women I knew would have let the thing go, but Delia wasn't most women. In fact, it was kind of sexy in a way.

All night I'd been terribly ambivalent about my immediate feelings toward her. All night—hell, for the past week—I had been, and felt all those dark clouds of tension building up again just as they had in the old days. Suddenly I just didn't have anything to say. My mind was drifting as I finished my veal.

She obviously sensed the silence and so leaned over and said, "Johnny, ask me a question."

"What question?" I said.

"Any question."

"Okay, who's buried in Grant's Tomb?" I replied dumbly. I didn't know what she meant.

"No, no, just a question. You look like your mind is someplace else."

"Are you happy?"

"Yeah, I suppose so," she said. "I guess I've got whatever it is I wanted."

I nodded. "Yes, I suppose you do."

We locked eyes for a long moment. My mind was racing. I had already noticed she wasn't wearing any wedding rings. The past week had been a jumble of emotions. There was obviously a part of me that was still hooked on Delia, though my better judgment kept telling me don't get stuck on that tar baby again. Then, suddenly, the filter in my brain that culls out what I say from what I am thinking went on the blink.

"Have you even seen the play *Same Time Next Year*?" I asked.

"No," she said. "I've heard of it."

The instant I asked that I wished I hadn't. But I had, and there was nothing left but to forge ahead.

"It's about a couple who've been lovers for years and they're both married to other people. But they never wanted to give up each other entirely, and so every year they meet for a romantic weekend someplace. That's the theme of the play—that the one weekend together is enough for them."

Delia absorbed this for a moment. "Oh God, Johnny, is *that* how you think of *us*?"

I backtracked. "Well, no, no, not exactly,"

"Then why did you ask it?"

"I don't know. You said to ask you a question and I did," I said. "It was just on my mind for some reason. Anyhow, in the play they decided to part ways for good. That's the end of the story."

Delia asked for another cigarette. "Can I talk to you about something, Johnny?" she said. I noticed that her brow was furrowed and there was a serious expression on her face, but even in seriousness she was beautiful.

"Of course," I said.

She hesitated a moment. "I'm not sure where to start. A few months ago, at the station, I began getting these, these . . . letters." She said the word *letters* as though she had a mouth full of dirt.

"What kind of letters?" I asked.

"I don't know," she said. "I mean, I don't know exactly what they mean."

"What are they about?"

"Well, they're . . . very explicit. They're embarrassing. They're . . . horrible."

I could see she was clearly upset.

"What do they say?" I asked.

"They . . . they say all sorts of things. Very personal things."

"Who are they from—I mean, from the same person?"

"Yes, I'm pretty sure they are."

"Pretty sure . . . ? How many have you gotten?"

"Five."

"Well, what's the purpose? I mean, do they want something?"

"I'm not sure."

"And they are addressed to you, personally?"

"Yes."

"At the station."

"Yes."

"Are they like crank letters or something?"

"Well, yes and no. I mean, I think they're from somebody I once knew."

"Who?"

"I don't know."

The waiter appeared at the table with Delia's chicken and put it before her.

"Why don't you go ahead and eat," I said. "We can still talk."

She cut a piece of the chicken and put a forkful into her mouth.

"It's overcooked," she said.

"Oh no," I groaned. "Well, we can send that back too."

"No, no. Don't bother. I'm not hungry anymore,"

she said. "Besides, I don't eat much anyway. I had my salad."

I poured her some more wine. "Well, are these letters threatening?"

"I'm not exactly sure of that, either," she said. "I mean, no explicit threats have been made, but the implication is there."

"Have you told anybody about this—I mean, at the station?"

"No."

"Why not?"

"Because they're so embarrassing. They'd want to call the police. And then the police would want to see the letters. And then somebody at the police would in all probability leak them to the press—you know the tabloids pay people in the police for tips—and pretty soon it would be all over everywhere."

"Have you told your husband?"

"Yes—sort of. I didn't tell him about the letters. I told him they were phone calls."

"Phone calls?"

"If I told him about the letters, he'd want to see them. I just couldn't have that. And I really wasn't lying, because there have been phone calls, too."

"Well who . . . what do they say?"

"Just a couple, and it's some guy, I think, but the voice seems disguised. I haven't the faintest idea. They're very brief, just a sentence or two."

"Was that one of them, at the bar the other night?"

"Yes."

"But how did he know you were there?"

"That's what scared me so much. But then I remembered that I'd left the number where I'd be on my voice mail. I do that a lot when I'm away from the office. So I guess he could have been anywhere. He phoned me at the station and got that number off my voice mail."

"Well, what did he want?"

"He wanted to know if I'd gotten his last letter."

"Had you?"

"I'm not sure, because the latest one I got came about ten days ago."

"So what did you say to him?"

"I hung up."

"And what did the letter say?"

"Uggh . . ."

"That bad, huh?"

"Well, they're—yes, they are—they are very explicit. About, well, my personal life, my sex life. About how I am."

"What did your husband say?"

"He was upset, of course. He said we should tell the station and go to the police."

"So?"

"I can't. Because then the police would want to tap into all my calls. I'd have no privacy, and besides, he's smart enough not to talk but a few seconds, so there'd be no time to trace the calls."

"And you have no idea what this person wants?"

"No, not really. I mean, it's all sort of veiled. But in the last one, it said that I was to . . . to wear an open jacket and to unbutton the two top buttons of my blouse during the last break before the end of the broadcast and . . ."

"And?"

". . . lean over just a little before I was off camera."

"Jesus," I said. "And what if you didn't?"

"Well, it was like . . . there was nothing special threatened. It just sort of ordered me to do it."

"Did you?"

She paused for a moment, looked troubled, and took a sip of wine.

"Yes. I didn't know what else to do. I was afraid."

"Of what?"

"Of somehow those letters getting out. Or their contents, or whatever."

"Getting out where?"

"I don't know, Johnny—the press, the media. I think this person has some plan, something he hasn't revealed yet."

"How do you know it's a he?"

"Because of what's in the letters. It's obvious he knows a lot about me. About . . . about the way I make love. He's got everything in there."

"I thought you made love beautifully," I said, but of course that observation didn't come out right and I thought I saw a flash of shock in Delia's eyes.

"What I meant was," I said, trying to recover—I always seemed to be trying to explain or recover or backtrack in my conversations with Delia—"that in my recollection there wasn't anything, well . . . unnatural with you."

Actually, I wasn't sure. Our lovemaking back in the old days was hammer and tongs and there was practically nothing she couldn't or wouldn't do and a lot of it was probably still cited in the criminal statutes of various states.

"But your husband, though," I continued. "I know you told him about calls, but how does he feel about it all?"

"Brad is upset, like I said. I told him I don't want to go to the police. He doesn't really understand, but Brad's got this friend—Rick Olsen. Maybe his best friend. He owns a big detective agency. It's nationwide. Years ago he was head of security at Brad's business and they got to be really close. Rick's offices are here in Los Angeles now. Brad told him about the phone calls and Rick talked to me and he's trying to figure something out. But, you see, it won't work, because he thinks they're phone calls—not letters."

"Did you tell him what was in the phone calls?"

"Not exactly—I was vague."

"Did you tell him about unbuttoning your blouse?"

"No."

"Why?"

"I was ashamed."

I noticed a tear beginning to form in Delia's left eye. She brushed it away with her hand. We sat looking at each other for a long moment. It suddenly occurred to me this was the first time since I had known her that I had ever seen her cry.

"What are you going to do?" I finally asked.

"I don't know. Wait, I guess."

"For the next letter?"

She was silent and took a puff of her cigarette.

"I hate these things," she said, snuffing it out half finished.

"Is there something I can do?" I asked.

"I don't know. I really don't, Johnny. Its just that when I saw you the other night, I . . . I felt, well, a kind of security. A kind of strength. I didn't have anybody to talk to about this. To really talk to, and I remembered that you've got such a good take on things. I don't know why I brought it up to you, though. There's nothing you can do. I'll have to figure it out. . . ."

"Well, maybe, maybe not," I said. "Look, do you have *any* notion at all who might be behind this?"

"No, except that it would probably have to be somebody I slept with. And not just for a night. I mean, somebody who knew me pretty well."

"I guess then I'd have to let my journalistic instincts guide me," I said. "Can you tell me how many people we're talking about? I mean, there's got to be some way to narrow it down."

This obviously upset her more and she shook her head. "I don't know—I mean, look, I was single for more than twenty . . ."

"When did you have your first lover?" I asked. I knew it was probably brutal, but it was a beginning.

"I was eighteen," she said softly. "But it wouldn't

have been him. This person—I mean, these letters, are sophisticated. They were written by someone who is very . . . worldly, very refined."

"Well, if you were eighteen, that was more than twenty years ago, wasn't it? So that person is twenty-odd years older now too. Maybe he's gotten worldly and refined during that time."

"No, no. It wouldn't be him. It would be somebody I knew later. I think somebody I knew for a longer period of time. Maybe in New York. Or Chicago."

"Not San Francisco?"

"I was only there six months before I met Brad. But of the other men, it wouldn't be all of them. It could only possibly be about half of them—even less, I think."

"Why's that?"

"Because of what was said in the letters."

"And how many is that?"

"Well, eight—ten maybe."

I cleared my throat and nodded. "There's something I don't understand here," I told her. "You say it's probably somebody you knew in New York, or Chicago—all back east. But if he's giving you instructions about what to wear and what to do on the air, he's got to be watching you here in L.A.—right?"

"Yes, I've thought about that."

"Well, are any of those guys you have in mind—do you know if any of them are living here now? Or do they spend time out here?"

"No. I mean, if that's so, I don't know about it."

"So it's got to be somebody then who's here—or

able to watch you here—but who you met back east? That's kind of strange."

"I know, but the letters are real. He's out there somewhere, Johnny, I assure you."

My stomach pangs had returned full force. The most irrational thought I could have ever had, of course, was that I'd been the only one.

"Listen," I said, "I've got a little time on my hands now. Let me think about it. Things like this can be figured out. Maybe you're too close to it."

I reached out and took her hand, which was resting on the table. I honestly didn't do it because it was obvious she was vulnerable right now, I did it because I knew she was upset and scared and I felt sorry for her. I wasn't sure what I could do, or how I could do it, but she was clearly in distress and I wanted to help.

"No matter what happens with any of this," I said, "it's not going to be the end of the world. He'll probably get tired of it after a while."

She didn't resist my taking her hand, but after a brief moment she withdrew it.

"It's getting late," she said. "I've got to get back to the studio."

I called for the check.

"I'll be watching you myself tonight," I said. "Do something nice for me. I promise I won't write you any letters."

She smiled, but I could tell she didn't really appreciate the last remark.

CHAPTER 4

T HAT NIGHT I went home more confused than
ever. It was my impression Delia's marriage was
not a thing of overwhelming bliss, and yet she had
parried every move or hint I made toward a reunion
between us of more than platonic dimensions. In my
later life I have developed two rules: First, never con-
fuse fantasy with reality and, second, always understand the consequences of what you do. As rules go,
they have saved me a lot of trouble. It concerned me
now that I might be on the verge of violating them
both.

There would have been times, years before, when
I would have told her to go screw herself if she had
come to me with her problems. She had toyed with
my feelings then—if not deliberately, at least care-
lessly, which might have been worse. Time heals
many things, though, and the wounds are gone now.
The scars, however, are still there.

I lay in bed pondering Delia's dilemma. The obvious thing to me was that whoever was sending
the letters most likely lived in the L.A. TV-viewing
area—if for nothing else, to see what she did or didn't

do. And yet she'd indicated that the culprit was somebody she'd known back East. Anyway, I made a mental note to ask her to get me a chart of the entire broadcast area—to its farthest reaches.

There was a possibility, of course, that Delia was being stalked. That someone from her past had not only gone to the trouble to track her down but was following her around. That was the scariest notion. Could have been the creep hadn't learned she was at the Peninsula from her voice mail after all, but had followed her there and placed his call from the hotel lobby phone booth. He might even have been among those dozens of Italian-suited lounge lizards standing at the bar, watching her reaction afterward. That's what they like, isn't it? The reaction? On the other hand, I could picture him in some cheap hotel room, sitting in the dark, glaring at her image on a television screen, getting off on the idea of writing her dirty letters and relishing the thought of upsetting her with them. And more, getting off on the notion of being able to control her, to get her to do his bidding sexually—at present, just little things such as unbuttoning a couple of buttons on her blouses. But later, what? Anyone who would go to all this trouble would probably have greater things in mind, especially now that he saw she was taking him seriously. It occurred to me to suggest to Delia that her husband get his detective-agency friend to provide her a bodyguard. But, of course, that would make a mess of any plans I might have had about her.

And maybe the letter writer wasn't sitting in a dirty

hotel room at all. He might have been sitting in the room next door to me, or at the Beverly Hills, or the Bel Air. There were wide possibilities. And another thing came to me. Where were these letters postmarked? Were they from L.A.? It was stupid of me not to have thought to ask that right off the bat.

It was eleven o'clock and I flipped on the television to Delia's station. There she was, looking just as I had left her an hour or so earlier. She went through her broadcast in the professional way I had seen before, but this time I noticed that when she spoke on TV she slowed down her words. Over the years some diction coach must have gotten her in tow. Delia talked fast in person and I always believed it was because she didn't think before saying things. It was her version of "honesty," to just let it all pour out.

I watched for some little something at the end of the broadcast that I'd jokingly suggested she do for me. For a moment I almost wished she'd unbutton those top buttons and lean over, but that was gross of me. This was no time for kidding around. Then, just as she signed off, I saw her look into the camera and give a tiny, almost imperceptible wink. At least I thought I did.

FOR THE NEXT two days I had a bunch of stupid meetings with the studio people on my schedule, all of whom were clamoring for my services. There were breakfast meetings here at the Peninsula or at the

Beverly Hills, lunches at the Ivy, dinners at Spago or Morton's or Mortimer's or wherever.

Then there was also the task of "writing up the girl" for the Warner's script. The "girl" in the present story was sort of cardboard—a prop that the protagonist could have a sex scene or two with to ensure that teenagers would buy tickets to the movie. Her only function was to look pretty and be a sounding board for the hero. Movie heroes always need somebody to talk to about their situations because you can't film an actor's thoughts.

Until now I hadn't had a clue how to handle it and I'd read the play three or four times. There had to be a way to give the "girl" some dimensions so they could show the script to actresses like Sharon Stone or Meg Ryan or Elizabeth Shue. Actually, I thought Anne Archer or Mimi Rogers might be good for the part. Anne Archer was older, yes, but she was pretty and exuded a sort of knowing kindness in her screen persona. Probably did in person too. I'd only been introduced to her once, briefly, at a party, but I kind of liked Anne Archer. Her eyes said a lot, and so did her smile. Like Delia, she was a woman of "a certain age" who had weathered well.

It suddenly hit me. A character like Delia, with all her complications, would have fit perfectly into what I needed here. Somebody who was a contradiction in herself—on the one side, kind, loyal, smart, honest, strong, bold, decent . . . and on the other, sometimes cruel, calculating, difficult, shy, insecure, and certainly wicked in bed. Hell, if I could write part of Delia's personality into this character, they wouldn't need to worry about finding somebody to play it. Actresses would be lining up outside the studio. It would be a role for a movie star! This was a very self-satisfying feeling for me. It occurred to me just then that maybe I really *was* worth all the money producers were throwing at me.

IT WAS LATE afternoon and I was working on the "girl" part when the phone rang. It was Delia.

"I got another one today," she said.

"Where from?"

"It was mailed from Boston."

"Boston? What about the others? I meant to ask you that."

"One was from New York, one from Miami, and one from Chicago. Then there was one from Atlanta and, oh, yeah, one from Washington, D.C."

"Well, whatever else he is, he's clever.

"Great."

"Was this one like the others?"

"Yes. Even more explicit. It's worse than bad fiction."

"Do you have it with you?"

She hesitated a moment. "Yes."

I could tell she wasn't exactly anxious to read it or show it to me, so I let that drop.

"Are you at the station?"

"No, I'm in Santa Monica. We're doing a live

broadcast from here in about two hours. Some kind of pollution in the ocean."

"Would you like to have dinner?"

"Sure," she said. "Would you like to meet me here?"

"All right. Where are you?"

"After we wrap it up, I'll be at Gleason's. It's right at the intersection of the boulevard and the coast highway. A nice little seafood place. I'll just wait at the bar."

"Fine, I'll see you there," I said. "I'll try to beat rush hour."

I GOT TO the restaurant in Santa Monica before her, and waited at the bar, sipping a glass of white wine. Along the mirrored counter were a dozen bottles of single-malt scotch, several of my favorite brands, before I quit drinking it. The bottles looked so inviting, Glenfiddich, Devon, Famous Grouse, Glenlivit—all twelve, eighteen, and twenty-five years old. I could almost taste them now and for an instant felt like ordering a double shot, just to calm my nerves. Then I reminded myself that that was where a lot of trouble lay. In the old days I'd calmed my nerves with those potions so much I often couldn't feel my nerves at all. I quickly perished the thought. I'd been there about twenty minutes when Delia swept through the door. There weren't a lot of people in the place yet, but she commanded the attention of all who were as she strode confidently toward me in a dark red suit with a closed-lipped smile and lush auburn hair bouncing provocatively around her shoulders.

"Hiii," she said sexily, kissing me lightly on the cheek. She hoisted herself into a bar stool with her long slender legs crossed and dangling in front of me. She put an elbow on the bar and rested her chin in her hand, looking at me with a smiling, come-hither expression I had seen many times before. I had a feeling she was giving off mixed signals again; anyway, I was certainly receiving them. I sipped my wine and ordered Delia a double scotch, on the rocks.

"So how was the story?" I asked.

"A little boring, actually. Somebody suspected sewer water was being leaked into the ocean. All the animal people were up in arms—the sea otter people, seal people, fish people, bird people. They were all lined up to get on camera. The only people who weren't there were the *people* people," she laughed.

"Maybe they *enjoy* swimming in shit," I offered.

She laughed again. I asked her if she liked what she did.

"Sure, it pays a lot and everything, but if I had it to do over, I think I'd become a writer, like you, Johnny."

This brought up painful memories, but I'd let it go at that.

"What I do is gratifying, but it's just not challenging," Delia said. "It's sort of like eating rice morning, noon, and night, you know?"

Yeah, I knew. I'd sometimes thought Delia could

have done practically anything she wanted in life, and now she was the biggest thing in L.A. television.

We had dinner and this time a broiled sea bass remained to Delia's liking, although she did send back a glass of white wine as tasting too sweet. We only engaged in small talk at the table. She asked me about some of my friends she had known when we were seeing each other. I had to tell her four or five had died since then. She'd known about a couple of them, who were pretty famous writers, but not the others. She seemed genuinely sad at the news. It was strange, perhaps, but at the moment it occurred to me I had never actually met any of Delia's own friends.

After dinner I suggested taking a walk along the big cliffs that overlook the ocean. The Pacific sun was setting low on the water as we crossed the street toward the palisades park. I put my arm gently around her slender waist to usher her across and at one point I could have sworn she snuggled against me. I was sorry when we reached the other side.

There was a path that extended for miles along the coast, just at the edge of the cliffs, and we walked southward down it. With the sun setting in the west, I knew we would be silhouetted against the ocean to anyone watching us from the restaurants and sidewalks across the coast highway. We were a handsome couple; that's what people always said. I made a mental note to use this one day in a scene somewhere. A handsome couple walking slowly alongside the sea, silhouetted black against an orange sun.

"It seems to me this guy sending the letters, he's obviously shrewd. Sounds like he's either got accomplices or he's a traveling man. Does that bring anyone to mind?"

"Well, not really. I'll think about it. I mean, most of the guys I knew were brokers or lawyers or mortgage bankers and some owned their own businesses. They were always flying off to someplace."

"But I think we can assume that whoever he is, he lives or spends time here," I told her. "So either he goes to these places where he can send letters or he has accomplices. You know, I wonder if he's shrewd enough to make sure there aren't any fingerprints on the envelopes or the letters themselves."

"Well . . ."

"If he did, and ever served in the army or something or had a criminal record, then we might put the proof positive to him."

"Yeah, but wouldn't that involve going to the police?" she asked.

"Maybe, maybe not."

"But wouldn't they have to see the letters?"

"We might just ask them to look at the envelopes. This is all a pretty new experience for me."

We stopped and watched the dying sun sink into the ocean, then headed back. Santa Monica is a pretty safe place, but I've learned that around L.A. no public place is really safe after dark, including Disneyland.

"Do you have the letter with you?" I asked.

"Yes."

"Where is it?"

"In my purse."

"May I see it?"

"Oh, Johnny, no. . . ."

"Hey, look, okay. I really didn't want to ask that. You mentioned that there was something 'more' in this one."

"There was."

"Want to tell me what?"

"He wants me to wear certain clothes on the show next Friday."

"Like what?"

"A red sweater—no jacket—and he wants me to wear my hair down."

"That's all?"

"Yes."

"Hummm—this guy's really kind of crazy, I think."

"I know."

"Are you going to do it?"

"No. I'm not going to be broadcasting Friday. Brad and I are going to Palm Springs for the weekend. I'm not on again till Monday."

I nodded. Palm Springs, I thought, a place for lovers. Why did she have to tell me that?

"Listen," I said, "I'm kind of in between projects right now. I've got to finish cleaning up a script, and then there's something else I'll get started on, but probably not for several months. If you like, I will take some time off and just work on figuring out who's doing all this to you."

"I couldn't ask you to do something like that," she said. "I really only needed somebody to talk to." She put her hand on my arm. I didn't try to hold it, though I wanted to. Delia looked absolutely sweet and innocent and vulnerable at that instant.

"Think about it," I said. Besides, I've always enjoyed a good mystery.

CHAPTER 5

WELL, I'VE CHANGED my mind," she said. "I've thought about it. I don't know where else to turn."

"Then I guess you're going to have to make me up some kind of list or something," I told her.

"Yes, I know," she replied unhappily.

It was two days later and Delia and I were back in the bar at the Peninsula, and in the same place—at Toby Burr's table, only he wasn't there. She couldn't have dinner because her husband was in town and she had to "hang out with him tonight," which was the way she'd expressed it. Anyway, she'd suggested drinks between her evening and late-night news shows.

"I think it would be good if you would put down all you remember about each one," I said. "At least what would be of any use to me. City they live in, addresses, phone numbers if you have them. Occupation. When you dated them, how long, and when was your last contact with them."

"I will," she said.

"And something about their personalities too. You know, 'nice guy,' 'asshole,' that sort of thing."

"Right."

"And I guess you'd better tell me whether it was you who broke it off, or them."

"It was mostly me," she said distantly. I couldn't get over the translucent look in her eyes and wished for a moment we could stop talking about this and start talking about something else—politics, sports, history, art, music. I really didn't know much about her views on things like that, which seemed strange, given my feelings for her.

"And also, any peculiarities," I said. "I don't know what they might be. Just anything you think of, you know. Like maybe if somebody had a thing for red sweaters or unbuttoned buttons.

"And also, if you noticed in the letters any sort of correlation between some, well, something sexual that might connect with a particular guy. Just anything you can remember. You don't have to tell me exactly what it was. Just something to give me an edge."

Delia nodded and fiddled impatiently with her scarf. "I already have," she said. Then she took a breath and glanced up at me.

"Johnny," she said, "I'd like you to meet my husband."

I just looked at her, dumbfounded. She wanted me to meet her husband? My mind began racing. I have never been with anyone's wife before; never wanted to be, before now, and I still wasn't comfortable with the notion. But at least if the husband stayed anonymous, I figured I could handle it.

"Why?" I asked finally.

"Well, I just think it would be a good idea. Brad's going to be down here all week on business. I thought you could come over to my place for lunch on Saturday. I was going to have Rick Olsen there too—Rick's the guy I mentioned, the one who owns the detective agency, a really good guy. If you're going to do this for me, I think it would be good for you to discuss it with Brad and Rick."

"Well, I . . ."

"Look," she said, "I know it might seem a little, well, awkward for you. I mean, seeing you again after all this time. But it'll be okay. Brad's a nice guy. I know he'll like you."

She picked up a book of matches from the table and wrote down her home address. *He'll like me?* I thought. That was the farthest thing from my mind. I began to feel like a creep, except it was also pretty creepy of her, I thought, to suggest something like this.

"Straight up noon," Delia said, handing me the matchbook with a smile.

"Do we mention letters or phone calls?" I asked feebly.

"Phone calls will do. Let's not make things complicated."

"Right," I said sourly. "Let's make things as uncomplicated as possible."

*　　*　　*

DELIA DEPARTED FOR her broadcast and I stayed at the table for a while, finishing my wine, the suggestion about meeting her husband still ringing in my ears. That was the way it was with Delia—just when you thought it was going one way, it went the other.

My thoughts drifted back almost twenty years to that weekend in Bermuda and later, that wonderfully happy winter and spring.

I had been right, on the beach that afternoon, that her noncommital murmur to my stated interest in making love to her was a yes on her part. We got back to the house and built a fire and sat in front of it on the floor. She'd put her head on my shoulder and we held each other for a long time as sunset turned to twilight. It wasn't long before we were wrapped in a passionate embrace. That night we had the most fabulous sex I'd ever known—intense, immediate, irrational, and terrific. And it went on that way for days.

I think every guy would somehow like to think he was the only one to have made love to a girl he had special feelings about. With Delia, of course, this would have been ridiculous. She obviously hadn't learned those sexual arts out of any book or boarding school conversation.

We stayed over another three days before heading back to New York, lying in bed or around the living room or taking long walks on the beach. We talked, we read, we went out to dinner or cooked at home. Looking back on it, these were some of the most memorable moments of my life.

When we returned to New York, I told her I'd call the next day. We hadn't made plans, but I didn't think they were necessary, but when I phoned her next afternoon, I got the answering machine. I tried again later that evening with the same result.

Her answering machine became my companion for the next week, although I'd long since stopped leaving messages. It was bewildering. I began to worry something might have happened to her when, on a Sunday night, she called me back.

"I had to go home to Kansas City for a few days," she said. "And then there was a wedding in Washington this past weekend."

"Well, I sort of thought you'd have let me know something," I said. "I was beginning to worry about you."

There was a moment or two of silence, then she said, "No, no, I'm fine. I just had other obligations."

That threw me. What other obligations? But I let it pass.

"Would you like to have dinner?" I asked hesitantly.

"When?"

"Tomorrow?"

"I can't tomorrow. How about, let's see, Thursday?"

"Okay, Thursday. I'll call you."

"No, no, why don't you just say where and I'll meet you."

"All right," I said. "Elaine's—eight o'clock."

"Where is it?"

"You don't know?"

"I've known *about* it. I've never been there."

"It's on Second Avenue at the corner of Eighty-eighth," I told her.

"See you there," she said cheerfully.

BY THEN I was more bewildered than ever. A week of bliss, then a week of uncertainty, and now, at least until Thursday, a week of doubt. I hadn't sensed that Delia was duplicitous; maybe a little odd, but basically I thought she was a straight shooter. I decided it was best to write it off as a miscommunication.

On Thursday she arrived at Elaine's forty-five minutes late. I was sitting with friends and getting more anxious as the time ticked by. She apologized, saying she had gotten home late from some appointment downtown. It was to discuss a position she'd applied for at a book publisher.

We moved to our own table and she appeared very glad to see me, frequently putting her hand on my arm while we talked. She was wearing jeans, boots, a white sweater, and a leather jacket and many a male eye in the place was turned toward her. That night was a hot one at Elaine's. Lots of writers and movie stars and other celebs. I knew many of them. Elaine's had become my club of choice over the years. You didn't just walk in and get a table and I was pleased when some well-known people came over to say hello. It wasn't because I wanted to show off, but because I thought Delia would enjoy meeting them.

When I was a young writer, I always liked to meet the Old Lions. To a one, they were all nice to me, and I felt exalted in their company and their conversation was always witty and charming. It never occurred to me that Delia would feel self-conscious around them, but I learned later that she did. It took me a while to understand that she had a fragile ego and the presence of so many accomplished people around her made her feel diminished. Including me.

After dinner, and a nightcap, I asked if she'd like to go back with me to my place. She couldn't, she said, because she had an early something-or-other in the morning, so I asked if she'd like to do something over the weekend.

"What?" she asked.

"Well, we could go to the country," I offered. I had friends down in Southampton who would always let me use their home there. It was a great, elegant Georgian manor on the ocean and I thought even in winter we could take walks along the beach and spend nights by the fireside, just the two of us, as we had in Bermuda.

"No, no, why don't we stay here," she said. "Maybe we can see a play."

"All right," I agreed. "Here we will be."

We saw the play on Friday and it wasn't very good. Some English version of a French farce. Afterward I'd been invited to a friend's party in his apartment overlooking Central Park. It was a big shot artsy crowd again, which I ignorantly thought Delia might enjoy, but she spent half the night talking with an out-of-work actor who mostly did stand-ins when he wasn't tending bar and the other half in what appeared to be flirting with several other good-looking wannabes. I was beginning to feel irritated and didn't say much on the way back to my apartment. At least, I thought, she probably wouldn't have any appointments on Saturday morning.

When we got there, I built a fire and offered her a drink.

"Why don't you kiss me instead," she said.

It was the last thing I would have expected at the time, but I did, and suddenly it was Bermuda all over again and later as we lay in my bed having coffee and toast, I said, almost casually, but in reality I just blurted it out, "You know, I think I could fall in love with you."

"Don't say that," she said abruptly. "You don't even know me."

She was right. I didn't.

I WAS STILL sitting at Burr's table in the Peninsula with an empty wine glass when a blonde walked by on her way back to her crowd by the bar—she couldn't have been more than twenty-five or so. She sort of looked like a movie star, but she wasn't. Movie stars don't hang out at bars, and this girl was, well, kind of plain, compared with most of the heavy hitters out here. Still, she had an interesting, handsome look, with blue eyes and a prominent, aquiline nose and a little smile that reminded me of Greer Garson in *Mrs.*

Miniver. She raised an eyebrow as she walked past, then stopped, turned, and came back to my table.

"You look a little lonely, sitting there all by yourself," she said. "Want to join me and my friends?"

That wasn't a hooker's line. A hooker would have asked to sit down. I was flattered by her approach. It made me feel I still "had it." But I smiled at her and shook my head.

"You're very sweet to ask," I said, "but I've got a big day tomorrow."

"Well, sorry," she said. "I just thought you looked nice."

"I am," I replied. "Maybe we'll meet again sometime."

She gave me a little ta-ta wave and walked back to her friends.

I paid the check and went out into the lobby. For an instant I thought about going back to that girl at the bar. She seemed sincere and bold—as Delia had so many years ago—even if she didn't have the same beauty. There was something about her that was, well, captivating, that made me think I'd be making a mistake not to connect with her in some way, even if it was nothing more than a phone number inside a book of matches.

But I didn't. My heart just wasn't in it tonight.

CHAPTER 6

N

O TRAP IS as deadly as the one you set for yourself, but I wasn't thinking about that as I drove
up under the portico of Delia's apartment complex
near the Hollywood hills. It was a big forty-story
affair and a valet dressed like a South American dic-
tator came out to park my car.

Her apartment was on the thirty-fifth floor, overlooking the city and the hills in the distance. It was a
brilliant late September day, no smog and only a
few high wispy clouds in the sky. I got off the elevator right into the foyer of Delia's place. I rang the
buzzer and a Spanish maid answered, directing me
through several well-appointed rooms with marble
floors and chintz wallpaper to a wide terrace with a
small swimming pool. The pool sort of threw me. I
wondered if the architect who designed this place got
an A or a C in his course on how much weight a floor
can carry.

She was reclined on a chaise lounge in an under-
stated green bikini, if such a thing was possible with
Delia in it. She immediately rose up and greeted me
with a little hug and cheek kiss. I could smell suntan

lotion and a hint of perspiration, but it was her smell, all right, beneath it all.

Just then I saw the two guys, walking toward me. I picked out who must have been the husband right away. He was fairly slender and clean cut, not terribly tall; in fact, I think Delia had an inch or two on him. He was wearing Bermuda shorts and a Hawaiian shirt and had some pinkish-looking drink in a glass and he reminded me of one of any number of those Hollywood actors whose faces you remember from B-type movies but can't place their names. The "Bermuda" shorts gave me a sudden flash of nostalgia, but I got over it. The other guy I took for Rick Olsen, the detective. He was dressed in tan slacks with a green polo shirt and was tall and blond and walked with a kind of Robert Mitchum gait.

We all shook hands awkwardly as Delia introduced us, but the men had smiles on their faces. Beneath a green-and-white-striped canopy where Rick and Brad had come from, a white-jacketed Oriental-looking barman waited patiently behind his bar. Without asking, Delia called over for him to bring me a glass of white wine. We sat for a while in a grouping of wicker furniture under an umbrella while jazz was piped out to the terrace from recessed wall speakers. I made small talk about how great her apartment was, the view, the weather, and so on, and Brad and Rick complimented me on my movies. Then the phone rang and Delia answered it at the table. It was for Brad, but he said he would take the call inside.

"Want to go for a swim?" Delia asked.

"Thanks, but I don't think so," I told her.

"Oh, c'mon," she said seductively. "The water's warm. We always swim here before lunch. It improves your appetite. Besides, I want to talk to you about T. S. Eliot."

"I didn't bring my suit," I answered lamely. Screw T. S. Eliot, I thought. What was I? "A pair of ragged claws/ Scuttling . . ."

"No problem," she replied. "Brad's got a bunch of them. I know one will fit you, slim and trim as you've kept yourself."

"Well, thanks, but I don't really . . ."

"No, no, no—I insist," she said. She was leaning over the table at me, providing an eyeful of what she looked like in a bikini. I hadn't seen that much skin on Delia in almost two decades and was pleasantly astonished. Only a faint wrinkle or stretch mark to be seen, but everything else taut and tanned. My protests notwithstanding, Delia got up and pulled me to my feet by the arm.

"Come with me," she said. "I'll take you to the dressing room."

I came out a few minutes later wearing a pair of Brad's swim trunks. She'd been right, they fit perfectly. Delia was in the pool at the far shallow end and waved for me to get in the water. I dived in, concentrating on using my best form. When I surfaced, she swam to me and we treaded water.

"See, I told you it's nice, didn't I? Now what about Eliot, you handsome thing?"

"I am a scarecrow. . . ." I said. "I march alone. . . ."

She was right, of course, the water was warm and relaxing. At one point she put her arm on my shoulder to keep afloat. We swam around for a minute or two, then both took to the side of the pool to hold on. It was obvious she now had something other than T. S. Eliot on her mind, if she ever had in the first place.

"Do you like Brad?" she asked quietly. Our heads were below the surface of the terrace and the water gurgled gently in the skimmer cup.

"I hardly know him."

"I haven't really told him about you, you know. I mean, I told him I'd met you back in New York years ago. But not anything else."

"Good," I said.

"I could, though, you know. I mean, he's not really the jealous type—but, of course, since I moved down here, I think he's a little . . . well . . ."

"I can imagine," I told her.

I kicked away and swam a lap or two by myself.

Rick, the detective guy, seemed especially pleasant. He had a funny sense of humor and I got a friendly, comfortable feeling with him. Most people who own big companies so often seem unbearably intense, especially out here in the movie business. Brad, meanwhile, had returned from his phone call and was squatting down saying something to Delia, who was still hanging on to the side of the pool. Suddenly she yelled over to me, "Time to get out now. Lunch is served."

I swam to the shallow end and walked up the steps. She had hoisted herself out and come over and tossed me a towel. The maid had laid out a typical California spread: prosciutto with basil, ricotta cheese, and sliced tomatoes and some kind of clear, cold unidentifiable soup. I figured it must be Oriental. Brad forked up one of the tomatoes and took a swallow of his tutti-frutti drink. He seemed decent enough, but, at that moment, I thought he had a sort of furtive air about him, like Farley Granger in *Strangers on a Train*.

"So, Johnny," he said, "Delia tells me you want to help her with this problem we've been having."

"Yes, I do," I told him. "I don't know how much good I can do. But I can try."

"She says you have suggested going to some of her, ah, old friends, and making inquiries."

"Well, it's a start. That's the only thing I can think of."

"Rick and I have talked about it. He doesn't think it's a bad idea."

"No, I don't," Rick said. "Actually, we thought of doing the same thing ourselves, because unless this guy shows himself more than he is now, it's the only way. But I think that you yourself going on this little mission would be much better than if I sent one of my detectives. A lot of these fellows, as Delia describes them, are pretty well up there in the pecking order. If I sent one of my people, chances are a lot of her friends would be reluctant to talk with him. But you, as an old friends of hers, might just be able to get in-side better than we could."

Actually, I was still wondering just how in hell I was going to get through the door myself.

Delia rose and excused herself from the table, os-tensibly to change out of her wet bathing suit, but I figured she didn't want to hear anymore.

"Where are you going to start?" Rick asked.

"I thought here, if there's anybody she can re-member who might have moved here." I told him my reasoning that the caller was probably in the L.A. television-viewing area. Both Brad and Rick nodded in agreement.

"You might have missed your calling," Rick smiled.

"I think we've just got through the easy part," I replied. "Somebody once said that writing is like try-ing to hold up a four-hundred-pound fat woman—there's a lot of things sagging all at once and you better figure out just the right place to put your weight."

Rick and Brad both laughed at that. "Now, of course," Brad said, "I am going to reimburse you for your expenses in this. It's a big undertaking."

"No, not at all," I said. "I'm doing this because, well, Delia and I are old friends. And, frankly, money is not a problem with me."

"Yes, I, well, I would have guessed that," Brad said, "but I wish you would. I'd feel better."

"And I'd feel worse," I said. "Let me worry about

that. If I run out of money doing this, rest assured I'll let you know."

They both smiled again. Outwardly they were a relaxed pair and even though things were jovial, I remained very much the outsider and sensed an undercurrent of collective wariness from them.

Delia returned wearing a yellow sundress and white sandals. She looked absolutely radiant with her auburn hair slicked back from the swim and a golden glow in her cheeks.

"Are you guys going to miss your tee-time?" she asked.

"Oh Lord," Brad said. "I almost forgot." He turned to me, "We've got to be at the club in twenty minutes," he said.

Rick started to rise too. "They make old duffers like us play at one-thirty sharp, while the scratch golfers are still eating lunch, so we don't hold them up on their afternoon round," he said wryly.

"Yeah," Brad laughed.

"It's time for me to go too," I said, getting up from the table.

"Oh no, Johnny," Delia said. "You don't have to go. Stay a little while. I'm being abandoned by these two cads."

"I've got some work to do," I said. Even though Brad seemed perfectly comfortable with me, I felt a little uncomfortable myself, being alone in a house with his wife.

"Please stay for just a little bit," Delia pleaded.

"There're some things to talk about, you know, about this . . . business."

"Yeah, no rush for you to leave," Brad said. "We didn't get you all the way up here to eat and run." He said it in an offhand sort of way, but I thought I might have seen a flash in his eyes—anger, angst, who knows?

"Well, okay," I conceded. "I suppose I can enjoy a little bit of a Saturday afternoon without pounding on a typewriter."

"Good," Brad said. "You guys have a nice time. We'll see you later."

He went in the apartment, I suppose to get his things, and Rick took me aside for a moment while Delia was retrieving something from the chaise lounge.

"Johnny," he said, "I know Brad really appreciates your doing this. I want to tell you that I do too. Brad is an old and dear friend of mine, and I know this has him worried. It's a very delicate situation, as I suppose you realize. Here's my card."

He scribbled something on the back of it. "That's my home phone. Anytime, night or day, that you find out anything, whatever, that might be a lead in this, call me. And I've put down all Brad's numbers too. We've got ways of checking out people that are almost beyond belief to the average person. It could be this bastard's done this kind of thing before. Matter of fact, I think there's a good chance of it. He's probably a borderline psychopath—maybe full blown.

Obsessive-compulsive, whatever. So don't hesitate to let me help."

"I won't," I assured him. Rick gave me a firm handshake and disappeared through the sliding glass doors, just as Delia returned.

"Now," Delia said, "how about another glass of wine?" She plopped down in a chair and before she crossed her legs, I observed that she wasn't wearing underwear. That was sort of a jolt.

"No thanks, if I do, my afternoon'll be shot. Like I said, I'm a working man."

"Oh, phooey," she replied with a mock pout. "I was hoping I'd have you all to myself today."

"I THINK I'm getting cold feet," Delia said. She held in her hand the list of old lovers she'd made up, but had not shown it to me yet.

"Listen, we have to start somewhere."

"I don't know . . . I just . . . Look, Johnny, you won't ask them anything personal, will you? About me, I mean?"

"Well, I'm going to have to ask *some* things," I said, "just to get them talking. I can't go in there and say, 'Hey, are you the one sending Delia Jamison ugly letters?' "

"No, I suppose not. But you know how I value my privacy. You remember that. I always did. I think it came from being a little girl—the nannies were always prying into things. They were worse than nuns. They'd always find my secret little hideaways where

I'd keep my dolls and little notes and diaries and they'd read them and then let me know they had. I don't know, I'm just really sensitive about my personal privacy, I guess."

"I'll be as discreet as I can," I said.

"Well, that's one reason I really didn't want Rick too involved in this. I mean, he's a good guy, but I could just imagine if he sent his detectives out and they'd get to talking and comparing notes and, well, you know . . ."

"Don't worry, whatever it is, it will stay with me. And he is a nice guy, Rick," I said, trying to change the subject. I remembered that when Delia got off on something like this, it was hard to get her to let go.

"Yes," she said, "but he's been a little down since his wife died."

"His wife died?" I said. I thought he looked pretty young to have a wife die.

"Couple of years ago."

"That's too bad. What was it?"

"Well, nobody talks about it much. . . . Suicide."

"Lord."

"She was Japanese. I understood she'd been having problems for a long time. He took it hard and I think if it hadn't have been for Brad, he might have gone off the deep end himself."

"Well, that's what friends are for," I said. "And you were right, I did like your husband."

"Thank you," she said.

"He looks so young, though."

"He is," Delia said. "He's thirty-five."

"Funny, I always thought you'd go for a younger guy."

"Why?"

"I don't know, I just always thought it."

In fact, I figured it was because Delia liked control, and she was never to be controlled, and it probably would have been easier for her to establish control— or at least her fierce independence—with somebody younger than with an older man.

"Well, I guess we'd better get on with it," Delia said. She got up and pulled a chair right next to me and set her "list" out on the tabletop. It looked to be several pages long.

"I've put down everything I could think of," she said quietly.

I glanced over it quickly. Almost all the names were people on the East Coast. I mentioned this to her again.

"I know," she said, "but these are the only ones I can think who . . ."

"But if they're all back there, I still don't understand how one of them could now be directing you what to do out here."

"I'm just telling you, Johnny, that from what was said in the letters, I think these people I wrote down here would be, well, the most likely."

She was so close her bare shoulder touched mine. Everything became unbelievably acute to me just then. I absorbed her smell, the sort of high-pitched treble of her voice, her long, delicate fingers with the same old family-heirloom ruby ring that she'd worn in Bermuda. I didn't look at the list again, I looked at her, and for an instant her deep green eyes locked with mine.

After a few moments she said, "Is something the matter, Johnny?"

I noticed that the Oriental bartender had gone on his way and the maid was no place to be seen.

"No. Nothing," I told her. "I'd better be getting along now."

When we got to the elevator, Delia said she'd ride down with me. We didn't say anything, and stood side by side till it hit the ground floor. As the doors opened, she gave me a hug. It was no society hug, but something more, or at least I thought so. I felt her take a deep breath against me. She took me by the hands.

"Thanks, Johnny, for everything," she sighed.

"And I guess this is where I get off," I told her.

CHAPTER 7

IT SEEMED ESPECIALLY ironic here in sunny California that during my drive back to the hotel I was feeling, to steal a line from Melville, "cloaked in a damp, drizzly, foggy November of the soul." My feelings for Delia were intensifying every minute I was around her, like a hurricane gaining strength, but I've still got sense enough not to dive into pools unless I'm sure they've got water in them. Still, she continued to give off what I took as mixed signals, and I had to be careful not to grasp at any false ones. One thing was for sure, though—Delia Jamison was a woman of impenetrable contradictions.

When I got to my room, there were two message envelopes under the door. One was from Toby Burr complaining I hadn't returned his phone calls. The other was from somebody called Meredith McDonald. I didn't know who that was. It just had a number and said, "Please call." I called Burr.

"I've been worried sick about you," he barked right off the bat. "Where the hell have you been?"

"I went to Australia for a few days, to shoot at kangaroos."

"No, you didn't. Something's going on, I can smell it."

"What's it smell like?"

"Shit," Burr grumbled.

"Then you must be reading one of your own scripts again," I suggested.

"Now listen, is it something to do with that television girl? I know you, Johnny. When you go underground, there's always a female involved."

"When I *finally* go underground, you can be sure a female was involved," I told him. "But until then, it's none of your business."

"Yes, it is," Burr continued. "You have that damned screenplay of mine to fix. I cannot have you mixed up with trouble—and from what I saw the other night, that woman is trouble for you."

"I'm a big boy, Toby."

"You are not. You're a child, just like all the rest of them. You've made all this damned money now and you can have whatever you want. So you don't care about that anymore, right? Now you only want what you *can't* have. Am I right?"

"You're as right as anybody in the film business ever gets," I replied serenely.

"I *am* right!" he yelled. I could almost see him kicking his wastebasket or pounding his thigh with his fist. "Are you getting involved with that woman? She's married, isn't she?"

"That 'woman' might just save your script," I told him.

"What! How? What woman? What the hell are you talking about?"

"Trust me," I said.

"Are you crazy!" Burr hollered. "There's fifty million riding on this goddamn movie and you say 'Trust me,' when you're letting some idiot TV girl work on a script that I am paying you to—"

"She's not working on the script," I cut him off. "She *is* the script."

"Now listen, Johnny, all I wanted you to do is write up the girl—that's all! This is a simple picture. I don't want you putting in a bunch of esoteric bullshit. This is not Academy Award time. Sarah wants that house on Beverly Drive so she can show it off to her fucking bridge club. And she's going to get it just as soon as the studio turns the money loose, and they have to see a sensible script before they'll do it. Understand?"

"What makes you think anybody in this town would recognize a sensible script if they saw one?" I said.

"Fuck you, Lightfoot!"

"I love you too. By the way, have you ever heard of somebody called Meredith McDonald?"

"Hell no. Who's that?"

"If I knew, I wouldn't be asking you."

"Do you know you're going to give me a heart attack!" Toby hollered.

"Trust me," I said.

*   *   *

I WENT TO the little refrigerator in my suite and took out a bottle of California white burgundy, poured myself a glass, and walked out through the French doors to the tiled terrace. The sun had gone behind the hotel now, headed toward the distant ocean horizon, and I thought of our little sunset bet of the week before, a man and woman silhouetted black against a fiery orange ball. A handsome couple, that's what people said about us in the old days.

I lit up an Upman Monte Cristo and sat in a chair, then took out Delia's list from my pocket and unfolded it. There they were, all the "lovers," laid out in print. I felt a vicarious, almost nauseous thrill, as if I was somehow a fly on the wall in her private affairs.

I checked down the order of dates to see who it had been during those years when she and I were still connected. Several fell into that frame. I shook my head. Hell, I knew a couple of them—one had been a tennis doubles partner of mine for six months, until he just sort of faded from our game. Now I knew why. I knew some of the others too, if not personally, by reputation. There were various "crowds" in New York—social, literary, theater, movie, artsy-fartsy— but ultimately they all overlapped into one big crowd and I'd been in it somewhere. Well, I thought sourly, at least she spread it around.

She had phone numbers and even addresses for them, though some had to be out of date. And as she had indicated, they were certainly a homogeneous bunch. Lawyers from old-line firms and brokers and bankers from the elite financial houses. They ranged from a few years younger to a lot older. There was a turd or two in there also, I noted. How she ever got mixed up with them I couldn't imagine, unless it was at a time her bullshit detector was out of tune. Or maybe she'd just decided they might have a good piece of ass. Who knows? I decided to torture myself a little by visualizing Delia going out with them to plays and parties and movies and having neat lunches and dinners in uptown society cafés, then returning to their fashionable apartments or homes for a night of romping in bed.

This was the same as beating yourself on the foot with a stick just because it feels good when you quit.

One thing that troubled me even more now was how somebody from New York might be able to give Delia orders about what to wear or how to act on her TV show in Los Angeles. Then it occurred to me that there were in fact *services* out here that would tape television shows and programs for people. I'd seen them advertised in the papers. I guess they were set up for folks like me who don't know how to set the clock on a VCR, let alone get it to record something. Maybe that was how it was being done! I went to the desk and got out the yellow pages. Sure enough, there were dozens of these outfits in the area. Apparently, they performed a useful function for all actors and other broadcast people out here by providing them accurate copies of their on-air time or something.

Problem was, there were so damned *many* of them! At least fifty, maybe more. And even if I visited them all, how could I pry out of them the names of any customers who matched the ones on Delia's list?

I put the phone book down. On the bar counter was the message from this Meredith McDonald. Not many people knew where I was, so I figured that at least Meredith McDonald was not somebody trying to sell me magazine subscriptions. I decided that whatever she wanted, it would take my mind off things for the time being, and dialed the number. A voice cheerfully answered at the third ring.

"Hello, this is Johnny Lightfoot," I said, "returning your call."

"Oh, hello, Mr. Lightfoot," said a soft feminine voice. "I'll bet you don't know who I am, do you?"

"I'm embarrassed to say that I don't."

"Well, do you remember last week when you were sitting at a table by yourself in the Peninsula, and a girl came up to your table and asked you to join her at the bar?"

"Yes."

"I'm that girl, Mr. Lightfoot," she said.

"Mr. Lightfoot is my father," I told her. If I sounded nonplussed, I was.

"Oh, then—John."

"Johnny."

"Anyway, after you left, I asked the bartender who you were. I mean, you sort of looked like somebody.

And he told me. I hadn't realized you were the . . . well, you were so famous."

"I am the least well-known famous person I've ever met."

"But you, you wrote . . ."

"Yes, I know I did."

"The bartender said you were living there in the hotel, so I just, well, this afternoon I was sitting around and I thought, Why not, and so I called."

"Yes, I know that too. It's why we are talking to each other."

"And I, I don't want to seem too forward, but I thought if I didn't call, then we'd never see each other again, and maybe that would be okay or maybe it wouldn't. Do you understand what I mean?"

"Yes, I've been in some of those situations myself."

"And I was wondering if you might like to have a drink with me sometime."

"I suppose I like drinks as well as the next fellow, but I have to eat too. Would you like to have dinner with me?"

"Sure. When?" she asked.

"Well, it's Saturday night and I don't have any- where to go. Would you like to meet me here at the scene of the crime?" I really didn't feel like going out, but at least I wouldn't have to sit here alone, gnashing my teeth over the painful conundrum Delia presented, with all its awkward history.

"Oh, ah, tonight?"

"Tonight."

"Ah, well . . ." There was that pause I'd expected. Then: "Okay, sure," Meredith said. "What time?"

"Eight." There was something in her voice, a quality unafraid, cheerful, and without guile, that made me want to know more.

"I'll be there," she said cheerily. There was a nice lilt in her voice.

"In the bar. At the same table where we met."

"Right," she said. "I know just where it is."

I SHOWERED FOR the second time that day, dressed, and went downstairs to meet Meredith McDonald. At least it wasn't a blind date in the literal sense. Meredith was most probably after me, but I in turn was after Delia, who wasn't after me but after her husband, or something like that. In the elevator I had the gloomy feeling my life was becoming a solemn and prolonged farce.

Meredith was standing at the bar when I walked in, looking resplendent in white slacks and a blue blouse that played well against her blond hair, pulled back with a clip. She gave me a big wave and a toothy smile.

"Hi," I said. "Why didn't you sit down?"

"I didn't know if I should," she said. "They're kind of stuffy about that sort of thing here."

"Well, they can stuff it if they want to, far

as I'm concerned." I led her to Burr's table. She ordered a gin and tonic and I ordered my usual. Wino Lightfoot.

"So . . ." she said.

"You want me to go first, huh?"

"Yep."

"Well, I'm not married. I'm forty-seven years old. I come from North Carolina. I live in New York but come out here a lot for work. I have expensive tastes and very few bad habits, but I'm about to indulge in one of them now." I took out a pack of cigarettes and offered her one. She declined. I lit mine.

"I've been a newspaper reporter, novelist, screenwriter, and all-around idiot for the past quarter century. In my spare time I play tennis, fish for trout, and hunt game birds."

She mustered up a feigned frown at this last revelation.

"I'm fairly neat and clean and try to be honest—except with myself sometimes." And with the evil angels, I might have added.

"That's about it. Now you."

"Can I ask questions first?"

"Certainly." I hoped she wasn't going to ask me what *sign* I was.

"Do you have a girlfriend?"

"No." And it was close enough to the truth.

"Okay."

"That's all?"

"For now," she said.

I liked her smile. It showed a lot of teeth and was very natural and there was a spark in her blue eyes that indicated something was burning within.

"I'm twenty-six. I'm from a little town in the San Fernando Valley near Sacramento. My dad's a lawyer there. I went to UCLA and studied set designing. So now I'm a set designer."

"What have you designed?"

"Well, actually, I'm just an assistant set designer for the moment. But I worked on *All of Heaven's Doors* and *Sometimes Strangers* and *The Squid.* I think that was my favorite."

"Why?"

"Because I got to do the squid—you know, when it busts loose out of the big tank."

"I'm afraid I missed that one. But now tell me again—you say you made the squid?"

"No, no, silly. I just *drew* it. You know, we paint mock-ups of all the scenes."

WE HAD A very pleasant and comfortable dinner in the hotel dining room, which is one of the better places to eat in L.A., I think. Meredith seemed unflappably cheerful and, what was more, didn't send any of her food back. Ah, younger women, I thought; there is much to commend them. It's not so much that they're trying to please, it's just that they're grateful for little kindnesses others often take for granted. And there was something else about Meredith I found different too. Delia had cleared her throat for years before she finally found what she wanted in life, but this one didn't even have to look. She wanted to draw and create and she just went out and did it, and apparently did it well. While I was at it, I decided another thing on the spur of the moment, perhaps dangerously, but this girl didn't seem at all like the sort who sooner or later was going to blow up in your face like a trick cigar.

"You know," she said, "when I first saw you sitting at that table that time, I thought you looked, well, sad."

"Maybe I was."

"Why?"

"It's a long story. Besides, it's the lot of most writers to be sad. It's why they drink so much."

"You don't."

"I did."

"You seem a little cynical," Meredith said.

"I think it comes with age." I'd had a nice time this evening, talking with this pleasant, intelligent young woman, but now I was sort of in a sinker. Getting down on myself, maybe. The afternoon's conversation with Delia was still not fully absorbed. Over the years I'd heard the litany of complaints about me from various women—I swore too much, drank too much, was sometimes unresponsive. Now I was cynical. Somehow I shook out of it and tried to end the evening on a lighter note.

"Well, you know what they say, don't you?"

"What?"

"Scratch the heart of a cynic and you'll uncover an optimist."

"Who says that? I've never heard it before."

"I do," I said. "I just made it up."

"Good for you," Meredith said. "I think you're right."

CHAPTER 8

PEOPLE ARE ALWAYS telling you to keep your ear to the ground, but they often fail to tell you it's not a very dignified position. I was beginning to realize that, after my latest conversation with Toby Burr.

He had insisted on a face-to-face after our Saturday phone call. I think the conversation had thrown him into a panic. We had lunch at Morton's, where he laid out in lawyerly fashion all sorts of snares and pitfalls I was headed for if I got involved with Delia.

"I've been checking things out," Burr said. "She's been seen all over town with different guys."

"Checking it out with who?"

"I have my sources."

"Seen with what guys?"

"Hell, I don't know them. I just hear she's been seen in public."

"How *many* guys?"

"How would I know, for chrissake? Isn't that enough?"

"Well, did it ever occur to you it might have been her husband, or some of her husband's friends, or her own business associates? Hell, Toby, this isn't nineteen *fifty-five*. After all, when we saw her first at the Peninsula, she was with two guys and another girl. She told me they all worked together at the station."

"And I'm telling you to keep your ear to the ground, that's all, Johnny."

"How about both ears to the ground, like an ostrich?" I said. "Sometimes ignorance is bliss."

"Very funny," Burr muttered. "Johnny, I know you better than you know yourself. What's going on between you and that woman?"

"If you know me as well as you say, you wouldn't have to ask."

"Bullshit. It's enough I know something is. I could tell it the moment you saw her in here that night. I can read you like a book."

"Read me, then."

"Son of a bitch! I'm your friend for nearly twenty-five years! We've done great work together. I remember when you used to practically live with me, working on those movies. You always shared stuff with me. Whassamatter, I'm not good enough for that anymore?"

"Toby, look, this is really a private thing. When it sorts itself out, I'll let you know, okay?"

"Not okay. I know for a fact that there are half a million beautiful girls in this town who would die a thousand deaths just to get you in bed with them. And when you've got a hang-up over this one middle-aged married dame, there's got to be some calamity attached to it somewhere, sooner or later. Am I right?"

"Well, maybe better sooner than later," I said.

"Maybe better never," he retorted.

"There are just things I need to find out. Listen, Toby, sometimes the sphinx has to solve its own riddle. Can't we leave it at that?"

"All right, all right. Just don't say I didn't warn you. Now what's all this shit about her saving the script?"

"Oh, it's simple," I told him. "Look, the female lead in what you showed me is as flat as her own shadow at high noon. She's just a sounding board. Sure I can write her in a few more scenes and give her some more dialogue—same old stuff, have her throw a screaming fit, cry, beg or plead—whatever passes for drama out here. So what? She's still a hollow character."

"That's unfair," Burr said, sounding hurt. "I thought she was a darling character. Why she's . . ."

"She's as shallow as low tide, Toby. What I want to do is give her some complexities, so we don't get exactly what we see in her at first. Make her a little mysterious."

"Jesus! That's what I was complaining about, Johnny. All your writer's dime-store psychology! Nobody understands it. It'll just clutter up the story."

"No, it won't. Not the way I'm going to do it. What I'm going to write is a beautiful, intelligent woman with interesting contradictions that are revealed as the story develops. It'll keep the audience on the edge of their seats. Hell, you won't have to worry about finding a movie star to play her. They'll be calling *you,* instead."

"Yeah, and I know exactly what's going to happen next, you ignorant shit-for-brains. Let me tell you. You write the girl like that and next thing you know I can't find a fucking movie star to play the *guy,* because as soon as he or his agent reads the script, they're gonna realize he's being upstaged by the fucking *girl*! Then where am I?"

"Then you'll pay me another hundred thousand to write up the *guy.*" I said serenely, "and sooner or later you might have a movie that'll open."

"Why, you detestable moron!" Burr seethed. "You probably *did* think of something like that! I ought to bring you up on charges to the guild."

"Forget it, my dues are all paid up."

"When are you going to finish it?"

"Whenever I'm done. I have to go to New York in a few days. I'll let you know."

"New York! Jesus Christ! When are you coming back!"

"When I'm finished," I said.

THAT SATURDAY EVENING I was on the California Zephyr, winding eastward through the spectacular precipices of the Sierra Nevada mountains. The tracks were so close to the edge at some points I could look straight down thousands of feet into the valleys nestled below snowcapped peaks. We were even higher than the eagles that soared above tall firs and redwoods.

It seems odd to some, but I love the train. Not many people know that long-distance trains have come back in this country. I was on a modern train in my private compartment, complete with double bed, chair and desk, and my own washroom facilities, including a shower. I had my own phone, though no one knew how to reach me on it, and my laptop to work on. At night, the porter brought my dinner to my room.

I picked Saturday to leave because I don't much like being by myself in L.A.—or, for that matter, much of anyplace—on Saturday nights. It's just kind of a lonely time, I guess, and there wasn't anybody I wanted to share the loneliness with. Anyway, before I left, I'd called Rick Olsen and told him my thoughts about somebody ordering tapes of Delia's news shows. He seemed very interested and said he'd get some of his men to start checking with businesses that offered such services. We both agreed, though, it was a very long shot.

I'd been studying the list of former lovers Delia had left me with. I hadn't heard from her since a week ago today and her silence was a little baffling. Something self-flagellating in me wanted to know what exactly was in those letters that was so embarrassing to her. I mean, if somebody had been sending *me* such letters, I couldn't imagine what could be said that would be so derogatory if it were made public.

But, of course, I'm a guy. Guys are supposed to pride themselves on their sexual acumen, even publicly— unless it involves sticking a broom handle up your ass or some kind of shit like that. Anyway, I figured she'd show them to me if she had to, but for now she didn't. I guess I couldn't blame her.

It was dark now and I'd ordered a steak and baked potato from the dining car and opened a bottle of pinot noir. I was trying to figure out which of Delia's former "companions" to look up first.

Here was one, Robert "Bo" Bothwell. I knew Bothwell a little. He had been a member of New York's upper East Side café society, the little cliques of successfully up-and-coming young men and women that met on Saturday afternoons for lunch and table-hopping at "in" restaurants, where it was impossible to get a table unless the owners knew you. Bothwell had been a pleasant enough fellow who played a lot of squash and even in the days before yuppies, dressed in the typical yuppie costume— dark suit with suspenders, polished Italian shoes, designer tie—and wore his hair slicked back like some New Orleans bartender. He'd always reminded me of Laurence Harvey in *Butterfield 8*. Delia had listed his old office number at a big brokerage house. It would be interesting to find out if he was still there. The home number and address were for an apartment on East Fifty-eighth Street. Chances were, in all these years, he probably would have moved. Yeah, I knew Bo Bothwell a little from the old days, but if I just phoned him up cold and said that's what I wanted to talk about, why would he give me the time of day? On the other hand, maybe if he smelled money . . .

ALL THE NEXT DAY we traveled through the deserts of Utah and the scrub grassland of western Colorado. Mine was the last car on the train and I had persuaded the porter with a twenty-dollar bribe to open the top of the rear-end door so I could stand there and smoke an occasional cigar. Out of Denver we hit what is the most breathtaking scenery of any rail route in America. For nearly six hours we wound our way alongside the magnificent Colorado River gorge, huge gray boulders deep below a frothing river with immense falls and rushing white water that over the miles settled down first to rapids, then riffles, and finally, late in the golden afternoon, to a wide, clear, meandering stream along which the only evidence of civilization was an occasional trout fisherman.

The beauty of the place made me think of writing Delia a letter.

It was that same insane impulse I sometimes got lately when I found myself in a nice place and thought she might enjoy it too. I took out a piece of railroad stationery that was provided in the room; *The California Zephyr,* said the heading, *Established 1931.* I began writing a first sentence but before I was halfway finished, wadded the paper up and tossed it in the trash. It came to me that there is a time to be eloquent and a time when eloquence is wasted, and this was one of those. Besides, I decided, she's getting enough letters at the moment without having to get them from me.

EARLY NEXT MORNING in Chicago I caught a plane to New York. One of the names on Delia's list, a lawyer named Frankie LaCosta, was in Chicago; she'd known him when she was a television reporter there, but he'd have to wait. I wanted to start earlier than that. Back in her New York days. That's what she'd suggested too. I'd ordered a car to pick me up at La Guardia, a luxury I'd indulged myself in since the movie money started rolling in. I'd always despised the crazed, jerky, dirty cab rides in the city and the illiterate ignorance and insolence of drivers who always seemed to be from Bosnia or someplace. When we pulled up in front of the Carlyle, I was glad to be home.

Doubly glad because as soon as I walked through the door, I got a stupendous, almost knockdown welcome from Gotcha. Gotcha is my big Old English sheepdog, right out of the movie *Serpico*. He's eight years old and still thinks he's a puppy. Has a nose like a black lightbulb and must have sniffed me when I came in the lobby. He'd been lying in the little bellman's booth with Brendan, one of the doormen. While I'm away, Brendan takes him home with him at night sometimes and the other guys always take him walking in the park. I tried for a few years shipping Gotcha out to L.A., but they had to put him in that tight cage on the airplane and then when he got there he had to put up with all that hot weather—with a coat like a Tibetan yak—it just wasn't working. So what I had right now was a hundred twenty pounds of love, excitement, and slobber and it was the best greeting anybody can expect or wish. No complications there. Gotcha's love is unconditionally unconditional.

I called the desk to check my messages. Two were from Toby Burr, wanting to know where I was. I hadn't told him I was taking the train. There were a bunch of others, but it was lunchtime and I didn't want to respond to them just now. I dialed the number of an old friend, Jay VanWiik. Jay was an older fellow, almost a father figure for me, who had been through some of the most pitiless battles of World War II. I always called him the professor. He came from one of the most prominent families in New York and was the most down-to-earth intellectual person I'd ever known. He was delighted to hear from me and immediately invited me to lunch with him at his club, arguably, the finest and most exclusive in New York.

"So what have you been up to?" Jay asked, after we placed our orders.

I filled him in blandly on a little of my work in California and then dropped the business with Delia—practically all of it. Jay was the one person I knew I could trust to keep it to himself. Besides, I might need his help.

"Oh my," he said.

"These things present their dilemmas, don't they?"

"Yes, they do," Jay said. "Sure, I remember that girl. I always thought you two made a handsome couple."

"Yeah, a lot of people said that."

"But there was trouble, as I recall."

"Big time. It sent me into a tailspin for three years. I couldn't write anything—but checks."

"Yes, I do remember that. She seemed a bit immature, as I recall. Playing games or something."

"She wouldn't remember it that way," I said. "She'd call it being honest, and it was."

"Being honest?"

"Yes. She prides herself on that. Besides, she was smart; she just didn't know where to stop."

"Sometimes being honest just means people give themselves a license for doing what they want," he said.

Whenever I saw Jay, I always thought of the Walter Pidgeon character in *How Green Was My Valley*. He had that air about him.

"I guess that was certainly so."

"I've sometimes found it can be a way of getting off the hook for hurting someone's feelings. People who say they're 'completely honest,' you've got to watch out for them."

"Like keeping your ear to the ground?"

"Well, yes, something like that."

As lunch was served, I told him the rest, about the letters she was getting and my role in it.

"Oh dear," Jay said. "Oh dear."

"Well, it isn't as bad as that. I just thought I could help her."

"Forgive me, but it sounds as if you're getting into something sticky here—both with this girl and with this task you've agreed to perform."

"May be," I said, "but I'm in it now for better or worse and I may need your help on a few things."

"Of course. But what could I do?"

"Well, it might not be necessary, but your family has run in the same circles as a lot of these guys she listed as former lovers. I may need some help tracking them down. After all, it's been more than twenty years since she's seen some of them."

"Whatever I can do."

It was true. Jay knew practically everybody worth knowing in New York; his people had owned the largest brokerage house in the city for many years. And if he didn't know any of these guys personally, a phone call from Jay would probably supply the information.

"Well, Johnny," he said, "you seem to have set yourself up for a herculean chore. I only hope you haven't set yourself up for a herculean fall, as well."

"I hope I haven't either, but I suppose when you climb the mountain, there's always that possibility."

"From what you told me, a lot of other people have climbed the same mountain."

"Thanks, Professor, for reminding me of that," I said.

CHAPTER 9

IT WAS A clear, cool, perfect October morning in New York as I rode down Fifth Avenue toward Wall Street and my appointment with Bo Bothwell. He'd seemed pleasant enough on the phone after I told him who I was and he remembered me. He also must have remembered reading about how much money I'd made on the last movie because when I told him I was interested in talking investments, you could almost hear his ears perking up over the phone. He had left his original brokerage house and was presently senior vice president of a big-time investment banking firm. I told my driver I shouldn't be more than an hour and entered the impressive stone building where Bo's office was located. Inside, a secretary led me down a hall to a comfortable corner room, where Bo sat ensconced behind his desk.

He rose when he saw me and shook my hand, indicating for me to sit in an overstuffed red leather chair. He hadn't changed too much since I'd known him; the attire was the same but the slicked-back black hair much thinner and receding. He now reminded me of an older version of Michael Douglas.

"So, you've done very well, congratulations," he said.

"I can afford a better brand of toilet paper now," I told him.

We chatted for a while about old times and then he asked what kind of money I wanted to spend and what sort of returns I expected and so forth. I gave him a figure that didn't disappoint him, about two hundred thousand, but probably wasn't nearly as much as he'd anticipated. I figured, what the hell, I could let him buy some tax-free bonds for me—some of mine were about to mature anyway. There wasn't much risk in that and as far as I'm concerned, one broker is about as good as another, for that kind of thing.

That's it, then," he said, making some notes. "We can discount some of this and it'll give you a nice little piece of security." He leaned back in his chair as though he was about to get up, but then I startled him into immobility.

"Bo, let me ask you something, do you remember a girl called Delia Jamison?"

I saw something flash in his eyes for an instant and his jaw sort of tightened. You couldn't read much into that, but I clearly got his attention. It took him a moment or two to recover, and then he shifted in his seat and nodded with a kind of forced smile.

"A blast from the past," he said awkwardly. "Quite a girl. Is she still here in New York?"

"No, she's in Los Angeles. She's the news anchor for a network TV station out there."

"Is she?" Bothwell said in a tone of astonishment.

"She's quite successful."

"She was a lot of girl back in those days. What's she look like now?"

"I doubt you'd be disappointed. I expect she's not too much different than you'd remember."

"She still married?"

"Still? Well, she just got married recently. A couple of years ago."

"Oh?" he said. "I thought I'd heard something about her getting married way back—years and years ago. I can't remember exactly. There was some tragedy or something not long afterward."

"She was married before? A tragedy?"

"Maybe I'm wrong. The husband died? You know how it is, you hear something and it goes in one ear. Could be I'm confusing her with somebody else. She'd sort of dropped out of our crowd by then. She have children?"

"Nope."

"Well, I wouldn't have thought so."

"Oh, why not?"

"Just didn't seem like the type. She was very self-absorbed."

"That so?"

"Well, yeah. And she was a lot brighter than you'd expect, but she'd go from guy to guy—at least the ones I knew—stay awhile and then she's gone. Made us all look stupid, I guess. . . . But she was direct, I'll say that for her."

"She hurt you?" I asked. A kind of ruminating

expression came over Bothwell's face and he leaned back in his chair.

"Not as much as she might have."

I didn't say anything for a moment as we, both old veterans of the same battleground, sat and looked at each other. I hadn't told him about my own affair with Delia, but I suspected he either knew or guessed it.

"She didn't stick around long enough for me to fall in love with her," Bothwell offered, "if that's what you're getting at. I thought we were going great, but found out I was wrong."

"How's that?"

"She was doing the old second shift on me."

"The what?"

"Late-dating me."

"Is that so?" I said, puzzled. That didn't really sound like the Delia I knew. She could be fickle, but somehow 'stepping out' seemed a little out of character for her.

"Yeah, that's it. There were times when we'd go somewhere—party, dinner, whatever—and then fairly early, she'd say she had to get home. Not every night, but often enough for me to take notice."

"Really?" I said.

"So one night after I dropped her off, I got back home and phoned her. No answer. It seemed odd, but I didn't think much of it then. Next time, same thing. I called till well past midnight."

"Ever ask her about it?"

"Not then. I tried it a few more times. She had an answering machine, but I didn't leave messages. Once I even waited around after I'd dropped her off to see if she left with somebody else. Far as I could tell, she didn't. But it was a big building she lived in, lots of people coming and going. I guess the guy was going up to her apartment.

"Finally," Bothwell said, "I confronted her. She claimed she'd been studying, but somehow I just didn't buy it. I mean, she'd always answer the phone every other time I'd call—studying or not. Somehow that drove a wedge between us. I was suspicious and she started getting testy and that's when it began to fall to pieces. To tell you the truth, I was sort of scared of her, myself. Not physically, of course. She was smart, beautiful, so . . . well, everything. . . . Problem was," he said, "she was what you might call a woman with 'issues.' Get her hackles up if she thought you were treating her as anything but a complete equal. Everything had to be on her terms. She seemed almost paranoid about anybody thinking she was a sex object or something. And there was all that *honesty* stuff too. I remember once I took two newspapers out of a stand because I didn't have the change for both and she raised hell with me about it. Made me go get change and put it in the machine. And she was hell-bent against drinking too—a regular Carry Nation. But the funny thing was, after we split up, I saw her with Arthur Dalton and she was choking down martinis like they were going out of style."

He paused thoughtfully for a moment and began tapping his pen against the desk pad and then went on.

"There was just something about her that was fascinating. She was terrifically different from the girls in our crowd. She stood apart, and I don't just mean looks. She was so, well, independent. I mean, she wasn't really looking for a husband like most of them. She wanted to make it on her own—and I guess now she has. But, I don't know, it seemed you just couldn't get close to her. If you did, she'd fly out the window like a bat."

"Tell me about it," I said. As I expected, this revelation didn't surprise Bo Bothwell; in fact, he seemed to welcome it.

"What did *you* make of her?" Bothwell asked.

"About the same as you, I guess. Of course, it was a long time ago too. She was young. Kicking up her heels, I suppose."

"She was something in bed, huh?" Bothwell said.

"Different?" I asked, but felt like I was betraying something.

"You could say that."

"Oh, how so?"

He looked at me as though he'd thought I'd understand it without saying, but now he realized I didn't. His brow furrowed.

"I don't think all that's worth getting into," Bothwell said a little uncomfortably, I thought.

"Like to tell me why not?" I asked. "After all, you

brought it up." Maybe I was onto something now—
what was said in the letters . . .

"No, I don't," he answered firmly. "Say, what's the
reason for all this about Delia Jamison?" He had
realized I hadn't just mentioned all this for an offhand chat, so I decided to throw all my cards on the
table.

"Somebody's been contacting her," I told him.
"Apparently a former lover. She doesn't know who.
Nobody's sure what this person wants, but the im-
plications are ugly. Intimations of her, well, sexual
life—veiled threats of blackmail, maybe worse."

"You don't say?"

"I do say."

"What? Obscene calls or something?"

"Yes, something like that. We have reason to think
it's serious."

"We—you and Delia?"

"And her husband," I told him.

"What kind of guy is he?"

"Seems nice enough. He owns a software company in San Francisco."

"Figures," Bothwell said. "I always wondered what
kind of guy she'd finally marry. I guess he's rich?"

"Seems that way."

"I'll bet he's pussy-whipped."

"I wouldn't know," I said, noting that Bothwell's
last statement was certainly evidence of hostility,
though how deep it ran I couldn't tell. This was a
tricky business.

"But wouldn't you guess it? When did you go out with her?"

"A year or so after you did."

"How did you know when I saw her?"

"She told me. She gave me a list of former lovers."

"Gave you a list? What? She suspects me of being involved in something . . . ?"

"No, no," I calmed him. "I just told her I needed to know the names of all the . . ."

"Hell, I've got a wife and children. I can't imagine her thinking I would be mixed up in some sort of business like this!"

"She doesn't. It's just that I thought you might be able to give me some leads. People you might have known who were involved with her that you might think would—no, not even that," I said. "Just people who you might have known who went out with her. Especially those who might have been hurt by her more than you."

"Well," he said. "I don't know. . . ."

"Look, if you give me something, anything to go on, it might lead to something else."

"I'll have to think," he said tentatively. "I mean, it was a long time ago. I don't want to get something wrong."

"Take your time," I told him. "By the way, just how *did* Delia get into your crowd?"

"Do you remember Homer Greer? Used to work for Merrill Lynch in the bond department?"

"The name's familiar, but I don't put a face to it."

"Homer found her first. He was separated from his wife at the time and I suppose was pretty vulnerable. One day we were at the Racquet Club, in the locker room, and he's going on about this great girl he'd been seeing. Turns out it was Delia Jamison. Bunch of guys were playing cards in there and at some point one of them makes a crack about her—some sexual intimation—and Homer just goes berserk. Dives on the guy and everybody had to pull him off. Lot of bad feeling about that. I think the club suspended him for six months."

"Where's he now? Still at Merrill Lynch?"

"Oh no. I don't know, actually. Something happened there. Dropped out of the club too. I haven't seen him around for years."

"Can you find out for me? Where he might be?"

"I can try. I still know a few of the guys over there."

"I'd appreciate it. Anybody else?" As Bothwell was talking, I'd quietly taken out Delia's list to look for Homer Greer. He wasn't on it.

"There was another guy, Arthur Dalton. He's the one I mentioned seeing Delia drinking martinis with. Used to play a lot of tennis. He got into her for a while."

"Yeah, he's on the list," I said. Actually, Dalton was the guy who'd been my sometime tennis partner when he was dating Delia and toward the end I was too, at least on those rare occasions when she still turned up in my life.

"He's still with Agee-Williams," Bothwell said.

"General manager of their international investments department. Stays gone a lot. He's just remarried and trying to support the first wife and four kids. Nasty divorce."

"Aren't they all?"

"I don't know. I haven't been through it, thank God."

"Anybody else?"

"Let's see. I think Worthy Hathaway had a fling with her for a bit. I saw them together at a party in Southampton once. Looked pretty lovey-dovey. Grapevine had it she shit all over him and he took it pretty hard. I remember somebody saying they used to see him hanging around on the street near her apartment or something."

"Really? That's sort of odd." This indicated something to me, like obsession maybe. On the other hand, Bothwell himself had confessed to doing the same thing, trying to figure out what was going on.

"Oh, yeah," Bothwell said with refreshed recollection. "One time Worthy and I were talking at some dance at the Brooke and she came in with somebody else and he said something to me like 'Fucking bitch.' I remembered it at the time because that wasn't Worthy's style. He was always a happy-go-lucky gent, you know. He might have loved 'em and left 'em—but he always left 'em laughing."

I remembered Hathaway's name from Delia's list. "Where's he work now?"

"He's gone," Bothwell said. "He left New York

about five years ago to be general counsel for the Richards Group. Oil brokers."

"Where are they?"

"Los Angeles," Bothwell said. "He got divorced and just split town. Told people he wanted a fresh start."

"Well, L.A.'s the place to get one," I said, stunned by this information. "Just go out there and reinvent yourself."

"It's C.R. Richards Group," Bothwell said. "Want me to look it up for you? It's in this book here. We do business with them sometimes."

"Thanks," I said. "That'd be a big help."

"Here it is," he said. "It's Worthington Hathaway; I'll write the number down for you. It's his direct."

"You've been a great help. I really appreciate your time."

"Not at all," Bothwell said. "And by the way, when you see Delia, remember me to her, huh?"

"I'll tell her," I said.

"Let me ask you something," he said. "Did you really come here to invest money or talk about Delia Jamison?"

"Both," I said, more or less truthfully.

"Why are you doing this, anyway?

"Friendship, I suppose."

"That's it, huh?"

"For the time being."

"Well, I was you, I'd watch my flanks and rear. She nailed some pretty good men in her time."

"Thanks, I'll do that. And keep my ear to the ground."

IT WAS STILL cool, so I rolled down the window in the car on my way home. The sounds and sights of New York never failed to astonish me, the street vendors and bunches of bustling pedestrians and honking of horns and rattle of jackhammers all combining into an intolerable din for anyone but natives, who think it's the way normal people live.

Bothwell had seemed forthright too—but perhaps a little too much so. He had willingly given me several interesting leads—was it *too* willingly? To throw me off the track? Oh, hell, I caught myself; don't start thinking like a detective. "Scratch a cynic and you'll find an optimist . . ." was what I had said to Meredith McDonald. Right.

It had been strange, almost creepy, sitting there discussing Delia with one of her old bedmates. And what was the sex thing with her he didn't want to talk about? That seemed peculiar, especially since he'd brought up the subject in the first place. And I didn't know what to make of his recollection that Delia had been married earlier either. I'd certainly never heard anything about it, but, of course, I'd completely lost track of her for years and years. And this "tragedy" he'd alluded to? Well, anyway, he said he might have been wrong—confused or something.

On an impulse I told my driver to turn west and go down the West Side Highway. In New York I didn't go downtown much, although these days it had become the place to be for night life—the Village, Soho, TriBeCa, all the trendy cafés and gallerys and clubs where younger people met and danced and found somebody to warm their beds in the morning. But I am an uptown guy, I guess. Like some ancient wag said once: "Nobody ever goes to the lower West Side unless it's to get on a boat."

Well, we were there now, passing the giant slips and docks where once upon a time majestic ocean liners were tied up row on row. Now it was mostly a few small cruise ships, freighters, and the old aircraft carrier from World War II. The rest was a rot of decayed barges and busted wooden terminal buildings with shattered windows, where so many years ago debarking passengers set foot ashore from points abroad, happily met by friends and loved ones. All those great ships had vanished now, like dinosaurs. I would have liked those times, I thought, old-fashioned as I am. Getting on a big ship with serpentine and confetti blowing in the breeze and a band playing. Off to somewhere. Maybe I was a dinosaur myself. People like me, at least when we were younger, thought we'd rule the earth, and for a while perhaps we did rule our little part of it. And then autumn comes.

I tried to think all sorts of things as we drove past the Battery and the Statue of Liberty out there in the harbor, but I still couldn't keep Delia off my mind. I had been through the uphill side, but the downhill was fast to come.

We had seen each other fairly steadily through the remainder of the winter and into the spring of 1979, but I sensed even then there was an unbreachable span developing between us. It never became a given anymore that she'd be available. I hadn't wanted to push the issue because by then I was beginning to get a sense of what I was up against. Frankly, it was an animal I'd never seen before.

When we were together for dinner or shows or movies or museums or whatever, there was a close and solid discourse, like two old pals who enjoy each other's company and learn from each other—she from me, the more experienced, perhaps—though now I sometimes wonder who was which. But mostly I was the teacher and Delia, provided you didn't cross her with some kind of perceived slight, was an able and willing pupil. And then there was the sex business, which was almost out of some kind of dirty novel you'd read as a teenager. But between those two she created vast distances I could not apprehend, as though she was something made of air and wind and any attempt to touch or grasp her became a practical impossibility.

And then the rift came not with wails of anguish or rages of anger but more a sort of whimper from two people riding off in opposite directions. Cautious as I'd been not to say anything that set her off, I had still spoken occasionally to Delia in the language of love, but it was a dead language, so far as she and I were concerned. And there were no interpreters.

The big split came in late spring, when she was to have met me in Stamford for a long holiday weekend in the Connecticut countryside at the home of a very famous scribbler pal of mine. I'd been delighted Delia had agreed to come and she'd seemed excited at the time. Then she called and said she would be out in Oyster Bay on the North Shore of Long Island and she'd take the train back to New York and then up to Connecticut. That's when the trouble began. I drove down to meet her at the station an hour away and when the three o'clock pulled in, she was nowhere to be found. I not only waited till the last passenger was off, I waited till the new passengers were boarding for the trip to Boston. I was totally bewildered. This simply wasn't like her, to stand me up. But what could I do? I phoned her apartment and got the machine. There was no place else to call. There was nothing else but to return to my friends' home, fifty miles away, and hope she'd call.

There'd been no messages when I got there, and I think they sensed I was upset, and tried to offer possible explanations. I'd been there for an hour when she finally called up. Her explanation was that during the ride from New York she'd gotten in a conversation with a guy she'd sat next to and simply forgot to get off the train and that she was now in New Haven and would catch the next train back. I was relieved I hadn't been stood up, but it sounded like a pretty crummy explanation to me. What place of importance did I hold in her life if she was so engrossed with talking to other men that she literally left me standing in the station? Anyway, that set the tone for the weekend.

When she'd finally arrived, she was full of apologies, but I sensed something was amiss. This was confirmed when she asked where her bedroom was. Of course there were many in this grand home, but my hosts had put us together in their loveliest guest room. When I showed her to it, she said, "Oh, well, maybe I can take this one across the hall." The mood of things was getting glummer by the minute.

It would have been a glorious weekend otherwise, but Delia remained aloof toward me, entertaining herself in conversations with others attending the house party or simply disappearing with a book out onto the lawn. After two days of this, I'd had enough.

I took her for a drive and asked what in hell was going on.

"I'm just keeping my distance," she said.

"What in the world does *that* mean?" I asked.

"Just that I'm keeping my distance," she repeated.

I can't exactly remember the rest of the conversation, but the gist of it was that we were no longer a couple. She was going back to take a few courses in English at Columbia and was really going to be busy for, well, the foreseeable future. She'd call me sometime when things let up. So that was it, and there wasn't a goddamn thing I could do about it.

I offered to put her on a train back to New York then and there, but she protested that it would look embarrassing for her to be leaving early, and so I spent the remainder of Memorial Day in a blur of misery. I thought tennis might take my mind off it, but instead I went out and got beat by a rinky-dink who in normal circumstances wouldn't have been able to stay on the court with me five minutes. When we finally left that wretched place, she was concerned all the way back to New York that she'd miss her dinner appointment with a faculty adviser.

It seemed strange to me at the time that faculty advisers would take their female students out on dinner dates, but it has become much clearer to me now. Among the names on Delia's lovers list was one Horst Vining, English Department, Columbia University.

CHAPTER 10

WHEN I GOT back to my apartment, there was a message Delia had called. She said she'd be at home, so I called her back.

"You forgot to give me your number in New York," she said. "I'm glad I remembered you were at the Carlyle."

"I'd rather expected to hear from you before I left," I told her a little grumpily.

"Well, I thought I'd hear from you too—I guess it was some kind of miscommunicaiton."

"I guess," I said. "So, how's it going?"

"I got another letter."

"Where from?"

"This one's from Atlanta."

"Oh? What's it say?"

"He's mad I wasn't on camera that night when I was away. Set a new date for the red sweater thing."

"When?'

"Tonight. But it gets worse. He says at some point I'm to lean back and 'stick out my boobs.' Do you believe this shit, Johnny! *He* said, 'Boobs'! That's what he *wrote*!"

"Humm . . ." I said, trying to picture it.

"It's worse than that too. Here's what he says, 'If I don't see that, the whole town is going to know a lot more about Delia Jamison than she would ever wish them to.'"

"That's pure blackmail then," I said. "He's just created a prosecutable crime, if he hadn't already."

"I don't know what to do," she said darkly. "You know, I'm not particularly scared, I'm getting mad."

"And I don't know what to tell you either. The thing about blackmailers, of course, is that they're rarely satisfied, and it can lead to more and more."

"I know."

"So I guess you can call his bluff and take your chances with whatever he says he's got."

"I've thought about that."

"But in that case, we may never catch him," I said. "I was sort of hoping he'd show his hand, somehow get bolder and bolder until we could lay some kind of trap."

"Thing is, if I do what he says tonight, I'm worried about, well, my job. I mean, the station manager didn't say anything about the buttons, and maybe didn't even notice. But sooner or later, if this keeps up, he will. They watch that sort of thing very carefully."

"You could always tell him about it," I offered.

"No, no, I've been over that with you. He'd want to

call the police. No police. No publicity. I know it would get leaked."

"So why don't you just let the bastard play his hand?" I said.

"Because I don't know exactly what's in it," she replied firmly. "Look, Johnny, L.A.'s one of the three major markets in the country—and it's actually the biggest. Do you know how sensitive the station is to any kind of bad publicity? Any kind of ratings drop and I'm gone. And my reputation with me."

"Well, forgive me, and I know this sounds pragmatic and maybe even indelicate," I said, "but I would think something of this nature would cause your ratings to soar. I mean, after all, 'Beautiful Top Anchorwoman Blackmailed by Sex Maniac' . . .'"

"Oh, yeah, right," she said, "maybe for a little while, until the contents of the letters leaks out and the press starts sniffing around and digging up dirt that isn't even there, and then the tabloids and the other TV stations. . . . You know how this kind of thing starts and gets worse and worse. We may just report the news on TV, but *we're* some of the biggest news of all ourselves out here, Johnny. It would turn into a scandal and the station deplores scandals."

"Well, what else are you going to do?"

"I don't know yet," she cut in. "I'll decide later."

"Well, Mrs. Lincoln, other than that, are you enjoying the play?"

There was a pause, then Delia laughed. "Yeah, yeah, but, well, you know, I miss our quiet little meetings. I wish you were here."

"They were fun," I said, scarcely knowing what to make of her last remark. I had made an ironclad promise to myself not to read more into Delia's statements than was actually there. I had done that years ago only to find I'd reached the acme of gullibility.

"I saw Bo Bothwell today," I said.

"You did?" She sounded tentative, almost shocked.

"Yes. Seems like a nice guy. He wanted to be remembered to you."

"What did you tell him?" She sounded anxious.

"Nothing, other than you've been receiving odd communications and that I was trying to find out who might be responsible."

"Nothing more? What did you talk about?"

"You, of course."

"Now, Johnny . . ."

"Well, who was I supposed to talk about? Elizabeth Taylor? I mean, that's what I went there for."

"So what did you think?"

"I think it might be useful if you would tell me what was said in those letters—the sexual thing, I mean, that tipped you off."

"I've already said I don't want to get into that," she told me coolly. "Besides, it doesn't matter, does it? I mean, it was the same with them all, so what difference could it possibly make?"

"I just thought it might help me."

"I can't see how," she said, "and I really don't want to discuss it anymore."

I knew from painful past experience that when Delia got this way there was no arguing with her.

"So what did you two do," she said, "talk about my sex life? What did he tell you?"

"By the way," I asked, "did you ever know a guy named Homer Greer?"

"Homer Greer? Why, yes, I did. . . ."

"He wasn't on your list."

"Oh, well, Homer. I mean, I just couldn't imagine. It, it was so short. And he was, well, he wasn't exactly married—I mean, he was, but he was separated, and when I found that out, that was the end of it for me. I don't date married men. Did Bo tell you about that?"

"He mentioned it," I said. "He recalled that Homer was, well, let's say he had a crush on you."

"Yes, but I just can't believe Homer Greer would be involved. He wasn't the type. He was, well, to be blunt, he was weak. Frankly, I'd forgotten about him. I don't think you have to worry about seeing Homer Greer," she said.

"You never know," I told her, wondering if Homer Greer had also forgotten. . . .

ON THE OFF chance that my old tennis partner Arthur Dalton was in town, I called Agee-Williams & Co. to find that in fact he was. He seemed surprised to hear from me, even more so when I revealed what I wanted to talk about—which was making some foreign investments—and he cheerfully agreed to meet me for lunch next day. I figured I'd done enough detective work for a while and went out for a walk. Madison Avenue was a rush of people coming home from work, but the air was still bright and cool in the late afternoon. I walked past the little outdoor cafés where I'd often taken Delia way back when and the old nostalgia reared its head again. One time in high school I had failed a vocabulary test by confusing nostalgia and neuralgia and sometimes I still can't tell the difference, except that they both involve pain.

THE LUNCH DALTON had set up was at some chic Italian place on East Fifty-sixth Street. I got there a little late and didn't see him until I noticed a big fat man motioning me over. My God, I thought, so this was what the great Dalton had come to.

We shook hands and he seemed earnestly happy to see me. Sitting across from him, I could tell Dalton's tennis days were long over. He must have weighed three hundred pounds, and even his sandy hair was thinning. In the old times, he'd resembled a young Charlton Heston, but now he looked more like Sydney Greenstreet in *Casablanca.*

"Johnny, I've been following your career and I think it's just grand," he said. "I saw the Academy Awards. Congratulations."

"Thanks, Arthur," I said. "And so how have you been?"

"Oh, all right, I suppose. They keep me busy these days. I never see my apartment but about once a month. I kind of live in airplanes and hotels. Just got back from Beirut yesterday—we're trying to revive some kind of business there. And day after tomorrow I'm off again for Holland."

"Sounds interesting," I told him.

A waiter came over and took our orders. Dalton took a martini and I my usual. We talked about me putting some money into his firm and he suggested a mutual fund that specialized in Asian markets.

"I've doubled my own investment there in nine months, Johnny," he said, leaning over conspiratorially.

"That's the kind of deal I like to hear," I said. "It makes me more comfortable to get into something when the broker's into it himself. You remember what Bob Dole said when somebody asked him if he wasn't too old to run for president? He looks at them and says, "I just watch old Strom Thurmond. He's ninety-two. If Strom Thurmond makes a speech, I make a speech. If Strom Thurmond eats a banana, I eat a banana. . . .""

"Well," Arthur almost screamed, "I love bananas, myself!"

We ate lunch and talked casually of old times, and then I sprang the subject, as I had with Bo Bothwell.

"Delia Jamison," he drew out the words seriously, taking a deep breath. He pursed his lips and shook his head, as though it was a matter he hadn't much taste for.

"You went out with her for a while, right?" I said, knowing damned well he had.

"Yeah, sure did, way on back there. For about fifteen minutes. Say, you dated her too, right?"

"For an hour or so," I said ruefully.

"I lost track of her about six, seven years ago," he said. "Why do you ask?"

Ah, I thought, at least here was someone who could fill in a gap or two that I couldn't. I told him where she was and that a person was trying to blackmail her.

"No kidding. About what?"

"Not sure. It has something to do with sex, I think."

"Well, for her, that would cover a lot of ground," Arthur Dalton said.

"Why do you say that?" Looking at him now, I simply couldn't imagine the two of them in bed together.

He stared at me for a moment and shrugged.

"Was there something peculiar with her about sex?" I pressed.

"That's something I don't want to go into," he said suddenly.

"But there must have been—"

"Skip it, Johnny," Dalton interrupted. I saw a glint in his eyes that told me he meant it.

"Anyway," I continued, "it appears whoever it is, he's someone from her past, someone she had a fling with—more than a fling, actually." I still couldn't bring myself to use the word *affair.*

"And so what are you doing, trying to interview all

her old lays?" Dalton said. There was a hint of pathetic amusement in his eyes.

"Something like that. Just looking for anything that might help get to the bottom of this."

"You might spend the rest of your life on that," Dalton chortled.

"Why do you say that?"

"Hey, look, you're not still seeing her, or anything, are you?"

"No, she's married."

"No kidding? That's something I just wouldn't have expected. Listen, you ever see a barracuda go through a school of mackerel. Just chops them up by the dozens and spits them out. Doesn't even eat them. Leaves them trailing blood and guts as they float to the bottom."

"That the way Delia seemed to you?"

"Not at first. I mean, at first I just couldn't get over it. Here was this gorgeous babe, well bred, composed, didn't take any shit. Why, I was on my way to falling in love. Might already have been."

"But you say you didn't fall in love?" I asked.

"I damned sure could have, if she had given me a chance—who knows? You have any idea what it's like to be eaten alive? Why, when she cut out, all that was left of me was bones."

"That so?"

"Just out of the blue one day, she says she's got to be honest. Says she doesn't want to see me anymore. I asked why, and she says, 'You drink too much.'

Now what was that supposed to mean? Hell, Delia could down half a bottle of vodka and now she's walking away because *I* drank too much? I thought it was totally sanctimonious and fake, but, anyway, that was that. For a few weeks I was really down, you know. I even dropped out of our tennis game because of that. My head wasn't in it for a while."

That was interesting. I'd somehow figured he'd dropped out *because* he was seeing her and maybe knew I'd been seeing her too. Not because he was feeling low after she broke it off with him.

"But you said you'd seen her after that, though?"

"Yeah. I sure did. I dated old Susan Taylor for a while and after that was over, I don't know, I sort of just drifted for a few years. Fell in with the nose candy crowd, if you know what I mean. We found ourselves in all those downtown clubs. You know the kind. Nobody gets there till ten or eleven and you stay out till three or four in the morning. Dance, screw, whatever. I was into that for a while."

"And?"

"She was there too, sometimes."

"Delia?" That truly surprised me, but I didn't let on.

"Yeah, she'd be out on the dance floor doing her thing—it seemed so out of character. Funny, though, on the few occasions she'd see me, she'd avoid me like the plague. Once or twice we'd bump into each other, but she'd just be cordial, nothing more. Like we'd just been casual acquaintances."

"And so?"

"Well, I'd seen her enough in those places to know she wasn't just there for the dances."

"No?"

"She had a thing with one or two of the bartenders in a couple of different places. I knew that because they knew I knew her and told me afterward—it was strange—like they were trying to find out from me who she was. Really was. You know, even after they'd done the big deal with her. I guess she kind of kept them at arm's length."

"Yes, I understand that kind of thing."

"And there were some other guys too. Those places are a mixed bag, you know. No telling who you'll find in there on a given night. I mean, writers, bimbos, publishers, movie people—as well as guys from fucking Brooklyn and New Jersey, you know— from plumbers and construction workers to Wall Street guys, you know?"

I humored him with a nod.

"And sometimes, well, I guess I'd gained a little bit of weight by then, and mostly I'd be hanging around at the bar, just looking. And every once in a while, there she'd be, especially during the slow dances, hanging all over some guy, and sometimes it would be somebody in a pin-striped suit and sometimes somebody in jeans and a tank top. It didn't seem to matter. And, well, it wasn't just some rare occasion when I'd see her leaving the place with them, you know?"

"So you think she was sleeping with these guys?"

"Well, what the hell else? She hadn't come with them. But she left with them after hanging all over them all night. What would you think?"

"Maybe she was going with them to another club?"

"Sure. This would be at three, four in the morning. Closing time. I'm not that dumb."

"So how long did this go on?"

"Oh, I don't know, five, six years, on and off, of course. That's when I made that scene. Then I married Alice and all that ended for me. I don't know what happened to her after that."

"Do you remember the last time you saw her?"

"Yeah, actually I do," he said, and he said it almost trancelike. "It was around Christmas, about five years ago. I was hanging out by myself like an asshole and in she walks with this guy. He's a nice-looking guy, really well dressed, sort of Italian-looking. And I remember it because she's got her hair piled on top of her head, which she usually didn't do, and she was decked out too, high heels, a short blue skirt, and a red sweater. And that was one of the few times she seemed to go out of her way to recognize me, you know? She was up near the bar where I was standing and she gave me that big old smile and waved 'hi.' Normally she didn't do that."

"You remember what she *wore*?"

"Yeah—well, you know Delia, she sure filled out those sweaters."

I tried desperately to think of some way to pursue this line but couldn't.

"What were these clubs? Their names?"

"Well, there was Zero's and the Cave. There was Rads and the Glitch. Those were the hot ones then."

"Did you know any of the guys you saw her with?"

"Well, just those couple of bartenders. They were the Euro-trash kind, you know. Big muscular Italians and Spaniards and so on with dark tans and that kind of sexy way about them. One of the owners told me once the only reason he hired them was because a guy will buy a drink from any fucking geek, but girls need something to attract them to the bar. You know?"

"Yeah, I think I do, Arthur," I said. "I guess that makes good sense. Do you remember any of their names—the bartenders?"

"Only their first names. That's all anybody ever went by down there. Who knows what's happened to them by now?"

"Do you suppose you could jog your memory and put a name with a place I can use?"

"Sure, I'll try," he said, and told me a few names he remembered.

"Listen," I told him. "Bo Bothwell told me something about Delia getting married a long time ago—some kind of tragedy involved. You know anything about that?"

"Nope. I never heard it. What kind of tragedy?"

"I don't know. Bo says he might be wrong about the whole thing. By the way, do you remember a guy called Homer Greer?"

"Greer—oh, yeah. He's the fellow got into some

trouble over at Merrill Lynch, right? Some kind of mis-trading."

"Did you know him?"

"Why, did he date Delia too?"

"I think so. How about Worthington Hathaway?"

"Worthy—sure. Now, I know he went out with her a couple of years after I did. She must have really done something to piss him off."

"Why do you think that?"

" 'Cause after it was over with them, every time he'd see her, you know, at some party or even a restaurant, he'd just slam out the door. Wouldn't be in the same room with her. He never talked about it, at least not to me, but he was burned, and that really wasn't like Worthy. He was a pretty easygoing guy."

"So I've heard."

"I guess I've gotta ask you, is she still good-looking?" Dalton said, but there was something in the way he said it that made me feel he was getting agitated, as though some burst of realization was just dawning on him.

"I'm afraid she is."

"Well," he said, shaking his head. "Say, you still play tennis?" he asked, abruptly changing the subject.

"A little," I answered.

"And I bet you're still pretty good." Now I detected a flare of harshness in his voice.

"I have my moments," I said. "Tell me—with Delia . . ."

"I don't want to talk about Delia," Dalton snapped

suddenly. "Say—you didn't come here to talk about investments anyway, did you? It was just about her, wasn't it?"

"Well, in a way. . . ."

"Well, screw you, Lightfoot," he snarled, "and her too! I don't like being taken for a sucker—especially where that woman's concerned. I've got my pride."

Dalton rose up from the table like some gigantic thing from the sea and threw his hand dismissively. "And who are you? Fucking Dick Tracy or somebody?" He turned and waddled out of the restaurant, sticking me with the bill.

CHAPTER 11

I HAD CONCLUDED BY now that the unforgivable sin in this kind of work is to form a rigid picture—to assume a person acts the way you want them to, when in fact it might be just the opposite. Sure, the 1980s were a time of self-indulgence and the pursuit of pleasure and Delia had been a young, beautiful single woman living through them by wit and instinct. But the picture I was seeing now was different from the one I'd imagined; almost like that bizarre turn-of-the-century trompe l'oeil in which the portrait of a beautiful woman, when looked at long enough, transforms into a ghastly skull—Doreena Gray, Dorian's kid sister. Well, maybe not quite that bad, but that's the drift.

There was a message at the desk from Bo Bothwell. He had tracked down Homer Greer and left me with his current phone number. I rang it and a person answered with the information that I had reached some kind of computer operation located in a small town in northwestern Massachusetts, about three hours from New York. Soon Homer Greer was on the line and I didn't see any way to ease into the conversation by offering to buy computer widgets and so I told him what I wanted to talk about. There was a long silence, then he said, okay, he'd talk to me, but that he was leaving first thing in the morning for a week's sales trip to various cities. What the hell, I thought, it was still early afternoon and a drive through the autumn countryside of New England might be nice.

Before I left, I dialed the number in Los Angeles for Worthington Hathaway. His secretary said he was in a meeting. I left a phone-tag message for him to call me back. He, of course, was my most interesting prospect, but three thousand miles away. I'd have to settle for some preliminaries for the time being.

This time I didn't call my driver. Actually, I love driving myself, except in Manhattan, and when I finally cleared traffic and pulled the big green Mercedes out onto the New England Expressway, I felt exhilarated as its power leapt to my command. Three hours later I turned off on the exit to Homer Greer's village. The beeches and maples were a riot of red, orange, and yellow and the road followed a clear rushing stream past hayricks and old red barns, just like out of a picture book. Homer's business was in a small frame building at the edge of town, with what appeared to be a warehouse in the rear. It was a casual place, and the several employees I saw were wearing jeans and plaid, a far cry from the stuffed shirts of Wall Street. A secretary took me back to Homer's office at the end of a long hallway. A windowless room cluttered with files and reports stacked everywhere, even in the chairs where you might have sat down. I waited a few minutes, then Homer Greer appeared in the door.

He was a lanky guy with a pudgy face and watery blue eyes. Years ago he might have resembled Ronald Colman in *Lost Horizon,* but there was a distasteful aspect to his expression now, as though he'd witnessed something unsavory and was always thinking about it.

"You're Mr. Lightfoot, I guess?" he said, extending a rather weak hand to shake. He apologized for the disarray and moved some piles of paper so I could sit down.

"Why is it you want to talk to me, I mean, about her?"

I got right to the point. I'd already gathered Delia Jamison was not a subject pleasant to his memory.

"And so you think it's me, huh?" he said with some finality.

"Not at all," I told him. "I'm just trying to piece some things together and find out who it is. The chips can fall where they may, but I understand you had an experience with her."

"Who told you about me—that I had an affair with her?"

"Bo Bothwell."

"Oh, good old Bo. Did he tell you he did too?"

"Yes."

"And what did he say?"

"Only that you dated her and it might not have ended too well."

"Might not have ended too well. . . ." Homer repeated, as if savoring the words in distant recall. "Yes, I suppose you could say that. You might also say that she wrecked my life."

"That bad, huh?"

"Every bit that bad."

"Want to tell me about it?"

"No, but I will, if it's any use to you," Homer said. "You see, when we started going out—"

"Wait," I interrupted. "How did you meet her?"

"She didn't tell you?"

I shook my head.

"Well," he said uncomfortably, "I'm not sure if I should go into that. Let's just say we met. . . ."

Instinctively I interrupted him again.

"Look, it might be important," I told him.

"Why don't you ask her?" he said sourly.

"Because I'm here and I'm asking you," I said. "Listen, I understand that your feelings for Delia might not be fond, but I think what's happening to her is serious and I'd appreciate any help you can give me."

He thought for a long moment, then said finally, "Well, I met her on the phone. One of those call-in services."

I was puzzled and frowned.

"It was phone sex," he said.

I still didn't get it.

"I was married, but separated from my wife," he went on. "Somebody told me about a number to call where they charge you so much a minute on your credit card. They said I wouldn't believe this girl, Sheika—that she was pure sex and sensuality. So I called. You couldn't imagine the voice—strong but very sexy. Like somebody in charge. You could tell you weren't talking to some bimbo or a sixty-year-old grandmother or something. . . . This girl was the real thing. After a few times when we got through talking about sex, we just started talking. About all sorts of things. Matter of fact, I ran up a hell of a bill. She was very funny and quick."

And this was Delia. The week had been full of surprises, but this took the cake.

"She wanted to know all about me," he said.

"Who suggested the meeting?"

"I did."

"And she wasn't averse to that?"

"At first she was, but as the weeks went by, I guess she was getting as curious as I was. Finally she agreed to have a drink. She told me to meet her at some place over on Lexington. To go sit at the end of the bar. I guess that was in case I was a troll or something, so she could just take a look and then walk out. But the fact is, we hit it off right away."

"And she kept up the phone sex job while you were dating?"

"Yes, I guess so. A lot of times she said she had to go home early. I figured that's what it was. But I wasn't calling her then. I didn't need to. I really couldn't believe it when I met her—she wasn't at all what I'd expected."

"What did you expect?" I asked. Now I understood Bo Bothwell's confusion over the late-dating.

"I don't know, but it sure wasn't her," Greer said. "I wish the hell I'd never done it."

"How come?" I thought he was going to tell me anyway, but I wanted to guide him along a little.

"She was very aggressive to me. I mean, in an exciting way. It was like I wasn't coming on to her, more like she was coming on to me. And I found that exciting."

"The sex, you mean?"

For the first time Homer looked me straight in the eye, and then totally brushed off the question.

"She sort of ran the conversations," he said. "And she knew things about the market, not specifics, but what drove it. And it wasn't bullshit either. It made sense, at least as much as any of that stuff made sense."

"Yes, I know."

"She knew I'd been married because I'd told her, and she mentioned it, and I said something like 'Peg and I split up a year or so ago.' It wasn't really a lie, and it seemed good enough for her, so we made another date."

Homer leaned back in his chair and looked at the ceiling and let out a kind of sigh, as though gathering his thoughts. I could see that at one point he'd been a large, good-looking man, probably confident and proud, but no longer.

"After that first date I was—what's the word? Smitten, I guess. She was, well, so perfect. Everything was perfect. We did everything together for five and a half months, and she was a helluva bridge player too—best I've ever seen. I mean, everything. Peg and the kids had moved to Florida to her parents' place after our breakup, so I still had the townhouse on Fifty-eighth Street. I knew we were probably going to have to sell it sometime, but in any case, I asked Delia if she'd like to move in with me. I think that's when it started."

"What was that?"

"She—she backpedaled. At first I thought she just needed more time to get used to the idea. But it was more than that. I think now it was almost as if I had slapped her in the face. And in the next weeks I found she seemed to be doing a lot of other things. Things we would normally have been doing together, but she'd tell me she did them on her own, movies and stuff like that. And then one day, it was right at New Year's, she just vanished. I mean, nothing.

"Right after the first of the year Peg and the kids came up for a few weeks and I moved into the Century Club during that time. I phoned Delia day and night, trying to figure out what happened. The answering machine was all I got. Then I found out what did."

"What was that?"

"Well, I went over to my house one afternoon to see the kids, and Peg wouldn't even let me in. Slammed the door in my face. You see, Peg and I had discussed getting back together; she was a wonderful mother, a wonderful woman—but, of course, that was before Delia came into the picture.

"Anyway, it took a lot of calls and stuff to Peg, but I finally found out what had happened. Delia had written me a letter. Basically, it was a Dear John, breaking things off. It said stuff like that she'd enjoyed our time together and was touched by the seriousness of my feelings toward her and that I wanted her to move in with me and all. But she went on to say she wasn't ready to make any kind of commitments with anybody now. Not just with me, mind you, she'd said, 'anybody,' as though that's what I was—an 'anybody.'

"Thing was, the letter was so cheerful. You know, here we'd spent nearly half a year together, and her tone was just so matter-of-fact, like she was a schoolteacher explaining something to a child. Firm, but honest, you know what I mean?"

"Yeah, honest. That sounds familiar. Did she mention knowing you were still legally married?"

"No, why?"

"Just wondering."

"Damn," Homer continued, "I just couldn't get over the *tone*! It actually sounded happy! Like she wasn't the least bit sad after all that time. Said stuff like 'I'm sure you will find someone soon who you will truly love and who will truly love you.' That kind of bullshit. Can you understand how *patronizing* that was for me? It was just like she took it for granted I'd understand, that everything was okay, now that she had explained it—like nothing had happened between us at all!"

"Must have been a rude awakening," I offered.

"Worse than that," Homer said. "The end of the letter was filled with, well, just chitchat. And do you know where she mailed the letter from? From fucking Bermuda, of all places—that's where Peg and I had spent our honeymoon! Wrote all about how pretty it was there and the sun and sea. Said she'd been spending a few days there with 'friends.' Didn't she think I'd pick up on that? *Friends,* my ass! She had to be there with some guy—and there I was freezing my tail off in New York. . . ."

Then it came all at once. *Homer* had been her date that New Year's Eve we'd met! So that's why Delia accepted my invitation to Bermuda—to put her space, her distance, between herself and a soon-to-be former lover.

"Well, what happened was, Peg had opened the letter," Homer said. "Her excuse was that it was her business because what was I doing getting letters from women in Bermuda if we'd been talking about reconciliation? So that was the end of it—for everybody. Peg split the next day back to Florida and I didn't hear from her again except through her lawyer. And of course he had the letter. It cost me everything.

"I was so rattled by it all that a couple of weeks later I really bombed out. It was a terribly busy day in the office and I made a big bond trade on the computer and, well, I accidentally put in some wrong figures. I just couldn't seem to concentrate during those days. I knew I should have asked for some vacation, but the notion of spending a vacation under those circumstances was almost unbearable. Anyway, my little gaffe cost the company two million bucks and I got canned. When something like that happens, on the Street, it means you're out for good. It wasn't long after that I moved up here. A friend of mine owns this little company. I'm the sales manager."

"Look at it this way," I said. "This is a lot prettier place to work than New York."

"I could have made millions by now," Homer said, ignoring my observation. "And Delia, she comes and she's gone, and all I ever heard from her again is a lousy Christmas card she sent me the next year—with a picture of herself on the cover! Can you imagine that? I might even have been back with Peg and my kids," he continued. "Now I only see them two weeks a year. And Peg's remarried. Almost sixteen years"—his voice drifted off—"sixteen years."

"What do you do as sales manager?" It sounded as abrupt as it was, but something had just occurred to me.

"Sell these hard drives," he said. "We've got our little share of the market, I guess."

"Travel much?"

"Good bit," he said.

"Big cities?"

"Yeah."

"Ever go to Atlanta?"

"Sure."

"L.A.?"

"Of course."

"Boston?"

"All the time."

"Miami?"

"Yeah, sometimes, why?"

I looked at him openly. "Those are the places some of these communications have come from," I said, almost hoping he would slip up and mention letters and I'd probably have my man. But he didn't bat an eye.

"And now she's on TV in L.A." Homer Greer shook his head. "Well, she was always smart. I thought she'd do good someplace, but that wasn't one I'd figured. She sure outsmarted me."

"Maybe someday she'll outsmart herself," I told him. I don't know why I said it, except I thought it would somehow make him feel better.

He asked how I came to be involved in it and I told him. "Just friendship," I added.

"She still pretty?" he asked.

IT WAS DARK when I drove back along the thruway and finally the lights of New York began to shine in the distance. The glow of a modern Gomorrah. Homer just didn't seem the type—Delia had been right about that. He seemed irreconcilably sad and in fact I felt sorry for him. But so far his travels to places where the letters had come from and his bitterness certainly didn't let me rule him out as a suspect. I'd have to do some more digging in that pit, or maybe Rick would. Naturally, Delia hadn't meant to send her letter where Homer's wife would read it, but she did. Things on paper can always be dangerous. Delia was smart enough to have figured out Homer probably wouldn't take things too well in a face-to-face confrontation and thought writing was the best way to end it. Honestly. Whatever the facts were, Homer Greer, in my impression, was a broken man, yet the shadow of my suspicion still hovered above him. He certainly seemed to have a motive to hurt her.

WHEN I GOT back into Manhattan, I turned off Roosevelt Drive onto East Ninetieth and then down Second Avenue to Elaine's Restaurant. I was up for a big veal chop. I double parked the car outside the door, went in and got a menu, and put it on my driver's side dashboard. Don't ask me why, but cops seeing such an exhibit when they are about to write a ticket mysteriously change their minds.

Elaine was by herself at a front table, looking jovial, when I came back in.

"Well, good to see you again, Johnny. I thought we'd lost you to those sunshine people on the coast."

"Never," I said, giving her a hug.

"So what have you been up to? More scripts?"

"Somebody's got to make sure the U.S. Treasury doesn't go broke."

She laughed. "I know exactly what you mean."

I ordered the veal chop and a bottle of Chianti, then pulled out a cigar.

"Hope this doesn't offend anyone," I said.

"Screw 'em," she replied. Good old Elaine.

"Listen, I want to ask you something," I told her. "I'm doing this script, okay, and there's a girl in it who's a real heartbreaker, you know? I mean, she's got dead and wounded all over the place—for years this has been going on. You know the type, don't you?"

"Know 'em? Hell, I see 'em in here every night of the week."

"Well, I've got my own ideas, but you might have a different take on it than me. What I'm trying to figure is, what makes them tick?"

"What makes a butterfly tick?" Elaine answered. "They just go from flower to flower till they've sucked it dry and move on again."

"What about smart butterflies? Wouldn't it make sense to just find one bush or tree and stay with it?"

"There aren't any smart butterflies," she said. "They're pretty, but they ain't smart."

I could see the metaphor had played itself out. "I guess what I'm driving at is, why? Would it probably be something that happened to them in childhood, or adolescence, that sets this kind of behavior off? Like getting dumped on by guys one time too many—something like that? Sounds too simple."

"Who knows?" she said. "Could be anything. Some people are afraid to settle down. Maybe they're not ready. Meantime, they got to do something. So go figure."

"You're not much help," I said jokingly. "But I'm talking about a girl who has this unbelievable attraction. Men fall head over heels for her immediately, and then it's like being caught in a spider's web. They can't get out."

"And then the spider eats them, right?"

"Exactly. But why?"

"Just write the damned story like you see it, Johnny, it'll turn out fine. Surprise me." Yep, good old Elaine.

"Say," I said on impulse, "do you remember a girl I used to go out with way back when. Girl called Delia Jamison?"

"Oh yeah," Elaine said. " 'The Looker.' Worked on you pretty good, I remember. Of course, those were your whiskey-drinking days," she laughed.

"Yeah, well . . ." Elaine didn't mince words. "You know, she went to work in radio here for a while."

"Yeah, I know. She used to come in with Max Weed."

"Max Weed?"

"You remember Max—he was a gossip columnist in those days."

"Oh, right," I said. I did remember Maxwell Weed. He was old New York society, but I could hardly imagine Delia being an item with him. They used to call him 'The Arm' because he was forever squiring around divorced or widowed socialites to functions where you get your picture in the newspapers. Maybe she was just along for the ride, as they say, because I remembered that when Weed wasn't escorting the obligatory socialite, he liked to be seen with pretty women, though I doubted he took any of them to bed.

"Yeah," Elaine said, "Max used to come in with her from time to time for a couple of years, I think. They'd been to parties and things. I think they had some kind of falling out or something, though, 'cause one time I asked him, 'Where's The Looker,' and he just sort of waved me off. You know how they do."

"He still come in?"

"Sometimes. Mostly he hangs out at the bar at Smith and Wollensky's—that's where a lot of the old Twenty-one crowd went, you know."

"When does he come in here? Often?"

"You never know," she said. "But he's at Smith and Wollensky's every afternoon about five."

"Thanks," I said, grateful she didn't really care why I'd asked.

CHAPTER 12

I WAS BEGINNING TO feel my life was full of snakes, and that what I was seeking here was not only Delia's tormentor but some kind of vindication for myself too. I guess I wanted to believe I'd meant more to her than the rest and not just been another victim of her siren's song, but in a temporary moment of mental clarity I realized how totally ridiculous that was.

The next evening I threw on my best banker's-looking suit and went down to Smith & Wollensky's, a venerable chophouse with an old-timey, comfortable wooded feeling. I spotted Maxwell Weed as soon as I walked in. He was at the bar holding forth with four or five guys surrounding him, New York political types as well as a newspaper columnist or two. As luck would have it, there was a vacant stool and I passed by Max as I went toward it. He recognized me all right, though he probably didn't remember my name. But we'd spent a night or two together at the tables in Elaine's in the old days and I could see a flicker of recognition in his eyes and he nodded as I went by.

I ordered a glass of wine and tried to look preoccupied as I listened to Max's conversation behind me. There was a lot of laughter and some feigned whispering, which is how those kinds of people communicate—as though there were big, important secrets in the air. After a while I turned around on my stool and sort of half faced them, and when Max noticed me, I saw again the spark of recollection in his face. For some reason he reminded me of a cross between a rat and a snake—an unctuous combination of Peter Lorre and Rip Torn. The ultimate ratsnake man. Suddenly a big grin spread across Weed's lips and he stood up and came over to me, bringing his vodka and tonic.

"Johnny Lightfoot," he said, "a million years ago!"

"Hi, Max," I replied. "You haven't changed a bit."

"Oh yes, I have. I'm fatter, older, meaner, and smarter. But you've done well too, my boy. Congratulations."

The others around Max started their own conversation or drifted off and he sat next to me as we caught up on old times. Max was the quintessential New York insider. He knew everybody and everything, and was mad when he didn't, and told me all the latest gossip. He'd already downed two more vodkas and I was on my second glass of wine when I sprang the question on him.

"Delia Jamison," he intoned. "The most fabulous piece of ass in New York City!"

I thought that was an inelegant thing to say but held my tongue. Besides, I'd be bowled over if Max had any firsthand knowledge of the subject. And, yes, he said, he'd dated Delia off and on for several years, apparently in between her other boyfriends.

"She used me, of course, my boy," he said, "but then we all use each other in our own little ways, don't we? She liked going to the functions, you know, and she met a lot of rich and powerful men on my watch. Dated some of them too, but I imagine nothing much came of it. She could be interesting company, though, when you needed it."

"That so. Why do you say?"

"Look, my boy, she went out with some of the *biggest* of the biggest in her day. I introduced her to most of them, of course, one way or the other. But as those things go, hers wasn't a long run on that circuit."

"When was that?"

"Oh, around the mid-eighties, I suppose."

"Who were these biggies?"

"You name them, my boy. Greek shipping tycoons, British media barons, cosmetic kings, Hollywood moguls, record company big shots—all the princes of capital who use this city as their whorehouse."

"And Delia saw these people?"

"Saw them, she screwed them, for God's sake."

"What makes you think that?"

"Because those people don't take out girls like Delia who won't—at least the ones who still *can* screw don't. Are you dense?"

"No. But why Delia? I'm astonished." Actually, I wasn't, but I *was* surprised she'd found her way into that group. She was in many ways an unpretentious person. It just didn't seem like her style.

"Whatever on earth for? She was superb, my boy! I mean, here's this gorgeous woman on their arm, and so they get attention at all the right places, Twenty-one, Le Club, Four Seasons, Mortimer's, Le Cirque. Even Elaine's, for that matter. And Delia played it like a pro." Weed downed the last of another vodka and motioned to the waiter for another.

"How's that?"

"Well, for heaven's sake, you've met a few of these people, I know you have! They spend the whole day playing God. Hell, some of them *are* God. And then they come home to their quiet little docile woman who goes to bed early so they can say they've got a business meeting that night and then drive off to pick up some chick in their limos and show her off for a while."

At this point I resisted a sudden impulse to order a vodka myself.

"Well, at first Delia was just a prop to them. Like something pretty on a stage set, you know, or an exquisite centerpiece on a dining table. If she'd been plain or mousy, nobody would have even spoken to her, of course—you know the scenario. But she wasn't, and then sooner or later one of the big shots would begin sounding off."

"About what?"

"Oh, everything and anything, of course, they always do—the junta in Argentina, the Mideast, Greece versus Turkey, the IMF, various trade agreements—you know how they are, lecture, expound, expect everybody to shut up and listen. One of them just goes on and on while the others nod in agreement, but Delia would just sit there, looking scrumptious, waiting for her time. And then, precisely when the speaker thinks he'd impressed her and everybody else, she'd jump right in!"

"Delia? When I knew her, she'd never do anything like that."

"Ha, ha, my boy! She'd obviously grown out of that phase! She'd wait till they had a few drinks, then make her move."

"And say what?"

"It wouldn't matter. These were guys who knew 'everything.' And so she'd invariably disagree with them. You know Delia, my boy, habitually contrary! Of course, those people weren't used to this; at first they'd think it was cute and be patronizing. My God, I saw it myself! But she could be absolutely tenacious; then they'd all get flustered and try to make a fool of her. Not used to a woman speaking up! Sooner or later one or more of them would try to 'persuade' her to his, or their, line of thinking, but by that time it was too late. They were probably drunk by then and maybe she was too, but they were *old* drunks, and couldn't hold it. She'd always manage to shift the argument around until at last even *they* didn't know what they were arguing about anymore; they were just trying to look down her dress or something!"

At this point Weed was giggling.

"Some of them were put off by her behavior, but she didn't care. But others were positively intrigued by it, drooling over this voluptuous beauty who could waltz into their poker parlor and beat them at their own game. Naturally, those were the ones Delia wouldn't give the time of day to. My impression was that she looked at it as a game, a cat toying with mice—whether it was instinctive, or only because she'd realized she could, who could say?"

"And this went on for . . . ?"

"Oh, a year or so, maybe more. She'd jump from one to the other, I don't know whether by her choice or theirs. Maybe they were just passing her around. But, my God, she was always off to someplace in those days, and she didn't have a pot to piss in of her own. The Mediterranean on Sam Spiegel's yacht, to France on the Concorde, or to the South Pacific. I remember once she got back from Saint-Tropez, for chrissake, and told me with a straight face she'd been parasailing and whitewater rafting and it 'wasn't scary enough' for her! Why, my boy, she was playing in the scariest game of all!"

"What happened in the end?" I asked. "Obviously she didn't stay in this crowd."

"Kicked out, I'm afraid," Weed said piously. "At first she'd be everywhere, all the dinner parties and stuff, but none of the older women, or the younger ones either, liked her, and for the same obvious reasons. She was a threat. A loose cannon. These people are what pass for international high society these days. Fifty years ago, the old crowd in New York wouldn't have had anything to do with them, but, anyway, there it was—Kansas City versus . . . well, 'the world as we know it now.' I don't know what happened really. I think the wives must have gotten together and somehow laid down the law. No more Delia! And so she came back to me, and back to her little junior society bunch, and from there she just seemed to gravitate downward."

Weed gulped the last of what I'd guessed was about his tenth vodka. "I had launched her, my boy, and she went up like a Fourth of July rocket," he gurgled, "but I'm afraid she came down like the stick!"

I realized Max Weed wouldn't be in condition much longer to tell me anything, let alone about Delia, but he was proving a fountain of intriguing information, even if it was only background. So I asked him for lunch the next day. He mumbled something about having another luncheon date but suggested a drink at his club. It wasn't a particularly good club, but that was okay by me, I wasn't in the clubby mood these days. I left him there at his table and as I looked back going out the door, he was hailing a waiter for another drink.

A LITTLE AFTER noon I found myself at Weed's club, off Park Avenue in the Forties. I walked in and was looking around at pictures when I heard his voice hail me from the bar.

"Hope you don't mind sitting in here," he said. "It's ever so much more pleasant."

I didn't, but I knew this club. Members who are posted for not paying their dues are allowed to pay cash at the bar for a while but can't charge anything else. I asked for a beer. Weed already was working on a Bloody Mary. Considering how I'd left him last night, I was surprised he'd showed up at all, but he was actually looking hale. As if on cue, he jumped back into the conversation as if it had never ended.

"I knew you'd taken her out at one time yourself, sure. She told me. But that was well after—"

"You know what's become of her?" I cut in.

"Yeah, sure, she's in L.A. on the television. Big star now. But of course you know that too, my boy, you're out there all the time."

"Do you still stay in touch?" I asked.

"Oh, no, no," he said. "We haven't seen each other in years. Had a little set-to and that was the end of it."

"Not serious, I hope."

"Oh no, of course not. You see, Delia—well, as I said, she saw me only when she thought she couldn't do better, at least that's how I'd put it, and then, after her demise in the big leagues, it seems she'd suddenly fallen in love with this *prick*. And I do mean that word. This guy was an aspiring movie director, standing in line with all the other aspiring movie directors—what they call underground movies, that is. Young guy named James Cornwell, I think. I'm not even sure that was his real name. And he was absolute trash. Came from Texas or someplace and was in with that lowbrow artsy-fartsy bunch that wore all-black clothes and those ridiculous high-top laced shoes and so on. But she fell for him like a ton of bricks and the next thing you know, she announces to me they're going to be married. It was absurd."

"Why was that?"

"Well, it was obvious she was feeling the—oh, whatever you call it when women get to be that age, she was about thirty-one or thirty-two then—the time clock or 'biological clock' or something. You see, Delia, I think, was torn between the notion of finding somebody rich and powerful and falling for a hunk. Part of her wanted one, part the other, and it's pretty difficult in this town to find them in combination. With the possible exception of JFK Jr., most of the money guys are old and hoary. The hunks, well, they're an uncertain entity. Maybe they'll make it or maybe they won't, but the hunks don't live in floor-through apartments on Fifth and Park Avenues and have limos and big mansions in the Hamptons, and if they do, there's a long line of women after them. Delia didn't like to stand in line. It wasn't her style.

"Anyway, I told her not to do it—to not marry this bozo," Max continued, looking more like the snake now.

"First, I knew something about this guy. He'd done a couple of cute little experimental movie shorts that got some recognition at one of the so-called film festivals and thought he was hot shit. Going all the way, you know what I mean? Well, he was also a druggie—big time. Delia didn't believe that—she could be obtuse that way. I tried to tell her, but she brushed it off as a rumor. He must have cleaned up his act for a while when he was around her, but this kid had Bolivian Marching Powder written all over him. Delia, as you know, could drink like a fish, but she didn't put up with any kinds of drugs. It was totally hypocritical of her, of course, but that's the way she was.

"Anyhow, they got married and I, well, I couldn't stand this kid. I didn't go to the wedding—I just arranged to be out of town, but I saw them once afterward. She took him up to Elaine's, thinking Elaine was going to give them a good table, because she had sometimes come up there with the big shots. But Elaine don't do that. Delia had totally forgotten she'd mostly been riding on my magic carpet with Elaine. Elaine, unless you're her special buddy, seats you as who you are, or who you come with, not who you've *been* with. So, anyway, I'm in there one night and spotted them back in the part of the restaurant they call Siberia—that's where Elaine had put them, God bless her. So I went over and tried to be nice, but the kid is obviously stoned out of his gourd and being rude and silly, so I just let them be.

"Next thing I hear, she's left him. She called me up one night late and left a message saying, yeah, I'd been right, he's a druggie, coke all over the place and so forth. So she packs up and leaves. They hadn't been married but six or eight months and were living over on East Seventieth Street or somewhere—with that address, probably on her money, such as it was, 'cause all this kid's dough went up his nose. Next thing, I read in the papers what happens. The shmuck jumps out the window of their apartment. *Splat,* fifteen stories below—a wonderful self-defenestration, I must say. No telling what caused it—was it because she left him or the cocaine snorting or both? But whatever, she doesn't blame herself at all. That was Delia. She called a week or so later and you've never heard anyone so calm and collected. She was just, well, philosophic. Like she hadn't even been married to him at all. Said the guy had a problem and solved it and she was going to get on with the rest of her life."

"You don't think she felt bad about it?"

"Oh, of course she did, but Delia was a tough woman that way—not merciless and not without pity or feelings—she just didn't like to show it. But she had an enormous sense of self and her own security. When she put you behind her, my boy, you ate dust."

As those words rang in my ears, Max jumped up from his bar stool and waved at somebody coming through the door.

"Well, my boy," he said, "here's my party, got to go. See you around, huh, kid?"

I sat there a few more minutes in Weed's club, finishing my beer and pondering his revelations. A lot can happen in people's lives as the years go by, but for some dumb reason I'd always thought I would have known if anything big or bad had happened in Delia's. I figured she would have told me about the earlier marriage if she'd thought it was any of my business. I guess it wasn't.

FOR THE NEXT two days I worked on my screenplay for Toby Burr, who'd left increasingly sardonic messages with the front desk. I had also set up an appointment with Professor Horst Vining of Columbia University, at his office on Friday afternoon.

None of my several calls to Worthington Hathaway in Los Angeles had been returned, even though I'd told his secretary what I wanted to talk about. I put in another one and was told, as usual, that Mr. Hathaway was in a meeting.

That evening, around eleven, Delia called.

"I got another one," she said. "This time it was mailed in town."

"From L.A.?"

"Yes. It was mailed from the main post office downtown, I think."

"What's it say?"

"He's unhappy."

"Did you wear the red sweater?"

"Yes, but I didn't stick out my chest, goddamn it."

"Well, good for you."

"Maybe not," Delia said. "He was furious. Listen to what he says: 'When you are asked to do something and you don't, this raises the specter of my royal displeasure.' Can you believe it!"

"Sounds like he's got a Napoleon complex," I said.

"He's got pictures, Johnny." I thought I heard her voice crack.

"What?"

"He says he's got photographs of me. He put in a cutoff piece of one in the letter. 'You can't believe how cute they are,' he says, 'even though they are a bit revealing.' He underlines *revealing*."

"Where would he have gotten photographs?"

"Who knows?" she said. "I certainly never had any 'revealing' photographs taken of myself—at least not that I am aware of."

"What's the picture?"

"Well, it's just a snip—no face or anything. Of somebody naked."

"You?"

"I can't tell. It could be. It's blurry."

"And you've never had any pictures taken of you like that?"

"Never. I mean, one time years ago I was at the beach and took my top off for a few minutes and then I saw somebody walking toward me from way away and put it back on again. Whoever that was, they couldn't have taken any kind of picture from that distance."

"Well, it doesn't sound like that's the kind of thing he's talking about anyway, does it?"

"No."

"What about at your apartment? By the pool. Do you sometimes—"

"No, never, there are five floors above me, looking

down. I wouldn't even swim in the dark of night without a suit on."

"Well, either he's bluffing or he's got something. That's the bottom line."

"Where would he get them?" she said almost frantically.

"I don't have a clue," I replied, "unless one of your former boyfriends—"

"What?"

"Well, I've heard of people setting up secret cameras in their apartments. In their bedrooms. Video cameras, even. There was even a movie about it once. With all this sneaky Pete business going on these days, they can do anything. They even have a big trade show out in Vegas every year, showing off stuff like long-range cameras, hidden cameras, listening devices, and all sorts of things like that."

"But who . . . who on earth would do such a thing? Nobody I ever dated. I can't imagine!"

"Well, it appears someone you dated is the one sending the letters. And he now says he's got pictures. You've got to draw some conclusion."

"Oh my God, Johnny. What do I do?"

"It might be about time to break all this to your husband," I said. "All of it. And maybe your TV station too. It's serious."

"No, no, I can't. I've explained that. All this just makes it worse."

"Well, what does he want you to do now?"

"The red sweater thing again—the whole business all over again."

"When?"

"Next Friday."

"Sounds like he's got a fixation on you with red sweaters. Can you think of anybody you ever wore a red sweater with? I mean, some kind of connection?"

"No. Of course I've had red sweaters. I don't even know how many over the years, maybe dozens of them. All girls have red sweaters in their wardrobes."

"Let me change the subject for a second," I said. During the conversation I'd been tempted to ask Delia about Max Weed and what he'd said to me, but I didn't. I couldn't see how it fit in right now. So I asked about something else.

"One of the guys is named Worthington Hathaway, right?"

"Worthy, yes. I dated him for a while—you knew that, he's on the list."

"Did you know he's living in Los Angeles?"

"What's he doing here?"

"According to Bothwell he got divorced and moved out there a few years ago. He's general counsel for an oil brokers company."

"I didn't even know he'd gotten married," she said.

"I've been trying to call him and so far he hasn't responded."

"Well, maybe he's still mad at me," Delia said.

"Why would he be mad?"

"Oh, it was silly of me. I was supposed to go somewhere with him, and I didn't."

"That would make him mad at you for twenty years?"

"It was to Rome."

"Rome, Italy?"

"He'd planned this big trip, you know? I mean, I'd hardly had time to consider it after he asked me. I think he believed he was in love with me or something, and he wanted me to be in love with him. But I wasn't. And all of a sudden, I just felt like I was getting sucked in. And he'd rented a big villa overlooking Rome on one of the hills. We'd just seen this old movie on television, *Rome Adventure,* or *The Roman Spring of Mrs. Somebody,* I don't remember which. And Worthy says, 'How would you like to go to Rome?' and I said, 'Sure,' because, well, I just thought he was sort of joking, and next thing you know, he's got the plane tickets and this expensive villa for three weeks and everything. It just shocked me, I guess."

"And so you backed out?"

"Well, I suppose it was worse than that."

"Meaning?"

"I just didn't go."

"I don't understand."

"I was going to meet him at the airport, because he was coming from downtown and—"

"You stood him up?"

"I suppose that's what you'd call it. I was nervous.

I was young then. I waited till the last minute to call him, and by then he'd already left his office. I really felt bad about it. In fact, I'm still ashamed of it in a way. I guess it was horrible of me."

"Jesus, Delia. . . ." The words as much for me as for Worthington Hathaway, who I didn't give a shit about. But I could have imagined his anger and hurt when she didn't show. I'd run that route with Delia myself, though not nearly as bad.

"Well, anyway, he's there, right in your viewing area," I said. "Do you have any more reason to suspect him than anyone else, now that you think of it?"

"No. I mean, I haven't really thought about it."

"Well do," I told her. "Because I'm going to come back to Los Angeles in a couple of days. And among other things, I'm going to go see this guy who's always in meetings and won't return my calls."

"Oh, Johnny, you're coming back!" She sounded delighted.

"Yeah, soon as I finish up some business here." Careful, I told myself. This was the woman who cut out on the grand Worthington Hathaway on a trip to Rome. "You going to be around this weekend?"

"Until Saturday or Sunday," she said. "Brad has a meeting down in San Diego. I'm supposed to meet him there."

"Yeah, well, don't stand him up," I said acidly.

"Don't be sarcastic."

"How about a late dinner Friday, after your show?"

"Sure."

"I'd sort of like to get a look at this red sweater my-self."

"Now, Johnny, that's not very—"

"Trust me," I said.

AFTER I HUNG up, I wondered what it was about her. Most people sniff around for a few dates, maybe go to bed, and then if nothing big is shaking, just drift away and settle back into being lonely again until the next thing comes along. But in Delia's case, she mostly had affairs of long duration, then abruptly trashed them soon as her partners revealed a serious-ness that was intolerable for her.

My case had been different. Or at least I wanted to think so, because even after that appalling weekend in Connecticut, and its aftermath, she still wasn't fin-ished with me.

After I'd dropped her off that night long years ago so she could have dinner with her "faculty adviser," I drove home in a fury of bewilderment and anger. It seemed clear I'd gotten the shaft, but it didn't make sense. Why had she agreed to spend a long holiday weekend with me if she'd decided it was over? I'd even said at one point: "I don't understand why you came here." And she'd replied, "Because I'd told you I'd come." But to what end? To make the weekend miserable for me? Certainly she must have known it would, given the circumstances. What I didn't know at the time was that a year earlier she'd stood up old Worthington Hathaway at the airport.

Maybe the unpleasantness of that episode was still on her mind. Then again, it was only ten years later I discovered that, on and off in her spare moments, she'd been screwing my good old buddy "the famous scribbler." He revealed this to me laughingly on his hospital bed.

So I guess that's what it was all about; I should have predicted it with him, it had always been his reputation. Big deal—I guess in the end that's what money is all about to them. Some buy professional ball clubs, others run for Congress, others buy newspapers or something to satisfy their egos—and others try to fuck their friends' wives or lovers. Anyway, he's dead now, and I hope he had a good time with it. Somehow I really didn't fault Delia, but I probably should have. She had a mind—or whatever—of her own, though. Still, there was something about it that never squared with my own notion of fairness—or "honesty," as she would undoubtably put it.

For the first week or two after that weekend in Connecticut I'd hoped she might call, but I knew in my head if not my heart it wasn't going to happen. I went out to L.A. for a couple of months to do a movie and the day I returned sat through most of an hour of my answering machine calls, hoping like a fool one would be from her. By then it was the end of summer and I went out to the Hamptons for a week with friends. At a big party over Labor Day I saw her standing in a group. She didn't seem to have a date and I was about to walk over when some guy joined them and handed her a glass of wine. I know she must have seen me, but she didn't do anything about it, and after a while I left, feeling forlorn.

Autumn came, a melancholy time despite its vivid splendor. I tried to engross myself in a new novel but just couldn't seem to get it going. I went home for a couple of weeks, went bird hunting, caught redfish in the marshes, got the usual lecture from my father about moving back and getting into the family business, and then returned to New York refreshed. I hadn't been there but a day when I answered the phone and heard her voice.

She sounded unusually cheerful and said she just wanted to know how I'd been. I told her fine. She said she'd been doing a little freelance work and we chitchatted for a while. I was trying to get a feel for what she wanted, but she gave me no clues. I finally decided to dive in and asked if she wanted to have dinner.

"Sure," she said. "When?"

I suggested Friday, but she was going out of town for the weekend. We agreed on the following Tuesday. That week was a little disconcerting and the question hung over me like a fog. When Tuesday came, she met me at my apartment right on time, unusual enough in itself, but she brought with her a small overnight bag. Her explanation was that the water in her apartment had gone out and that if I didn't mind, she'd like to shower and dress in mine. Of course I didn't mind. It was almost like old times.

Dinner was a pleasant haze of catching-up conversation. Delia thought she might have landed a job and

I was pleased for her. She really didn't talk too much about the past five months and I didn't ask about them either. She did mention seeing me at the party in the Hamptons and said she'd looked for me later, but I must have left. I just nodded.

Afterward we walked the few blocks toward my apartment. This was crunch time. If we got to my corner and she took a cab, that would apparently be that. Just an anticlimax to the whole affair. If I asked her up for a nightcap, and she accepted, I was still in the ball game. Turned out, an invitation was unnecessary. I'd forgotten she'd left her overnight case at my place. When we got inside the door, I offered her a glass of wine. As I opened the bottle, she came up close behind me and when I turned around, she was right there.

"Why don't you kiss me first?" she said.

We kissed and touched, standing there for a long while, until she said, "You know, Johnny, you look tired. Like you need some rest. Would you like to get into bed?"

It was of course terrific again, just as it had been. Afterward we lay in bed, smoking, as we both did in those days. Everything seemed comfortable, as though nothing strange had happened over the past five months. "Why did you pull away from me?" I asked finally.

"Pull away?"

"Yeah, last spring. Did you forget that?"

"Oh, I see—no, no, of course not. I'm just not sure how to answer you. It was a lot of things."

"Such as?"

"Listen, Johnny, I'd really rather not get into this kind of conversation. Okay?"

"Sure, but it sort of leaves a gap, don't you think?"

"Look, without getting too deep, like I said, it was a lot of things, you, your friends. . . ."

"Did I do something wrong?"

"No, of course not. It's just that you're so . . . well, strong. And your friends . . . they're wonderful, but they're almost overwhelming, at least to somebody like me, who's only getting started."

"What? Did someone say something to you?"

"No, never. They're as kind as they can be. That's not it."

"Are you saying you're intimidated by them? By me?"

"Maybe it's something like that. I feel . . . I don't know exactly what it is. Sometimes, though, I sort of felt like a hanger-on. It's not my way."

"Oh my, no, I know that," I said. "That's silly. Why, everybody adores you, and I'm not just making that up. They've told me. They think you're witty and smart and nice."

"That's good," she said, but her voice was distant. I could tell she'd said about all she was going to say.

Next morning I fixed coffee while Delia was dressing. When she came out, she had on a different getup from what she'd worn the evening before. It didn't occur to me until afterward that she'd planned to spend the night all along.

"Well, thanks for everything, Johnny," she said cheerfully. "Gotta go now." She had her bag and was headed toward the door.

"Want to do something this weekend?" I asked.

She barely turned around. "Oh, thanks, I don't think so," she said. "I've got a lot of things to do and then I'm going up to Rhode Island for a week over Thanksgiving."

I should have just saluted and marched off in the opposite direction, but again, I couldn't help myself. Where was she going? To Newport? Fishers Island, Watch Hill, or only to Providence?

"Well, should I call you sometime?" I said pointlessly.

"Sure, if you want to."

"Or maybe I should wait for you to call me?"

She gave me a peck on the cheek and laughed. I didn't hear from her again for more than a year.

CHAPTER 13

I THOUGHT THE SCREENPLAY for Burr was going pretty well and a few days later when it had turned quite chilly, I found myself climbing up the stairs of a building in Columbia University's College of Arts and Sciences. I located the English department and introduced myself to a secretary.

"Yes, Mr. Lightfoot," she said, "Professor Vining should be here any time. Please have a seat."

A few minutes later an imposing figure stood in the doorway. He was tall but bent and walked with a cane; time had not been kind to him. Still, he somehow gave off an air of cunning and calculation that reminded me of the actor James Mason.

"Professor Vining," said the secretary, "here is Mr. Lightfoot to see you."

I rose and walked over, extending my hand. Then I noticed his free arm was drawn up and atrophied, so instead I simply said, "I'm glad to meet you, thanks for sparing the time."

Horst Vining nodded with a sort of grimace. The right side of his face was slack. It was apparent this man had suffered a stroke. He indicated for me to follow him into one of the small offices off the main reception area. It was cluttered with books and papers, as one would expect in a college professor's digs. He lowered himself somewhat painfully behind his desk while I sat in a stiff wooden banker's chair. His hair was white and his face craggy, but there was still a kind of twinkle in his eye. I guessed he was in his early seventies.

"So you want to talk about Delia Jamison," he said matter-of-factly.

"I do, sir," I said.

"Mr. Lightfoot, I know your work. First book was very good. Second, well, I'm not even sure why you wrote it."

This, of course, took me off guard. In the circles I traveled, compliments were the order of the day, but criticism such as this was whispered to others. . . . But I was now in academia. They did things differently here.

"Why haven't you written more?" he asked.

"I do a lot of screenplays."

"Oh," he said dismissively. "Well, so how can I help you about Miss Jamison?"

Jesus, I thought. So this had been my competition that dreadful evening when I returned Delia to New York from Connecticut so she could have her "meeting." Of course, that had been almost two decades earlier. He would have been in his early fifties then, and I could see that he had probably still been an attractive man in those days.

"She's been having some problems," I told him. "She's trying to find out why."

As I laid out the situation, Vining absorbed it with nods or grunts.

"And so do you think I am the man behind this?" he said when I had finished.

"Well, you weren't in L.A. a few days ago, and that's where the last letter was postmarked. I'm just investigating all leads, hoping something will turn up to help."

"And what is your interest in this affair?" he asked.

"Old friendship. That's all."

"Old friendship," he intoned. "Yes, old friendships are important, aren't they?"

"I think so."

"And you want to know about Miss Jamison and me, is that it?"

"Whatever you care to tell me."

"Well, I thought she was exquisite. And quick—so very quick. But she didn't really apply herself as I thought she should. I don't think she studied as much as she should have. But then, I expect she didn't have to. And she liked to argue—with me, as well as her classmates. When she thought she was correct in a point, there was no shaking her from it—right or wrong."

"Well, that sounds familiar," I said.

"Yes," he said. "She was defensive in her arguments, even combative. Unlike a lot of colleges, we encourage that here, to a point, but she was so firm in her convictions, so strident, I felt . . . well, I felt there a sense of impeccable honesty in her— but it was almost as though it was an obsessive thing, something on the verge of pathology. But I sensed something else there too. Someone troubled with herself. I think that was where the defensiveness lay. She wasn't really happy in her life, and could lash out."

He fumbled with a pipe in his jacket pocket and put it between his teeth.

"They won't let you smoke these things inside anymore," he said. "Can you imagine it, a professor of English without his pipe?" He chuckled at his own joke. "But to go on, there was something else there I saw. A sincerity in her—yes, that's it—maybe a kindness, but I'm not sure of that. I've always wondered what became of her. But television—oh dear!"

"Well, she's good at what she does," I said.

"Yes, I'm sure. Maybe that was where she was destined. She had that kind of tenacity I suppose it takes."

"Did she ever date other students, that you knew of?"

"No, not that I was aware of. Even though she was the same age, she seemed more mature than they were, at least in her own way. I tried to bridge the gap, you see. She was like a person split, though you couldn't see that right away. Fighting something within herself. I never quite understood what it was. I would take her to the ballet, the symphony, the opera. It was wonderful, seeing her trying to appreciate the nuances. But sometimes, I felt she wanted to be someplace else. Like so many young people those days—and these."

"But you, well, you 'dated,' her too," I said. "I mean, on another level?"

"Yes, yes, of course. She was my first student. I mean, the first student I had a romance with in more than twenty-five years of teaching at this university. And she was the last, as well. It was ecstasy, sexual and otherwise. You see, my wife had died a few years earlier. And when Delia and I . . . well, I had never known a woman who could do such things. It was a whole new experience for me. You see, I teach English and this has always been a cloistered environment. Naturally I'd read Proust and D. H. Lawrence—and there was *Ulysses* too—Joyce knew these things. But I never thought I'd actually have it in the flesh. Of course, things have changed now. I don't think you could get away with being romantically involved with a student these days. You'd probably get fired—even prosecuted."

I wanted to go further into the sex thing, but somehow it didn't seem appropriate. Besides, I just couldn't figure out a gentlemanly way to ask the question. The old man pushed himself up and leaned on his cane, turning slightly to look out the window, and he laughed ruefully to himself.

"But," he continued, "it wouldn't make any difference to me anyway. I'm just a cripple now, with fading memories."

"I'm sure you're much more than that," I said. There was a long moment while he looked out the window at students crossing on the quadrangle below, so I went on.

"So you—you couldn't think of anyone who might want to be doing this to Delia?" I asked.

"No, no one," he said.

I nodded my head in acceptance.

"Well, give my best to Delia," he said. "Tell her I think of her fondly sometimes, will you?"

"Certainly." I rose to leave.

"You know," he said quietly, "Delia told me about you, after I got to know her. She said she knew you. That's how I came to read your first book."

"Really?"

"She never said she'd been involved with you, but I guessed it from the way she spoke of you."

I wasn't sure how to respond to that, so I thanked Professor Vining and said good-bye.

"I preyed on her, you know," he said as I was leaving. "She was looking for an older man then. Perhaps a father figure, I suppose one calls it. I think she had trouble with her own father—I don't know what."

"I understand," I said, opening the door.

"I felt bad for a while at first. And then, you see, I realized it was not me who was doing the preying, it was she. I began to feel like . . . well, have you ever read Thomas Hardy?"

"A little."

"In *Far from the Madding Crowd* there is a cautionary tale. He thinks he's in control, but slowly he loses that, you see. Until it's all her—he's, he's . . ."

I saw he was becoming upset and tried to change the subject. "How long did it last with her?"

"Oh, it was a summer and then the autumn. Oh my, that was a lovely time. And then winter came. I had taken to writing her letters. I think that became the end of it. They were wonderful letters, if I say so myself. I wish I had copies of them now. Will you please come back in and close the door."

I did. "Did she write you back," I asked.

"Once. It was only a short letter, but I could see she was agonizing over it. Over me, I guess. You see, I think I was coming very close to touching something. Something she had hidden, and she didn't want that. I think by then she'd already decided to end it."

"But she did."

"Yes, the semester was over and one day she came to my office. It was in another building then. She came in and she . . . she sat me down. She *sat me down*! In my *own* office! I remember she was wearing a short brown skirt with those long, slender legs, and a red sweater—a very bright red sweater—and all her loveliness was in it. And she said, 'Now, Horst, I just want you to know that I've really had a great time being with you. But I think it's getting a little out of hand.'

"And so I asked what she meant by that. And she said to me, 'I just want to be honest with you. I think you need to know that I tried to love you, but I just can't, and I don't think things can go on with us any longer.' I asked why not, and she said, 'Because it wouldn't be right. I really hope we can be friends.' And after that, she just got up and left."

"And that was it?"

"Friends! That's what she said, as though she was collecting them! I was too stunned to do anything. I just sat there, where she had told me to. Where she'd sat me *down*! Afterward, for weeks, I wrote her letters, but she never replied."

I could see the professor was tormenting himself to a point of distraction. I could see the expression of deep fury that had come over his face.

"Why, I've never been treated that way in my life. In my *life*!" He raised his voice. "I've devoted myself to *truth* and *honor* and with her it was all so . . . so *cold* and calculating! There was no compassion— and whatever *tact* there was seemed feigned! Never, never in my *life*!" he spat. Supporting himself with a hand on the desk, he began tapping his cane against a chair. "And for months—years—afterward, I wondered where I'd gone wrong! I felt like she'd used me, grades, father figure, intellectual linchpin, whatever!"

"You didn't really go wrong," I told him.

"I didn't?"

"You just picked the wrong mushroom to eat. Some of the deadliest ones in the forest are also the most beautiful, the most seductive."

When he turned directly toward me, I could see small tears of outrage welling in his eyes. "Sometimes I hate her," he said quietly. "I've never really been able to get her entirely out of my mind. After all these years."

He looked at me for a long moment, and then his mouth turned down on one side and began to open and close, as if he was searching for words.

"And now *you* come along," he hissed with renewed fervor, "at her bidding. . . . What do you want with me! Get *out,* please, leave!"

I opened the door again and took a step into the hallway.

"Why have you come here!" he seethed. "Did you want something of me, for her?"

"Nothing," I said.

I turned and walked through the reception area. I could tell the receptionist had been listening to whatever she could and I could hear Professor Vining shouting after me.

"She's one of a kind, you know! She could have been one of the greats—you just remember that, my young movie-writing friend! With my help, she would have been! But never with people like you. . . ."

CHAPTER 14

IT'S STRANGE HOW the mind works, how time and distance suppress things over years, then something comes to set them off all over again, as if the battle was still being waged. I would have immediately crossed Professor Vining's name off the list, except for one thing: his vivid recollection of the red sweater Delia had worn the day she broke it off. Ordinarily, of course, this would be no big thing, but I knew I had to look at the Vining situation more closely. But judging from his performance with me, if he was the sender, he was a damned good actor—Broadway quality. It still didn't make sense, though, because why would he make demands of her on television when he couldn't even see the program, unless, of course, he'd flown out to L.A. and then back again many times?

Anyway, these things were on my mind as my airliner cruised high over the Nevada desert toward Los Angeles. If New York was Gomorrah, L.A. was certainly Sodom. What I'd learned so far was that Delia had not exactly left behind her a wake of happy memories but rather a trail of broken hearts. If she'd been beautiful but dumb or frivolous, she'd have been much easier to dismiss. But she wasn't. Delia had beauty *and* brains, as well as charm and integrity, and there was even, as Vining had noted, an odd sort of kindness in her, although I believe it was often superficial. Still, I was beginning to think a lot of the anguish her lovers endured was self-inflicted. Myself included. A failure, perhaps, to read the signals. It was hard to fathom that after those affairs of months and months she would always just decide one day it was over and walk out.

I had made a date with Delia for that night and she was to call me after the early news broadcast was over. I had also arranged for a meeting with Rick Olsen, the detective. It had come time to lay out a few things. Besides, I'd decided to ask for his help.

When I got back to the Peninsula, there were a pile of messages, among them a note that Meredith McDonald had called. I only had time to shower and change before meeting Rick at a bar he'd suggested in West Hollywood. When I got there, he was standing by the service counter, having a beer.

"Delia tells me you've been finding out things in New York," he said. Rick was apparently not the kind of guy who wasted words.

"A few," I said. "Nothing you could hang your hat on." I told him about my interviews. He was, of course, interested in Homer Greer because of the bitterness of Homer's experience and because he often came to L.A.

"They're all bitter," I said. I related my meeting

with Professor Vining but didn't mention the red sweater business because I didn't think Delia had yet unveiled those demands to either her husband or Rick. But it sure had me chewing over the fact that people remembered her in red.

Rick was particularly interested in Worthington Hathaway because he was actually living here in L.A. and could watch her every night on TV. I explained that Hathaway would not, or at least had not, returned my calls and asked if Rick could find a way for me to get to him. He said he'd put his people right on it, and also suggested that his company could run a check on Hathaway to see if anything turned up, and I thought this was a good idea.

"You know, Johnny," he said, "Brad's really been anxious about all this—even if she hasn't had any more calls lately."

"I know he must be," I said, taken aback that Delia had not revealed to her husband anything of what she had recently revealed to me.

"You must be an awfully good friend of Delia's to be doing all this."

"Well, we go back a long way."

"You mind if I ask in what way you go back?"

"All the way," I said uneasily. This was one of those very delicate things I hated to dance around. But telling the husband's best friend I had once had an affair with his wife was awkward.

"Look, I won't say anything to Brad. I just want to know myself. I feel protective toward Delia," Rick said. "I realize she comes off as very confident and self-reliant and all that, but I think she has some insecurities. I don't think she's ever gone through anything like this mess—matter of fact, I'm sure of it—and I think it makes her vulnerable."

"And then I show up?" I said.

"Something like that. Of course, I'm not suggesting there's anything going on between you two. If I thought that . . . well, let's just say I wouldn't approve. But, you see, the move she made down here from San Francisco has put a strain on Brad. Not that there's anything wrong with their marriage. At least not as far as I'm aware. But he waited a long time to get married. I've known him for nearly fifteen years and he worked night and day to build up his business and now when he's finally reached his goals and aims, Delia moves away to take this job."

"Delia waited a long time too," I suggested, deliberately omitting what Max Weed had told me about Delia's earlier marriage. But, like I said, maybe it wasn't any of my business. Who knew if she'd ever told Brad about it?

"I know she did. I don't begrudge her coming to L.A. and of course Brad doesn't either. After all, this is probably the most prestigious broadcast job in local television in America. But it's just sort of strange for him. After all, the normal thing is for a wife to live with her husband."

"Modern times," I said.

"Nobody understands that more than Brad," Rick

said. "Me, I'm a little more old-fashioned, but that's not important. But I'd still like to know what your relationship with Delia was."

"Why don't you ask her?"

"Because I'm asking you," he said. "I don't think it would be appropriate to ask her."

"Is this something Brad wants you to ask me?"

"No. I'm asking it on my own," he said. "Look, Delia starts getting these calls one day and then all of a sudden you turn up back in her life. Is it just a coincidence . . . ?"

"I really hope so, don't you? What, do you suspect me . . . ?"

"Look, Johnny, I think you're a nice, personable guy, but my business is investigations and security. I'd be remiss if I didn't ask questions."

"Well, us scribblers are suspicious-looking fellows. Always snooping into people's closets and then using it in some book."

"Let me put it this way," Rick said, "and I'm just reciting a scenario: Delia is sitting in the bar there at, where, the Peninsula, and all of a sudden you walk in, and then you renew a friendship with her that's been defunct for what, ten or fifteen years? With all this other going on with her, doesn't that seem a little odd?"

"It might," I said, "if it wasn't for the fact that I *live* at the Peninsula when I'm in L.A., as I have for five or six years. And it wasn't me who went over to her table, she came to mine."

"And so then you take her out on dinner dates. . . ."
Rick said.

"She didn't like the food," I replied, a little short.
"Why didn't you ask Delia about it?"

"Let's just say I'm keeping an eye on her," he said.
"Brad asked me to."

"Have you told her that?"

"Brad doesn't want me to. She's . . . well, you
know her a bit, she can be funny about that sort of
thing."

"Well, let me ask you this," I said. "If you think I
could be the caller, how in hell could Delia not recognize my voice on the phone?"

"Johnny, I don't think you're the caller. I'm just
asking the normal questions. But in case you don't
know it, there are a variety of devices on the market
that will disguise a voice so well a person could never
recognize it as someone they knew. Johnny, look, I
asked you not to take any of this the wrong way. Why,
hell, do you think I would reveal I was keeping an eye
on Delia if I thought you were the caller?"

Rick put a firm arm on my shoulder and squeezed
it. I could feel the powerful grip of a man who handled himself well.

"Listen, Johnny, I normally wouldn't say this to
anyone—maybe you, especially—but I know Delia
pretty well myself. You get what I'm saying?"

"Well, yes and no. . . ."

"What I mean is, I was the first one to meet her
when she came to San Francisco."

"You mean before Brad?"

"Exactly."

"And so you two were . . . ?"

"Let's just say that I know Delia and leave it at that. I know how she is. She is a very seductive woman, you know? I was married then, but, well, she's an awfully persuasive person too. And now my wife's dead, and now she's married to Brad. End of story, okay? Frankly, I don't know if she's good for Brad or not. I know she's got him all twisted into knots. Maybe she doesn't mean to, maybe she does, but Brad's my friend, and, as I said, I know Delia. Do you get my meaning?"

"Yes, I think I get it," I told him.

"Okay, good. Now," he said, "about this Hathaway guy, you got his office address and all?"

"Yeah, in my pocket." I gave him the information and he copied it down.

"I'll get my people on it. We'll have something for you in a few days," Rick said. "And, listen, I'm glad we had this talk."

"Yeah, me too."

THAT WAS A hell of a note, I thought, driving back to the hotel. Followed—he was having us followed, or at least having her followed. I was damned glad nothing had happened. I could imagine the fallout if Delia had gone up to my room and not come down till morning. Sometimes I felt invisible wings were beating over me.

Rick came across smooth, but something in his demeanor seemed to be trying to make you believe he was your friend. Beneath the suave polish, however, I sensed an undercurrent of unctuousness, as though he knew a lot more than he was telling and wanted you to think he was on your side so as to get you to divulge something he wanted to know. Then again, that was the nature of Rick's occupation, wasn't it? And that was a helluva surprise that Rick possibly had slept with Delia before she met Brad. Something must have happened there, because for all his professed protectiveness I sensed that he really didn't care for Delia at all.

Delia called me about seven, just after her early news show. She said she was going to San Diego in the morning to meet Brad, but that she had taken the night off from her late broadcast, thus putting off having to deal with the red sweater thing. She suggested I come to her apartment and we'd have supper there. I wondered if I should read anything into that and also wondered about Rick's revelation of this afternoon. Would I be watched? Should I tell her that Rick was "keeping an eye on her" or not? Finally I wondered, given what I recollected of Delia's culinary skills, what dinner was going to consist of. All in all, it was a lot of wondering for one day.

IT WAS DARK when I pulled into Delia's apartment complex. Instead of driving under the canopy and letting the attendant park the car for me, I parked it myself way out in the lot. I didn't see any other cars moving and concluded I wasn't being followed. But Rick had said he was keeping an eye on Delia, not me. Anyhow, I gave a wave to the parking lot in general, just to say, "Hi." In the lobby no one was there but the desk staff. I gave my name and after a phone call the clerk nodded to me to go on up. Delia was waiting for me at the elevator door.

She was wearing yellow slacks and a sleeveless beige sweater and looked sumptuous, as usual. She gave me a brief hug and led me inside. The dining table was set up a step from the living room and places had been set for two with silverware and china and flowers. There were candles. The kitchen door was closed, but I could hear activity behind it, which told me she had a cook to prepare the meal.

She brought me to a table on the terrace where a bottle of Chardonnay Pinot Grìgio was chilling in a silver cooler. The lights of the immense city glowed and twinkled below and beyond us and a cool far-off ocean breeze made the night very pleasant indeed. I glanced up at the wall of windows above, wondering if there was someone there watching us.

"Well, I postponed it again," she said with a sort of sigh, referring, of course, to her absence from the late news tonight, where the red sweater trick was supposed to be performed.

"Be interesting to see what his reaction is," I said, thinking that somewhere out in this city, our creep was waiting, expectantly, for eleven o'clock to roll around.

"Well, I don't think he can do anything if I'm not on the air. It's not like I'm defying him or anything. This is so ridiculous, isn't it?"

"It is, but you've got to figure that if you keep off the air every time he makes one of these demands, he's going to wise up."

"I thought about that too, but at least this gives me space to think."

"What have you been thinking?"

"Well, I was wondering, and I know this sounds silly, but would there be some way to trap him? I mean, if I was to make some kind of reference on the air. After all, that's the only way I can communicate with him. I don't know what, maybe just say something like 'I've been getting some pretty interesting fan mail lately, and . . .'"

"And?"

"I don't know. That's as far as I've got, and it would be hard just to get that far—just to raise that subject—without management wondering what the hell was going on. They do give us some latitude in what we say; as a matter of fact, they encourage chitchat. It's supposed to make the audience feel a part of the show. But I'd probably only have one shot at anything like that before the station manager or the news director would come up and ask what the hell I was talking about. But maybe it was a thought."

"No, no, it might work—but the question is how to trap him."

"I wonder how it's going to end," she said

distractedly. "These so-called pictures. I just can't imagine who."

"I had a talk with Rick this afternoon," I said.

"Rick. Oh?"

"I filled him in a little on what I've been doing."

"What'd he say?"

"He found it interesting. He also wanted to know about us."

"What about us?"

"Whether we'd ever been lovers and, I think by implication, whether we were now."

"Why?" she asked nervously.

"I'm not sure. He said it was because, well, he said he was just doing what he considered his job. And he thought it a strange coincidence that I reappeared in your life just when all this was going on."

"You mean he suspects you?"

"He says he doesn't. Rick may be just the kind of fellow who likes to know everything. Detectives, gossip columnists, and, I may add, writers are very similar in that regard."

"Well, he certainly doesn't have any gossip on *us* these days," she said.

"Yeah, we're pure as the driven snow."

"So what did you tell him about us before?"

"I think he's got a pretty good idea," I said.

DINNER WAS A delicate Oriental something with shrimp, lobster, and vegetables, served by a couple I took for Vietnamese. Afterward we stepped down into the living room while they cleared the table.

"Johnny, you really look tired, do you want to play some bridge? Might wake you up a little. Can you play two-handed?" Delia asked.

"No, thanks. I am tired, though. This morning I was in New York trying to make a two P.M. flight and now here I am three thousand miles later. I hate flying, even in first class. It makes your muscles stiff."

"Well, here," she said, "you sit down here and I'll give you a massage." She motioned me into a low overstuffed chair and kneeled behind me. I felt her long, slender fingers on my shoulders and neck, kneading and gently rubbing, and I closed my eyes and just let the feeling seep down. I could smell a hint of perfume and makeup and even feel her breath on the back of my neck.

"Your shoulder muscles are really tight," she said. "Does this feel good?"

"Oh, not at all." I said, "I hate being touched by you."

"Hush. . . ."

I sat up and took her left hand in mine, pulling her gently around beside me until she was sitting on the left arm of the chair and we were looking at each other with that kind of intense gaze-lock that bespoke things to come. Just then the kitchen door opened and the Vietnamese man said, "Miss Jamison, would you like the coffee served now?" Delia quickly rose to her feet and indicated for the coffee to be brought. I could have killed the son of a bitch on the spot. No wonder we lost that damned war.

In any case, there wasn't any way to recover the moment and little else to do but get to other matters at hand.

"I saw Homer Greer when I was back east," I told her.

A look of stunned mortification crossed her face. She reddened. "Look, Johnny, I appreciate what you're doing, but I didn't expect you to pry into my life," she said. "This has nothing to do with that."

"How do you know?"

"I just know."

"Sounds like you know more than you're telling me."

"I might, but my life is my own affair."

"Nobody's business—that it?"

"Yeah," she said, "that's it."

"Well, Homer Greer's still not particularly enamored of you. And I'd say from what I've learned so far, he's the guy who has the most reason to do something like this."

"He didn't."

"And just what makes you so sure of that?"

"Because I am. Because of what was said in the letters."

"What's that?"

"As I explained to you, Johnny, the writer of those letters is someone I've been with."

"And you weren't with Homer Greer?"

"Yes, of course I was, but the letters mention something very personal. But I never did it with Homer Greer, so he couldn't be the sender."

"And you still won't tell me what it was?"

"No."

"This isn't much help. If I'm going to resolve any of this, I need to know what you know. I can't be of much assistance if I'm flying blind."

"I'm sorry."

"Well, let's suppose that good old Homer just imagined whatever it is you do with certain men in your life. Then we can't rule him out, can we?"

Delia, ignoring the question, got up and stood in front of the window. "And I suppose he also told you how we met?" she asked.

"He did."

"Well, I can't worry about that," she said with a certain resignation.

"Is that why you didn't put Homer on your list for me?"

"No, I've already told you why. Look, Johnny," she said, drawing herself up, "I did it because I needed the money. I was putting myself through school. It was expensive. At that time my parents didn't have a lot of money. My father was having business problems. I needed to be in class during the day. What was I supposed to do—be a waitress? It was easy and I could study between the calls. And it was good money too—twenty bucks a call and sometimes I could do five or six calls a night."

"Wasn't it creepy?"

"Actually, a lot of the guys weren't creeps—they

were like Homer. Anyway, I didn't talk to the creeps more than once. I'd steer them to somebody else after that."

"How long did you do this?" I asked.

"On and off, three, four years."

"You were doing it when we were dating?"

She hesitated and lowered her eyes. "Yes. Sometimes."

I couldn't resist pressing it. "Did you find it exciting?"

She glared at me and for a moment I thought she was going to explode into anger and for once I wouldn't have blamed her. Instead she shook her head and looked at me with an air of withdrawal and let out a deep breath.

"Occasionally, yes, it was. Okay? All the guys were anonymous and, well, in a way it was like being an actress. In fact, after the first year I branched out on my own."

"Branched out?"

"Look, the guys paid the service about three bucks a minute to talk to me—usually for about twenty minutes. But I only got a third of that. The big money went to this woman who owned the service and she was a real bitch. Always thought we girls were going out on our own and stealing her customers."

"But I thought you just said you did."

"Yes, I did. Over time I had about six or seven guys—the ones I really enjoyed talking to. They just sent the money straight to my post office box. I gave them a good rate too—a flat fifty bucks an hour. That was a third of what they had been paying and also three times what I'd been netting from the service. Besides, we could prearrange the times of the calls so I could pretty much keep my own schedule. Toward the end, I was making over twenty thousand a year. Now, are you satisfied? Have you heard enough?" Delia said tensely.

"Did you pay taxes on it?"

"Oh, for chrissake . . ."

"Why did you stop?"

"Because I didn't want to do it forever. And, yeah, it was a little weird. But the one thing everybody kept saying over and over was what a great voice I had. In fact, that's what made me decide to try for a job in radio."

"I told you you ought to do that myself, remember?"

"Yes, I know you did," she replied.

CHAPTER 15

I GOT UP NEXT morning still cursing the Vietnamese cook for his *coitus mentalis interruptus* of the night before. Shortly after we finished coffee, I went back to the hotel, leaving her to spend another romantic weekend with Brad at the fabulous old Coronado Hotel on San Diego Bay. Typically, she had to let it drop that's where they'd be staying. I'd once taken a girl there myself, long, long ago. It's where Billy Wilder shot the movie *Some Like It Hot*.

I hadn't told Delia about Rick's "keeping an eye on her," but I saw a problem developing over just whose side I was on. Rick and, I suppose, Brad seemed to take the view that I was on their team, not hers. It was a sort of patronizing position; they knew what was best for her. In the end, I decided not to tell her because I wasn't sure how she'd react. Besides, I also concluded that, for the time being, it was not important for her to know, it was only important for *me* to know. And the fact that I did was enough for me to steer us clear of trouble.

After breakfast I returned to my suite and reviewed the messages I'd gotten while I was away. None of them seemed very pressing, especially for a Saturday morning, but I did set aside the one from Meredith McDonald. I waited till noon, then called her.

"You've been a stranger," she said.

I told her I'd been away and she filled me in on her latest project, which was designing a part of a new Spielberg movie. I wanted to ask her out for dinner that night, but didn't. Asking a girl for a Saturday night date two times in a row on Saturday afternoon seemed presumptuous. Besides, I figured she'd already had a dozen offers and most probably had accepted one, so I let it pass. Toby Burr was a member of a swank beach club near Malibu and I thought that would be more appropriate.

"Do you like the beach?" I asked.

"It's my favorite," she said.

I told her about the club and suggested I pick her up about eleven next morning.

"I'd love that," she said. "Can I bring my drawing stuff?"

"Of course," I told her.

"Well, I thought I'd better ask. I've never been to a beach club before, but I've seen them from the highway. I thought they might not approve."

"When they get a look at you, you could have arrived with a trained animal act and nobody would object," I said.

"Flattery will get you everywhere," Meredith said.

I spent that Saturday night alone in my room, mostly watching television. For a while I tormented myself with the notion of Delia at the Coronado but was redeemed by the idea of spending tomorrow with Meredith. I amused myself by wondering what *she* would do if somebody started sending her dirty letters. Probably just laugh it off. But again, with Delia, the stakes were higher.

MEREDITH LIVED IN one of those neat little Spanish-style apartment complexes built in the thirties on the outskirts of Hollywood, sort of like the set they used in *The Day of the Locust*. She'd made it quite homey, with good art and comfortable furniture in the living room. One of her two bedrooms had been turned into a studio and I was impressed by the quality of her work. She was one of those artists who could actually draw things recognizable to the normal eye.

When we came out to my car, as luck would have it, somebody had wedged me in from behind at the curb. I had leased an old red Caddy convertible out here—the perfect L.A. car—and today with the top down it promised to be an exhilarating drive. But first, how to get out of this squeeze. I put Meredith in and got into the driver's seat and began cautiously pushing up against the car in back when without warning a sprinkler system erupted on the lawn next to us. The first blast soaked Meredith as though she'd been hit by a bucket of water. She couldn't get out on her side because that was where the deluge was coming from and by the time I got out and let her exit behind me, she was thoroughly drenched and howling in laughter.

She went in to change, still laughing, while I got the top up on the car and somehow worked it free and into the street. As I waited for Meredith, it came back to me that the last time something like this had happened was with Delia, years before, but there was no laughter then. I had an old Cadillac DeVille then and once, on the way to the shore, we stopped by an automatic car wash to clean it up for the weekend. Delia and I had just started seeing each other then and were rapt in conversation as the car began to go through the wash. Then I realized all the windows were down and just as the automatic tow took over, I frantically put my fingers on all four window buttons to roll them up. But suddenly the engine quit and we were propelled with unimaginable astonishment into the wash.

The experience was almost unbelievable. Fierce jets of warm water hosed us down and next, huge soapy brushes came right into the car and thrashed us. Delia began to holler and scream and tried to get into the back seat, but it was just as bad there. The noise was beyond description. At one point I looked at her and she was completely covered with suds and cursing wildly. I couldn't help laughing, but Delia entirely failed to see any humor in it. By the time the wash was finished with us, we'd been soaped, rinsed, waxed, and finally blow-dried. There was six inches of water on the floorboards and Delia stayed pissed-off all day. Inexplicably, the car started right up outside the wash. I think that was the first time I realized she took herself very seriously and didn't enjoy things not going her way.

Meredith and I drove to Toby's club and went in to change. She reappeared in a red two-piece bathing suit that complemented her figure, and she had let her hair down. It was quite lovely, swept back by the Pacific breeze. She had her easel and paints under one arm and we were led by an attendant to a row of wooden chairs facing the ocean. We ordered a couple of beers and walked down to the water's edge. The sea was calm with only faint waves breaking against the sand.

"So tell me about New York," she said.

"New York is New York," I answered. "Three parties, a dinner, and a dance every night."

"Really? I've never been there."

"Actually, it was pretty there, now that it's the beginning of fall. Lots of color."

"Do you go to plays?"

"Sometimes, but not this trip."

"What did you do?"

"Well, I was doing a favor for a friend," I said. "It took up most of my time."

"That was nice. Something important?"

"Fairly."

"Sounds mysterious."

"It is."

"Oh? Now you're beginning to get me intrigued. Can you tell me about it?"

"A little bit, I suppose. You see, this is a friend I've

known for a long time. And she's got a very high profile. And somebody's trying to blackmail her."

"My goodness—that really *is* intriguing! Why?"

"Not sure yet," I said. "It's apparently some guy—one of her old lovers—and he says he's got something on her and is threatening to expose it."

"And he wants money?"

"No, at least he hasn't demanded any yet. We don't know exactly what he wants."

"And she's in New York?"

"Well, no."

"Out here?"

"That's something I'd rather not go into right now," I said. "I probably shouldn't have told you this much. I think the thing will shake itself out pretty soon."

"Must be a pretty good friend, for you to go all the way to New York," Meredith said.

"She used to live there. We go back a long way."

"Something that was serious?"

"She's married, if that's what you mean."

"Oh," Meredith said.

WE HAD A lovely afternoon. Meredith set up her easel and spent most of the time drawing bathers near the water. I do not understand the compulsion of painters to paint but figure it must be akin to a writer's need to write. The sun was sinking on the horizon and I walked down to where she was working.

Every once in a while she'd look over at me and wave and smile. Thing about Meredith was, she was comfortable. Comfortable and easy to be around, unlike Delia, who always seemed to create an atmosphere of tension and vibrancy wherever she was. In a way, that's what made Delia exciting. Comfortable, she wasn't. Meredith, on the other hand, maybe didn't take my breath away, but she damned sure made me smile. One day, I thought, she'd make somebody a good wife and be a good mother.

It was deep twilight as we drove back along Palisades, and Meredith leaned back on her passenger-side door with her hair blowing in the breeze and her bare feet in my lap. It was comfortable in one way but less so in another. When we arrived at her apartment, I got out to open her door.

"Want to come in?" she smiled. She was standing close to me, looking into my eyes with an expression I took as expectant.

"Thanks," I said. "I've got a long day tomorrow. I'd better get home early."

"Can we have a kiss good night?" she asked, moving even closer. I took her in my arms and for a moment was about to kiss her, but instead I held her and said, "Meredith, you probably ought to know something."

"What's that?" she asked.

"When you asked if I had a girlfriend, I said I didn't. That's true, so far as it goes. But what I didn't tell you was that I've got, well, what you might call a hang-up."

"You're not gay?" she said saucily.

"No. Nothing like that. It's just that there's some-body I have some unfinished business with. And until that's over, I think it's only fair that you know it."

"Will it be over soon?" she asked.

"Probably. I'd like to keep seeing you, but my head's not quite straight yet. I don't think all you want from me is just some casual fling."

"I might settle for that," she said cheerfully.

"Well, I don't know if I would," I told her.

"Okay, that's cool. Call me sometime," she said, and bounced into her apartment with her drawing stuff under her arm. I stood there for a few moments before driving away. Her reaction had surprised me. It intrigued me too.

NEXT AFTERNOON THE front desk called to say I had a package. Rick Olsen had been good to his word and quick about it too. He had messengered over a folio on the elusive Worthington Hathaway. Hathaway's divorce in New York three years earlier had been a messy affair. Court papers showed the wife had ac-cused him of spousal abuse. Not only that, but shortly after the decree was granted, Hathaway had been in-volved in a fracas with his wife's lawyer. According to a clipping from the *New York Post,* Hathaway had encountered the attorney in the street, assaulted him, and administered a kick in the rear. Charges had been filed, but there was no later account of their disposi-tion. That Hathaway was prone to violence certainly didn't square with Bo Bothwell's recollection that he was such a happy-go-lucky "gent." Rick's dossier also revealed that other lawyers considered Hathaway an extremely combative litigator. How Rick had managed to come up with all these things over just a weekend, I couldn't imagine, but it was obvious his people knew their business.

Rick had also divined—from heaven knows where—that Hathaway was in the habit of stopping off after work at a watering hole near Brentwood called Conneger's. That at least was a start. About five I drove over to the place. It was an ordinary little neighborhood saloon that served hamburgers. I sat at the bar and ordered a beer. After a while I asked the bartender if he knew Worthington Hathaway.

"Worthy, sure," he said.

"Comes here a lot, huh?"

"About every day, when he's in town—matter of fact, here he comes now."

A tall, lean man strode through the door, looking like a kind of aging Richard Widmark from his Tommy Udo gangster character in *Kiss of Death*. He walked right past me and sat at the other end of the bar. Luckily, there was a second bartender down there, so I didn't have the embarrassment of my conversation with the first hanging over me. I studied Hathaway from my distance. He ordered what looked like a double bourbon. His hair was straw-colored and his burnished red face covered with some freckles. Somehow it reminded me of an ear of corn.

The place was beginning to get crowded, so I

thought I'd best make my move before people occupied all the bar stools. I took my beer and came up on the opposite side from where Hathaway was facing. He paid me no attention and took a couple of deep gulps of his drink.

"Excuse me, you're Worthington Hathaway?" I said.

He looked at me with cobalt eyes, no smile. "Yeah, I am."

"I'm Johnny Lightfoot," I said, extending my hand. He stared at me for a long moment, not taking it.

"You the guy who's been wanting to talk to me, huh?"

"Yes. I left some messages."

"I thought you were in New York."

"I was. I'm back here now."

"Something about, ah . . ." He almost didn't seem able to pronounce her name.

"Delia Jamison," I said.

"What about her?"

"You know her?"

"I did."

"You know she's in town?"

"I've seen her on TV."

"But you knew her back in New York?"

"What the hell's this about?" he asked.

"I'm an old friend of hers. Like you. From a long time ago. Somebody's been trying to blackmail her. I'm trying to find out who and why."

"Friend of hers," he said distastefully. "Well, she's

no friend of mine. Who told you about me, and how did you find me?"

"Delia, for one," I said.

"She thinks I'm a blackmailer?" he sneered.

"No. But I'm trying to find out who is. It's apparently somebody she knew before she was married. Someone she dated."

"Oh, really? Well, she accused me of stalking her once, if that's any help. It was total bullshit, you know."

"She thought you were stalking her?"

"So she said. I think she saw me on the street near her apartment after we broke up. Got a curt letter from her a few days later saying somebody was leaving obscene notes under her door or in her mailbox or something. The implication was obvious. What a crock."

"So what did you do?"

"Not a goddamn thing. I personally think she's half nuts. I might have been in her neighborhood for a minute or two. What the hell, she doesn't *own* her fucking neighborhood, you know. And I certainly wasn't leaving her any kind of notes. I didn't want anything to do with her. By that time, she wasn't my idea of fun."

"Well, I gather you two had a falling out, but I thought maybe you could help me anyway."

"Why would I want to do that?"

"Out of decency, I guess."

"Yeah, the same kind of decency she showed me, I imagine? She tell you about that too?"

"A little."

"Like what?"

"Like you two went out for a while and then she stood you up, and that was the end of it?"

"Stood me up! Now that's a really polite way to look at it," he said with undisguised sarcasm. He put his empty glass on the counter and motioned for the bartender to refill it.

"Look, I don't know what happened between you, but . . ."

"What happened? I'll tell you. She put every move she ever knew on me. I must have been the biggest fool in Christendom. One day I asked her to go to Italy with me for a couple of weeks. Rented a big place there. Most romantic spot in Rome—cost a fortune. And you know what she did?"

"She didn't show."

"Goddamn right she didn't. Left me standing at the fucking airport with my thumb up my ass."

"I think I know something of how you must have felt."

"You do? Oh, really? Well, let me go on. I'm calling her from a pay phone every five minutes. The flight's about to leave, so I didn't know what to do, right? I figured something must have happened. I mean, she'd never pulled this kind of shit before. So I go ahead and get on the plane; next thing you know, I'm in Rome. I go to this place. Must have been the most beautiful villa in Rome. Right out of the movies. Overlooked the whole city, terraces and gardens everywhere. And it's just me, by myself, and a bunch of fucking servants, staring at me. I try to call her from there, okay? You know how the phone service is in Rome. I finally get through. What do I get— her goddamn answering machine again!"

I nodded. The answering machine was a scenario I was beginning to know well.

"So for three or four days, I'm trying to reach her. And thinking maybe anytime she'd just show up. Not a peep. Finally it sinks in. She's not coming. Nothing! No sorry, no nothing!"

"Well, I can understand. . . ."

"I doubt it," Hathaway said. "And I'll tell you something else too. Before I left New York, I'd gone over to Tiffany's. Do you know what I did? I bought her an engagement ring. It was the most beautiful engagement ring I'd ever seen. Forty-six thousand dollars—and that was real money in those days. I was going to give it to her over in Italy. That's how close we were—or at least how close I *thought* we were. Ha! First time in my life I'd ever really been in love."

"Did she ever say she was in love with you?" I asked. It seemed important for me to know that, just for personal reasons.

"Maybe not in so many words, but she didn't need to. We were . . . we were that close! You could tell from the sex. It was just spectacular. She was really something special in that department. Hell, I've been with a lot of women in my life. Women don't screw like that unless they're in love."

"Something in particular that she did?" I ventured.

A look of dead contempt spread across his face.

"What? Does it get you off asking questions like that?"

"Not at all. I'm just trying to find out everything I can. It's a complicated situation."

"Yeah, well, what Delia and I did is nobody's business," he said sharply. "Besides, how do I know you are what you say you are? For all I know, you might be some kind of nut."

I started to say, "Trust me," but thought better of it. "Look," I told him, "I might be nuts, but I'm trying to help her. And I appreciate your candor. Would you go on?"

Hathaway studied me for a moment, as though I was some kind of exotic snail, then put his palms in the air and shook his head. "All right, there was more to it than sex. I mean, she'd even mend a missing button on my shirts—stuff like that. I'm not that much of an idiot, I've been around—this was love."

"For you?"

"For me, you're goddamn right it was! I never figured out how it wasn't for her—unless she's the best fucking actress in the world. And she made so much of her goddamn being honest. Always talking about it, you know—'I'm the most honest woman you'll ever meet,' that sort of shit. I guess that was her version of being honest. No beating around the bush, just wham! Stand you up and disappear. I'll have to give her credit, that's just about the most honest statement anybody can make—the unspoken 'good-bye and good luck.' "

"Maybe she just got cold feet," I said.

"Bullshit. She didn't even have any idea I was going to ask her to get married." Hathaway turned for a moment to the bar and shook his head. I could see the expression of disgust on his face in the barroom mirror.

"So you know what? There I was and there I sat. I hadn't even taken a vacation in more than three years except a couple of long weekends. You know how it was in those days. The market was incredible—mergers and acquisitions every fifteen minutes—and I was up to my ass in legal papers. And so I just sat there in that goddamn villa, on my vacation, looking out over Rome day and night, servants bringing me food I wouldn't eat. I wouldn't even go out into the city. Couldn't bring myself to do it. I was so hurt I couldn't even cry.

"And then one day, toward the end, I went for a long walk. I walked all over Rome. Looked at all the old stuff, you know, things that she and I would have enjoyed if she'd been there—the Vatican and all that shit. And by that evening I found myself on a bridge across the Tiber, and I was so disgusted I . . . I don't know what. And I had that goddamn engagement ring in my pocket and . . . to this day I don't understand it, because I'm a pretty practical person . . . but I took it out and thought about tossing it right into the river and before I knew it, I did. Right down to the bottom—gone.

"And you know, I think it made me start feeling a little better, doing that. Crazy as it sounds. Forty-six thousand bucks. It took my trust fund a year and a half to build back up—I'd borrowed the money against it for the ring."

"Can you think of any reason she'd do that?" I asked. "I mean, had you recently had words or something?"

"No, never. That's what was so strange about it. Until then, we never had words. Delia was one of the most accommodating women I've ever gone out with. We never had an argument. She never raised her voice."

"That surprises me," I said. Actually surprise was a mild way of putting it. I couldn't imagine anyone being with Delia for any length of time without some kind of eruption. In a way, it might have been part of her allure—the strong, dominant woman who could only be tamed in bed.

"It's true," Hathaway said. "Rarely a cross word, even if I was in a pissy mood from the office. She was almost unflappable."

"*Unflappable* isn't a word I'd think of using to describe Delia," I said.

"I remember one time I'd taken her to dinner at Veau d'Or," he said, "and we were going off to a party later. She was wearing a new light pink dress— that was her favorite color—and this waiter spilled half a bowl of soup on her, gazpacho, for chrissake! She didn't flinch; shrugged it off, smiled, went to the ladies' room, and never mentioned it again. Hell, I think I was madder than she was."

All of a sudden, I was beginning to wonder if I really knew Delia at all.

"You say pink was her favorite color?" I asked.

"Yeah. That's what she told me. She liked those little pink roses and I'd send some to her every so often. She said she thought of pink was nice and 'girlish.' "

Hathaway was on his third double bourbon now. Even after all these years his bitterness seemed as undiluted as the whiskey he was drinking. Despite my preconceived notions about him, I felt myself empathizing.

"I never really got over it. A few years later I got married, but I guess I was still on the rebound. Every time my wife and I went to bed, it was her, instead. But of course it wasn't the same. Changed my life in a way. I used to think I was a pretty nice guy. Now people think I'm a shit. And I probably am."

"Well," I said, "somebody's still trying to blackmail her."

"I wish I'd thought of it myself," Hathaway scowled. "There she is, every goddamn night, sitting up there on the tube, looking good as she ever did. Probably gloating over all the guys out there who'd like to get into her pants. You know, she acts so prim and proper—wears all these unrevealing clothes and stuff—I wonder what people would think if they knew what she was really like?"

"Did you ever confront her about it—about Italy, I mean?"

"Hell no. What was to confront? By the time I got back she was already hooked up with somebody else. In my crowd too—would you believe it? Didn't even have the courtesy to find some other crowd to ass around with. Half the time she was with that fat-slob gossip columnist Max Weed—what does that tell you? So I had to look at her at all the parties and restaurants and clubs we all went to. Every once in a while I could tell she was trying to catch my attention, but I wasn't having any of it. She even sent me a Christmas card once. Had her picture on it, but screw that. I finally couldn't stand it anymore and I stopped going to that shit altogether. And then I got married and moved to Connecticut. Finally couldn't stand that either and moved out here. And what happens? I get to look at her on the television every night."

"You don't have to," I said.

"Well, I do it anyway—the fucking bitch."

CHAPTER 16

AN IMAGE CAME to me that when Delia was born, seraphim hovered over her cradle bringing gifts—intelligence, beauty, strength, character, humor—and then a dark angel swooped down and declared, "Not so fast!" and added to them insecurity, carnality, a certain amount of ruthlessness, plus that inflexible "honesty" of hers. I didn't begrudge her any of it, good or bad, but the notion was growing stronger with each of these encounters that I was barking up the wrong tree in hoping to find I'd been any more special in her life than the others.

When I got back to the Peninsula, I called Rick Olsen and told him of my conversation with Hathaway, who had several earmarks of being our man: his history of violence toward women as well as men, his unrelenting bile toward Delia, and, foremost, his presence in L.A. Yet if he was the one, I would have thought he'd have been a lot more circumspect with me. Instead I got what I took as unvarnished candor. Still, our culprit was obviously a man of shrewdness and deception; perhaps, as a lawyer, Hathaway realized he'd spewed out enough bitterness toward Delia to others by now that if he played the role of just another old flame, something would seem amiss.

Rick seemed concerned and suggested putting a tail on Hathaway. Wasn't that pointless, I said, given that you couldn't tail a man into his own bedroom where he kept his phone. But Rick observed that if Hathaway was the caller, he'd probably have better judgment than to make the calls from his own home for fear of being traced or monitored.

Meantime, Rick had come up with other information. Homer Greer, it seemed, had made two trips to the Los Angeles area about the same time as Delia received at least two of her "calls." How he found this out I don't know, except I suspected he must have had some sort of plug into computer records of the airlines or credit card companies. Rick suggested that when I went back to New York, I interview Homer again—this time taking a sterner line.

I HAD A date with Toby Burr that night for dinner, and as I showered I began again to think of Worthington Hathaway and his experience with Delia. It was nothing like my own because, after disappearing from my life, she then turned up in it again. I had come to liken our relationship to a pair of comets pulled toward each other by some kind of gravity but moving so fast we just went spinning off in opposite directions. If we could only slow down . . . But this completely overlooked an immutable truth of astrophysics: Comets are always predictible.

After our last little evening in New York a year had gone by. I had stupidly called her once or twice after the night we spent together, but only got her answering machine and when my messages went unreturned I quit trying. My ego had been bruised enough and besides there was no sense beating a dead horse.

Then one day she just popped up again on the phone, as if no time had passed. We engaged in what was for me a disembodied conversation; it was amicable but completely strange, talking with her as though nothing had happened between us. It was the dead of winter again and I mentioned I was planning to go to Bermuda again in a few weeks. Actually, that wasn't quite the truth because the idea had planted itself in my head as we spoke, but she didn't ask how *long* I'd been planning it.

She remembered our last trip fondly, she said. Such a lovely place it was and a relief to be out of the cold of the Northeast. I asked her, casually as I could, why didn't she come along? To my astonishment, she said that might be fun. She didn't commit but at least she hadn't pooh-poohed the idea. I said I'd call her in a few days to see if she'd made up her mind.

It turned out we went on separate flights because Delia first had to go home to Kansas City for something. I didn't quite understand it all, but it was enough that she'd agreed to come and, besides, that would give me time to get there first and open up the house. For two days I scurried around the Hamilton

Harbour area, buying flowers, cheeses, wines, cakes, and goodies. After a while I began to feel like one of those lonely widowed mums in old British movies who putter around their houses for hours on end to make them inviting for some elderly gentleman caller.

If I'd known about the Worthington Hathaway business then, I would have gone to the Bermuda airport with far more trepidation, but in fact as the flight taxied into the arrival gate, Delia was the first one off. I'd brought her a yellow hibiscus from our lawn, which she immediately fastened in her hair.

She was full of chatter, compliments, and gratitude on the ride back through town and when we got to the house, I showed her to one of the guest rooms. I didn't want to make presumptions for her, and she apparently thought nothing of it. The water was still too cold for swimming, so we again took a long walk on the beach. On the way back the sun was dropping low on the horizon and a slight chill filled the ocean air. At one point I moved close and put my arm around her waist. She didn't remove it or pull away, but I didn't sense she welcomed it either. Nor did she put her arm around me, as one might expect of affectionate people, and so after a while I let go and walked apart from her.

That night I made a dinner of fresh rock lobsters cooked over an open grill and a salad I thought was first rate, served with a bottle of chilled Bergerac Sec. I had a fire going in what my family had named the

Ocean Room and through big glass windows we watched occasional twinkling lights of ships passing by.

We stayed up and talked for a while. Delia wanted to discuss literature, mostly mid-twentieth-century women writers of whom she had become fond. It was a subject of which I was not particularly keen on, but I can't say I wasn't enjoying myself. It was delightful to see Delia animated about these things. Most women I had met until that point in my life—at least those with whom I contemplated romance—spoke mainly of mundane stuff: parties, gossip, trends, new restaurants and clubs, and if they spoke of politics, one side or the other, they were often so strident it was unpleasant to deal with. This made me reflect that I might have been running with the wrong crowd.

But Delia already knew a lot and, good for her, she wanted to learn. And she had a way of asking you questions; whether or not she was actually interested in the answers, she made you feel she was, and that counted for a lot.

It wasn't very late when she announced she was going to bed. I wasn't invited, and so stayed up by myself until the fire was very low, wondering what any of this meant. Next morning Delia announced she wanted to go into Hamilton to visit some stores. As a British protectorate Bermuda has some duty-free shops with goods from Harrods and other fancy stores: great bolts of Scottish tartans, Waterford crystal, and Wedgwood ware. There are few automobiles allowed on the island, but we kept several Vespa motor scooters in the garage and I showed her how to ride one. She left just after breakfast with a cheerful "See you in a little bit" and didn't return until nearly dark, by which time I was feeling concerned.

When I asked her how the day had gone, she was evasive. I could see she had bought nothing, and I wondered aloud how she had spent her time.

"Oh, I just wandered around," she said.

"All day, in the harbor?"

"Well, I went on a ride to the other end of the island," she casually informed me.

That was a long way, in fact, but a beautiful trip. It was the sort of romantic adventure meant for two, crossing narrow bridges over crystal coves with breathtaking surf breaking on the pink coral rocks at the water's edge. I could only think she had wanted to be away from me.

"I stopped for a while and read my book," she added. She kept a half-finished Edith Wharton novel in her purse.

"Where?"

"Oh, some quiet little parklike spot. There was a table with benches and I just lay there and read and then fell asleep for a while."

"I had a lunch ready," I said, trying not to sound miffed. "If I'd known you were going to be gone all day, I'd have packed it up for you."

"Oh, that's okay," she said offhandedly. "I don't

eat much lunch these days, you know? Got to keep off the pounds."

Foolishly, I wondered for who.

That night I'd planned to steam a big pot of jumbo shrimp I'd arranged to be sent over for the occasion from the Carolina mainland. These were the days when express messenger services such as FedEx were just getting started and I had called my mother and asked her to go down to the docks when the boats came in and get FedEx to fly the shrimp over next day. Large almost as lobsters, they arrived while Delia was on her excursion. I have a special way of cooking them, an old recipe from the Carolina lowlands: Steam quickly in a half-pint of beer with celery and onions as garnish. It's quite a treat when they begin to turn pink from the steam and are served up with hot lemon-butter.

But somehow that night I just wasn't inclined to go to the trouble. She was "keeping her distance" again. I felt like I was putting up some innocuous tourist from Norway or someplace, or perhaps running a bed-and-breakfast where polite conversation was expected and nothing more. Frankly, it pissed me off.

I suggested without mentioning the shrimp that we go out for dinner. Delia of course agreed, so we went to the Coral Beach Club down the road, a private place where my family were members. It was a tense evening, at least for me, and I expect for her as well, though she didn't show it. In fact, she tried to be cheerier and more animated than usual, I imagine to make up for my clearly dour mood.

We hadn't been there long when we ran into a couple I had met during previous visits to the island—Rennie and Phippie from Charleston, whose relatives had a home here too. Nothing would do except that we all join together at a table. I had planned over dinner to confront Delia, but naturally this was now foreclosed and at least we all had a respite from the looming "honest hour."

Afterward we walked home along the beach again. A full January moon was shimmering off the water and a true chill was blowing in off the ocean. I noticed that this time she walked briskly ahead of me, whether to get home out of the crispy weather or to keep me at arm's length, I could not know, but I suspected the latter.

I was building another fire when she announced she was going to bed.

"Before you do, I'd like to ask you a question," I said.

"All right."

"Why don't you sit down."

Her resigned expression told me she understood this was to be a heavy conversation she'd been avoiding.

"What exactly are you doing here?"

"I've been enjoying myself."

"By 'keeping your distance'?"

"Look, Johnny, I've thought about all this and it's just . . . that I don't share your feelings toward me. I've wanted to and I've tried. But I can't."

"We've been over that before," I said, "and it's

never made any sense to me, then or now. How can you say you 'try' to fall in love with somebody? It sounds totally calculating."

"It's not, but it's the way it is."

"Well, that aside, I'd settle for sex." I knew it sounded pathetic, but I thought maybe I could salvage something from the trip.

"Now, Johnny . . ."

"It didn't stop you a year ago—you weren't in love with me then either."

"Listen, I like you and I admire you and I respect you. Can't that be enough'?"

"Passion is an emotion that's truly honest and hard to fake—I like it a lot better than respect and admiration."

"I'm giving you as much as I can feel."

"And you came all the way out here knowing that? What did you expect when I asked you on such a romantic trip? That we'd spend our nights in separate bedrooms?"

"No. I wasn't sure until I got here."

"That's nice. What made you decide, just taking your first look at me?"

"No. Actually, I think I decided on the flight over. Looking down at the ocean . . . with all those whitecaps."

"What the hell do whitecaps have to do with it?"

"I don't know, I'm just telling you what I felt."

"So why did you stay? Why didn't you just turn around and go home? Don't you understand how awkward and tense and uncomfortable all this is?"

"For you?"

"Of course for me. Isn't it for you?"

"A little. But I was enjoying your company."

"Yeah? By riding off all day by yourself?"

"I needed a little space."

"You needed to get away from me."

"I sensed a confrontation coming," she said.

"Like now?"

"Yes."

"So you just postponed it?"

"I suppose. I'm only trying to be honest."

"Right, honest. Well, frankly, Delia, I don't believe you. I believe that you decided your feelings about me a long time ago."

"I had, but I thought they might change."

"And they didn't."

"I'm afraid not, in any important way."

"And so now you have to have some sort of . . . 'emotional attachment' to sleep with me?"

"In a way."

"How come you didn't before?"

"When?"

"Like last year, for example?"

"I don't know. Sometimes I start . . . thinking about you. And it gets me excited."

"But not now."

"Not now."

"And so you just turn up in my life whenever you

want and wait to see whether you'll blow hot or cold, huh? And what am I supposed to be doing all this time?"

"It's not that way. It's more."

"What's more?"

"You're one of the people I keep thinking about."

"One of them? You mean there're others?"

"Look, Johnny, I can't explain it, and it's not going to do any good to talk about it all night. I've said everything I know."

WE BOTH WENT off to bed, but it was a sleepless night for me. I was into scotch in those days and probably drank half of the bottle I brought to my room. When I woke up next morning, of course I felt like shit. I went to the kitchen and made coffee and put some sweet rolls in the oven. I could hear her shower running. I cut up a melon and set out two plates for breakfast. The day was gray and a strong wind was kicking up the ocean. I started to build a fire but then figured, what the hell—what was the reason for being cozy?

At one point I went back to my bedroom for something and as I passed hers, I saw her door was wide open and Delia was standing in front of her mirror brushing her hair, wearing nothing but panties and a bra. I know she saw me in the reflection. Well, goddamn, I thought. When I returned, I pointedly stopped and shut her door.

I stormed out of the house, furious. What the hell was she trying to do? This was more than I was willing to put up with. I stood for a long moment on the cliff overlooking the violent sea. The waves were grayish black; a salt spray was blowing in the air and it had begun to drizzle. I started to walk off down the beach, but, when I turned, Delia was standing in the open doorway, leaning against the door frame, her long, slender legs crossed and her auburn hair blowing in the breeze. She was still wearing nothing but underwear. I looked at her with a frustration bordering on disgust, but she was smiling.

"What are you doing?" I snapped. "Why don't you put some clothes on?"

She raised her hand and beckoned me to her.

"What is this? Charity?" I said with astonishment.

"Why don't you come inside? You'll get wet."

"So what? I feel like getting wet. It's a wet day, it's a wet time of year—it's a wet life. It matches my mood."

"I can improve your mood, I think," she said. She began rubbing her hands along her thighs and hips.

"This is not necessary," I informed her. "If this is supposed to be gratitude or guilt or obligation or something, I want no part of it."

"It isn't," she said. "I've been thinking. . . ."

"I thought you'd already done that."

"I had other thoughts, last night, after we went to bed."

I walked up to her. This was completely seductive,

and I felt myself unresistant to the siren's song. When you mount a wild horse, you know you'll probably get thrown, but you do it anyway, just for the thrill.

"I want you to take me into the bedroom," she said. "Just like the old times."

CHAPTER 17

WHILE I WAS still mentally trapped in Delia's endless non sequitur, the phone rang. I answered it, wearing a towel. It was Rick Olsen again. He said Delia's husband, Brad, was in town after their San Diego trip and wanted to talk to me. He asked could they come over in a little while. I told him I had a dinner engagement and suggested we meet next morning. But Rick said Brad wished to speak with me tonight, so I told them to meet me in my room about ten. That would give me time to finish with Toby Burr.

Burr was downstairs in the restaurant at his usual table when I came in. He had in his hand a sheaf of papers, which I took to be my first revisions of part of the script he had hired me to rewrite.

"Dammit, Johnny," he said as a typical greeting, "I was afraid of this. Are you trying to turn this whole story around?" He slapped the pages on my side of the table as I sat down.

"I'm trying to turn it in the right direction, if that's what you mean."

"The girl," he said, leaning over, clenching his

teeth, and throwing up his hands, "is not the star of this picture!"

"Why not?"

"Because I said not, that's why! It's my picture, not hers and certainly not yours."

"I'm sorry you don't like it," I said with feigned contriteness.

"I didn't say I'm not liking it. It's just not the picture I pitched to the studio."

"What do they care—as long as it works?"

"They care because they got fifty million smackeroos riding on this thing, that's why! It's like if you made contract for somebody to build you a fifty-million-dollar house and they give you plans, and all of a sudden somebody comes along and changes all the plans. It makes people nervous. You been out here long enough to know that, Johnny!"

"Look, Toby, I wouldn't know where to live in a fifty-million-buck house. Besides, it's a better script now, isn't it?"

"But how do I sell it? They were expecting the *guy* to be the star. You know how hard it is to find a bankable woman star, don't you?"

"With this script, you don't even need a star," I retorted. "Any good actress'll do and when it opens, she'll *be* a star."

"What is it with this project?" Burr continued. "It has to do with that TV girl, right? What? Are you obsessed with her or something? I mean, look, this is heavy material, Johnny. You've created a very complicated character here."

"That's what I said I was going to do."

"And that's exactly what I told you *not* to do, right?"

"It'll be okay, Toby, be patient," I said.

"Look, what I want to know is, what's with this girl? I mean, is she in love with the guy, or isn't she? Did she ever love him, or is she just jerking him around? I don't understand."

"You're not supposed to yet—that's the beauty of the thing."

"But goddamnit, I'm the producer! I *have* to understand everything, all the time! That's what producers do!"

"It's not important what you understand," I said serenely. "It's what the audience understands." I could see he was becoming apoplectic.

"Who pays your salary?" he demanded.

"The studio."

"Bullshit! I pay it!"

"Yeah, but you get the money from them."

Burr collapsed backward into his chair and rolled his eyes. A waiter placed a bowl of soup in front of him, but he seemed not to notice.

"Johnny—this girl, she's full of contradictions, am I right?"

"Yes."

"Do they get resolved?"

"Of course, to the audience at least."

"How?"

"I don't know yet."

"What!" Burr cried, sitting up straight. "You're

making experiments with fifty million of somebody else's hard-earned money!"

"Hard-earned, my ass. I'm not finished yet," I told him.

"Well, can't you give me a hint?"

"No, not yet. Trust me," I said.

I WAS BACK in my room a little before I was supposed to meet Rick and Brad. At ten on the dot the front desk rang, announcing I had visitors. A few minutes later Brad and Rick were at my door.

"Johnny," Rick said, "Brad wants to know whatever you know about this Hathaway character."

"Just what I told you, Rick," I said. "They dated back about twenty years ago, he was going to ask her to marry him, but she stood him up. He's still holding a grudge, it seems."

"What kind of guy is he?" Brad asked.

"I don't understand what you're saying."

"Well, describe him."

I found this a little puzzling but tried to paint a picture of Worthington Hathaway—tall, fairly trim, blond, direct to the point of curtness, and so on.

"So he's a good-looking fellow, huh?" Brad said.

"Not bad. I mean, he's no beach boy. At least, not anymore."

"And comes from a well-to-do family?"

"Yes, I think you could safely say that. His name alone would—"

"I don't give a damn about his name." Brad was pacing the room.

"What I think Brad's driving at," Rick said, "is, would he be the kind of guy Delia might, well, be interested in?"

"Well, I guess . . . she was, of course—but that was years ago."

"I mean *now*," Brad interjected.

"Now? Why, that would seem ridiculous," I said. "He hates the thought of her, unless he's lying. And she didn't even know he was living here in L.A. Hadn't seen him since nineteen seventy-eigh—"

"How do you know?" Rick said.

"Because she told me. What makes you think she might be?"

"He's here," Brad said. "And so is she."

"Well, what does that have to do with it? I mean, there are five million guys who are also here. Why him?"

"Old flame, maybe," Rick said.

"Look," I said, "this conversation seems preposterous, given what I understand is happening. I mean, your wife is getting these calls from somebody and we're trying to find out who. Is there something I don't know going on?"

"We're not sure they're calls," Rick said.

"Not calls?"

"We think they're letters or something."

"Why?"

"Delia said so; she told Brad while she and Brad were in San Diego."

"Hummm . . ." was all I could think of to say at the moment. I was treading water and decided to play dumb.

"She told me there were letters as well as calls," Brad said. He looked uncomfortable, so I offered him a drink. He took a gin and tonic and Rick settled for a beer.

"What do the letters say?" I asked.

"Same as the calls."

"Did she show them to you?"

"She said she threw them away."

"But she told Brad these pictures were more than what the guy said during the calls," Rick said. "That he wanted something from her, sex—"

"Pictures?" I asked. "What—"

"Letters, I mean," Rick corrected himself. "I understand there was a reference the guy made in the letters to pictures or something."

I saw Brad look at Rick with an expression as though Rick might have said something he wasn't supposed to.

"But he said that he'd like to meet her for sex or something?" I asked.

"No—not yet exactly. He wants her to perform intimate things on the television broadcast."

"Seems like that would be pretty hard to do," I said.

"They are little things, things not particularly noticeable to anyone who's not watching for them," Rick said.

"Well, how does that connect to whether or not

Delia might be seeing this guy Hathaway?" I asked. "I don't see . . ."

"Because she wasn't telling the truth from the start," Brad said.

"She give you a reason?" I asked.

"Yes. That it was embarrassing to her. That I'd want to see the letters and she didn't want me to. That it was her business."

"Sounds reasonable."

"Yeah, unless you've spent three years listening to her go on about how honest and straightforward she is."

"Well, that always did seem to be her trademark," I said.

"Don't you find it strange?" Rick asked.

"Not particularly. I mean, this is a delicate situation, isn't it? She's a woman. It must be embarrassing for her."

"Why?" Brad said.

"I suppose because the letters are coming from somebody who she knew well at one time," I said. "I think anybody is entitled to their own secrets about that kind of thing. It was evidently a piece of her past life. Not the one she's leading now."

"We've never had secrets," Brad said.

"Do you have any reason to suspect she's having an affair?" I asked, knowing damned well there were secrets between them.

"No, but I never had any reason to suspect she'd been lying to me about these . . . letters either."

"That's a pretty far leap," I offered.

"Leap or not . . ." Brad said bitterly, "there are things about this I don't understand."

"Well, if you'll forgive me, I've always prided myself on being a pretty good judge of character—so far as it goes. If you ask me, I'd think the most far-fetched thing imaginable would be that Delia is somehow involved with Hathaway or—for that matter—he with her, unless he's the letter writer, or caller, or whatever."

"I hope you're right," Brad said.

"Keep your eyes open, will you, Johnny?" Rick said. "I assure you, we're going to get to the bottom of this sooner or later."

"Let's make it sooner," I said.

NEXT DAY, THE opéra bouffe opened again, with folly unveiling another act. I'd just returned from lunch and was headed out for a meeting at Fox when the desk called with a message from Delia saying she needed to see me as soon as possible. I phoned her at the TV station, but she was doing a radio newsbreak taping, so I left word for her to meet me in the bar at the Peninsula at seven. She was waiting in the lobby when I came downstairs.

"Thank you for this," she said, giving me a little peck on the cheek as I led her to Burr's old table. I began to order a bottle of wine from the waitress, but Delia stopped me.

"I don't want to talk here, if that's okay," she said.

"Would you like to go do dinner—someplace else?"

"No, thanks. I'm not sure I could eat anything."

"Well . . ."

"Could we go to your room, maybe?"

"Sure," I said, and for once I did not sense this was some kind of good-time proposition on her part.

On the elevator Delia didn't say anything. She looked drawn and upset.

"We can go up to the roof garden," I suggested. "There's a nice view from there and I don't think anyone else will be around this time of day."

"No, no, I think your place is better."

We got off and walked down the hall. As luck would have it, a door opened and a guy I knew from New York appeared, on his way downstairs. He had some kind of job that took him coast to coast. He was effusive in his greetings despite our obvious embarrassment but didn't seem to recognize Delia. I extracted us from this encounter quick as I could.

"Oh, this is really nice, Johnny," she said when we walked into my suite.

"Yes, isn't it? A two-room—just like the old New York place of mine you probably remember."

"But it's a lot swankier than that," she said, admiring the paintings, decorations, and other perks the hotel provides for its most favored customers. "It's almost like home, isn't it?"

"Yeah, except Mom's not here to bake an apple pie."

She gave a little laugh and I was glad. Maybe it lightened the tension a bit.

"Would you like a glass of wine or something?" I asked.

She said yes and while I poured it, she fiddled with something in her purse, finally taking out an envelope that contained a letter.

"This came today," she said, handing it to me.

The envelope was postmarked New York, a week to the day after she skipped the late news show. I removed and unfolded the letter. It was a single page on nondescript stationery. Someone—I assumed Delia—had pasted little strips of white paper blanking out parts of the text, which were typed, probably by a computer printer.

"What are these?" I asked.

"They're . . . well, private, I guess you could say. They don't mean anything. It's just his dirty mind. It wouldn't tell you anything."

I read the uncovered parts of the letter aloud.

I can begin to see, it opened, *that you are avoiding me on the air. How many times will you do it? A few maybe. So I've decided to give you something else to think about.*

Just look at your face, it said. *You should see yourself.*

"What does this mean?" I said.

"There was a picture with it."

"A picture? You mean he has something that you can tell is actually you?"

"Looks that way."

"Where is it?"

"You don't want to see it," she said.

"But you've saved it."

"Yes."

I went on: *We'll do it again, when you're not expecting it. Sometime I'll be there and you'll just do it because you want to. Because you miss it. I know you. You're not what you try to make people believe you are. And when you're ready, just remember, I'll be there.*

Delia had sat down in a chair and was staring out the window, away from me. I continued reading:

Tell anyone about this and you'll get to see a lot more pretty pictures. This one doesn't show much because I've fixed it that way. You won't remember where they were taken. But I do, and there's a lot more to it than that. You don't understand the half of it.

"This is worse than I thought," I said.

Delia nodded but still didn't look at me.

"The picture," I said, "what is it?"

"Just my face. It looks like he's cut out anything else I might recognize."

"A camera?"

"I'm not sure, but it looks more like a piece of videotape frame."

"It would be useful to have it," I said. "Police have ways of identifying a lot of things like that."

"I know they do," she said, "but that's still the problem. No police."

"It doesn't show anything? No background or something like that?"

"No, nothing. I imagine he's smart enough to have considered all that."

"I expect you're right."

"How about your—your looks? I mean, can you tell when it was done?"

"I've tried. It's sort of blurry. You can't even see what hair style I had, except . . ."

"What?"

"It's pulled back, I think. Most of it's cut out of the picture."

"Does that ring a bell?"

"No. I wear it back a lot."

"Always did?"

"Yes."

"Well, maybe he just videotaped you on your show and doctored up the thing and had a frame printed. If all he has is your face, that doesn't pose much of a problem."

"I think it's more than that—that he has more."

"Why?"

"I just do. I can tell."

"And you have no idea of where or when it could have been made?"

"No, not really."

"Not really?"

"Frankly, not at all."

She crossed her legs and finally turned to me.

"Johnny, this is scary."

"I know it is. I really think this is the time to go to the police or somebody."

"No, no. I've told you . . ."

"It's a threat. This guy sounds like some kind of rapist, maybe—no matter what he says he thinks you'll feel."

"I keep hoping he'll ask for money," she said.

"He hasn't so far. What makes you think he will?"

"I said I was hoping."

"Have you told anybody else about this?"

"No, why?"

"Because your husband was here last night, and he said you told him about the letters."

"Here? With you?"

"He was. Rick brought him."

"But why?"

"Well, he seemed to be checking up on how I was doing."

"He never mentioned it to me. When was he here?"

"About ten."

"While I was doing my show?"

"Yes. And said you told him about getting letters instead of calls."

"I told him I got both."

"Yes, that's right, that's what he said. What made you tell him?"

"I was frightened. It just sort of slipped out. He's always asking me about it—ever since it started. I think he thinks I know more than I'm saying."

"Well, you do, don't you?"

"Yes, but no more than I've told you."

"Do you know more than you've told me?"

"No, why?"

"Because you're right about your husband—he thinks you know more."

"Why do you say that?"

"He thinks you lied to him."

"I know, about the letters."

"You did."

"I've told you about that." She got up and walked around the room, one hand on a hip. I felt something stir inside me. Here was someone I found passionately attractive, walking around in my own hotel room, so, so . . . Well, obviously this was neither the time nor place. Besides, Rick most likely had his people "keeping an eye on her." It could look sticky.

"Listen," I said, "why don't we both sleep on this. I'll talk with you in the morning."

She rubbed the back of her neck and shook her head, as if she was trying to exorcise an ugly thought. "All right, I'd better go."

Again, I thought I saw something in her eyes, but it was probably a misreading on my part, like so many times in the past. I phoned for an attendant to bring Delia's car around and walked her down through the lobby.

"This means a lot to me, what you're doing, Johnny," she said. She put her arm on mine and leaned over for another cheek kiss and stepped out to her car. I watched her drive away. As she did, lights came on in a nondescript sedan across the street. It pulled out after her and I figured Rick's men were on the job and at least she'd be safe tonight. It also meant they knew Delia had come to my hotel.

CHAPTER 18

I T HAD BEEN quite a couple of days. I felt somehow that seeds of hypocrisy were beginning to sprout. Instead of worrying about his wife's safety, Brad seemed consumed with suspicion of her fidelity. And she, the self-described paragon of veracity, had been lying to her husband over the matter of phone calls versus letters. That was more or less understandable, however; honesty's a fine virtue but can be carried too far. If she'd had a checkered past and these letters revealed it, then why subject Brad to that humiliation? Maybe it was better untold. I deal with actors and fictional situations all the time, and this rang the least true of any scenario I ever concocted. Nevertheless, stranger things have happened in the world. And what the hell was this peculiar sexual thing nobody wanted to talk about? That was another aggravating mystery.

Could it be that Delia was *faking* getting these letters? To go to all that trouble—why? You would have to go through a litany of explanations and still nothing makes sense.

And Brad—what was his deal? Why suspect Delia

of being unfaithful in the face of apparent threats from some unknown kook? In the end, I concluded that, until I could prove otherwise, both were most likely acting in good faith. Delia was getting real threats and Brad was reacting like a confused husband living apart from a beautiful wife while she was an object of craving by countless TV viewers in a city where craving is elevated to an art form.

Worthington Hathaway still seemed suspect; he had motive, presence, and, until this latest letter, opportunity. I had seen him Friday afternoon; the new letter to Delia had arrived next Friday, postmarked New York. Unless he had an accomplice, there was no way he could have mailed it after we spoke, unless he had flown to New York and back. Anyway, there wasn't much at this point I could do about Hathaway. Rick had put a tail on him; so, for all temporary practical purposes, that base was covered.

But there was still unfinished business left in New York.

Bo Bothwell and Arthur Dalton seemed the least likely so far, but I hadn't eliminated them. Both bore Delia at least some hostility and Dalton, before he stalked out on me, had even mentioned the red sweater. Homer Greer also remained a mystery, as did Professor Horst Vining, who, on the face of it, seemed even less likely, but, again, there was his recollection of the red sweater thing. And there were also the "downtown" people described by Arthur Dalton. All that struck me as strange; no one on Delia's list matched anybody of that stripe, and yet

Dalton had no reason to fabricate such a tale. Problem, of course, was how, after so many years, to locate any of them. I hadn't done this kind of legwork since my newspapering days.

Restless as all this was making me, I violated a long-standing practice and caught the red-eye, first class, of course, to La Guardia, cursing all the way at those environmentally righteous who had nixed transcontinental flights by the SST. I arrived home in a foul and testy mood, but seeing Gotcha again quickly pulled me out of it.

After a few hours' sleep I showered and went out for a late lunch. At the restaurant I spread before me the notes I had taken during my conversation with Arthur Dalton. There were the names of some of the downtown clubs he—and Delia—had frequented, along with some of the bartenders who he'd remembered only by their first names. At my request, a waiter brought me a phone book, but none of the clubs was still listed. I'd rather expected this. In New York, as in L.A. when a hot spot opens up, everybody who's anybody in that crowd flocks to it; fortunes are made, money is skimmed, and so forth until the owner concludes he's reached his peak and sells the place to an unsuspecting fool who thinks the gold will flow forever.

After lunch I stopped by the New York Public Library and dug back in the stacks for old phone books from ten years ago. Sure enough, several of the clubs Arthur mentioned were listed and I jotted down their addresses. Most of these club owners know each other and I thought maybe I could work some leads that way.

About sundown I headed down Broadway to the now modish neon district of clubs, restaurants, and lofts around Soho and TriBeCa. My first stop was at an address now called Contacts. It sounded like a spot for assignations, but once upon a time it had been the Cave, which Arthur had remembered. It wasn't open yet, as I'd suspected, but I managed to sweet-talk my way past a setup guy who was sweeping the floor. A bartender who looked like Mischa Auer, the eternal butler in old movies, was behind his counter, measuring liquor bottles. I asked him how many years he'd been there.

"Six months," he replied.

"So I suppose you weren't familiar with this place before it became Contacts?"

"It was a lot of things," he said.

"Remember the Cave?"

"No—but I know a guy who used to work there."

"Yeah? Know where he is now?"

"What for?" he asked.

"I just want to see if he'd remember somebody— somebody who used to come in here when it was the Cave."

"That's a long time ago, seven or eight years, I think."

"Well, maybe he's got a good memory. Can you tell me where he is now?" I laid a twenty on the bar.

"Name's Frankie. He works the bar over at Slanders."

"Where's that?"

"Market Street."

I thanked him and left. Slanders was a step or two up from Contacts. At least it had a wood floor instead of concrete. A couple of fellows were behind the bar and I asked for Frankie.

"In the back," one said, nodding toward a double swinging door.

"You Frankie?" I said to a guy piling limes and lemons into a bowl.

"Yeah."

"Worked at the Cave?"

"Why?"

I introduced myself and told him briefly why I was there.

"I'm trying to find a girl named Delia Jamison," I said.

"Don't know her. She work at the Cave?"

"She was a customer—back in the mid-eighties."

"Don't remember the name."

"Not at all—not even the first name?"

"Hard to recall," he said. "So many girls, you know."

I put a twenty on his counter too.

"She apparently came in a lot—for a few years."

He shrugged. "Why you looking for her?"

"Old friend."

Frankie shrugged again.

"You remember any of the other bartenders from back then?"

"Sure—two or three."

"Know where they are?"

"Yeah—Carlo's working at DanTonio's and Phil's at Hobart's."

I put another twenty on the counter and was about to leave.

"Let me ask you," I said, "maybe it would help to see a photo?"

"Yeah, maybe," he said.

I nodded and walked out. Told my driver to go back uptown. In my apartment I rummaged through a closet where I kept a box with old photographs. There were half a dozen I'd taken of Delia on that first trip to Bermuda. I selected a couple and slipped them into my jacket pocket, then headed back downtown.

Frankie was behind his bar now and I put the photo in front of him. He was more cordial this time, re- membering as he did the double sawbuck I'd laid on him.

"Yeah, she used to come in," he said. "A real babe."

"You ever take her out?"

"Me, no. She went out with Carlo, though—I think."

"The guy who works at . . . ?"

"DanTonio's. It's a real restaurant, you know."

I got directions and headed over there. Behind the bar was a handsome swarthy-skinned guy of about forty who looked like he spent all his tips on improving his teeth. By now the place was beginning to fill up and there were several customers at the bar. I waited until he'd taken care of the drink orders and then asked for a beer. I laid another twenty on the counter, along with Delia's photo.

"You remember her?" I asked. "From about ten years or so ago?"

Carlo studied the picture carefully, looked at me, and nodded.

"Uh-huh."

"Know her well?"

"Did, for a little while. But not really well, I guess."

"No?"

"Flake," he said, flashing a Burt Lancaster smile.

"What makes you say that?"

"Sheika? She was slippery, man. One night here, one night there—and then she don't even know your name."

"Sheika?"

"That's her name—at least the one she told everybody. She come from uptown."

"She have a last name?"

"Nobody got last names down here," Carlo said.

"So you took her out?"

"I took her home a few times—my home, I mean. My pad."

"Got to know her?"

"Nobody got to know her, man. I mean, she ain't got no phone number or nothin' that she'll give you.

She just comes in once or twice a week, and about closing she hangs around the bar and you take her home, you know? Or you don't. But I give you this, she was different."

"How's that? Something unusual she did in bed?"

"Nah, not particularly nothin' like that. I been with so many women, I seen it all, I guess."

"What, then?"

"Well, she was *sophisticated* or somethin', man. I don't know. Had a funny sense of humor. She knew a lot of shit too. Always asking questions, like, you know, what's it like to be a bartender or what's it like coming from Spain—that kind of shit.

"Was she mostly in at the Cave, or other places too?"

"Oh, she got around, man. I mean, I heard she spent a lot of time at the Hellfire Club—you know, whips, leather, all that stuff. But I ain't into that shit, man."

"And you haven't seen her since . . . ?"

"Hell, I don't know—six, eight years, maybe. Why? What become of her?"

"She's on the coast. Doing television."

"A movie star or somethin'?"

"Yeah, something like that."

"Well, good for her. Why you interested, man? She dump on you too?"

"You could say that. By the way, do you remember anybody else she went out with?"

"She went home with a lot of guys, man. I mean, it's a wonder she didn't catch something."

"I'm talking about for any length of time."

"Yeah, a few. Why?"

"Remember their names?"

"Yeah, a few."

I laid another twenty on the bar. This was getting expensive. Carlo took no notice of it, of course.

"Well, she gone out with a movie guy for a while. He was kind of an asshole, if you know what I mean, but she seemed to dig his act."

"Was his name James Cornwell, by any chance?"

"Nah—not him. She went out with him too, but he's dead, man, years ago. Killed himself, I heard. The guy I'm talking about's name was Rex Ober. I remember 'cause he's always handing out his business cards to people. Every night he comes in and gives me a card—Rex Ober—like I couldn't remember him from the night before, bullshit."

"He still come in?"

"Nah. He moved out to the coast. Gone two, three years. Says they got better weather for making movies. What movies? I never seen any movies he's made."

"Anybody else?"

"Well, there's this one guy I remember best. He was a big shot, you know? From Chicago. I think he was connected. Expensive suits and little rat-sticker shoes. Used to come there a lot and one time she hooked up with him. A pretty nice guy, actually. She'd meet him there more than any of the rest, you know? I think for a few months. Then I didn't see neither of them again. That was the last time."

"You remember his name?"

"Just Jackie, Frankie, somethin' like that—he was Italian, I think. That's all I remember."

"No last name?"

"Like I said, man, nobody got last names down here," Carlo said.

And so it must have been Frankie LaCosta—he was on Delia's list as the one Chicago entry. That lasted most of a year according to her story. It was difficult to imagine Delia spending a whole year with some gumba called Frankie LaCosta, but she'd put him down on paper herself—even gave an address and phone number.

THAT NIGHT I went up to Elaine's for a late supper. The place was crowded, but there was always a space at the "orphan's table," the big old round center one up front she reserves for out of town pals like me and other waifs and strays who remain in her good graces. Lo and behold, who was sitting there but Max Weed, drinking stingers and smoking a cheap cigar. He welcomed me heartily, I guess because he wanted company.

"We don't see each other in decades and then twice in a few weeks," Weed said. "We're almost getting to be old pals."

"I was just thinking the same thing," I told him

with a straight face. More than a little irony was buzzing through my mind.

"Still stewing over our lovely Delia?" he asked lasciviously.

That he would return to the subject was almost beyond coincidence, but I decided to run with it. "Well, my curiosity is piqued," I said. "I mean, about her being married, and then what happened to her husband. I run into her now and again on the coast. She never mentioned it."

"Perhaps she isn't proud of it," Max said. "Wouldn't be surprised. After all, it was a sordid affair. Matter of fact, after it happened, she literally dropped out of the scene altogether, you see? I heard she'd started hanging out downtown."

"Downtown? You mean those clubs?"

"Yes, of course. I'd have seen her around if she'd stayed in our crowd, but the truth is, I never saw her after that. I'm sure she felt the sting of scandal and it weighed on her. Delia was immensely sensitive to that, you see. After all, that business about her upbringing alone raised a lot of eyebrows among the so-called old guard in this town."

"What? Because she was from Kansas City? Half the people who call themselves socially prominent around here are from someplace else."

"Oh, not just that. I mean, Kansas City may be outlandish in itself, but it was the whole business about her father and what happened to him that started people talking."

"Her father? I thought he passed away at some point, but . . ."

" 'Passed away' is a pretty sweet euphemism, my dear boy," Max said. "He was murdered, you know."

"Murdered—no, I didn't know."

"A mob deal out there, I'm told."

"He was in the mob?"

"I don't think so, exactly, but he apparently was in heavy dealings with them. The mob in the Midwest isn't just guineas, you know. Lot of Irish—with names like Jamison, I'd suspect."

"What happened?" I asked, stunned.

"Well, he had some contracts with hotels. He was supplying linens or something. My understanding is that some muscle man tries to horn in. So Jamison goes to his own mob connection and tries to have the guy rubbed out. They bungle it and the next thing you know, Delia's daddy himself winds up buried in a cornfield with his tongue cut out. It was all over the papers out there."

"Good heavens," I said. "I always thought she came from good people."

"Maybe they were good people," Max said, "just not the sort that gets you into the Colony Club, honey. And, I mean, Delia already had her own baggage to carry around when it came to the level of the game she was trying to play in. It was just a rerun of her fling with the jet-set bunch. First, she was just too goddamn beautiful. And maybe even worse, she had a shrewd tongue and didn't really give a rat's ass what she said to people—even though most of it was true and probably fair too. But it was as if she didn't have that little filter in her mind the rest of us do that distinguishes between what we think and what we say. Those were two strikes already—and because of that, a lot of women resented her. And what was more, she went straight after what she wanted, in this case, men. No beating around the bush with our Delia; she'd see somebody who appealed to her, march over, and make a fairly obvious pass. Just not done in our crowd, my boy. I spoke to her about it once, but she pooh-poohed me."

As Weed talked, it certainly brought back memories, of the first time I'd met Delia at the party, and I suddenly wondered what would my life have been if I'd gone someplace else that night.

"So then," he continued, "when her father gets whacked, the gossip people put it in the paper. I was writing my own column then, you know. I tried to put a good face on it, but I had to write something—she'd had too much exposure on the social scene by that time to ignore it."

At the moment Weed seemed to resemble a rat.

"I never heard about any of this," I said. "I guess I was in California then."

"I was still seeing something of her in those days," Max continued, "and I watched some of her 'competition' at the parties and openings and so on do their best to cut her out. Delia wasn't rich like they were—she just *looked* rich, talked rich, acted rich, and had a good address, even if it was a tiny apartment. And she dressed well, despite the fact that she wasn't wearing Arnold Scaasi gowns. Actually, I think she made some of her own clothes. Scaasi hated her of course because she was so georgous she didn't need his talents to look like a million bucks. A lot of the girls in our crowd had grown up together and they'd all be in a group over in a corner, laughing at some in-joke, while all Delia could do was stand around and try to be nice to the men, because they were the ones who were paying her attention, and that of course just made it worse. People were saying she was a fraud—like those Vandigriff twins or whatever they called themselves, ten or fifteen years ago. You remember those boys, couple of good-looking young fellows who just appeared on the scene one day and got in with the crowd claiming they were society people when in fact their family ran a filling station up in Rye."

"Well, I knew Delia pretty well," I said, "and she never really claimed to be high society—I mean, not in so many words."

"No, of course not. She was too 'honest' for that. She never faked it with me either—never actually reinvented herself like so many of them do, but she'd always let it drop she'd gone to Miss Porter's School or whatever and then let people draw their own conclusions. And there was the matter of her accent too—I don't believe she actually took elocution lessons, she just had a good ear and picked it up. But it was naturally assumed that she was, well, from 'somebody,' and that's what made it so bad, because, as you know, people in this town love it when somebody fancy gets caught living a lie. And that's what happened to Delia."

"Honesty was a big deal for her, wasn't it?" I said.

"Naturally, my boy, but she wasn't, really, you know."

"No? Not honest?"

"Well, she made a lot out of it, of course, but in fact I always thought she was something of a fraud in that regard. Not that she was a professional liar or anything; Delia was no mythomaniac, but she used people whenever she could. Led them on to believe certain things and then professed shock when they tried to take her up on them. I'd call that dishonest, wouldn't you?"

"What kinds of things?"

"Oh, I know a number of the young fellows she went out with. Why don't you ask them?"

"I've already talked to a few," I said. "You see, somebody's trying to blackmail her, out on the coast. She thinks it's somebody she once knew. That she once went out with."

"Whatever for?" Weed asked.

"It's uncertain, actually." I proceeded to give him the barest bones of the situation.

"Well, it really doesn't surprise me," Weed said piously. "But sometimes I got the sense she was just itching to put those guys down. She talked to me about it. When she was ready to be finished with one or the other, she'd call me to see if I'd take her out someplace. Then she'd tell me her tale of woe—the guy was too much of this, or too little of that—she'd had enough. It was as though she was looking for the tiniest slight. She'd say she didn't know how to break it off, but I suspected she knew exactly how she was going to do it.

"In fact," Weed continued, "after the scandal about her father, I think that's when she first started going to those downtown places in earnest. Maybe just to gain anonymity, but that's where she met that degenerate turd she married. It was, in a sense, the beginning of the end for Delia—at least here in our crowd. Still, in a way I felt genuinely sorry for her."

"Anyone you can think of she had a really close relationship with?"

"Well, in that earlier group, she saw Jimmy Starvos for a while. That didn't end well, though."

"No?"

"She dumped on him, of course. He wasn't used to that."

"How's that?"

"How's that! He was Jimmy Starvos, for chrissake! At one point, one of the richest men in the world. Starvos Shipping. She got wind of a picture in *Paris Match* of Jimmy on his yacht with some half-naked broad on his arm, so Delia pulled the old split-o. No amount of explaining would satisfy her. He sent his driver around every day with flowers or something, but no dice. Finally he goes to see her himself, in her silly little apartment, and she won't even let him in. Word was, after that he bought her whole goddamn building and had her evicted. Don't know if it's true, but I do know she moved about that time."

"Yeah? So where's this Jimmy Starvos now?" I asked.

"Six feet under," Weed said. "Died about five years ago, fucking a Swedish woman in the shower at his suite at the Waldorf. What a way to go!"

Well, at least that saved me time. Dead men tell no tales.

"And you have no idea of anyone else in particular who might be pulling this kind of thing on her?"

"Oh no, my dear boy. Why, I'd guess it could be anybody. Sooner or later, we all reap what we sow, don't we?" said Maxwell Weed.

I HAD A few more things to do before Chicago, though. First there was the matter of Homer Greer. Rick's intelligence net had placed him in the Los Angeles area about the time the letter to Delia postmarked L.A. was sent. This was too important to let pass, so I phoned his office to make sure he was in town but didn't set up an appointment. I thought surprise might be a better tactic here.

Next afternoon I drove up the New York Thruway, then onto the New England Expressway, toward

Homer's little hamlet. It was the end of leaf season now; most of the trees were bare and a chilly rain was falling. Somehow this was what I remembered most of autumn here. When I pulled up in front of the little computer company, I was surprised to see Homer Greer himself coming out the door wearing a rumpled and stained suit with his tie half undone and his hair disheveled. He looked like the last ten miles of a Greyhound bus to Pittsburgh.

He saw me as I got out of the car and he came over. The watery eyes were more watery than ever and he had a drained look about him.

"I was coming up this way anyhow and thought I'd stop by," I told him. It was a disgraceful lie, which I'm sure he saw right through.

"Want to get some coffee?" I said.

He pointed me to a little restaurant down the block, where we found a booth.

"I've had a rough week," he said. "Just got back from L.A."

Naturally I perked up. "Business?" I asked.

"Yeah, not very successful, though. I lost a big order. My fault too."

I nodded sympathetically but figured this a good opportunity to raise the subject I had come for.

"You see Delia out there? On the television, I mean."

"Nope," he said. "I was kind of busy."

Of course, that didn't sound right. However she had hurt him, you would have thought at least out of sheer curiosity he would have turned on the tube. I remembered that during our first conversation Homer had even asked what station she was on out there and whether she was still pretty.

"Never gave it a thought, huh?" I continued.

"Not really. We had a lot of night meetings and dinners. It's why I'm so disgusted at losing that order. We'd counted on it. I don't even know if I can keep my job after this."

"But weren't you even curious what she looks like now?" I pressed. "I remember you asking me if she still looked good."

"I know she does," he said.

"Really? How's that?"

"I see her from time to time."

"You what?"

"Yeah, every once in a while I'll watch her."

"Watch her what?"

"On television. Her show."

"I don't understand. She's in L.A."

"She's here too. The DSS, you know."

"The what?"

"DSS—satellite dish. Those little ones they're selling now. I've got one."

"And you get her broadcast?"

"Yep. See, we've got no cable here. And the little dish is perfect for TV. You can get three or four hundred channels. But because it's pointed at just one place in the sky, you can't get your local news. Know what I mean?"

"Not exactly."

"Well, normally you could pick up Albany or even Hartford for news—you know, the network stuff. But because the dish is only pointed at one place in the sky, you can't, unless you switch to rabbit ears or something. And so the DSS people put on network news and the local news shows from different affiliates around the country."

"You mean you get L.A.?" I said, astounded.

"Every night. That's on Delia's network. On the others I can get the local news from Seattle or from New York."

"And so you can see her. . . ."

"I tuned her in a few times after you came here. At first it was a little spooky, seeing her. You're right. She's still pretty. But after a while, you get used to it."

"But you never tuned her in before we talked, is that right?"

"Well, no. You see, she's three hours different from here because of the time change, you know? So her midday broadcast would be about three in the afternoon my time, when I'm at work, and the six o'clock, about nine, and I usually watch the sitcoms then. You ever watch *Chicago Hope*?"

"No. I'm embarrassed to say I haven't," I told him.

"Anyway," he said, "by the time her late news show comes on, I'm in bed."

"How come you didn't mention any of this to me before?"

"I don't know—I guess I thought you knew about the TV. Besides, you didn't ask."

This news simply bowled me over—that *anyone* with one of these satellite dishes could be picking up Delia all over hell's creation. It blew my thinking right out of the water—that the sender had to be someone who could frequent her L.A. viewing area. Why the hell hadn't anyone *told* me! Not Delia, not Rick . . .

CHAPTER 19

ASTONISHMENT WAS ALMOST an understate-ment. How could I have missed such an obvious thing as satellite broadcasts? Well, the truth is, I am ignorant of all this technological gadgetry; I resisted computers over typewriters, still don't fool with the Internet, and was probably one of the last people to avail themselves of faxes, cell phones, and even answering machines.

In any case, if Homer Greer was picking up Delia's broadcast, so, theoretically, could any of the others. It occurred to me perhaps Rick might have some connections with the companies that vend these DSS programs and maybe he could ascertain if any of our subjects had one hooked up to his home. But just as quickly it occurred to me that that wouldn't necessarily prove anything. They could have had access to one someplace else.

Back in my apartment at the hotel, I ordered dinner from room service and ate by myself after building a fire. Outside the cold rain continued to patter against my windows. Down below, the streets were slick and a wind was blowing. Here and there couples

tried to hail cabs or bustled along, all headed somewhere for evening appointments. This was party
season, but I hadn't responded to any invitations.
Somehow I wasn't in a partying mood lately. About
ten I called Delia. She'd just wrapped her six P.M.
broadcast and seemed glad to hear from me. Hadn't
gotten any more letters.

"I think you ought to be prepared," I said, "for him
to try to make some kind of personal contact pretty
soon."

"I realize that," she said. "But until he does, I don't
suppose there's anything I can do. Until he makes his
move, I mean. Rick's got somebody watching me."

"He does? How do you know that?"

"I asked him to," she said. "At least I asked Brad to
ask him a couple of days ago. I thought it would be
safer that way."

"I do too," I said.

"You sound tired."

"I am. I just got back from Massachusetts. Saw
Homer Greer again."

There was an awkward silence, then she said icily,
"Oh, didn't you get enough dirt the first time?"

"Did you know he's been watching you?"

"He's what!"

"Watching you. On your show. There's this thing
called a DSS—a little satellite disk. They broadcast
your news program in a lot of places around the
country—including Homer's little town."

"They—well, yes, I knew they were doing something like that. There's some deal with the network

where we were simulcast, I think. I don't know much about it."

"Well, there you are every night," I said, "in living color right in Homer's living room."

"Oh."

"And a lot of other people's living rooms too—who have that particular setup."

"So that means . . ."

"It sure does. That anybody with one of these things can be watching you. Not just in L.A. but a lot of different places all over the country. I think there's probably more than one system. I've got to get Rick to look into it, find out how it works and who can actually get your program."

"Well, I . . ."

"And you weren't aware of this?"

"No—not really. We don't get any kind of extra air-time royalties or anything. I think it's sort of like a newspaper story that gets reprinted in other cities."

"Yeah," I said—which was all I could muster.

"What's the weather like there, Johnny?"

"Rainy, cold. Winter's coming on."

"I miss that sometimes. Sometimes a lot."

"New York winters? Why?"

"Do you remember when we used to build a fire in your apartment when it was like that?"

"I have one going now," I said, wondering if this was the beginning of another Chinese Torture of the Thousand Cuts.

"You were working on your second novel then, remember? And you would read me passages."

"I remember."

"What ever happened to that?" she asked. "Did it ever come out?"

"No, I scrapped it," I told her. What I didn't say was that she played a big part in the scrapping. It was not a comic story, but there was humor in it, at least up till the point when Delia began jerking me around. Reading over it one day, I realized the whole mood of the book had changed at that point. It's hard to be funny when you're all torn up inside and hurting. I'd put it aside for a few months, hoping I might lighten up, but I didn't; as a matter of fact, it got worse.

I even thought about ripping into the first part and making it dark too, just so it would match up with the second, but that wouldn't have worked either. I'd lost touch with my characters—they all went flat, just like I had. This was about the time I began working on my first screenplay, and going to California a lot was a tonic in many ways. I finally told my agent to get me out of the book contract. In a way it was probably a good thing. Novel writing isn't a hugely profitable undertaking except for a very few, whereas I had made half a fortune in the movies. Maybe I should have thanked her for that.

"Sometimes I think about those times and miss them. Do you ever, Johnny?"

"A few of them," I said. "But not most. It wasn't a very pleasant period in my life."

"Why? Because of me?"

"Oh no, Delia. I never gave you a second thought."

"That's not a very attractive thing to say."

"It's a lie too. Something you despise."

"I know it's a lie but not the kind of lie that matters, because I know what you really meant."

"Well, the problem for me is that the good old days and the bad old days are still somewhat with me. I thought they were long dead and buried, but when Count Dracula comes out of his grave, he's just as real as he was a hundred years ago."

"Does that make me Dracula, or the Bride of Dracula?" she asked. I detected a giggle.

"No, it makes you the bride of Brad," I said.

"And do you want to drive a stake through my heart?"

"Maybe—if I could find it," I told her.

"I should have known better than to parry with you," Delia said. "You should have been a lawyer."

"No," I said ruefully, "I probably should have been a monk."

A FEW MINUTES after I rang off with Delia, Rick called.

"Delia just told me about the satellite thing," he said. "It was completely stupid of me. I just never thought of it. We've got all sorts of satellites working for us, but that new little one isn't the same kind."

"Puts a kink in our theory, huh?"

"It expands the chase somewhat," Rick said.

I told him my suggestion that he try to check into any of our boys who might be connected with such a device and he said he'd get right on it. I also told him

I thought the satellite revelation ratcheted down Homer Greer a few notches on my list of suspects. After all, *he'd* been the one to tell me about it, hardly something one would do if they wanted to keep secret the act of watching Delia on her show.

"Anything else you can think of?" Rick asked.

I told him no. Maybe later I would go into things I found out about Delia and her downtown episodes, but I assumed whatever I told Rick probably went straight to Brad—in one form or another.

"Delia hasn't gotten any more of these letters," he said. "I've been hoping she would, because we could try to test for fingerprints."

"Yeah, what'd she tell you? She's been throwing them away?"

"That's right. What an idiot thing to do," Rick said.

"Well, I imagine she felt she had her reasons."

It suddenly occurred to me maybe now I could persuade Delia to give up one of the letters—or at least an envelope, as I'd once suggested. Maybe she could tell Rick she found one of the envelopes she hadn't thrown away. It was a very outside chance, but with all the automated mail sorting these days it just might be that the sender's prints would not have been obscured.

"Are you going to be in your office tomorrow?" I asked. "I'm going to try to find out a little more about this satellite system. There's a store selling them not far from here."

"Actually, I'm not," Rick said. "I'm going up to San Francisco for the day. It's . . . well, it's the second anniversary of my wife's death. I go out to the cemetery."

"That must be hard," I offered. "Delia told me."

"Did she?" Rick's voice seemed strained and he took a breath. "Well, yes, it is hard, but I guess it gets easier every time. But was there something else you wanted me to do?"

"No," I said, "not really."

"Just call the office number. I have a pager. They'll find me."

I wished him luck in San Francisco, which sounded kind of dumb, but what can you say to a man—especially one you hardly know—whose wife committed suicide?

NEXT MORNING I called Delia at her apartment and asked her to give up one of the envelopes. She was reticent, of course, and it seemed curious that she appeared even more reluctant when I told her Rick had brought up testing for fingerprints.

"Why don't you just send it to me, then?" I told her. "Maybe I can find a way. After all, it's just the envelope—not the letter itself. There shouldn't be any embarrassment in that and it could possibly solve the whole thing, if this guy's got a fingerprint on any record anywhere." She hesitantly agreed to forward several of the envelopes overnight by FedEx. She also wanted to know if it was still raining in New York.

"Only in my heart," I told her. We both laughed.

Something else had occurred to me during this time. In a way it was out of line, but I felt I needed to know more than just what I was being told. A trail often leads many places and the only way to really follow it is put your nose to the ground and not rely on where somebody "says" the trail goes. At least I wouldn't have to follow it with my *ear* to the ground.

Many years before, Delia had let it slip that she sometimes saw a psychiatrist. I never asked why. But I remembered that it was a woman psychiatrist and that she had a practice somewhere in Delia's old neighborhood. Since that was not an office district, but residential, it seemed to me there couldn't have been many female psychiatrists in that relatively small area, so next morning I made another trip to the New York Library.

There in the stacks among the old phone books from back during the time we had dated, I searched the pages for female psychiatrists who might have lived in the area. Sure enough there was a Jennifer Flaggler within a couple of blocks of Delia's old apartment. The only female shrink in that neighborhood. Naturally, when I looked up Dr. Flaggler in a recent book, she was not listed. On a chance I checked the other boroughs, Connecticut, and New Jersey, and, bingo, there she was, out in a little town near Short Hills. When I got home, I dialed the number for an appointment but got only an answering service. I left my message and after an hour or so Dr. Flaggler called back.

"Why do you want to see me," she said pleasantly, "if you live in Manhattan?"

"I have some work I have to do for a week or two out near your town," I lied. "It's an emotional problem of sorts. Not really a big deal, but I wanted to talk with somebody."

I was becoming quite an accomplished liar, but it seemed to do the trick, and Dr. Flaggler set up an appointment three days later.

Meanwhile, I had another fish to fry. A big one, in fact. A United States senator who was the only well-recognized name on Delia's list. I had already set up a meeting with him. Soon as I mentioned Delia's name, he agreed to make time, so I had my travel agent book me on the nine o'clock Metroliner to Washington next morning.

The train pulled out of Penn Station promptly and soon was flying across the Jersey meadows and down through Philadelphia, Wilmington, Baltimore, to the capital. It's a pretty nice ride and center city to center city not much longer than a plane shuttle. An attendant brought coffee, breakfast, and *The Washington Post*.

I was as curious about Senator Charles Awling as he must have been about me. He'd been a fortyish rake in those days, apparently a confirmed bachelor often photographed with a beautiful woman on his arm. I'd had no idea Delia had dated him, but according to her they'd been an item for a while— apparently sometime after her "club scene" period. It seemed inconceivable that a U.S. senator could be mixed up in a scheme as sordid as this, but then I recalled some of the deeds congressmen had got caught doing. And, besides, several of the letters were postmarked from Washington. And it was interesting that Homer Greer, the most traveled of my little group, had replied when I asked him, that Washington was not in his sales territory, although other places where the letters came from were.

I was actually surprised that Senator Awling agreed to meet with me. He'd realized who I was all right—something of a celebrity. I had let on in our brief conversation that I might turn out to be a Hollywood contact for some campaign money. That got his attention. At the same time, I couldn't really fudge my real reason for wanting to see him, like I had with some of the others, so I mentioned Delia. There had been a silence at his end of the phone at first, then he asked me what about her I wanted to discuss. I told him I'd rather not get into it on the phone, but that I'd be coming to Washington in a few days. Awling graciously suggested lunch in the Senate dining room.

He was pleasant and businesslike, aging gracefully into his sixties, a kind of Walter Huston look about him, right out of *Dodsworth*. He got quickly to the point.

"And so you want to talk about Delia Jamison?"

"Yes," I said. "Somebody seems to be trying to blackmail her—talking ugly. And we think it's someone she knew, someone she once dated for a period."

I hadn't mentioned the letters, because I thought I might learn more that way.

Not unexpectedly, he seemed taken aback. "Why would they do such a thing? What do they want?"

"That's a little murky," I told him. "But the threat is very real. I'm an old friend, just trying to help. To see if maybe somebody like you, who went out with her, might have a lead or two about who might be behind it."

"Not a clue—that is, off the top of my head. I really didn't know anybody else she'd dated. Some, I guess, by reputation—you, for instance—but not personally. But it's strange you mention it, because this sort of thing has happened before, you know."

"Oh, how so?"

"Well, her getting obscene messages."

"On the phone?"

"Yes, years ago. They started after we'd been seeing each other for a few months. That's what she told me. Some guy was calling two or three times a week, talking dirty, that sort of thing. He'd leave the message on her answering machine, she said."

"Somebody she knew?"

"No, she hadn't any idea."

"Did he want anything?"

"No, not that she told me. Just one of those perverts that got her number, I imagine. Just wanted to talk dirty. She didn't seem to think it was such a big deal. Of course, she lived in New York, where all sorts of those things go on."

"What did she do?"

"She switched to an answering service. That cut out the obscene messages, but sometimes she'd answer the phone herself, and he'd be there. I told her to call the phone company, the police, whoever, but she didn't want to. Said it was too much bother, and, besides, they'd have to tap her phone or something, and she didn't want that."

"Did they stop, or what?"

"Well, actually, they went on for some period," Awling said. "I tried time and again to persuade her to go to the authorities because I was getting worried, but she wouldn't. Said she just hung up when he called and he'd get tired of it sooner or later and that would be that."

"And he did?"

"I guess so, because at one point I took the bull by the horns. I've got a little clout with some people and I made a call and got them to listen in on her line and see if they could trace this bastard. She wasn't going to do it herself, but I would and I could."

"So what happened?"

"Nothing. They put a tap on her phone for three months and didn't find anything unusual. I'd just supposed the guy stopped calling. Maybe it was a coincidence that he decided to just at that moment."

"You don't think she was making it up, do you?"

"No, I didn't. Of course not. Why would she?"

"I don't know. Did you tell her what you'd done?"

"No. I thought she'd be angry about it. Delia was a

very private person, you know. But I'd satisfied myself. That was enough."

"Satisfied yourself what?"

"That the guy had stopped calling."

"And she didn't mention it again?"

"No, she didn't."

"Well, the guy who's doing this to her now is still
in business," I said.

"She isn't in danger, is she?"

"Maybe."

"My word," Awling said. "You know, I saw her
briefly in San Francisco a few years back. I didn't
know what became of her for years after we stopped
seeing each other, except I think I got a Christmas
card from her not long after we split up. But when I
got to San Francisco, there she was on the news show.
I called and took her to dinner. She brought her
boyfriend along—nice guy, I thought."

"Yeah, she married him," I said.

"Did she? Well, good for her. I never thought she
was the marrying kind."

"She apparently struck a lot of people that way," I
told him.

"Well, she was so independent. That in itself was a
wonder because in this town so many of the women
are devious. Now, Delia could be a user in her
own way, though. She was looking after herself first.
Often I'd take her to parties or dinners where she
spent a lot of time chumming up to people—fairly
important people. It left me with an impression she

was 'making contacts,' so to speak. Nevertheless, she had convictions and the courage to stand up for them—to a fault, sometimes. More than once she got in way over her head with somebody who knew a bit more than she did. But even back then, you could tell she was going to make something of herself. She had that air about her. Still, I always felt there was something in her that was a little 'off.' "

"How's that?"

"She just seemed to live in her own world, and there was part of her that you could never reach. She had these little traits—inappropriate laughter, stuff like that. She had a weird sense of humor, almost childlike in a lot of ways. She'd just crack up at the oddest things, almost as if she was seeing things that you didn't."

"Such as?"

"Oh, I can't really remember. It might have been something on television—the silliest thing imaginable—and it would have her in stitches. Or she'd heard a joke and would tell it to you and it was the dumbest joke imaginable, but she'd think it was the funniest thing in the world. She actually liked to watch sitcoms, for God's sake."

"Yes," I said. But that was something else new to me.

"She was smart, though," Awling said, and then he hesitated and scratched the side of his face, as though to correct himself. "Actually, I don't know if *smart* is the right word. Maybe *shrewd* is better—what we used to call *sharp*. She read a lot, but the thing was, she was young and tended to believe most of what she read, and when she'd take a position, why, you just couldn't get her off it—she could be tenacious. That was back then, though. I'm sure that's changed now. But, anyway, I think it's what ultimately caused us to drift apart."

"And it was not an unpleasant drift?"

"She told me about you, by the way," he went on. "She was proud she had known you. She even gave me one of your books. Very good—I enjoyed it."

"Thanks," I said. "But you didn't have a rough breakup, huh?"

"Not at all, really. We'd see each other weekends or on trips. For a while I found myself really falling for her. She was of course quite a looker, but . . . well, we don't get much time in this business. And I also had a feeling that deep down she wasn't really interested in what I did. Naturally," he chuckled, "I consider it rather important, myself."

He stopped and shook his head and for a moment a look came across his face as though he was staring into a great distance.

"You know," Awling said, "in some ways she seemed sad, like one of those people struggling with something inside—bright, decent, whatever, but they aren't really able to love anybody else."

That was something I couldn't disagree with.

"Maybe that's not the right way to put it, though," Awling ruminated. "I think it was more that she couldn't love *unconditionally*. There were always conditions—hers. She didn't like this or that or the other. And there were a lot of implied 'or elses.' She was almost completely self-absorbed with her looks and I think that was in direct conflict with what she perceived as her image. Another thing was that she had so many issues; they'd invariably get in the way of her happiness and, by extension, the happiness of anyone else in her life unless, of course, she found the perfect match. And that, we all know, can sometimes be a practical impossibility. Truth was, she was becoming a very difficult person, and more's the pity."

I thought Awling was summing it up pretty well and wondered if I actually needed to pay a visit to Delia's psychiatrist.

"You know," he continued, "the interesting thing was that we never really had many cross words. Sometimes I thought it might have been better if we had. Her way of dealing with unpleasantness was to withhold herself. I say it was interesting because you could almost tell there was something beneath the surface ready to erupt. It was practically as if she was restraining herself with me."

This was the second time I'd heard this kind of thing about Delia and was beginning to think she was one of those people who sometimes play the opposite of themselves—like an actress training in the Stanislavsky method. On a hunch, I asked the senator a question.

"Do you remember what her favorite color was?"

"Why—it was blue, I think. I remember she liked irises. At my summer place over on the shore in

Maryland she'd collect them from the woods around the water and have them in vases all over the house."

"It wasn't red?" I baited.

"No, no, it was blue. Once she appeared in a blue outfit, slacks and a sweater with a yellow color, and I told her she actually looked like an iris. She laughed and told me blue made her feel—well, sensual.

"She broke it off with me, of course," he continued. "I let her. I knew it was headed for the end. One day she called up and said she wasn't coming for the weekend. It got me a little miffed because we were supposed to go down to Virginia for a house party. Lots of people, fancy horse country, all that. And she said she wasn't coming. Nothing else. And when I asked why, she didn't even sigh or anything. Just blurted it out—romance not working, I was too busy for her lifestyle, felt awkward around my crowd—that kind of thing. All very underkeyed, but she said she wanted to be 'friends.' I said, 'Okay,' but I had the impression that really startled her."

"Because you weren't upset?"

"Maybe. I think she expected she'd had a more profound effect on me—that we'd talk about it more, I guess. She just said, 'Well, good-bye,' and that was it—at least I thought that was it at the time. After a few weeks I got a letter from her, then another. Wanted to 'talk it over.' I didn't respond. Then one day I was walking to the floor and there she was, dressed to kill, talking with Billy Dowell, the congressman from Ohio. I'd introduced them at some point. Apparently, she'd called him and told him she was coming to town. It was Dowell's impression, because I asked him about it later, that she wanted to 'put herself in my way,' so to speak. One day she called on the phone. I told her I thought the thing ought to be put to rest—and she flew into a rage. First time I'd seen that. Accused me of 'using her.' It struck me as humorous because I thought it was the other way around."

"That was the last time you spoke to her?"

"I didn't hear from her again and never knew what happened to her until I went to San Francisco. I gather after she left New York, she was in Chicago for a while—with a TV station."

"She was," I said.

"Well, anyway, I'm glad she married that fellow—they seemed pretty lovey-dovey."

"Brad's a nice guy. I think he treats her well."

"Brad? I didn't remember that being his name."

"No?"

"I thought it was something else, but maybe not. It's been a few years now."

I decided to try something else.

"You ever think about her?" I asked.

"Delia? Why, sometimes, I suppose. I don't mean to say I'd ever like to get involved again. Couldn't anyway, now that she's married. But she was, well . . . she was pretty good company for a long weekend, if you know what I mean."

A kind of leering twinkle flashed in his eyes. I knew what he meant, all right.

"Let me ask you something, Senator," I said.

"Of course, but the name's Charley."

"Do you have any connections in the FBI?"

"Well, I guess I . . ."

"I'm sorry," I said. "Naturally you do. What I meant was, and if this is out of order, I want you to tell me . . ."

"I will."

"Part of this, this scheme with Delia, involves somebody sending her letters. Demands, as I told you. If I brought you a few of the envelopes, do you think the FBI could check them for fingerprints?"

"I thought she'd been getting calls," he said.

"No, I didn't mean to leave that impression. They're letters. But what I want is for somebody to test one of the envelopes."

"What about the letters themselves?"

"She doesn't want that. They're of a personal nature. She's afraid something will leak out."

"Something sexual?" he said hesitantly.

"Yes, that's it." There was something about the way he asked it that made me want to go on. "When you two were . . . together . . . was there anything different? I mean, different from other women?"

"Well . . ." the senator said, looking at me strangely, "you dated her as well as I, didn't you?"

"Whatever you can tell me might help," I said.

"I don't know," he replied with an uneasy haste, adjusting his tie. "She was, well, just Delia."

"And there was nothing unusual?"

"Forgive me, but I really don't think this should be a part of our conversation."

Something in his demeanor, like the others', told me I'd again run into a brick wall. Delia had probably been right that whatever it was, it wouldn't be of much help in finding the blackmailer. It wasn't important that I knew, it was only important that *she* knew. Still, it was tantalizing, because it made me realize that perhaps I wasn't in the same club with all these guys after all.

"All right," I told him. "But, as I said, Delia's a pretty big name in L.A. right now, and she's deathly afraid of any kind of scandal."

"I can appreciate that," he said. "If you get me the envelopes then, I'll get somebody on it. And they'll be discreet. That's one of the perks we politicians get. The FBI always remembers budget time."

I thanked him and got up to leave.

"By the way," I said, "have you ever seen Delia on her news show—recently, I mean?"

"Me? Why, actually I did, once or twice."

"You have one of those new satellite receivers, then, I guess?"

"Well, not here in Washington. But I do have one at my place over on the Eastern Shore of Maryland. I go over mostly for weekends."

"And you've seen her?"

"Just a couple of times. I can pick up the L.A. network news. She doesn't seem to work most weekends."

"Do you remember what she was wearing the last time you saw her broadcast?"

"No," Awling said a little uncomfortably.

"I was wondering if you ever remember her wearing a red sweater?"

He looked at me for an instant as though he'd connected with what I'd said. There was that brief hesitation politicians use when they've been asked something disagreeable at a news conference.

"No," he said, "I don't. I'm not very good at remembering women's clothes."

He seemed a little flustered at this line of questioning.

"But I get the local L.A. news, if that's what you mean. It's on the network I watch most. Why do you ask?"

"I was curious," I said, "if you thought she was any good."

"My, yes. I think she's superb," he said.

CHAPTER 20

I T'S THE CRAZY ones who somehow make you think *you're* the one who's crazy. This was on my mind as I drove out to New Jersey to meet with Dr. Jennifer Flaggler. Delia had made me feel I was crazy more than once. On that final trip to Bermuda, she'd not only arrived by separate flight, she'd departed by one too.

Originally it was planned she'd stay a week. And after those first two days of tension and angst, we fell back into bed with a lusty vengeance, and for two more days it was as though we'd never left each other at all. It's amazing what sex will do for a relationship. It's the great temporary leveler and vindicator where ego and one-upsmanship don't matter. Nothing, in fact, matters, but the immediacy.

During that time I began to convince myself something might have changed with her. One moment she was removed, unapproachable, telling me I was no good for her, the next we were in bed. Those brief days were terrific for me. We rode horses along the beach and went for picnics near Briars Head or on the beach. Delia was a born horsewoman—"born to the saddle," as they say. Once on a warm day we pedaled on bikes down to the harbor, where I rented a little sloop, and we sailed to a deserted cay, had lunch, and made love in the sand among the pine trees and sea oats. I asked if she was happy. We seemed to ask each other that a lot.

"Sometimes—maybe most of the time," she said. "I'm never sure what it is. I think you have to stay in one place to be happy."

"Do you mean like in a city or a town?"

"No, just not be moving. Just be stationary."

"With someone?"

"Maybe."

"Would I do?"

She looked past me, off toward the ocean, her crystal green eyes sparkling in the sun. It almost seemed I was as translucent as the water and she was staring right through me.

"I don't think so, Johnny. Maybe if it had been another time or place in my life."

I vaguely understood now that I was diving into a pool with no water in it, but I plunged in anyhow. Maybe I needed the pain in my neck.

"I'm going to say it anyway," I told her. "If you'll let us, I think we could have one of the great loves of all time. Do you know how rare that is?"

"I can only imagine," she said distantly.

"So what's wrong with it—with us?"

"I don't like my men perfect."

"What's that supposed to mean?"

The sun was shining on her tanned face, her eyes

still fixed on the sea. She seemed to be smiling, but even when she wasn't, she always seemed to be.

"You see, you've got everything," she said, "and I . . . well—"

"You've got everything too," I interrupted. "Brains, beauty, and breeding—that's what my mama always told me to look for. We Lightfoots have been successful in that for years."

"What about kindness?" she asked.

"You're kind, Delia. I think sometimes you don't think so, but I see kindness there. Besides, it doesn't begin with a *b,* like the other three."

"I don't feel very kind. I don't want to hurt people, but sometimes it's the only thing to do."

"Hurt them how?"

"By not being for them what they want me to be. By not being able to return what they feel. And when I don't, they can't understand."

"Did you ever try to just let yourself go—to not overthink the thing too much?"

"Look, Johnny," she said. "Maybe I did love you— or at least felt myself falling in love with you. . . ." She stood up and faced the ocean, away from me.

"But?"

"But whenever I do, I seem to lose other interests after a while."

"What interests?"

"Sex, for one. Maybe it's always greener pastures, the far side of the hill. But I don't want it to be that way with us."

"Sex? I don't understand that. Why in hell was it

so good for us then and now, what? Can you explain that?"

"The only thing I can think of is that it's good because it's bad. We're both so angry and frustrated we can never be what the other wants, and that's why it's good. Does that make sense?"

"No. That actually sounds perverted. And so what next? You just want to reappear in my life from time to time and have a roll in the hay for a day or so and then vanish again?"

"It could be, but probably not. I think I really want to move away from New York."

"That will solve something?"

"Who knows? I might give it a try."

"This is like Groucho Marx said—you'll never join any club that would have you as a member."

Delia picked up a towel and used it to slap sand off her legs.

"Maybe," she said indifferently. "Do you think we can go back now? It's getting a little chilly."

We repacked the boat and I shoved us off into the water. A stiff afternoon breeze heeled the little sloop to the gunwales and we pounded along in a chop. Delia sat with her back to the cockpit coaming, eyes closed, catching the warmth of the fading sun.

"Johnny," she said, "let me ask you something."

"Sure," I replied dismally. I knew I'd crossed the line today, but by now it had almost become blurred beyond recognition.

"I've been doing a little writing on my own. Some short stories."

"Fiction?"

"Yes. I wonder if you'd take a look at them sometime."

"Of course. Did you bring them here?"

"Yes, they're in my suitcase."

"Well, I'll read them tonight," I said.

AS EXPECTED, IT wasn't a great evening for either of us. The old tension had returned, though at least now things were out in the open. I made supper—grilled yellowfin tuna and a cucumber salad—though I doubt either of us really enjoyed it much. We sat up reading for a while and talked awkward small talk, then Delia went to bed. I had built a fire before dinner and piled on a few more logs. From a manila envelope I took out her stories. A couple were only three or four pages—far too sort for commercial publication. The third was longer. I sat down with a pencil and began to read.

It was well past midnight when I finished. As with most beginners or amateur writers, she had used herself as the protagonist, thinly veiled, of course. The stories weren't bad, but they weren't particularly good either—what would probably be called "promising" by some editor trying to find a way not to let someone down.

I'd made a number of marks on the pages. Suggestions as to content, style—even wording, which I normally wouldn't do. Finally I went to bed and slept the sleep of the fitful dreamless, trying to keep my eyes closed in hopes of finally drifting away.

Next morning when I went in to squeeze juice and make toast, Delia had preceded me. Her stories with my markings and criticism lay strewn on the floor around her chair. She was looking out the window and didn't turn when I came into the room.

"I think I'm going to fly out today," she said flatly. "I need to get back to New York."

"Today? I thought we were going to be here till the weekend."

"You can," she said, "but I'd better get myself packed. Doesn't the flight leave at two?"

"Yes, but why go? I mean, I'll go on with you if—"

"No, I'd rather you didn't," she said.

"What is it?" I asked. "Was it yesterday on the beach?"

"No."

"So what then?"

Suddenly she tore into me, like a jaguar dropping down from a tree.

"I guess now you think you're pretty superior," she said with barely concealed contempt.

"I what?"

"My stories—I asked you to read them! Not rip them to pieces!"

"I did read them. I thought you wanted my opinion."

"I didn't want you to make fun of them," she spat.

"You're the big important writer, I'll give you that—but it's sad you felt a need to show me just how bad I am."

"For heaven's sake, Delia, I thought you wanted some constructive criticism. That's why I stayed up half the night—"

"Bullshit! You were hurt by what I said yesterday, and decided to get even, didn't you? Everything I've written here, you think is crap! You were even so small you had to try to correct my grammar and choice of words!"

"I was just trying to show you some shortcuts," I protested. "You can't take criticism personally. Not this kind, anyway. I did it as a favor—to a friend, you."

"Some friend! You did it to make me feel bad. To make me feel cheap and stupid and you know you did."

"That's preposterous," I countered, "because if you look at what I did, it really isn't that much at all. I wish you'd read my comments again. Nothing I said changes the basics of anything you wrote."

"That's just . . . well, anyway, I'm going to get ready," she said, rising up. "I'd appreciate it if you'll call a taxi."

"But it's only nine," I said. "The plane doesn't even leave till two. . . ."

"I've got to get checked in," she said, "and, actually, I like waiting in airports. It gives you time to think."

A more miserable day I've never spent.

The cab picked Delia up an hour after that nasty scene and I spent the afternoon on into the evening and then the night in a kind of lifeless shock, staring into an empty sea. Her revelations of the previous day were bad enough, but at least they'd gotten us talking, which I idiotically thought was a beginning instead of an end. And then there were the stories . . . but the moment was gone now. It was only later I figured out, like I said, that it's always the crazy ones who make you think it's *you* who's crazy.

I PULLED UP to Dr. Jennifer Flaggler's office with all this on my mind. She operated out of her home, a big Victorian affair set up on a ledge overlooking a tree-shaded street in Short Hills. I rang the doorbell and Dr. Flaggler answered it herself, an elderly woman, stout, and with a kindly smile, but sort of wild-eyed, like the wonderful old actress Ruth Gordon, or maybe even Josephine Hull in *Harvey*.

"I'm more or less retired now," she said. "I just take patients on an interim basis. Anything complicated, and I refer them to someone else. It's easier working in my garden."

She led me into a large, comfortable room just off the hallway. It was decorated with Persian rugs and the obligatory leather couch, but there were several big leather chairs, and I eased into one as Dr. Flaggler sat behind her desk.

"So, Mr. Lightfoot, what is it you came to talk about?"

I took a deep breath, as if I was about to bare my soul. "It's about a woman," I said. "We aren't actually seeing each other right now, but a few years ago she hurt me pretty badly. I've just run into her again recently. And I think that, to put it bluntly, my defenses are down a little. I'd just like to get another opinion, and," I said, "to make matters more complicated, someone is trying to blackmail her, and I'm trying to help find out who."

Dr. Flaggler slipped on a pair of half-glasses, the kind used for reading, and peered at me over the rims in a dubious way.

"So you have strong feelings still for this woman?" she asked.

"I do."

"Do you think it will lead to something?"

"I don't know. We ended badly, but it was a long time ago."

"How does she feel about you?"

"She's married."

"And that doesn't bother you?"

"Only if it bothers her."

"Yes, I see . . . well, you mentioned something about blackmail? What's that?"

"I don't want to get too deeply into it. She's kind of high-profile. Somebody's been sending her letters."

"And what do they say?"

"They make sexual suggestions and threaten her with some kind of exposure unless she cooperates."

"Are *you* writing the letters?"

"Me? Of course not."

"I just had to ask," Dr. Flaggler said.

"I understand."

"So what is it you feel toward her?"

"Me? Frustration, confusion, I suppose."

"Would you feel better if she wasn't around?"

"I don't understand what you mean."

"Well, if she was, let's say, dead or something?"

"Of course not. What are you driving at?"

"It's just part of my job," she answered.

"To ask if I might harm her?"

"It's happened before among people. I expect it will happen again."

"Well, let me put that notion to rest," I said. "The answer is no—not in any way. I'm trying to help."

"Look, Mr. Lightfoot, I don't like having to ask questions like this. But what if we did have that sort of problem? I would need to know it, right? Because it could quite obviously lead to matters much more serious. Don't you agree?"

"Yes, I understand, and the answer is still no. Emphatically. I'd never even think of anything like that."

"No," Dr. Flaggler said, "I don't think you would. So now why don't you tell me what's on your mind?"

I spent the next twenty minutes describing my subject in thinly disguised but real enough terms so that if she was actually the one who'd counseled Delia way back in those days, she might recollect the similarities without putting two and two together. I knew I had to be careful because outsmarting a psychiatrist is tricky business. But after a while I began to notice in Dr. Flaggler's questions a particular sort of refraction that made me believe she was possibly drawing on her past experiences with Delia in exactly the way I wanted.

"So after she went out with these fellows from Wall Street, or wherever, she met you?" Dr. Flaggler said.

"More or less—I think I was sort of squeezed in between."

"And that didn't last, correct?"

"No, but it dragged out a long while—on and off."

"And you have reason to believe she took off on a, well, what we used to call a 'bender,' and frequented these places in downtown Manhattan where there were liaisons with a great many men?"

"I know it," I said.

"What did you make of that?"

"Nothing, then. I just learned it."

"So what *do* you make of it now?"

"I don't know," I said. "That's why I'm here."

"Do you mind if I smoke?" Dr. Flaggler asked.

"Of course not. Do you mind if I have one too?"

She opened a desk drawer and pulled out a pack of Gauloise, half empty, and offered them to me.

"Hadn't had one of these in many a year," I said.

"I find it relaxing," she said. "Not very chic anymore, but what the hell?"

We talked for a long time, the doctor and me, long past the forty-five-minute appointment she'd set up. I told her things about myself I never thought about revealing. I told things about Delia I never thought about revealing either. In the end, she seemed confidently to sum it up.

"This personality you're concerned about," she said, "is not unfamiliar to me. I've had cases like this before."

Time had passed. We were now on about our fifth Gauloise. There was a cut-glass brandy decanter on a table, surrounded by crystal snifters, and for a moment I thought she was going to offer me a drink. She didn't.

"I don't think there's anything radically wrong with her," Dr. Flaggler continued. "Not in a clinical sense, anyway. There is no split personality or anything like that. It's just that she did or does live two lives—each separate from the other. One an inner life, which is real, and the other an outer one, which is just as real—and not just to her. Real in the actual sense.

"But the inner life is secret. She doesn't deny it, she just chooses not to make it public. The public one, well, you've seen it. And at times it's in conflict with the other one. That's when it all gets volatile, that's what you've probably seen when the times were bad—two emotions, lives, if you will, struggling with each other, as if an outgoing tide meets a strong wind, lots of waves and thrashing and danger."

"Sort of like putting a lion and a tiger in the same cage?" I mused aloud.

"You could use that analogy too," she said. "It is

also possible she actually finds a thrill in this. It's the same thrill schizoids have when they go nuts, but nothing anywhere as serious."

"If you knew this sort of person," I said, "would you think she'd be capable of writing these letters to herself?"

"Maybe, but I sort of doubt it. From what you say, she makes much of being totally honest. That would be in conflict with both her selves, unless she's gone off the deep end. My guess is that she uses all this honesty as a shield. A shield is used mostly to move around and protect body parts, but in her case it protects her psyche. If I didn't know better, I'd think she must have gotten involved with this new therapy that's become fashionable these days."

"What's that?"

"It's called Radical Honesty," Dr. Flaggler said. "The theory is that you just say whatever's on your mind to people, don't worry about the consequences. Very confrontational, but it's supposed to make you feel better."

"What, like if I think somebody's an asshole, I just go up and say so?"

"That's it."

"Doesn't that cause trouble for people?"

"Of course, it does. It's crackpot psychiatry. The people who preach it ought to have their licenses lifted."

I was beginning to like Dr. Flaggler. "And you think this person might have gotten mixed up in—"

"Oh no," she said. "This is a relatively new horror

in the therapy racket. Just the last couple of years. But that isn't to say your friend didn't figure it out on her own a long while ago, and fit it into her personality. I think what you were dealing with—what was it, twenty years ago?"

"Almost." It seemed strange she'd asked that—originally I'd told her it had been only a "few" years.

"Yes, she would have been quite young then—at least from my perspective, and yours too, I imagine. I think she was just kicking up her heels. She didn't know what to do with her life, so she did whatever she felt was necessary. There would have been, of course, a certain turbulence. Women of that age are normally thinking of getting married, having babies, and doing all the things their upbringing expects. But in this case, there was friction and it went unresolved and I would expect you, and the others you've described, simply happened into the middle of it and got burned."

"Burned pretty bad too," I said. "And there is something else too, something sexual."

"What's that?"

"I don't know. It's something that's being recalled to her by whoever is writing her those letters, but she won't tell me and, for that matter, neither will anybody else I've talked to. Must be pretty strange."

"Like what? Like whether she's a swallower or a spitter or something?"

I almost choked on Dr. Flaggler's directness, and it took me a moment to recover. "Well, yeah, I guess, something like that. I don't have the faintest idea."

"She obviously has a powerful allure," the doctor continued, unperturbed. "Some people have it more than most, sexual and otherwise. I've seen this before. It can be almost spellbinding—and that's an observation from someone who doesn't believe in spells."

"Enough for somebody to instigate this incredible plot? I wish you were psychic and could tell me who the culprit is."

"I do too," Dr. Flaggler said. "But are you sure it's just one person?"

"I can't see how it could be otherwise—what do you mean?"

"Well, from what you've told me, a number of men were involved with her. A number had reasons. The letters came from various places. Her TV show can probably be seen in any of them. I'm just thinking out loud."

"That what?"

"Well, that somehow these guys got together and decided she was a naughty girl and it's payback time."

I sat in silence as we both contemplated that disturbing notion. The early November evening was now upon us. I wasn't sure I'd plumbed Dr. Flaggler for all she knew, but I had the comfortable sense she was withholding nothing of importance from me. She finally came around the desk and we shook hands. She had a firm and reassuring handshake, like that of your old high school principal, or a deacon in the church. She walked me to the door and, stepping out onto the wide porch, we were both illuminated by an enormous harvest moon looming silver in a clear black sky.

"I'm sorry," I said, fumbling in my coat pocket. "I almost forgot. I need to write you a check."

"No, you don't, Mr. Lightfoot. It was actually a nice afternoon to be talking about all this. And by the way," Dr. Flaggler said, "good luck. And when you see Delia again, please give her my best."

CHAPTER 21

PALE LIGHTS ALONG the Jersey Turnpike gleamed against Manhattan's skyline as I drove back into the city. I don't know what astounded me most—the fact that Dr. Flaggler had figured out it was Delia Jamison or her suggestion that a number of people might be involved. Something from T. S. Eliot kept revolving in my head: "Between the idea/And the reality . . . /Falls the Shadow." After seeing the senator, I'd felt the shadow creeping in, but it had only been a shadow until the weight of Dr. Flaggler's suggestion sank in.

Practically all these guys I'd interviewed so far had an ax to grind with Delia and for several of them, she literally changed their lives, mostly for the worst. But was it really possible that many or *all* of them were somehow in this together in a nasty little conspiracy reaching from Wall Street to the United States Senate—and who knew where else? It was almost mind-boggling to contemplate that a cabal of grown men with nothing in common except a long-ago relationship with one girl had banded together after all this time to cause her anguish and fear.

But why? Had some one of them, through the same sort of legwork I'd been doing, pieced together the mosaic of Delia's love life? Could she have left an aftermath so dark and bitter to compel men to such extremes? Was it really imaginable that they sat around little satellite receivers waiting for her to perform some veiled act of sexuality they had extorted—to finally exercise the control over her they'd never had in real life? It seemed like a colossal fantasy, but the possibility refused to leave my brain all the way back into town.

The big silver moon moved westward in the night and bathed my apartment and the streets in its glow. I sat in near dark in my living room, thinking it was about time I paid a visit to Mr. Frankie LaCosta in Chicago. He'd been with Delia longer than any of them—nearly a year. And he had the least connection with the others.

Next morning, a Thursday, I decided to call my friend Jay VanWiik, the "professor." Jay was as sensible a man as I knew and I wanted to get his take on all this. We agreed to meet for lunch, at his club, of course. It was pouring rain when I arrived.

"This would be astonishing," Jay said, after I brought up the conspiracy suggestion, "if it's true. I haven't heard of such a thing since Teapot Dome."

"How about Watergate?" I suggested.

"It's not only the scope but the vileness. I simply can't believe some of these people would be involved in such business."

"It's just a theory."

"How could you prove it?" he asked.

"Well, I got the envelope from her yesterday and mailed it off to Senator Awling. Be interesting to see what he does with it."

"And the girl—how is she taking it?"

"About as well as the time she said something you didn't like, and you told her: 'Listen, and you'll learn something.' "

"Oh my, did I really say that?"

"It was in your drinking days. You were right, of course, but she took it badly. Matter of fact, she wouldn't see me for a week afterward."

"I'm sorry about that," Jay offered. "I could be an awful boor in those days."

"No matter," I told him. "Anyway, I'm sure it's hard on her now, but she's tough. I think she's more worried about scandal than actual harm. That's a little scary."

"You think something might happen to her?"

"How can you rule it out? He or they or whatever is obviously obsessed—I can't imagine somebody like Awling resorting to violence, but I wouldn't put it past some of the others."

"No, no, you can't. As long as there's the possibility. But I still think it absurd not to go to the authorities. The priorities are wrong here," he grumbled.

"I've done my best."

"What's next?"

"I'm off to Chicago, to see a guy I can't imagine Delia ever going out with, but she did."

"Who's that?"

"His name's Frankie LaCosta. A gumba I hear maybe has connections."

"I know Frankie LaCosta," Jay said.

"You do! How on earth?"

"His grandfather was my father's bookie, back in the thirties. Must be the same one. His father was an accountant for the mob for decades. He made a lot of money and sent Frankie off to prep schools and, if I'm not mistaken, he graduated from Fordham Law."

"You're kidding?"

"I think it has to be the same one. I met little Frankie about twenty years ago, not long after he passed the bar. Nice kid. He wasn't exactly going to be invited into a Wall Street law firm, but he practiced here in the city for a while. I've heard he's made a good career lately representing all those gambling operations down in Atlantic City."

The professor continued to amaze me. For somebody so impeccable he seemed to know everybody who was anybody.

"So he's there now?"

"I don't know," Jay said. "I'd heard he moved to Chicago. That's why I think it's the same guy."

"I'll be damned," I exclaimed. "This at least gives me an entrée to get to him."

"Careful you don't get what you ask for, Johnny."

WHEN I GOT back to the Carlyle, Rick Olsen had called. I phoned him back, but his office said he was en route from San Francisco to Los Angeles by private jet. When I identified myself, I found myself patched into a midair conference call.

"Brad's here with me," Rick said. "I'm giving him a lift back to L.A."

"Looks like Rick might be onto something," Brad said. "His man followed Worthington Hathaway to a post office yesterday. He was in and out before our guy could get close enough to see why he was there."

"Where was the post office?" I said.

"Off La Brea," Rick said, "near Sunset. Interesting thing is, it's not really near his office or his home. So what was he doing there? You'd think if he went to a post office, it'd be close to him."

"So we wait and see if another letter turns up?"

"Yep," Rick said. "Thing is, that post office probably ships all its mail to the main one downtown, so that's where it'll most likely be postmarked. But maybe Hathaway doesn't know that. But, anyway, if she gets another one in the next few days, it'll be mighty suspicious."

"Matter of fact," Brad said, "I'd say we'll have our man."

"Well, I wouldn't go quite that far," Rick said, "but it'll be interesting to see if she does."

"What about the satellite connection?" I asked.

"It's going a little slow," Rick said. "Our people are working on it, and we've pinpointed all the areas of the country that can receive Delia's broadcast from L.A. But getting the names of subscribers is a lot harder. The companies don't seem to have all that information on one computer. And we're getting a little resistance trying to get them to cooperate. We'll work it out in time, though."

"Well, there's another guy who I know picks it up," I said.

"Who's that?" Brad asked.

"United States senator Charles Awling."

"You're kidding," Brad said.

"I gather you met Awling once—with Delia a couple of years ago."

"Me? No," Brad said. "I know who he is, but . . . did you say a couple of years ago?"

"That's right—maybe three years ago. Before you two were married."

"I never did." There was a note of bafflement in his voice. "Why do you think I have?"

"The senator," I said hesitantly, "just thought he might have remembered you. I think he was out in San Francisco for a day or so and, well, as I understood it, he saw Delia on television and looked her up and took her to dinner."

"And I was supposed to be there?" Brad asked

"Maybe I'm mistaken," I said. This was very touchy for me. I didn't want to make trouble for Delia if it had been somebody other than Brad she was with, but I'd probably put my foot in it already.

"I don't remember that part of the conversation too clearly," I fudged. "Anyway, he seemed both surprised and pleased that you and Delia were married—and I didn't detect any sort of animosity there—but he did tell me he has one of those satellites at his vacation home away from Washington. And so he has picked up her broadcast a few times."

"That's suspicious too," Rick broke in.

"Maybe, maybe not," I said. "I don't know for a fact, but I'd suspect that the Congress probably has access to those satellite programs. I'd be willing to bet that somewhere in the Capitol there's a place they can watch live local news broadcasts from their home districts."

"Yes," Rick said, "that's probably true. But it's still interesting."

"Well, I've been thinking about something along those lines that might be even more interesting than that." I told them the theory that there might be more than one person involved in this.

"That's crazy," Rick said.

"It's wild, I know, but it's just something to consider."

"It's practically beyond belief!" Brad remarked.

"Well, like they say, anything's possible," I told them. "Whether it's likely is a different matter. But I believe we'd better keep it in mind. Especially if Rick finds out that all these guys have access to this satellite thing."

"So what do you do next?" Rick asked.

"I'm going to Chicago," I said, "as soon as I can set up an appointment."

*   *   *

IT WAS STILL dark and damp outside and I had built a fire to sit by. Gotcha was lying next to my chair and I absently petted his big shaggy head as I glanced over the *Times*. Rainy days in New York affect different people different ways; me, I get a sort of bittersweet feeling, especially this time of year. Thanksgiving was coming up and I really hadn't made any plans and, in fact, didn't want to. On an impulse I had called Meredith but got her answering machine. It was Saturday, and I thought she might be home, and I was beginning to feel a little blue when my phone rang.

"I was in the shower," she said.

"Are you decent now?"

"No, never with you."

"What are you wearing?"

"Imagine it," she said.

Meredith always had a certain abandonment, a different kind of honesty I wasn't used to; not confrontational but normal and touching.

We talked about things and she asked me about my "mission"—though I didn't tell her much more. In the most subtle way she let me know she wanted to do the sketches for the movie I was writing for Burr, but, of course, I couldn't guarantee her the job, though I'd sure do what I could when the time came. By now the fire was low and Gotcha was lying on his back in front of it, rubbing himself against the carpet. I thought Meredith would like Gotcha and vice versa. Some women don't like dogs. Generally, those are the women I want nothing to do with.

"When are you coming back to L.A.?" Meredith asked.

"Not long, a day or so, maybe."

"Will you call me?"

"Absolutely," I said, and the word came out a lot more certain than I felt.

LATER THAT AFTERNOON I phoned the office of Frankie LaCosta and was told he was with clients. I left a message that I was a friend of Jay VanWiik's and was going to be in Chicago for a day or so and would like to meet with him, but by late the next morning it had not been returned, so I phoned again. Now he was at a meeting. I asked if my first message had been delivered and was told it had. I left a second one and went for a walk down Fifth Avenue, along Central Park. It was still drizzling rain and the sidewalk was strewn with wet autumn leaves. I turned my collar against the cold and tried to shut everything out of my mind, but failed miserably. I kept going over Delia's list, as though there was something I had missed.

First there was Hathaway, the ruthless, unforgiving lawyer who admitted watching Delia on television all the time and hating her guts every moment of it. And sad old Homer Greer, broken, reduced from a successful career as a Wall Street tycoon to a peddler of computer parts, watching her too, on his little satellite system. Not only had he been in Atlanta at the time one of the letters was postmarked, but he'd been in the L.A. area when one came from there too. There was old Professor Vining, who clearly described the red sweater Delia had worn the day she gave him the shaft. I wondered if Columbia University had one of those satellite systems too. And Bothwell and Dalton, still players in the bitter picture. Then there was Senator Awling, who also watched her on TV from time to time. There was no outward animosity there, but how could I expect the real culprit to reveal that to me? Carlo, the bartender from Delia's "club" period, had seemed pretty philosophic, but again, there was something slick about him that couldn't help make me wonder if he knew more than he was letting on.

I stopped off at the bar at the Sherry Netherland Hotel, one of my favorites, and had a glass of wine. Out on Fifth the pedestrians streamed past the plate glass windows as if framed in a movie. After a while a tall beautiful woman with auburn hair walked by slowly, unlike the others, peering inside at us cozy patrons, as though she was contemplating coming in. She looked amazingly a lot like Delia and for a split second I thought it was. But she was somebody else, younger, another New York face in millions. Still, I thought, such a pretty girl. Such a pretty, pretty girl.

CHAPTER 22

I'VE ALWAYS THOUGHT Chicago was a terrific town, at least parts of it, but this was one time I wasn't looking forward to being there. After two days of waiting for Frankie LaCosta to return my calls, I took the bull by the horns. Next afternoon I checked in at the Drake, on Michigan Avenue. The day was sunny and cold and the wind was blowing in off the lake, but LaCosta's law offices were nearby and I decided to walk.

A receptionist greeted me in a waiting room and I asked her for a piece of message paper. On it I identified myself and said I'd come from New York, and that I was a friend of Jay VanWiik's. The receptionist rang for a woman I suppose was LaCosta's secretary, who glanced at me skeptically as she disappeared through a door with my note. The offices seemed to have only one door to the hallway and I was prepared to wait all afternoon if necessary. It wasn't. Five minutes later LaCosta himself appeared in the waiting area with a big hundred-dollar smile and a warm handshake. He led me to a spacious office with tall windows overlooking Lake Michigan, where the wind was churning whitecaps and blowing foam over Lakeshore Drive.

"So," he said, seating himself behind a huge walnut desk, "you're a pal of Jay VanWiik's?"

"I am," I told him.

"Did he tell you about him and my father—and his father and my grandfather?"

"He did."

"Those must have been the days," LaCosta said. "My grandfather only handled the horses, and Jay's dad, that was all he'd ever bet. My grandfather knew horses inside out. Not like today—bookies gotta know baseball, football, basketball, tiddledywinks, and horseshoes. It's ridiculous."

He was a large, jocular sort of guy, tanned and with flecks of gray in his jet black hair. He dressed impeccably, dark pin-striped suit, white shirt, gold cuff links—not at all gaudy—a silk paisley tie, and oxblood shoes with a deep, rich shine.

"I think Jay's old man won so much from my grandfather on the horses that he asked my father to give him accounting advice," LaCosta chuckled. "My father was a CPA, you know. Grandfather didn't want him mixed up in the gambling business. So what does my father do? He becomes the accountant for practically every mob guy in New York. Never got caught doing anything illegal, though. My old man was a stickler about that. Everything strictly on the law, but he knew all the angles."

Frankie LaCosta struck me as an amiable guy as he warmed to his subject. He leaned back in his chair and put his hands behind his head. He reminded me of Omar Sharif, but with a better haircut.

"So how do you know Jay?" he asked.

"Through friends. I've known him for years, maybe twenty. Just after his divorce we got to be drinking buddies. That was before he stopped drinking, of course. We sometimes stay out in bars till closing time, just shooting the breeze about everything under the sun."

"Fascinating man, Jay is," LaCosta said. "Very cultivated."

An awkward moment ensued. We'd just about run out of things to say about Jay VanWiik and I knew LaCosta was canny enough to know I hadn't come all the way to Chicago and looked him up just to talk about him. And he knew I knew it too.

"Well," I said, "some years ago, I introduced Jay to a girl I was dating called Delia Jamison. I understand you knew her too."

There was that same electric moment as with the others, as if the air was suddenly filled with ozone before a lightning bolt. I saw LaCosta's fingers tighten reflexively on his desk, and he sort of sucked on his lower lip, pondering a reply.

"Yes, for a long, long time," he finally said with almost a sigh. "Lovely girl—or she could be, anyway."

"Do you know somebody's trying to blackmail her?"

"To blackmail . . . ? No. How would I know that?"

"I'm just trying to find out who does."

"Blackmail her over what?" he asked. He was

leaning forward on the desk now, an intense look on his face.

I explained some of the story to him.

"And so she thinks it's one of her old flames, huh?" LaCosta said.

"Yes. But she hasn't any idea of who. So it's not as if she suspects you."

"Well, that's nice to hear. Even though I'm a lawyer, blackmail's not my game—outside the court-house, that is."

"I don't know what else to do but ask questions. I agreed to help her, I hope you understand."

"Fire away," LaCosta said.

"I understand you dated her—or went with her—a few years ago. About four or five, to be exact."

"That's true, but it goes back a lot longer than that. Didn't she tell you?"

"No—tell me what?"

"Oh, hell, I've known Delia since, well, since we were children."

"You were kids together?" Now I was confused.

"Well, almost. You see, when my grandfather made my father study accounting, he had hopes he'd be the straight arrow in the family. And, as I told you, it didn't exactly turn out that way. So when I come along, my old man, he's gonna go even further. He decides I've gotta start young on my climb to the top of society and gets me enrolled in one of the fanciest prep schools in the East. You believe that?"

"Sure," I said, a little surprised.

"And do you know who arranges for me, a wop

two generations off the boat, to get in this splendid place? Jay VanWiik's father."

"Really."

"Really. And there was this sort of sister school to us, over in Massachusetts, a girls' boarding school—and who enrolls there the same year as me?"

"Delia?" I asked, like a straight man.

"We were both fifteen," LaCosta said. "She'd come out from Kansas City—and I was from Queens—and between us we had about as much polish as a pair of shit-heeled stable boots. Those were the days before they started recruiting smart kids from poorer backgrounds. Most of the students were legacies. And I think both of us took a lot of grief because of that. I know Delia did."

"But she wasn't from a poor family," I said.

"Heavens no. Her folks seemed to have money and class too. I met them once or twice when they came to visit her. It's just that she was from Kansas City and that was enough for the other girls to make her feel self-conscious, like a Midwestern rube. Same with me. I mean, almost all these kids knew each other from the time they were born. Their families knew each other's families, they vacationed the same places. All that stuff. We were outsiders."

"I think she felt that way when she came to New York too."

"Really, well, anyway, Delia and I sort of gravitated to each other. There'd be interscholastic mixers and dances and the two of us got to be an item, I guess you'd say. Just kid stuff, though, there wasn't any real screwing around at that age in those days. She was really something, though. She was so much brighter than me, it was almost scary, but she tried to hide it a bit from the rest of us. I think she wanted to fit in."

"So you were her boyfriend, huh?"

"Yeah, for a couple of years," he said, nodding.

I waited for Frankie LaCosta to continue, but instead he got up and went to a low bookshelf and pulled out what looked to be an old preppy annual.

"Here's what we were like in those days," he said, opening the book to a page he seemed to know by heart.

"That's the two of us together."

The picture was taken at a dance. Though it was nearly thirty years old, you could easily tell the couple standing together were Delia and Frankie, he with an arm around her waist, she with her head on his shoulder. There were other memorabilia too. Letters in envelopes he didn't open, and a handful of pictures of Delia back then. Already she was quite striking.

"It ended, though?"

"It did. It did. I wish it hadn't, but it did. One weekend she'd signed out to go visit a classmate up near Boston. That's the way we got around things in those days. The sign-out rules were strict, and the girls were supposed to be exactly where they said—in this case, at the classmate's parents' home. Of course, I'd signed out too that weekend, and was staying with a classmate of mine not far from Delia.

"We played everything by the rules the whole

weekend, until the end, that is. I got her home at eleven every night or whatever and we'd spend the days, just a few couples, lying around the banks of the Charles. She was as sweet and smart as she could be. Had a great personality too—sort of innocent in, well, what you might call a Kansas City kind of way. Big laugher, I always remember that—her great laugh. For that age, I was definitely in love, and I think she was too.

"It was late springtime, just about the end of school for the summer. It was warm and lovely and we'd spent this great afternoon with the others just talking and lying around on blankets and about sundown somebody suggested it was time to go. Well, Delia and I said we'd be along later, and the others left.

"Actually, we'd meant to. But, I don't know, we got to fooling around and necking and at some point pulled our blanket up under a big lilac bush and, well, we didn't do anything, but that, but . . ."

He closed the book and replaced it on the shelf and sat back down.

"You know how long you can lie there with a girl at that age, just kissing and all. It didn't seem like much time had passed, but before we knew it, it was late. I was supposed to have had her back to her friend's place, but it was way past curfew. We didn't know what to do. People were going to be mad. So I suggested that she call the friend and tell her or her parents that she'd decided to catch the train from Boston back to school early—to study or

something—that she'd forgotten she had an important exam first thing in the morning. There was a train
that left about a hour before, and I said for her to tell
them she was on it and calling from one of the stops
along the way and not to worry and to ask her friend
to bring her things along when she caught a later train
in the morning.

"Delia didn't want to do it, but by now she was beginning to panic over the curfew, and so she did. In
fact, the next train didn't leave until next morning—
really early—about six, but it would get her back to
school by seven-thirty, when the dorms opened, and
we figured nobody would know the difference."

"But it didn't work?"

"Wouldn't you know it?" LaCosta said. "Somebody from the school called up the friend's parents.
Apparently it was their policy to do some spot checks
to see if the students were where they were supposed
to be. I took Delia to a hotel near the train station. It
cost me nearly fifty bucks, but my grandfather had
just sent me a hundred dollars. We didn't do anything
in the hotel room either. I think by this time we were
both scared and stayed up most of the night. I really
didn't have to worry about myself much. The rules
were easier at my school. And yet I guess I was as
scared as she was, but she calmed me down, quoting
things to me from *Macbeth* and *Hamlet,* right out of
her head, till dawn. Anyway, when she finally got
back, they were waiting for her."

"Lot of trouble, I suppose."

"Big trouble. They had an honor system there like

they did at my school, and they hauled her up in front of it. I could imagine how scared she was. Anyway, she apparently made it worse at first by fudging the truth, but at some point she broke down and told the whole story. The upshot of it was, they let her finish out the school year, which was only a week or so away, but they suspended her from coming back next year for a semester. Naturally, she was humiliated. To make things even uglier, as I understood it, her so-called friends shunned her that last week or two. Made her feel cheap and common. Really came down on her. It was a big deal in those days. They began calling her 'the K.C. Liar.'

"I tried phoning her any number of times, but she never returned my messages. I wrote her letters all summer, but she was definitely off my case. She finally came back to school the second semester of the next year. I don't even know why she did. Maybe her parents made her. That sort of 'teach you a lesson' kind of thing idiot parents sometimes do.

"I saw her at a school mixer not long after that. It was obvious she was trying to avoid me. She even left the room several times when I started over to see her. Finally I caught her in the hall and we had it out. She was blunt to a fine point. She'd been dishonest, she said. It had almost ruined her life. She had to make atonements. I wasn't to blame for it, but she couldn't forget that us being together was the cause. The long and short of it was, she didn't want to see me any-more. I tried reasoning, arguing, and finally begging. No dice.

"Of course, I was crushed, but what can you do? I got over it. Took a while, but I did. I graduated next year and went on to college and then to law school and worked for a New York firm for fifteen years before I came out here to Chicago. One night I was assing around in one of those downtown clubs with some of the other guys in the firm and this girl comes in. I nearly dropped my teeth. It was Delia. I hadn't seen her in what—twenty-something years! She was absolutely gorgeous. She was talking to one of the bartenders, but I went over after a while and told her who I was. It felt a little strange, but she was really happy to see me. She'd become a truly beautiful woman, but there was something different about her. I mean, her dress, the demeanor, all of it. She seemed very cosmopolitan, if you will. Had one of those upper-class eastern-type accents, but it sounded as natural as if she'd been born into it. She was working as a reporter for a radio station then. She told me she sometimes came to these places 'incognito,' was the way she put it at the time.

"Well, we talked for a while and then she left. We agreed to meet at that same place a few nights later. She was evasive about where she lived, no phone number either. I wondered if she was on drugs or involved in something shady—you know?"

Darkness was closing in quickly in the late autumn sky. The lake itself was almost obscured except for the whitecaps that still raged on angry surf. Frankie LaCosta had to take a telephone call and I waited in the reception area. Afterward he came out and said,

"Say, it's about closing time here. Do you want to go someplace and have a drink, or dinner, or something?"

I knew he wasn't finished with his story and so I agreed and, frankly, I found him to be good company. We walked down to a Chinese place he knew off Michigan. I don't normally like Chinese, but this place was splendid. Frankie ordered a martini and when it came, it looked so good I could almost taste it. I hadn't been big on martinis either, scotch had been my game, but every once in a while in the old days I'd have a couple. I settled for my usual wine.

"Just seeing her again that one night was enough to get it started all over for me," he said, picking up suddenly, just where he'd left off. "It was as though none of those years had passed."

I nodded. Delia could do that.

"We met in the club a number of times. At first I think she was holding off on me—in fact, I know she was. I think when Delia burns her bridges, she likes them to stay burned. But after a while she seemed to get closer and the barriers started to come down. We fell back into it. She liked the clubs, though. She seemed to know a lot of those people. I didn't care for them much myself, it was just a way to meet women, but when you've got one, what's the point?

"Anyway, we began seeing each other sort of seriously. I was in the process of moving out to Chicago. I'd already given notice at my firm. One of my new partners did some work for the local television affiliate out here and I mentioned Delia to him. He made a call and said the people at the station would be glad to interview her. To make a long story short, she came out and got a job right away. They had a radio station as well, but when the manager got a look at her, he hired her straight for TV. She wasn't a reporter but six months before they gave her an anchor job. She was terrific, a natural, she just took off. I'm amazed she hadn't tried it sooner. I think at one point she was probably the most recognized face in Chicago.

"I had bought a nice apartment on Lakeshore Drive. Forty-eighth floor, overlooking the water. She decorated it for me—good taste too. We lived there more than a year and I think she was happy. Me, it was the happiest time in my life. Now don't get me wrong, she could be difficult. A lot of it was all that 'being honest' business. What it really was with her was saying whatever she felt like, no matter how hard it cut, and, boy, you'd better like it. But I can deal with that. Hell, I'm a lawyer. I hear that kind of stuff every day—people trying to be tough and bluff and inflict their views on you. It runs off me like water off a duck's back. In a way I think it was what kept us together as long as it did.

"I'm not sure she ever figured me out. She'd get in one of those moods where she put in the barbs and I'd just laugh and lay back. It infuriated her, but that was okay. Thing was, she was so good in bed and, for her, that just made it better. That's where we spent a lot of time. And of course we took a lot of trips back to Atlantic City because that's where most of my business is—the casinos and all. She seemed to like that too, though I wouldn't have guessed it. She never gambled, but she liked to watch. Could sit all afternoon watching people winning and losing at dice or cards. I think maybe she played the slots every once in a while, though.

"Then one day she comes in, and out of the blue asks if I represent the mob. I said, 'Whoa—who told you that?' and she says she just 'heard it around.' See, because of her job and looks and everything, we'd gotten ourselves photographed some in the papers— at parties and charity things and stuff like that. And, frankly, if you ask me, it was some bastard at her TV station who put the bug in her ear, hoping she'd break up with me.

"Anyway, she keeps on about it. Says she'll have nothing to do with anybody associated with gangsters. I said, 'Me either,' but it didn't do much good. Maybe she watched too many movies. But she wouldn't let it go. Said her reputation was on the line. I pointed out it was my firm who got her the job in the first place. Looking back, I guess that was a mistake, because she threw a crazy fit. Said it was her personal integrity that she was talking about. She doesn't deal with dishonest people and that's that. I asked if she was talking about me, and the gist of what she said was that if I represented dishonest people, I was tarred with the same brush, or some such. Do I ever represent dishonest people? Can you imagine asking something like that to a *lawyer*?"

I thought about interrupting him to ask if he knew that Delia's father had been involved with the mob in Kansas City and in fact was killed by it. But I figured either he already knew that and didn't want to say anything to me about it or, if by some chance he didn't, what good purpose could be served by revealing it to him now? I also thought about trying to work in a question on the sex thing, but couldn't find an angle. So far, LaCosta had kept the conversation on a high level and I thought I'd seem like a turd if I just raised it out of nowhere.

"Well, it wasn't long after that she announced she was moving to San Francisco," LaCosta continued. "Said she'd sent some tapes to the station out there and they'd hired her. I think it was her way of ending it with us. Her story was that she actually wanted to become a writer or something—like you—but I never believed it."

He stopped for a moment and shook his head. A waiter came by and he ordered another martini. "This place has some wonderful chow," he said. "It's the best in town. Even the high-class Chinese eat here."

"Were you upset? Angry?"

"Lawyers don't usually have that luxury," he said. "I asked her to marry me before she left, though, and she turned me down. I just tried to be philosophical about it."

"Those pictures you have of Delia in your office," I said, "they the only ones—or did you take more?"

"Pictures? I've got lots of them. You mean more recently, right?"

"Well, when you were seeing her here in Chicago?"

"Sure, you want to look at them? They're back at my apartment."

"Videotapes?"

"Yeah, a few. We made some at parties we gave and on a vacation to France. And I think there are some on the beach at Atlantic City and around the casino."

"I hear those casinos of yours have pretty fancy video equipment," I said. "Even in your hotel rooms, they can take your picture."

"Well, yes, we have some of those facilities," he said, looking puzzled. "For security reasons. We don't use them much, but you can imagine some of the sorts of people we get staying there."

"Do you think it's possible somebody taped Delia in one of those rooms?" I asked. It was a hunch that had just come to me, and I decided to follow it through.

"Taped her? Why? Who would?"

"I don't know," I said. Then I decided to level with him. "But somebody—this extortionist—hints he's got tapes of her in bed. Sexual things. And he's indicated he'll make them public if she doesn't do what he wants."

"No, no one would have done that there. I can't imagine it."

"Well, she believes the only way it could have been

done was with a hidden camera. And you say you've got 'em."

"The casino does," he said defensively. "I'm not even supposed to tell you that. But, like I say, it's for security."

"Suppose somebody got nosy?" I asked.

"It's all done through computers," LaCosta said. "Anybody doing that kind of thing, what we call 'intrusive surveillance,' would have to be cleared by his supervisors and every time that's done—and it isn't done much—a request has to be made to the legal office."

"And who's the legal office?" I asked.

"Well, me," he said. "I mean, me or somebody who works for me."

The waiter came up with Frankie's martini and we sat and looked at each other across the table.

"How do you feel about her now?" I asked.

"Delia? To tell the truth, I'd give anything to have her back," he said.

CHAPTER 23

J OHNNY, I'M FRIGHTENED." Delia's voice was quavering over the phone. "He found me."

"He did what?" I asked. "He's there—in L.A.?"

She had left several messages for me in New York,
but I didn't get them until I returned from my meeting with Frankie LaCosta. I called her back at home.

"When I left the station this afternoon for lunch,
there was another picture—he put it in my car."

"Of you?"

"Yes. And this one's, well, it's very explicit—
very."

"Can you tell from it anything more about where it
might have been taken?"

"No."

"Not at all?"

"I've tried. It's just too blurred, except for what
you see of me. It's disgusting."

"How did he leave it in your car?"

"I don't know. It was locked. And it was in the station's parking garage, where there's a guard. It was
on the seat."

"Did you ask Rick where was his person who's supposed to be looking after you?"

"No."

"Why?"

"Because then I'd have to tell him about the picture. He and Brad don't know about them, remember?"

"But I remember Rick saying to me when he and Brad came to my place that you had told them something about pictures."

"No, no. I just said the letters 'referred' to pictures. I never told them they actually existed."

"Look," I said, "if this guy's that close, then I think you've got to assume he means real business. I will say it again, you've got to go to the police."

"There was a note with it too."

"Saying what?"

"The red sweater thing again. He wants it on Friday night."

"Okay," I said. "Look, I'm coming back to L.A. I'll be there tomorrow."

"Thank God. You're the only one I can really talk to about all this."

After we hung up, I thought, *Then why the hell are you married?*

I TOOK AN early flight and got back to Los Angeles before lunch. First class was booked and I had to ride coach, where the stewardess treated us like we were all terrorists. On the flight I pondered the things I'd learned about Delia from Homer Greer and Max Weed and Frankie LaCosta. It wasn't that she'd lied about any of it to me, she'd just never mentioned it. As Weed observed, maybe she just emphasized the positive. Still, I wondered heavily over Senator Awling's disclosure that Delia had previously received anonymous obscene phone calls.

There was a fax waiting at the hotel desk for me from Senator Awling about the envelope of Delia's I'd sent him. The FBI lab said no dice. Too many "handlers" on the thing. They couldn't get a print. Another dead end.

I decided to order lunch from room service—a club sandwich. The waiter came presently with his big silver tray and I told him to put it out on my balcony.

One thing seemed sure: Since it is impossible to be in two places at the same time, whether it was a single or group perpetrator, either he or an associate was right here in L.A., and not back east.

Frankie LaCosta, of all the ones on the list, actually had access to the kind of photographic technology that could have taken those pictures. Would they be pictures of him with Delia? Or did she perhaps have a dalliance with someone else while she was at the casino and he found out and had the cameras turned on?

I'd just finished eating when the phone rang. The hotel concierge said a package had arrived for me and did I want it brought up? A few minutes later there was a knock at my door and a bellman handed me a brown envelope with my name and room number typed neatly on a mailing label. To my shock, when I opened it, out dropped a black video cassette and a photo of Delia, as "explicit" as the one she had told me about. It was an eight by ten, in color, but somehow all the surroundings were blurred, so you couldn't tell much. She was nude and seemed to be on her hands and knees. Appearing vaguely in the background behind her, there was a man, standing over her, obviously in the process of a sex act. But someone had airbrushed it, or blurred it, so even his lower figure would be almost impossible to identify.

A typed note was also in the envelope. It said, "Pretty pictures? You keep out of it. Understand?"

I put the picture back in the envelope and stuck it in the desk. I felt dirty just looking at it, so I could imagine how Delia must have reacted. I sat there a long time and felt myself getting madder and madder until at one point I said almost aloud, "This son of a bitch has got to be stopped." There was a video player in the television cabinet in my room and I put in the cassette and turned it on. I pretty much knew what to expect. It wasn't a long piece of tape, just ten or fifteen seconds of the same scene in the photo. You could see Delia's face and an indistinct shadowy figure in the background, but it was clear what was going on. So he really had tape.

I marched down to the concierge's desk and asked where the envelope came from. He didn't know— one of the bellmen outside had brought it to him. We walked out and interviewed the three bellmen on duty. One of them said he'd found the envelope just sitting on the bell desk and took it to the concierge.

I asked for my car to be brought around and I headed up toward Sunset Boulevard to an outdoor sporting goods store. They had guns there and I bought one. This bastard was not kidding around, but neither was I.

I'D MADE A date with Delia on the car phone for after her late-evening broadcast and got in touch with Toby Burr because he'd been hounding me with messages. I'm not big on pistols, but I know how to shoot one, and what I bought was a .32-caliber Smith & Wesson revolver that was small enough to stick in a waistband, or even a pants pocket. When I got back to the hotel, I laid the gun on my desk and I have to admit it made me feel more powerful.

I met Burr for dinner at Morton's, at his suggestion. When I arrived, he was rubbernecking the room for celebrities and tossing down Rolaids as if they were candy.

"Where's the rest of that script," he demanded. "You only sent me those ten pages from New York last week. You were supposed to be finished with it by now."

"It's slower than I expected," I told him.

"What about the girl—what's her story? Is she going to love the guy or not?"

"See," I said, "it's already got you on the edge of your seat. You just can't wait to find out, can you?"

"You bastard!" Burr seethed. "I'm not worried about that, I'm worried about the people at Warner's! We got a green light here! You want it to turn back to yellow? Or red, for God's sake!"

"I'm working on it, Toby," I reassured him.

"But how does it turn out? That's what I want to know."

"Still don't know yet," I said calmly.

"Don't know! I'm not paying you not to know! I'm paying you *to* know! Don't you understand that?"

"It hasn't quite developed yet," I said. "I think it won't be long before things clarify themselves."

"*Things* clarify!" he strained. "*You* are the one who's supposed to do the clarifying! What is this, a goddamn soap opera where you just write whatever comes in your head?"

"Look, Toby, I'm trying to do something different here. I need to feel it. I can't turn on an audience's emotion without turning on my own. If I get mad when I write the scene, they'll get mad when they see it. If I cry when I write it, they cry when it comes on the screen. That's the way I do things."

"Different!" Burr sputtered. "Different!"

Several heads in the room turned toward our table. Burr noticed this and lowered his voice to a barely contained snarl.

"Have you thought anymore," I asked him, "about Anne Archer or Mimi Rogers or anybody else for the part?"

"Goddamnit, Johnny, how can I show a girl a script that isn't finished!"

"I just thought you could plant some seeds with their agents, that's all. Stir some stuff up."

Burr threw up his hands. "You ought to know how this business works," he said dejectedly, "but you don't have the foggiest idea."

"About the business, no, maybe you're right. About the screenplay, yes, I do."

"You ought to buy some stock in Rolaids," Toby said.

"Let me ask you a question."

"Sure—you want *me* to tell you how the girl comes out, right?"

"No, I need to know something about film."

"You're damned right you do!" he said. "You don't know shit!"

"It's not that kind of film. It's video film."

"That's not film, Johnny, that's tape."

"Well, tape then. Who is the best—and I mean the *best*—videotape guy in L.A.? Somebody who can look at something and be discreet, and tell me something about the tape itself. Where it might have been made, who might have sold the tape itself, all that sort of thing."

"Why would you want to know?"

"I got my reasons."

"Well, I don't deal in tape. In case you've forgotten, what we deal with in this business is thirty-five-millimeter film. Tape is for the assholes in TV or taking pictures of your baby or something."

"So you don't know anybody?"

"I didn't say that. Go over to HRS Processing. It's down near Studio City. There's a guy there named Kevin Jackobsen. If anybody knows about tape, he does. He's the best. Maybe the best in the world. Say, what's all this about, anyway?"

"It's a secret," I told him.

"We've never had secrets between us, Johnny," Burr said, sounding a little hurt.

"Toby," I said, "I've always found it fascinating how well men can keep secrets they haven't been told."

I MET DELIA at her TV station a little after eleven. I was led back to her office, which was decorated with lots of plaques and pictures and memorabilia and notes posted all over the place, but I didn't notice any photos of Brad. She got up from her desk and closed the door, then gave me a hug. I held her for a few moments, but I'll be damned if I could tell what kind of hug it was.

"I'm glad to see you," she said finally. "How was your trip?"

"Interesting," I said. "I'll tell you about it. Want to go get some dinner?"

"I'm not hungry," she said, "but, yes, let's go somewhere."

I walked her down to the parking garage and waited till she pulled out behind me. I saw no sign of the tail Rick was supposed to have on her. I led her up Sunset to the Bel Air Hotel, which has arguably the most intimate bar in the city. We sat at a quiet table and I ordered wine, but Delia asked for a scotch on the rocks, single malt. Just the notion of it made my taste buds stir.

"So how're you doing?" I asked.

"Hanging in there, I guess."

"Decided what you're going to do on Friday?"

"Not quite," she said.

"What does that mean?"

"Well, remember what I suggested a while back?"

"A trap?"

"Yes, if that's what you call it."

"How're you going to do it?"

"I'm not exactly sure. He'll be watching, and I'm going to figure out a way of telling him to contact me. I couldn't do this more than once, but I want this over. Do you think it's worth a try?"

"Yes, but we also ought to have a definite plan if he bites. We can't make a mess of it."

"I know," she said. "Maybe I should just quit and go someplace else."

"That wouldn't solve anything."

"I know that too," she said.

"Why didn't you tell me you'd known Frankie La-Costa since boarding school?" I said.

"I thought he'd probably tell you about it," she said. "But then I thought maybe he wouldn't."

"Something you didn't want me to know?"

"Maybe you most of all."

"And you didn't tell me about your New York life in the clubs downtown either."

Delia reached for her glass of scotch and downed the rest of it. "How did you find out about that?" she said.

"Arthur Dalton told me."

"Oh," she said.

"Did you know he was an old tennis partner of mine?"

"No, I didn't."

"After you stopped seeing him, he dropped out of the game."

"I'm sorry."

"But the clubs—that didn't seem very much like you."

"It wasn't. But maybe it was," she said.

Noticing Delia's drink was empty, the waiter came up. She nodded when he asked if she wanted another.

"Johnny, I just got tired of my life. I got tired of involvement—of hurting people—it just began to seem that I had that kind of effect on guys. I needed a time out. Just to be anonymous for a while, no connections."

"Well, you apparently connected with somebody during all that time. You remember a bartender at the Cave called Carlo?"

"Yes. I saw him a few times."

"And were there others?"

"Yes, there were others. I'm not enjoying this, are you?"

"No, but the sort of people you knew down there, they're into some pretty kinky things. Maybe making clandestine videos of their sex exploits was one of them."

"I never went out with them more than a few times," she said.

"Went out with, or went home with?"

"Please, Johnny . . ."

"I mean, for chrissake, you went to that Hellfire Club place, I understand. That's supposed to be one of those dens of leather and lashes and all that kind of stuff—males, females, running around naked. No telling what else went on there."

"I had my wild fling. I'd just spent so much time in that old crowd—all the dances and parties and the scene in the Hamptons or Newport or wherever. I felt like I'd sort of worn out my welcome. I needed to get away, to do something different. I even wanted to *be* somebody different. There were too many people I'd—oh, I don't know, it was awkward and strange— one weekend you'd be staying at so-and-so's house in the country who was good friends with thus-and-so who you'd just broken up with two weeks before and you were going out with whatchamacallit who was friends with the other so-and-so you'd dated who kept on calling you up. It was—well, can't we just leave it at that?"

"Sure," I said. "But think back. It might be any one of those guys you met downtown."

"I will," she said.

I'd decided not to tell her about the videotape I'd received today, but there was something else I could bring up.

"I had a conversation with Senator Awling, you know."

"How was he?"

"Very pleasant. Sends his best."

"He was a nice guy."

"He told me about the obscene calls you'd been getting."

"The what?"

"He said that when you two were going out, you were receiving obscene phone calls in your apartment in New York."

"That's ridiculous," she said. "Why would he say that?"

"You tell me. You mean it's not true?"

"No, I've never gotten an obscene call—not then. Oh—well, except in my, ah, former line of business, but that would be different."

"Awling says you told him you were getting dirty calls from somebody and that you wouldn't report it to the police or the phone company."

"That's total bullshit," Delia snapped.

"He also said you threw yourself at him, after you guys broke it off."

"What!"

"He said you wrote him letters trying to get back together and at one point arranged to 'put yourself in his way,' as he characterized it, at the U.S. Capitol."

"That's just a lie," she said furiously. "I never went back to the Capitol in my life after I quit seeing him. And I certainly never wrote him any letters."

"He says different."

"I don't care what he says. It's not true."

"Why would he say that?"

"All I can tell you is that it isn't so," she said.

"And another thing," I told her, now rankled, "Worthington Hathaway says you once accused him of stalking you."

"That's—why, that's not true either. Not exactly, anyway. Look, I noticed Worthy a time or two walking around outside my apartment building. I just wrote him a note. A nice note, saying how sorry I was about the whole Italy deal, and told him I hope he wasn't mad."

"He was. Still is."

"Well, that's . . . life, I guess," she said.

"By the way, Delia, what's your favorite color?" I asked.

"My favorite . . . what's that supposed to mean?"

"Nothing. Just curious."

"I don't have one," she said. "It changes."

She seemed drained now and I figured we'd both had enough for one evening. We finished our drinks and left and I followed Delia back to her apartment. I hadn't seen any sign of Rick's people, but just as we pulled into her building, I noticed a car behind us. It pulled slowly into the parking lot and stopped, but nobody got out. When Delia handed over her keys to the valet, I gave her a little wave and she went inside. I pulled into the street and the car in the parking lot turned on its lights and followed me.

CHAPTER 24

THE CAR FOLLOWING me stayed right on my tail, but I couldn't see who was behind the wheel. I'd left the gun back in my room and felt defenseless. If it was Rick's guy, why was he following me? If it wasn't, was it the blackmailer? And if that was so, what did he intend? I turned off on Beverly and headed down Richards and he was still tight on me. At Vine I saw a service station with one of those all-night convenience stores and abruptly turned in. The tailgater kept going. There were two guys in the car, a late-model sedan with California plates. I sat in my car watching until they were out of sight. They made no move to turn around or double back. Maybe it was just a coincidence that they got behind me, but it sure didn't seem like it. When I got back to the hotel, I made sure to dead bolt the door and also locked the French doors to the balcony.

In the morning I worked some on Burr's script and in the afternoon I drove out to HRS Processing and asked to see Kevin Jackobsen. A woman led me through dark hallways to a small shabby room crammed with all sorts of videotape equipment. At what I took for some kind of editing table sat a guy peering into a machine. "Kevin, there's somebody here to see you," the woman said.

I'd expected some kind of nerd or troll, but Kevin was a clean-cut fellow who looked to be in his mid-thirties. His clear blue eyes seemed to have an expression of perpetual surprise, like Montgomery Clift's.

"Toby Burr says if anybody can tell me something about videotape, you're the one" was the way I announced myself.

"That was nice of him. What can I do for you?"

"I'm looking into something pretty serious," I said. "It involves a blackmailer who sent this piece of tape to a friend of mine. It was taken of her, but nobody knows when or where or how. I know it's a ridiculously long shot, but I was wondering if by some miracle you could tell me anything that might help identify it. I mean, when it might have been taken, how it was taken without the person knowing it, just anything at all.

"It's not much," I said, "just a few seconds." I knew I was taking a risk he'd somehow recognize Delia, but the picture was so blurry I'd had trouble knowing who it was myself.

He put the thing into a machine and studied the image carefully for a few moments. "Good-looking chick," he said.

I didn't answer him. He was running it back and

forth slowly, looking at it through a big magnifying glass.

"Well, this is just off the top," he said, "but I'd say this thing was reproduced from DXT tape, wide band, commercial quality. From the look of it, the camera was about ten to fifteen feet away. You can tell that by the sync of the focus. And you can see somebody's doctored up the backgrounds. I'll need more time to look at it. Run it through some tests. I don't know if I'll be able to find much more."

"I'd certainly appreciate it," I said. "I'm sure you can understand this is a sensitive matter. Do you have any idea when you can get to it?"

"Sometime this week, I think. Tapes leave little track marks all their own, sort of like ballistics. Of course, you've got to have something to compare them with, which, in this case, you haven't got. But I'll give it a shot."

I thanked him and gave him my number.

"Say hello to Toby Burr. It's been a long time," Kevin said.

"By the way," I said, "how did you two know each other?"

"Used to work on nudie movies for him years ago."

"Nudie movies—you mean porn?"

"Oh yeah, Toby made a bunch of them, back in the early seventies, when videotape began replacing film. Using tape let him make 'em a bunch cheaper.

Course, it was a new medium then and he had a lot of kinks to iron out. I was his ironer."

"Why, that dirty old bastard," I laughed. For an instant it flashed before me that Toby might be—no, of course not, impossible, wrong timing, no motive—God, I'm getting paranoid, I thought.

"He was high-class, compared with most of 'em," Kevin remarked.

I thanked him again and drove back to the hotel. When I got there, Rick Olsen and Brad were waiting for me in the lobby.

"Could we go someplace and talk?" Rick asked.

"Sure," I said. "How about the bar here?"

"Maybe someplace a little more private," he said.

"We can go up to my room."

"That'd be fine," he said. As we rode up in the elevator, I sensed an air of seriousness and tension.

In my living room Rick sat down on the sofa and made himself comfortable, but Brad hung around in a corner, quiet and nervous, like a dog about to be sick on the rug.

Rick got right to the point. "Brad doesn't think you ought to be involved in this anymore."

"Really?" I said, astonished.

"Yes. I think he feels, well, that you've done enough. We can't thank you too much, but he'd like you to bow out. I think we can handle it from here."

"You mind telling me why?" I said to Brad, but he turned away and looked out a window.

"Brad just thinks that you, well, you've gotten too close to Delia."

"What's that supposed to mean?"

"Just what it says."

" 'Close' has a lot of meanings."

"I think you get the one intended," Rick said.

"That what you think, Brad?" I asked.

"That's what I think," Brad said.

"Mind telling me why?"

"You know why," Brad said flatly. "You don't just go out with another man's wife for half the night."

"Look, if you're talking about last night, I took Delia to the Bel Air for a drink after she finished her show. That was all. And I followed her back to her apartment to make sure she was safe. I didn't see anybody else keeping track of her," I said, looking at Rick, "that is, until we got there. And then the bastard followed *me*."

"We *were* keeping track," Rick said. "The fact that you didn't notice just means that we were doing our job."

"What does Delia have to say about this?" I asked.

"Nothing," Brad said. "It isn't her business. It's my business."

"So what are you suggesting? That we're having some kind of affair?"

"I think we've suggested that you stay out of this and stay away from Delia," Rick said. "That ought to be enough."

"Well, she's the one who brought me into it," I said, "and I think she's the one who's going to have to tell me to get out."

"Look, Johnny," Rick said, "we know you're a

good guy. But you're making matters worse for Brad and Delia. That's the bottom line."

"Or what?"

"Let's don't get into that," Rick said. "Brad's asking you like a gentleman and so am I. I'd like to keep it on that level."

"And if I don't, then I gather there's some sort of veiled threat?"

"Like I said, Johnny," Rick said, standing up, "you're off the case. That's just how it's got to be."

When they left, nobody said good-bye. This was one of the strangest developments of all. Had they somehow found out who it was—that it was Hathaway or somebody?

I was furious and yet I probably didn't have a right to be. The truth was, I was looking for an affair with Delia and would have felt few compunctions about having one. I wasn't very proud of that, but I somehow justified it with the notion that Delia wasn't particularly happy in her marriage. That seemed to make some small moral difference. Besides, I was still infatuated with her and there is an old Anglo-Saxon saying they use to justify that. All's fair . . .

I sat back in a chair, trying to recapture the way it used to be. Our relationship—if you could call it that—didn't end following the hideously strained final trip with her to Bermuda nearly fifteen years earlier. Back in New York, I didn't call her and she didn't call me. A part of my mind—the rational one—said stay away, even good riddance. Anybody who would throw such an uncalled-for hissy fit over what was intended as honest literary criticism was obviously going to be trouble to anyone except the most placid and submissive personality, and that wasn't me. I wasn't one of those people whose philosophy was to eat a little shit every day just so you make sure you don't lose the taste for it.

But a year later she did call, in the height and glory of autumn in New York. Again it was out of the blue. She said she'd just seen a movie I wrote and wondered how I was doing. I tried to be cool about it. I'd gotten my hand slapped too many times to stick it out again, but she sounded so pleasant and inviting that after a while I let my guard down. I wasn't sure what she wanted, but I was determined not to to put myself through some obligatory courting reprise of dinners and dates, only to find that nothing had changed and that she just wanted to be "friends." Hell with that, I thought. I've already got all the friends I need.

So I played a heavy card. I asked her if she'd like to go with me to Maine for a weekend—Bermuda had sort of run itself into the ground. To my surprise, she readily agreed, and so we set it up for three weeks down the road. I knew a grand old hotel on the coast, absolutely first-rate with big fireplaces in the rooms, gorgeous decor, and food to die for, and it would be a spectacular time of year. I made the reservations and arranged for travel and even went out and bought some new clothes. As the days approached, I found myself getting excited and expectant and had visions that we would somehow pull things together again, that maybe time or something had intervened with her and she had changed her mind about me.

Then one morning when even in New York City the fall weather was too perfect to describe, the phone rang. She couldn't come, she said. A job opportunity had come up, it was too important to delay, there would be interviews conflicting with our time schedule, so on and so on. There was an edge in her voice that didn't ring right with any of it, but like an idiot I asked her about the next weekend. No, that wouldn't work either. She had plans to visit her family in Kansas City. Just to make a point to myself, I asked her about the weekend after that—or even during the week. No dice. Delia seemed to be booked up for the foreseeable future and I never found out what caused her change of heart.

I hung up more disgusted with myself than with her. I should have known better. Not only was the rug pulled out from under me for the weekend, I also had to eat five hundred bucks in nonrefundable hotel reservations. Obviously, *something* must have come up with her—a new boyfriend, cold feet, who knew? But whatever it was, it was bad form, and I vowed never to put myself through it again. She's off the list, I declared, and so she was.

And so now where was I, more than a decade later? Mixed up in it again right up to my neck. I'd told her I'd try to help and now I was privy to facts that even her husband didn't know.

All this was depressing stuff and I didn't feel like being alone in my room. Surrounding myself with strangers even seemed a more pleasant prospect, so I went down to the bar at cocktail time to have a drink. When I walked in, I was surprised to see Meredith McDonald standing amid a bunch of young men and women, stunning, to me, in a black sheath. She had her blond hair down as I'd never seen it before and it framed her face in an elegant, sensuous way that made her look both younger and older. Certainly it made her more alluring, at the same time.

"I just got in from New York and was thinking about calling you," I lied. Actually, I wished I *had* thought about it. Meredith was good company and that's what I needed right now.

"I got tired of waiting," she said with what I took as a mock pout. "Since you're spoken for, I thought I might meet some other nice man here."

"I'm not spoken for," I told her.

"What about your 'unfinished business'?" she asked.

"I'm winding it up," I said.

Bland Christmas music was playing in the bar and they had already put up a few tinsel decorations, though not yet a Christmas tree. I hated Christmas out here.

"Good," Meredith said.

"Want to have a drink?"

"I'm having one."

"No, with me. We can sit over there." I nodded toward Burr's old table.

I ordered a bottle of Pinot Noir while Meredith went to the powder room. When she came back, she looked even more radiant.

"So how's your little investigation going?" she asked.

"Curiouser and curiouser."

"The mystery thickens?"

"Definitely."

"I love a good mystery," she said. "Why don't you make me your sidekick?"

"Good detectives always work alone," I said. "Like Sam Spade."

"Bullshit, what about Sherlock Holmes and Dr. Watson or Charlie Chan and his Number One Son?"

"How would you know about those old fogies?"

"I can read, can't I? Actually, I'm a big fan of old flicks on TV."

"The only reason Holmes had Watson or Chan had Number One Son was so the writer could bounce off dialogue," I told her.

"Yeah, and the reason Sam Spade worked alone was because he always got involved with some beautiful client so they could bounce the dialogue off her—is that what's happening to you, Sam?"

"Touché," I said.

"I guess that answers my question."

"Want to have dinner next week?"

"Sure, nobody else asks me out. I'm the living example of a wallflower."

"I believe I heard the word *bullshit* used a moment ago."

She smiled and leaned toward me conspiratorially. "Will you take me someplace fancy, dark, and quiet and ply me with romantic talk?"

"I might even bring you a corsage," I told her.

CHAPTER 25

NEXT MORNING I got a shock and shock is not an emotion I take well. A bellman delivered me my mail and when I got to a letter postmarked Los Angeles, my mouth literally dropped open.

It was a Christmas card from Delia, but that wasn't the thing. The front of the card was a picture of her—a painting, actually, and not particularly a good one—but it showed her, somewhat younger looking, standing on a winter hillside beneath a big leafless tree, wearing a long white skirt—and a bright red sweater!

There was no personal message inside, just a printed "Merry Christmas and a Happy New Year—Delia Jamison."

Did she know what she was doing? I phoned Delia at her office.

"Are you free for lunch?" I asked.

"Sure—about one-fifteen?"

"I'll meet you at Inman's—it's close to your studios."

"See you then," she chirped.

I looked at the Christmas card again. Yes, she was

definitely younger looking in the painting. It was an oil or acrylic and it was obviously by an amateur. But there was a sort of mystical quality about it too, as if whoever drew it was trying desperately to capture Delia in some exalted form.

"I got your Christmas card this morning," I said when we met in the restaurant and seated ourselves in a booth.

"Oh, good. I started sending them out early this year."

"Doesn't anything about it strike you as odd?"

"What?" she said, almost as though she was about to be offended.

"The red sweater, Delia. You're wearing a red sweater in the picture."

"Oh, that? I really hadn't thought of it. It's such an old painting. My father did it, years ago, not long before he died. He liked to paint and mostly what he painted was me," she said almost wistfully. "Ever since I was a baby. One year he suggested I have it put on my Christmas cards. Sort of in his memory, I suppose. In a way, it makes me timeless, don't you think?" she laughed ruefully.

"And you don't see any possible connection between the red sweater business that's going on now and this card?"

"Why, no, Johnny. I . . . like I said, I've been sending these cards out for, well, ten years or more."

"Did you ever send them to any of the guys on your list? The ones I've been out seeing?"

"Well, yes, I did, I guess. At some point—but not for years, now. Years."

"Forgive me for being blunt, Delia," I told her, "but did it occur to you that maybe you've left a path of hurt behind you—because that's what I've been finding out—and that maybe one of these guys saw this card as a kind of icon or something, and that's what all this red sweater thing's about?"

"Why, that's . . . why, I wear red sweaters all the time—at least until a few months ago. I only thought of my father, then I sent them out. We didn't have a very good relationship when I was growing up. And when he died, I thought it was something that . . ."

"How did your father die, Delia?"

"Well, he . . . why does it matter?"

"It doesn't, really," I said. "I saw Maxwell Weed in New York. He told me."

"Oh," she said, suddenly looking deflated, sad, and her voice trailed off. "I guess you're determined to pry into my life, even though I've asked you not to."

"Look, you're right, it doesn't matter," I told her, then I plunged ahead. "No, maybe it does matter. What I'm asking is whether or not that might have something to do with this, I mean, the mob. Is there any possibility . . . ?"

"No, I've already told you. . . . It's one of the guys on the list."

"You're sure?"

"So what else did Max tell you?" she asked, her tone now steely.

"That's about it," I lied.

"C'mon, Johnny. He didn't tell you about my earlier marriage?"

"He mentioned it."

"And now I suppose you want to know why he wasn't on my list?"

"No, I think I understand why he wasn't."

"Thank you," she said. She took out a handkerchief and blew her nose. At first I thought she was crying, but she wasn't.

ON MY DRIVE back to the hotel I decided maybe she was telling the truth—that it just never occurred to her. And yet in my suspicious mind I could just see some creep harboring that Christmas card in a sort of lascivious shrine and scheming about how to bring his perverted fantasies to life. And, in fact, a couple of these guys had actually told me they'd gotten Christmas cards from Delia after she broke up with them. In any event, I told Delia to see if she could come up with the names of other men she'd sent the card to in years past that might coincide with the names she'd already given me.

NEXT DAY I looked in the phone book for a Rex Ober, the "film producer." Carlo, the bartender back in New York, had remembered Delia being with him for a while. He was listed in Sherman Oaks and he answered the phone himself. He immediately picked up on my name, just as I figured he would. You could almost hear his breathing get harder.

"I've been interested in some of your work," I told him. "You've got style."

"Coming from you, that's a great compliment."

I asked Ober what projects he had in the pipeline and he gave me half a dozen films he intended to make. They all sounded preposterous, but I picked one of them—something called *Oh, Silly Day*—and feigned interest.

"Maybe there is some way we can talk about it?" I said.

Ober was drooling by now and said he could see me anytime. I pretended I was tied up on a script but that by chance I had this afternoon free. I was there within the hour. He lived in one of those nondescript split-level slab-type houses on the outskirts of Ventura and his office was in his garage.

Rex Ober was a sort of greaseball-looking guy but had a certain goofy charm, like Donald Sutherland. He was dressed in jeans and a tank top that showed off a tattoo of an eagle on his upper arm. A Harley was parked in a corner of the room. He was bigger than me—well over six feet—but looked a little gummy. He showed me his file on *Oh, Silly Day,* which I glanced over. It was just a treatment, not a script and definitely not a movie. You could have shot the whole thing in a couple of hours. Ober became extremely oily as he plied me with questions about what I'd do with this thing. I made some sug-

gestions, then he popped the question to me that had
been on his mind, I'm sure, since I'd called him.

"Would you be interested in doing this script?"

"Maybe," I said. "It has potential." Any numskull
would have noticed my insincerity in this, but not
Ober. We talked for a while longer, about scripts and
movies, and when he mentioned New York, I showed
interest. He had lived downtown, he said, making short experimental films after graduating from
NYU's film school. I dropped the names of some of
the clubs and bars Delia had hung out at and he began
to brag about some of the wild times he'd had. Then
I asked if he'd known an underground film director
called James Cornwell.

"Sure, I knew him," Ober said. "Too bad what happened. He had some talent, but I think he let the nose
candy get in his way."

"You know his wife too?"

Ober jerked upright and I saw his face flush a little. He rubbed his jaw and eyed me. "Delia, sure," he
said haltingly. "Matter of fact, I took her out after . . .
after it happened."

"A big affair?"

"No, not really. She was pretty much in a funk
then, I guess. She was having a hard time. When I ran
into her, she was waiting for a bus. She looked like a
bag lady."

"Delia looked like a bag lady?"

"Well, of course not, but that was my first impression," he said, wiping a few beads of sweat off his
brow. "She was running errands at some local radio

station and had a part-time second job at night. Wouldn't say what it was. Cornwell had left her in a world of debt before he took the big leap, and she was having a hard time with bill collectors and tax people on her ass and so on. Her landlord even locked her out of their apartment because she couldn't pay the rent. Kept all her furniture. And besides all that, her old man had died or something. She was in pretty sorry shape. I gave her a job working with me."

"Doing what?"

"Hell, anything at first—gofer, typist, receptionist—but finally she showed some talent in film. She had great ideas and was becoming a hell of a good film cutter. I couldn't pay much, of course, but my people didn't go hungry. After a while I started taking her out and we got involved. She was some piece of ass."

"Is that so?"

"Well, yeah," he said, squirming a little in his chair.

"Why? She have something peculiar that she did?"

"Hey, man, that was a long time ago, you know?"

"No, I don't know," I said to him. "You want to tell me about it?"

"No, I don't," Ober replied almost in confusion. "Like I said, it was a long time ago."

"Why don't you want to talk about it, then?" I pressed him. But I sensed he was getting the picture of why I might have come here, and when he didn't answer, I slid off the question, figuring I might come back to it later.

"So did it last long between you two?"

"Not very. By that time, Delia found a job with a new radio station. They made her a reporter and she started to make good money. Next thing you know, she's on the air a lot. I was shooting something down on the Jersey shore, near Margate, and was gone a couple of weeks. I get back and she's being a little distant, I could tell. The movie I was doing—it was one of those kinds of things like *Maidstone* that Mailer used to make back in the sixties—I tried to put her in it. God, was she gorgeous. But she wouldn't do it because there was some nudity. Not much, but any nudity was too much for Delia. I said to her, 'Hey, for God's sake, you got a spectacular body, why not?' and she says, "Yeah, and it's mine.' "

"You ever see her out here?" I asked.

"Nah. I called her a couple of times after first I saw her on TV. Left messages, but she never returned them. She's too hot shit for me now, I guess—say, what's this about, anyway? Why're you asking all this about Delia?"

"You ever take pictures of her when you two were seeing each other? Film or anything—in the nude?"

"What the hell is this?" Ober said, rising from his chair. "What is it you're getting at? Why'd you come here, anyway?"

"I asked you a question," I said, rising too.

"Look, I don't like this," he said, shoving himself close to me. "You come here asking these questions. You didn't come here about movies at all, did you?" He put his palms up toward me as if to shove me toward the door, but I came up between them and took him by the collar of his T-shirt and stood him up straight.

"Listen, you dip shit, did you or did you not take pictures of Delia without her clothes! And, goddamnit, don't lie to me!"

"Hey, hey, man!" Ober said, in an alarmed voice.

"Tell me!"

"No. Nothing like that! I already told you, she didn't do nudity."

"But maybe you did it without her knowing it!" I said, tightening my grip on his collar and putting my face so close to his I could smell garlic on his breath. "You're a cameraman, aren't you, Rex? In your studio, or in your apartment, you had a little hidden camera—maybe? Just to take some sexy pictures in bed, right?"

"No, that's nuts. I never did that."

"I told you, don't goddamn lie to me," I growled, "or you're gonna need a new set of teeth. . . ."

"I didn't take any pictures of her," he said in a quavering, high-pitched tone. "I'm telling you the truth!"

"Well, let me tell *you* something, Mr. Cecil B. De-Mille, if you did, and if you've got some kind of scumbag scheme to send her letters and shit, you better get rid of it right now, because when I come back—and I *will* come back—I'm gonna kick your asshole up around your eyeballs!" I shoved Ober hard and he stumbled back over a cheap desk cluttered with papers. His eyes were wild. As I stalked out and slammed the door, I heard him yelling, "I'm gonna call the police!"

On the drive back to Beverly Hills I noticed my hands shaking at the steering wheel. The revealing thing about this grotesque little incident was Ober's reaction when I'd brought up Delia's name. It was the most emphatic and obvious of any I had seen so far. Still, she hadn't put *him* on her list either.

FINALLY FRIDAY ROLLED around, the day Delia intended to set her little trap. I wasn't sure what she was going to do, but she'd asked me to meet her at the station again, before her late-evening broadcast. I decided I'd wait and find out like everybody else. Instead of taking my old Caddy that Rick's surveillance people surely knew by now, I arranged to be driven to the TV station in the hotel's big green Rolls-Royce and have the chauffeur take us around. I could tell the driver to pick me up at a side entrance.

That afternoon the phone rang in my room and it was Kevin from the videotape place.

"Maybe we're in luck," he said. "But maybe not."

"You got something?"

"Well, I've been going over that tape pretty carefully, and I'm about ninety percent sure it's something pretty unusual. You see, it was reproduced from that kind of continuous-running DXT tape I told you about. Lays on a very high quality picture, not like the usual surveillance tape that's black-and-white and all fuzzy-looking and jerky. But it's even more special because it's the kind of stuff they use for wide-frame, small-lens, stationary-ability 'waffle,' they call it. It's designed not to be used in a movable video camera but from a fixed station and still pick up a big spread."

"Like some kind of hidden camera?"

"Yes, but I don't think that's what it was really designed for. It was really developed for what they're doing now with those mounted flexible video cams that local TV stations use way up on buildings to bring in pictures of a whole city—traffic reports, weather, that kind of stuff. Except this particular tape began being manufactured about ten years ago, before they had those cameras that pan around everywhere, so it was usually used in conjunction with several fixed cameras to get a full pan."

"You mean they don't make it anymore?"

"Oh no, they still make it—just one company in the whole country still makes it to supply the customers who haven't got or don't need the mechanical cameras. They're based up in San Francisco. It's a very small part of their whole operation."

"So who uses it now?" I asked.

"Well, I think some nightclubs use it, and promotional events and stuff where they want to get good-quality, industrial pictures of patrons and people who attend things without having to hire a camera crew or install one of those rotating cameras, because they're expensive."

"How many customers do you think they'd have?"

"Oh, probably not many," Kevin said. "Only reason they're still making the tape is because they can probably sell enough of it to the few people who do use it—you know, twenty-four hours a day, so many feet per hour. If there's a market, I guess they'll still make it, but sooner or later it'll go the way of eight-track sound tapes and Betamax videos."

"You think there's any chance of my getting a list of the customers?"

"I don't know. Maybe. I've got some pals who work for the main company, but I don't think they work in the division that makes this stuff."

"Could you try to get in touch with them? I'd really take it as a personal favor."

"Well, sure, I can try. But the police ought to be able to get a list of customers pretty easy."

"It may yet come to that. But for the moment it's you and me."

"Okay," Kevin said. "By the way, you see Toby Burr, give him my regards."

"The porn king—I sure will," I said.

THE ROLLS DELIVERED me to Delia's TV studios about ten and I was taken back to her office. When I got there, she was out doing something, but a few minutes later she came in wearing the red sweater.

"It made my flesh crawl, just putting on this thing," she said. She looked preoccupied and strained but kept her composure. "You want to come down to the studio or wait here?" she asked.

"Whatever you want."

"Why don't you just wait here. You can turn on that monitor on the table. I'd better go now to read over some copy."

She left me alone in her office and I thumbed nervously through broadcast magazines, just like I would in a dentist's waiting room. What we'd more or less agreed on was that if the trap worked—if the guy actually got in touch with her—we'd try to set up a meeting between the two of them and then I'd try to catch him. Somehow. It wasn't exactly the kind of operation you could plan much ahead for. Whether he'd call at all, what he'd say, what he'd suggest—all of this was unknown. We'd just have to play it by ear, but I thought it might be worth a shot.

After about fifteen minutes the logo came on the set for the evening news. It was a half hour show and I watched expectantly for Delia to make her move but saw no signs of it. Then, just as they were signing off and there was a little chitchat between the people on the anchor desk, she sort of straightened up and threw back her shoulders a little, and with a big perceptibly strained smile on her face said very quickly: "And now for my special fan out there, get in touch soon, here at the station," and then she turned back to her partner and made a disparaging comment about tomorrow's weather. It was fast, and the other reporters didn't seem to notice and I watched on the monitor as they began to wander off the set. As Delia walked away, a guy in shirtsleeves and a tie came up to her. I could see him gesturing with palms up and shaking his head and she was nodding and shrugging, but after a few moments they too departed and she came back into her office.

"I knew that was going to happen," she said in resignation. "He doesn't miss a thing."

"I saw it on the monitor here. Who was that?"

"The night news director. Naturally he wanted to know what that was all about. I told him a little old lady in her nineties had sent me a sweet note and apparently forgot to put her return address on it and it was the only way I could think to get it so I could reply."

"You lied? My word, Delia . . ."

She didn't seem to take that remark with humor, so I quickly changed the subject.

"I guess the message is sent now," I told her.

"Let's hope so. So what do you think? Should we wait here and see if he calls?"

"I seriously doubt he'll call right away. I bet he was startled out of his mind. He'll have to think it over pretty carefully, figure out all the angles."

"You want a cup of coffee?" she asked.

"No, not really."

"Neither do I. I need a drink."

"Why don't you ride with me?" I told her. When we got to the big Rolls waiting in the parking garage, Delia did a double take.

"Hop in," I said. "I'll tell you why in a little while." I told the driver to take us to Fascio's, a neat little Italian place not far from the station. Originally I'd planned to take her back to the Bel Air but decided against it on the chance Rick's tail might catch on and follow us. He'd be watching Delia anyhow, but at least they wouldn't see us going to a hotel.

"Okay," I said after we'd ordered a drink. "It's not just to show off. I guess I need to explain."

"Shoot."

"Brad wants me to stay away from all this—and from you too."

"He what?"

"He and Rick showed up at my hotel a few days ago. Seems Brad suspects we're having an affair or something."

"How could he? We aren't."

"It's what he thinks. He didn't say it in so many words. He let Rick be his messenger boy."

"That's his jealous streak. It's been worse since I moved down here."

"I thought you'd told me he wasn't jealous," I said.

"It wasn't completely true. Frankly I never wanted to believe it, but I know now that he is. We had a row about it down in San Diego a few weeks ago. But this is ridiculous." She said it with such emphasis that I took it personally.

"Thing is, now we've got Rick following you and, apparently, me too, so it's going to be hard for us to see each other without them knowing about it. I don't mind—to hell with them—but don't you think you'd better come clean with Brad about all of this and let Rick spring this so-called trap? After all, he's a professional. Or better yet, go to the police? I don't like sneaking around—even if it is in a Rolls-Royce."

"Oh, please, Johnny," she said, reaching for my

hand across the table. "Just let's try this, and see if he calls. If he does, and I can arrange a meeting of some kind, maybe we can identify him and the whole thing will be over."

"How did you meet Brad, anyway?" I asked. Truth was, I just wanted to see if she'd tell me straight.

Delia took a swallow of her drink—scotch again.

"Well, it was actually through Rick," she said. "I ran into Rick not long after I got to San Francisco. His offices were based there then. We went out for a while, a few months, and then I discovered he was married."

"He hadn't told you?"

"In a way. I mean, he was at a party I was invited to. I didn't know many people in San Francisco and he was there and I asked one of the hosts who he was and she said he was Rick Olsen, president of this big private detective agency, and was a friend of the girl who had brought me to the party. It was a pretty fancy affair, at the Fairmont Club, and after a while we found ourselves talking and right away he said he'd been married but that his wife had some kind of emotional problems and, well, he wasn't wearing a wedding ring or anything, and I just assumed . . ."

"That he wasn't married."

"Yes. And so we started going out and in fact I really liked him then. He was a lot of fun. And then one day, by accident, I met his wife."

"That must have come as a shock."

"It sure did. There was a big luncheon benefit for saving sea otters and I was there—not as a reporter, but I'd been invited. This woman came over to me. She was Japanese—very pretty and younger than me—and right then and there announced she'd heard that I knew her husband. When she said it was Rick, I was floored. I was mortified. I told him of course this had to end and he was apologetic and said he was in the process of getting a divorce, but it was, well, that was where it ended for me."

"And then you met Brad?"

"No, we'd already met. Brad was his best friend and two or three times we'd had dinner or done things together. I thought Brad was super too, but I was with Rick. And a month or two after Rick and I split up, Brad called. It was so neat. I mean, Brad and I just had this kind of karma—that's what they call it out here."

"They call it that back east too," I kidded her.

"After that, there wasn't anybody else but Brad. It was perfect. It was a purely mental, intellectual, emotional, and, well, physical experience. We got engaged two months later and were married that summer."

"So I guess you and Rick had to make your peace."

"It's funny, Rick's a nice guy. He's hard to stay mad at. And after his wife died, he wasn't around much; I think he took it pretty hard—besides, he was in the process of moving his operations to L.A."

"Let me ask you something," I said, "just out of curiosity. Was it Brad or Rick you were with when Senator Awling looked you up in San Francisco?"

"It was Rick. I think that was even before I'd met Brad for the first time."

I DROPPED DELIA off at her car back in the studio parking garage but followed her home in the Rolls at a safe distance. I saw no sign of Rick's people but didn't go into her apartment drive once she'd made the turn. Next afternoon, Saturday, she phoned me, distressed.

"Can you believe it! He's got my home number! He just called."

"And said what?"

"He got the message. Wants to meet me tomorrow."

"What'd you say?"

"I didn't know what to say, but I tried to hint I wasn't horribly opposed to the idea."

"Where? When?"

"He wouldn't say. He said he'd contact me tomorrow and let me know."

"He's being careful, just like I said."

"That's what I think. He said he'd tell me where to go to take the call, and to be prepared to leave directly from there to where he'll set up the meeting."

"What about the voice? Anything you recognized?"

"No. It was funny. It didn't sound like anyone. I mean, almost not any human at all."

I remembered what Rick had reminded me about

those voice-altering devices. This guy was probably just smart enough to have used one, and telling her to go to a phone drop and then take off straight from there to the rendezvous meant he was obviously concerned about phone tracing.

"You want me to come over?" I asked.

"No, Brad's coming into town in a little while. He called this morning. He'll be here till Monday afternoon."

"Okay," I said. "Whatever you do, if you're not going to tell Brad about it, then stay in touch with me. I'll be here at the hotel. I'm not going anywhere; I'll take meals in my room. And if he calls, whatever you do, don't dare go out by yourself."

"I know that, silly," she said. "I wish you could be here right now."

"Right," I said, "but your husband will be. And I'll be here."

"Sometimes, I wish it had been you," Delia said.

"Well, it wasn't, and I'll speak to you later," I told her.

I knew she was upset, but this line of talk wasn't going anyplace. At the moment, I felt I needed something more than just being depended on. After all, I'm not a camel, though I had to wonder if Delia ever saw it differently.

CHAPTER 26

A T FIVE, JUST as the sun got low in the winter
sky, she called me.

"He says I'm to go to a pay phone on Wiltshire and
wait for it to ring. Says to leave right now and to put
the top down on my car. I told him I would."

"Is Brad there?"

"No, he's out playing golf."

"Okay," I said, "you know what to do." Kind of
made me wonder, though, why in hell was Brad always out playing golf? Didn't he know what Delia
was going through?

"Yes," she said.

"Then let's do it."

Ever since yesterday when Delia told me the guy
had called, I'd been working on a plan, and Delia and
I had talked it over last night on the way to her TV
studio. Part of the problem was to shake the tail Rick
had put on her. Now that I was *persona non grata* so
far as Brad and Rick were concerned, it seemed to me
that if Rick's boys started following her around they
were just going to muck things up. In a way, it might
have been nice to have them close by just in case

more trouble broke out than I could handle, but I couldn't figure any way to get them involved without blowing the whole thing. I thought I'd worked that out. I hired the hotel's Rolls again to go to Delia's apartment building. The driver was to wait by a side exit, all day if necessary. When the time came, she would sneak into it and it would bring her back to me at the Peninsula, which was not far away.

Meanwhile, that morning I rented myself a green BMW convertible just like hers and picked it up yesterday evening. Since the creep had put the latest envelope in her car, he obviously knew what she drove, and I was proud of myself for predicting that he'd make her keep the top down so he could be sure nobody would be hiding in the backseat. This way, when we showed up at the phone booth, wherever it was, the creep, if he was watching, would think she was alone in her own car. Not only wouldn't she be, but I'd be in the trunk of the rented one, with Delia at the wheel, waiting. I hoped, for the chance to bring this to an end.

Luckily, in the BMW convertible, the top sinks down behind the seat, so there's air to the trunk. I had instructed Delia, when she arrived at the ultimate meeting place he'd undoubtedly direct her to, to be absolutely sure to pull the trunk-release latch on the dashboard. Meantime, I had bought a length of lamp wire from a hardware store to tie down the trunk lid so it wouldn't pop up all the way, but instead only an inch or so, until I was ready to make my move. I'd also bought a neat little battery-operated intercom hookup that the clerk said would transmit her voice from the front seat to the trunk without her having to talk right into it. This way we could stay in communication with me hiding in the trunk.

There was, of course, an element of danger in all this. But I concluded that if this lowlife had wanted to harm Delia, he already had opportunities. So what he wanted now, from the tone of his letters, was some kind of sexual liaison. In his twisted mind, he apparently believed Delia must be turned on by his squalid intrigues, which was exactly what we wanted him to believe.

Whatever happened, she was not to get into a car with him, or enter any building, or go anyplace where I couldn't clearly see her. To ensure against this, at the hardware store I bought not one but three warning devices for her to carry. A whistle around her neck, tucked into her blouse, a sort of wristwatch siren that could be activated by simply pulling a little fob, and a larger alarm she could carry in her slacks pocket that the hardware clerk said sounded "like all hell was breaking loose." I'd also added a small can of spray Mace designed to look like a tube of lipstick.

In addition, I was delighted to discover when I'd rented the BMW that for a little extra it came with a portable cellular phone, which I could stick in my pocket in case 911 was needed. I would, of course, also have my gun. I slipped it into the waistband of my pants and went downstairs. In a few minutes the Rolls pulled up, as instructed, into my hotel's parking garage where I'd left the identical BMW.

"All right," I said, "are you sure you want to go through with this?"

"Yes," she said, and gave me a tight hug.

I climbed into the trunk and she got into the car.

"Hit the trunk release," I said into the intercom.

She did and it opened. I made her do it one more time for good measure. I pulled it shut, then the car started and we were on our way. From the time she left her apartment to where we were now couldn't have taken more than fifteen minutes and Melrose was just a few blocks away. The timing so far was good.

"I see the phone booth," she said. "I'm pulling over."

I heard the door shut and waited in the darkness of the trunk. I didn't hear a phone ring, but I did hear her get back into the car.

"It's the beach," she said. "Near Malibu."

"Good," I said. "It means he wants to get a look at you in the clear too—make sure you're alone and not being followed."

It took about forty minutes to get there. At the ocean road intersection Delia was to turn right and go exactly 6.3 miles and turn in on a gap in the sand dunes. She was then to get out and walk north along the water's edge for ten minutes, until she came up perpendicular to a beach house with a red roof. If lights were on in the house, she was to walk toward it and go in; if it was dark, she should wait in front by the water.

It almost seemed too perfect. While she walked

down the beach, I could get out of the trunk and, in the near dark, follow her on a parallel path along the dunes. She wouldn't be out of my sight for an instant and I'd have a clear view of the creep if he made any move toward her. Since we'd agreed that she wouldn't go into the house, I felt she was safe as could be under the circumstances.

"Okay, I'm going," Delia said through the intercom. The trunk lid popped, I heard her door shut, waited a full minute, and then lifted the lid just enough to slip out into the ground. I crouched and turned toward the ocean and my breath caught in my throat. Something I hadn't counted on. Mist!

It was rolling in off the Pacific and draped the beach like a pall. I could barely see Delia, walking slowly by the water's edge. My heart was racing as I bent low along the dunes only faintly lit by the dying sun, which appeared sickly white through gaps in the soup. Delia didn't look back even though she knew I was close by and it seemed to take forever to get to the appointed place. I looked at my watch and trailed behind her by twenty or thirty yards, trying frantically to keep her in sight. The only good thing about this was that the creep would have trouble detecting me too.

Finally she stopped and looked up at the dunes toward a house with a red roof you could barely make out. No lights were on. She waited and I stopped, expecting at any moment to see the scumbag come walking out toward her. Minutes passed and I could actually feel the blood pumping in my temples. So far as I could tell, the beach was empty, except for us. I sank back against the sand and tried to make myself as invisible as possible. A few cars passed by on the road, but none stopped. We waited longer; now it was almost dark. A car went by on the road behind the dunes and I heard it slow down. I thought I heard it stop near where the red-roofed house would be but couldn't be sure. Moments later I heard it take off again, accelerating rapidly. We continued to wait. My watch said she'd been standing there for twenty minutes. I figured it was enough and snaked along the dunes toward Delia until I was nearly opposite her. She was looking up toward the dunes. I didn't know if she could see me, but I motioned for her to start back for the car. The creep hadn't told her how long to wait, but I figured if he hadn't made his move by now, he wasn't going to show.

I was about to move closer to Delia when something suddenly caught the corner of my eye, beyond her, in the mist. A shape appeared, walking briskly up the beach. At first I thought it was two people, but it was only one, wearing some kind of knee-length cloak and carrying a stick or cane. Delia saw him too—at least I guessed it was a him—he couldn't have been more than a few yards away from her. I saw her turn and step back abruptly. I didn't wait. I raced toward them, feet barely touching the sand, and the two of us converged on her almost simultaneously. He saw me rushing too and it startled him, because he stopped, and as I flew into the scene, he instinctively raised the stick. I took no chances but dove at him thigh-high. I heard Delia scream. My blow bowled him over in the sand just at the water's edge. He began to holler and flail at me with the stick. By then I was on top of him, my hands at his throat and my fist cocked; in that same instant I felt myself sag. I was looking into the terrified face of an old man. He must have been in his eighties. His eyes were wild and he was crying, "Please! Please!"

I was too stunned for a moment to let go. He was certainly nobody I recognized. Delia was there too, standing over us, speechless. The water was lapping at the old man's head, and he was trembling. I got up slowly, leaving him cringing in the sand, still pleading.

"I'm sorry, I . . . I thought you were somebody else . . ." I said stupidly.

"Please," he continued.

I tried to help him up, but he shrank away from me and began to beg again, "Please! Please!"

Finally he allowed us to help him up. He didn't seem to be hurt.

"I'm very sorry," I repeated. "Somebody's been trying to attack this lady. I thought it was you."

"What? Are you some kind of nut!" he shouted.

"I can't tell you how sorry—"

"Get away from me!" he said, backing away down the beach. In a few moments, he was lost in the mist.

"Jesus," I said to Delia.

"Jesus," she said.

When we got back, I climbed into the driver's seat and backed into the road. I drove down to where the red-roofed house was and turned into the drive. It seemed completely deserted and, in fact, it was. I got out and peered into a window and there was no furniture inside. The screens were locked and there was sand on the decks and terraces. It hadn't been lived in for a while. I went back to the car.

"It may have been a test or a trick," I said. "He might have just wanted to see if you'd do it."

She shook her head. "I was so scared."

"It had to be a test" I said. "I heard a car stop on the road for a moment or two near the house, where there's a big gap in the dunes. He could have just hesitated for a few seconds and had a clear view of you standing on the beach. I'd say he checked you out to see if you'd come alone, but he didn't have any intention of making his move tonight. Just wanted to see how far you were prepared to go."

"This is just, just . . ."

"I expect you'll hear from him again," I said. "Fairly soon. If I suspect right, and it was somebody in the car, he'd gone before that mess on the beach."

"What about the house?" she asked.

"Nobody home. It's empty."

"Was there a name or anything?"

"I didn't see one, but it wouldn't matter. He's not going to use a house he has any connections with. He just picked it because of the red roof and because he knew he could see you on the beach from the road from there."

I got back into the driver's seat. "Need a drink?" I asked.

"No—well, yes, I do, but, no thanks. I'd better get back home. I left a note for Brad that I was just going shopping for a while. I think we're supposed to go out to dinner."

I took Delia back to the hotel, parked the car in the garage, and sent her home in the Rolls. When I got back to my room, I saw my shirt was stained with sweat. This butthole was smart and he was careful and I figured next time wouldn't be so easy. Hell, he might even have been in some clandestine perch where he'd watched me get out of the trunk, but I thought the guy in the car was more likely. I ordered a bowl of soup from room service and drank a whole bottle of wine, but I couldn't get to sleep until the early hours of morning.

NEXT DAY ABOUT ten the phone rang. It was Kevin, the videotape man.

"Well, that was easy," he said, "for what it's worth."

"What's that?"

"I got your list of DXT customers," he said.

"Already?"

"Yeah, pal of mine that works there—the one I told you about—he knew somebody in sales and they just gave it to him. He faxed it to me a few minutes ago."

"Great. How many customers are there?"

"Eight or nine hundred, I guess. There's another list with foreign customers, but he didn't get that."

"That's okay. I'm pretty sure what we're looking for is in the States."

"You got a fax? I can send it to you now."

"Yeah, great. Hang on and let me call downstairs and get the number."

I told the concierge I'd be having a fax coming in and to get it to me as soon as possible.

"Listen," I told Kevin, "I don't know if anything's going to come of this, but I want to thank you for your help."

"No sweat," he said. "But let me know how it turns out, will you?"

Fifteen minutes later a bellman brought Kevin's fax to my door. It was about six pages long, a computer printout, but it gave names and addresses and phone numbers for all the company's DXT buyers. Problem was, most of them were corporations. And they were spread out all over the country. I put the list on my desk, took a yellow highlighter pen I kept for scripts, and began to highlight all the users in New York City, Chicago, San Francisco, and L.A. There were about fifty possibles. Next I called Delia at the station and asked her to lunch. It was the longest of long shots, but maybe something would ring a bell.

"Do you think he'll call today?" Delia asked.

"Your guess is as good as mine," I said. "But I bet he can't stand waiting too long."

"I still can't figure out how he got my home number."

"Yeah, that's interesting. Have you ever given it to any of those guys on your list?"

"Nope."

"When you get a chance, why don't you look over who does have it and see if anything comes to mind."

"I was going to do that," she said.

We were seated in a back room of a place I knew near Rodeo Drive. It was nondescript and I don't think many of the patrons even recognized Delia.

"Has Brad said anything to you about telling me to stay away from you?"

"No."

"You say anything to him about it?"

"No. I'd planned to, but it never seemed the right time."

I nodded. "Well now, I've been doing a little sleuthing on my own," I told her. "I don't want you to get upset, but I've got to tell you something. Last week the slimeball sent me one of his videotapes."

"Sent you one?"

"He left it at the desk at the hotel. There was a note telling me to get uninvolved."

"Oh no, he's actually got a tape—was it . . . ?"

"Yes, and don't worry. You're not that recognizable."

"Well, you recognized me."

"I've seen you before, remember?"

"Yes, of course, but it's so . . ."

"It's sickening, what this guy will do," I said, "but there are a couple of things that came to me, but after last night I'm not so sure. So far, we've been talking about one guy, right?"

"Yes."

"Well, what if it's more than one?"

"More?"

"What if a couple of those guys you went with—and threw over—what if they got together in some way and are having some kind of perverted 'revenge,' if you will?"

"I don't understand—who?"

"Well, I know for sure that Hathaway, Greer, and Awling see you on televison. And that's just the ones I know of. Some of those guys were hurt pretty bad," I said. "And with your show appearing all over the country by satellite broadcast, it sure doesn't limit whoever it is to the L.A. area."

"That's a perfectly hideous thought," she said.

"I know it, but it might explain some stuff."

"What?"

"Well, for one thing, how those letters came to be mailed from different cities. If it was only one guy, he'd have to be a real traveling man. Didn't Brad mention any of this to you?"

"No."

"Well, it's just a theory—and maybe a bad one—but I told him and Rick about it before I left New York to come back here."

"But what about last night?" she asked.

"That's what I meant about not being so sure."

Delia rubbed her forehead with her hand and

shook her head. "I'm beginning to feel like this is making me crazy," she said.

"Well, there's something else. Like I told you, I've been doing some sleuthing. I took the cassette to a guy who's supposed to know everything about videotape. . . ."

"Johnny, you—"

"No, no, don't worry. He didn't recognize you. Anyway, this guy was able to establish that the photo was made from a certain type of commercial videotape that can be used in a hidden camera fixed someplace—in a wall maybe. And the interesting thing is that this type of videotape is very uncommon because it's basically about to be obsolete. But, in fact, there's one company that still manufactures it and I've managed to get a list of all their customers who buy this kind of tape. They are all over the country, but I've narrowed it down best I can to the ones located where you spent the most time. Like I say, it probably won't turn up anything, but it's worth a try. I have the list in my car and I want you to look at it carefully. See if you recognize any of these names as being someplace you might have gone and—"

"You don't have to say it," she finished the sentence for me.

CHAPTER 27

WHEN I GOT back to my hotel, there was a message that Kevin, the videotape man, had called again. I phoned him back.

"Man, what kinds of people are we dealing with here?" he asked tensely.

"What kinds . . . ?"

"I just came back from lunch and two guys were waiting for me in the parking lot. Big guys, and one of them grabs me and the other one puts a knife in my stomach and says if I ever get involved in this thing again, he's gonna cut out my asshole and nail it on his wall! Who are these people? Who did you tell you'd been talking to me!"

"Kevin, I didn't tell anyone except the woman in question. And your name wasn't mentioned. I promise."

It suddenly occurred to me Toby Burr also knew about Kevin because he was the one who'd referred me to him in the first place. And Toby had been a pornographer at one point . . . no, that's crazy. That's just crazy. I *am* getting paranoid, damnit!

"Well, somebody sure figured it out. I'm calling the police!"

"I don't blame you," I said. "But, look, did you maybe mention it to somebody yourself?"

"Nobody, man. I mean, this was between you and me. Except I told the guy I know up in San Francisco, so he could get that list for you, but that's all. He's an old friend. I don't think he would have said anything. Besides, I didn't tell him really what it was about, or anything. I just asked him to do me a favor."

"Well, look, I'm sorry," I said. "I don't know what's going on here. Did these guys say anything about who they were or why or anything?"

"Nothing. Just what I told you. It all happened real quick, and then they were gone."

"Did you see what kind of car they were driving?"

"Man, I didn't look back. I couldn't wait to get out of there. You should of seen these guys."

I tried to make the best of it. "Well, whoever they were, if they were going to do anything else, I expect they would have done it."

Kevin wasn't comforted. "I guarantee you, they meant business."

"Yes, I don't doubt it. I'm really sorry about this. Do whatever you have to. I'll be here if there's anything I can do—just call me."

After we hung up, I stood dumbstruck for a moment. Two guys—then it wasn't just some crackpot getting his jollies. But how in hell would they have known about Kevin? Only thing I could think of was that fax he'd sent me this morning—it had his name and number on it. Or was somebody tapping my phone? Or somehow listening in? Jesus! How in hell could they tap a phone in my hotel room? I went downstairs to see the concierge.

"A fax was sent to me this morning," I said. "Who brought it up?"

"Sir, I'm not positive, but I think it was Julio. He was assigned to me then."

"Could I talk to him?"

"He's already gone for the day, Mr. Lightfoot. He comes in at five A.M."

"I have reason to believe that somebody else got a look at it before I did. You know anything about that?"

"Sir, that couldn't happen here."

"Well, maybe not, but stranger things have gone on."

"I will certainly look into it, Mr. Lightfoot. I will call Julio at home."

"I'll be in my room," I said.

I stopped at the pay phone next to the bar and called Delia at her office. She was out, they said, so I left a message for her to call me soon as she got back. Then I rang her at home but got her answering service.

TWO HOURS LATER, just as I finally sat down in exasperation to fiddle with Burr's script, Delia called me in near hysteria.

"Johnny, I'm really frightened now," she said in a trembling voice. "I don't have much time, Brad's due back any minute."

"Where are you?"

"Home."

"I'll call you back in two minutes. Stay by the phone."

"No," she said. "I can't—"

"Do it," I told her, and hung up. I ran back downstairs to a pay phone by the dining room and dialed her number. She didn't answer right away and I began thinking the worst, when she picked up.

"What is it?" I said immediately.

"I can't talk," she said urgently. "I've got to go. I'm putting some things in a bag right now."

"But what is it. Delia?"

"It's—your *list*! Listen, I'm coming over to you now. I'm—"

"No—what about Rick's guy who's watching you? He'll follow you, you know."

"I don't care. Oh yes, you're right. What do I do!"

"Okay, listen. Get in your car, drive to the service station at Beverly and Wiltshire. It's about halfway between your place and my hotel. When you get there, pull around to the side where the air pump is. Get out and look like you're putting air in your tires. I'll be there."

"Hurry, please," she said. "I'm walking out the door."

"Wait," I said. "I want you to put the top of your car down," I told her. "Be sure to do that."

"See you," she said, and hung up.

I called and told the hotel parking attendant to bring around the BMW convertible I'd rented, pronto. I'd planned to take it back this afternoon, but I was damned glad I still had it. What I had in mind was that if Rick's guys were following her, they'd see her car with the top down. I kept the top up on mine. Just a little edge. Maybe they'd be confused for a moment or two. I grabbed the gun and ran downstairs. Thankfully, the BMW was ready when I arrived. The service station was only five minutes away. It was the one I used regularly whenever I was in L.A. When I got there, I pulled around back where there was a heap of old tires and scrap stuff. I figured if Rick's guy showed up, he'd probably park somewhere across the street where he could watch her check her tires. But he wouldn't be able to see me from there.

I got out and went into the station. The manager was a guy named Tom.

"A girl I know is going to be here in a few minutes," I said, "out by the air. I want you to give her car a full lube, brake, shock inspection, and then fill her up and check everything under the hood. She'll be back later to pick it up."

He agreed cheerfully just as Delia pulled into the station. There was a door from the garage that led to the air pump area and I waited a minute till she'd had time to get out and start checking her tires and then opened the door and called to her to come over.

"Come on, we're going now," I said as she stepped inside the garage.

"My bag's in the car."

"Forget it," I said. "There isn't time. I don't want him to see you getting it out."

"But it's got all my stuff in it."

"We can buy you more stuff, damnit," I told her. "Come on."

As we walked across the cash register area, I noticed through the plate glass window a car pull up across the street. Rick's people.

I led her through the garage to another bay and to a door at the rear where I'd parked. Soon as she got in, I took off from the side of the station that would be screened from anyone watching Delia at the air pumps.

"So what's this about?" I asked.

"First let's get out of here," she said.

I headed out on a cross street toward the wide stretch of Mulholland, where I knew the BMW would be able to outrun the kinds of low-end sedans Rick's people had been using. Once on the drive I flew past any number of cars until I felt safe, then made a series of twisting turns on side streets till I found one that put me on the way back toward the Santa Monica Freeway. I was sure no one could have followed me.

"Where are we going?" she asked finally.

"Where do you want to go?"

"I was coming to your hotel. I thought I'd take a room there—maybe next to yours."

"Why?'"

"Because"—she took a heaving breath—"because I think it might be Brad," she said.

"What?"

"Can we wait to talk about it until we get to your hotel?" she asked.

"My hotel? What about Brad and Rick? I mean, first place they'd look would be my hotel. Why do you think we played this charade in the first place?"

She stared straight ahead. "God, you're right. I'm not thinking straight. I just had to get out of there. I've got to have time to think."

"Why Brad?" I asked.

"I never wanted to believe it. Don't want to now." She was still staring ahead.

I didn't prompt her. I thought it would be best to let her get it out her own way.

"The night . . . that I went to the beach. He was there when I got home," she said. "But there seemed something the matter. He didn't seem mad or anything, but he asked what I bought shopping and when I said nothing, he sort of laughed and said, 'That's a first,' or something like that. It didn't mean anything to me at the time, but, well . . ."

She hesitated for a moment and I kept my eyes on the road.

"You see, it's that satellite dish thing too. When you told me about that, I didn't think much of it, but I remembered later that Brad said he was going to put one in at his office, so he could watch sports stuff whenever he wanted to. I remember him saying he could get anything anywhere, but it never registered on me. But now that I think about it, it was almost the same time I began getting the letters."

She hesitated again and I could hear her taking deep breaths. We were passing by some little strip mall and I saw up ahead a sign over a store announcing Beer, Wine, and Liquor.

"You want a drink?" I said. "Might do you good. Here's a place."

She said she did, so I stopped and got a bottle of scotch, a paper cup, and a bag of ice. She poured herself a stiff one and took a couple of sips and began talking again.

"When I looked at that list of people who use that kind of tape, I didn't see anything at first," she said. "I mean, there were places in New York and Chicago, but I'd never been to them and certainly not for any kind of picture taking or whatever.

"But then when I came to the ones in San Francisco, it hit me like a bolt. There was one. The Onion Dungeon."

"Onion Dungeon?"

"Yes. It was a really funky place down near the Presidio. All sorts of people went there—and I mean *all* sorts. It was gay, straight, bi, everything—even drugs, I suppose—but it wasn't particularly creepy or anything. At least not in the main rooms."

She carefully poured herself another shot of scotch and leaned back with her head tilted toward the roof of the car, eyes closed.

"Brad and I had only been dating a few weeks, but

we were pretty hot and heavy by then. One Saturday night he suggested taking me there—to the Onion Dungeon. We danced and had a good time till all hours. He knew the owners. I think Rick might have done some work for them at one point. Bouncers, maybe.

"And so we went back a few more times. And once, it was very late, and I guess we'd both had a few drinks, Brad said he wanted to show me something. There were stairs down to a basement, where there were more rooms. Some had glass windows on the doors and inside you could see people doing, well . . . I was flabbergasted, but in a way it was sort of a turn-on and Brad seemed to be into it. And then he opened a door to a room where there was leather stuff hanging all over the walls. Whips, masks, odd body thonglike things—whatever. I mean, some of it, I didn't have any idea what it was for. The walls were black and there were track lights from the ceiling and paintings of people doing—well, you get the picture.

"Brad locked the door and said no one could get in. He said it was a 'private room' that the owners used. Well, we started playing around a little, and I guess one thing led to another. It was so different. I mean, it started to be a serious turn-on, and after a while we tried out some of the leather things. To make a long story short, we spent the whole night there, just . . . I don't know. It was daylight when we walked into the street."

This was the damnedest revelation imaginable.

I began to picture the scene but shook it out of mind.

"And this Onion Dungeon is on the videotape customers list?"

"There's a company on it called RayJeff Enterprises. Those are the first names of the two guys who own the Dungeon. Brad introduced me to them. It's the only place possible. It just can't be a coincidence, if they had this kind of tape. It just can't be."

"And they probably had a hidden camera in that room, huh? So the owners could get their jollies." I felt myself burn at this notion.

"They must have."

"And Brad must have got hold of the tape somehow, you think?"

"I can't think of anything else."

"But why would he do it?" I asked. It seemed the unlikeliest of unlikely scenarios.

"It started when I took this job in L.A. He didn't like it, I know, but it was a hell of an opportunity. And, well, we'd been married a year by then and, oh, you know me, Johnny, I need my space. Maybe it's why I never could keep a long relationship going. After a while I just feel smothered."

I could tell she was getting worked up and I had to make a decision. We were on the freeway now, but I couldn't just drive aimlessly forever.

"Look, I have an idea, even if it's only a temporary solution," I said. "You want to get away to think, right, so we can talk about this? Someplace secure.

There's a neat place I know up in Big Sur. And no-body finds anybody up in Big Sur."

"Well, yes, but what about my things? I don't have anything but the clothes on my back."

"Neither do I," I said. "but anybody can buy new clothes. We can stop up in Santa Barbara. There's a Bloomingdale's right off the freeway. In an hour you'll be decked out like Ivana Trump."

"I've got to call the station. Tell them I'm sick or something. I'm on air in three hours."

"Ah," I said majestically, "that's another reason I kept this little toy car. There's a cellular phone in the glove compartment."

"Well, I guess then . . ."

"Let's go," I said, and hit the accelerator.

IT DIDN'T TAKE long to get free of L.A. traffic and shortly we were cruising north along the Pacific Coast Highway, high above the white beaches and blue ocean. At Santa Barbara we stopped and bought out Bloomingdale's, including clothes, toiletries, cos-metics, bathrobes, shoes—even luggage. Must have been the fastest shopping spree in history.

"It's kind of like we're starting a whole new life," I remarked as we loaded the car, but Delia was not in the mood for jest. She remained pretty much lost in her own thoughts until the highway narrowed to a winding, twisting ribbon in between the ocean and the Santa Monica Mountains. It was truly a beautiful drive as the sun sank over the Pacific casting a golden glow across pastures and farmlands. After a while Delia started talking again.

"After a while I noticed Brad was becoming jealous. I know I told you at one point that he wasn't, but I really didn't want to admit it to myself then. It wasn't overt in the beginning, just little hints I picked up on. Looking back, I think it evolved into real jealousy, that he knew that wasn't going to change anything and in fact he was just making things worse, but he couldn't help himself. But Brad is devious. I've learned that too. I thought he must have got that way building up his business. Anyway, I can't see any explanation than that he cooked up this whole scheme to scare me into leaving here and going back to San Francisco, or maybe if that didn't work, he'd actually send those pictures to the tabloids to either get me fired or to shame me so I'd have to quit. Oh, I don't know, I don't know . . . it's really almost too much to comprehend. It's so, so . . ."

"Delia, listen," I said, "you may very well be right about this. You know Brad, but I just can't believe this."

"Oh, I know it's him! I just know it!" she said, and for the second time since I'd known Delia Jamison, I saw her cry.

VENTANA WAS THE name of the place we pulled up at a little while later. It was a grand little resort that offered exotic asylum to celebrities and the rich, set on a hillside near the ocean and surrounded by towering firs. I'd called ahead from the car to make reservations and a bellman led us to our rooms, each of which was paneled in polished wood, and each with a fireplace. Typically, Delia insisted on paying her own way, and after we got situated, she said she wanted to take a hot bath. I told her I'd see her in an hour or so for dinner.

I took a shower and then lit a fire. I could hardly imagine what must have been going through her mind. If it was all true, this kind of squalid disloyalty had to be the work of twisted desperation.

She hardly touched her food, which was a shame, since the inn had a five-star dining room. It was late in the year and Christmas decorations were already put up. Even though Big Sur's climate was a lot chillier than L.A.'s, Christmas decorations on the Pacific Ocean just seemed out of character to me. East Coast snobbery, perhaps.

"Well, what happens next?" I finally asked.

"I don't know. I can't go back. I won't go back. I called the station manager again a while ago and told him I had to have a vacation—a couple of weeks. He surprised me. He just said okay, didn't even ask why or anything."

"We can stay here as long as you want to, but the best thing right now is to get a good night's rest and then we can start sorting it out in the morning. But at some point, though, you're going to have to confront Brad with this."

"I know," Delia said flatly. "I just wonder if there's any way to make absolutely sure."

"Let's sleep on that," I told her. As I looked at her sad face, I couldn't help thinking how beautiful she was, even at a time like this.

It also was not lost on me that this new development would probably spell the end of her marriage. I had never contemplated that before, and it left me with mixed emotions.

Our rooms were next to each other's and as I walked her back, a big silver half-moon loomed over the mountains. It seemed grimly ironic that this was just the kind of romantic hideaway I'd dreamed of taking Delia to for so long. And now that I'd succeeded, the circumstances made it all grotesque.

CHAPTER 28

WE STAYED AT Ventana three days and I watched Delia's outlook turn from melancholy upward as the days passed and she tried to come to grips with the hideous dimensions of her situation. The morning after we arrived, she emerged from her room in a far better mood than the night before. We had a good breakfast and then she came with me to my room, where we sat out on the wide terrace in big bentcane chairs, basking in the warm Pacific sun as it climbed above the mountains.

"I'm thinking of writing him a letter," she said.

"That's one way," I agreed.

"I just can't imagine facing him about it. It would be so horribly embarrassing for both of us."

"You don't think he'd harm you, do you? After all, he's had endless opportunities to do that already, and hasn't."

"I don't think so," she said. "But he does have a violent side. He's never hit me or anything like that. But sometimes he throws things and breaks them and kicks at stuff. One time he kicked his dog all the way across the room. That really shocked me."

It was still a little hard to believe that Delia, with her impeccable shit-detector, hadn't picked up on something along these lines earlier. She was by nature a suspicious woman. Maybe she was blinded by love, but I doubted it. She didn't act to me like a woman in love.

"Sometimes I don't know what he's capable of," she said. "Sometimes I think the man I married was not the man I fell in love with. It's like the man I fell in love with isn't here anymore and he's taken his place."

"This came on suddenly?"

"No. Over time, months."

"But I don't understand how—if he actually is doing this thing—you wouldn't have had much stronger feelings. I mean, for a person to do this, he has to be totally warped. Almost insane. You didn't see any of that?"

She shook her head. "No, but we were only seeing each other weekends, and he played golf a lot and we went out to dinner and did things with other people. But then, I wasn't looking for it either."

There was still coffee in the pot they'd brought me when I got up that morning and I poured another cup. She went into the bathroom. All the things I'd heard about Delia began to come round again. Whenever she split from guys, almost always there'd been something forced about it. She'd claimed Arthur Dalton drank too much. Got mad at Bothwell because he'd suggested she was late-dating him, and she'd split from Homer Greer after he asked her to move in. Likewise, Vining had apparently "gotten too close," and she'd accused LaCosta of representing crooks. And she flew off the handle with me because I'd edited her stories. Made me wonder if she wasn't just looking for another excuse. It was preposterous, but who could help but wonder.

"Well, there's one way we might find out," I said after she'd returned to the porch. "Suppose we go up to San Francisco and visit this Onion Dungeon place? Sniff around and see if we can find that room you described and if it has hidden cameras. That would pretty much cinch it."

"I don't want to go there again. It's just too disgusting and—"

"No, no, you're right. But suppose I go myself?"

"I'm not sure how you'd go about getting into that room. Like I said, it was my impression from Brad that it was private—that you had to know the owners or something, like he did."

"Wait a minute. Didn't you say Rick had some connection to the place too?"

"Yes. He had something to do with security. Bouncers or whatever."

"I guess it doesn't matter. I'm supposed to be off the case, unless you want to call Rick yourself."

"And say what?"

"I see what you mean."

"Johnny," she said, "can I use the car this afternoon? I'd like to go for a drive, just by myself."

* * *

SHE LEFT JUST after lunch and didn't return until nearly dark. She seemed refreshed. After dinner we went to my room again and I lit another fire and we watched TV for a while and read books from the inn's library. We tried to talk about things unconnected with present events.

"Johnny, are you happy?" she asked.

I remember she'd asked the same question the first night I'd seen her in L.A. when we'd had dinner. We always seemed to ask each other that when there wasn't anything else to say, as if in fact we weren't, and needed to know why.

"Sure. Shouldn't I be?"

"It's just that it seems we all press so hard to get ahead, be successful, live the kind of lives we think we're supposed to, that sometimes we forget to ask ourselves that."

"Well, I'm not doing exactly what I really wanted to do," I told her. "I always wanted to be a great novelist—or rather a really good novelist. But it looks like that's not in the cards. I'm not ashamed of anything I wrote, but I'm probably doomed to what publishers refer to as mid-list, which means no matter how good it is, they most likely won't promote it much with their sales staff or in ads and everything, and it becomes a self-fulfilling prophecy."

"But does that matter?" Delia asked. "I mean, if you think it's good, what's the difference if you don't sell a jillion copies?"

"It ought not to matter, but it does. I guess that's where writers' egos need to be massaged. It's the acclaim, I suppose. It's the difference between a pretty good football player for the New York Giants who's sort of second string versus the hero of the Super Bowl."

"I never thought you felt like that," she said.

"And you," I asked, "I know all this business occupies you right now, but before, weren't you happy? I mean, months ago?"

"It's like I told you, I think I was rushing so fast I never stopped to ask the question."

"If I ask it again, would it make a difference?"

"I guess I'm happy, in some ways, just like you. I've got all the success I suppose I can expect in this business—at least at this level. I guess the top would be to become another Tom Brokaw or Diane Sawyer, but somehow that doesn't thrill me anymore. Sometimes I get tired of working at all, just to be rid of the pressure and settle down in the little cottage with the white picket fence."

"Do you want to stay out here on the coast?"

"If I had my choice, I'd be back east. I feel more comfortable there."

"So do I," I told her.

NEXT MORNING I had a surprise. I told her to bring a book and that we were going for a beach picnic. The dining room fixed us a super lunch basket and we took some blankets and drove to a spot I knew where you could go down to the ocean. After a walk we emerged in a calm secluded little cove of clear blue water surrounded by huge evergreens. Out toward the sea, breakers exploded on the beach, and out further from that were huge conical rock formations, silhouetted against an azure sky.

"Oh, Johnny, I'd love to just dive in right now."

"You'd dive out a lot quicker if you knew how cold this water is."

"It just looks so tempting."

"Well, there's a great heated pool back at the inn with a secret grotto. I'll stop off and buy us some swimsuits if you want."

The winter sun was warm and we found a spot in the lee of high banks and spread our blankets. I had found a good California Chardonnay and we lunched on fresh tomatoes and cheeses and avocado dip.

"It's like there's nobody else in the world, out here," Delia said afterward. "The sun is heavenly." Without further comment she pulled off her sweater and unbuttoned her blouse and took it off too and lay back in the sand, wearing only a bra. This development of course left me confused. During these past days I had felt protective toward her more than anything else and the undercurrent of sexual tension hadn't been present. At least not until now. Was she sending a signal or just indulging in West Coast hip? Whatever it was, it reminded me of that first winter we went to Bermuda when she'd lain on the beach with her face to the sun, except then she'd kept her shirt on. I buried myself in a book and tried not to look and the afternoon wore down, slowly, quixotically, painfully, and with an aura of imagined bliss.

When we finally left the beach, the sun was sinking again. On the way back to the inn we picked up the swimsuits and after we'd changed, she met me at the pool. The suit she'd chosen was a modest black one-piece, but on Delia it became deliciously sumptuous. It was one of the things that had always intrigued me about her. In public her dress and often her manners were demure, even prudish at times, but alone she could be astonishingly wicked.

The water was warm and the contrast between it and the cold Pacific air was refreshing. Steam poured off the top of the pool, which was empty of swimmers except for us. We swam around for a while, and then she ducked under a stone bridge that led to the grotto. I followed. It was close and comfortable in there and the water seemed super-heated. It was about shoulder-deep and after a few moments I felt hands around my waist and then was pulled backward against Delia's chest. I felt her legs against my thighs and heard her giggling.

"Did you ever see porpoises play?" she asked.

"Sure, but they don't grab each other unexpectedly, do they?"

She turned bottoms up and came beneath me and popped up in front.

"Let's swim like porpoises," she said, and dived under the stone bridge again. We swam the length of the pool several times, side by side, rising and diving and occasionally rubbing against each other. Finally, exhausted, we hauled ourselves out at the end of the pool and toweled off in the chilly air but still warm from the water.

"What time's dinner?" she asked.

"How about half an hour?"

"Good. I'm famished."

I TOOK HER away from the inn this time, to a kind of Bohemian restaurant overlooking the ocean a few miles away. We had schnitzel and German potatoes and hot sauerkraut and a bottle of German wine.

"Even with all that's happened," she said, "I actually feel a little relieved. I mean, I still feel terrible in a way, but somehow I think I'm coming to the end of it. I want to thank you for everything, Johnny." She reached across the table and took my hand in both of hers.

Afterward, as we walked back toward our rooms, I asked her if she wanted to come over to mine for a nightcap.

"Sure. But I think I'll change first," she said.

I lit a fire and put some ice in a bucket. I'd brought in the bottle of scotch from the car and also opened myself a bottle of Spanish port I'd found in a little wine store down the road. Presently there was a knock on the door and Delia was standing there, one hand on her hip, her head cocked to the side, wearing a gray silk robe with tangerine trim. She looked like a billion dollars.

"Want to buy some ladies' lingerie?" she laughed.

"Only if it's in my size," I said. Despite my earlier uneasiness, I somehow sensed this could be a long and productive evening. Delia suddenly seemed vibrant with terrific energy; her deep green eyes had a glow and sparkle I hadn't seen in years.

She plopped herself down on the sofa and drew her legs up under her in front of the fire, staring intently into it.

"Johnny," she said, "how many times have you been in love?"

"Well now, that's—do you mind if I count on my fingers?"

"Go ahead, just be honest."

I thought for a moment.

"Let me put it this way," I said, "I probably *thought* I was in love maybe five, six times in my life. The times I've actually been in love, maybe once."

"With who?"

"You."

"Now that wasn't really love," she said authoritatively. "I think you just *thought* you were in love with me too."

"No, it was real," I said.

"How can you be sure?"

"People know these things."

"So why didn't you tell me so?"

"I did, once or twice, at least I tried to. But after that I got tired of getting my hand slapped every time I even hinted at it."

"That's not fair."

"It certainly is."

"Then it wasn't honest," she said. "If you'd just gone ahead and admitted it, even if I'd rejected it, it would have been . . . noble."

"If that's your notion of nobility or honesty, I want no part of it. If I'm going to get kicked in the teeth, I'd as soon not do it on bended knee. You never gave it time."

"I was young."

"Yes, you've said that before."

I got up to pour another glass of port and when I did stopped behind the sofa and put my hands on her shoulders. She leaned back as I massaged her, murmuring in pleasure. I touched her gently but firmly and she seemed to totally relax. Her robe fell open, exposing an expanse of breast. After a while I leaned over and put my cheek against hers. This didn't seem to bother her, but when I moved to kiss her, she turned away.

"No, Johnny . . . I'm married . . . thought we'd . . ."

"Okay, okay, I'm sorry," I said, straightening up. "But there's something I don't understand. What was all that today on the beach with taking off your blouse, and then in the pool, all the touching and rubbing and, and that business a while back about you wanting to remember the 'old times,' and then showing up here in your nightgown and—"

"Oh, c'mon—I was just playing, having fun."

"Just a game, huh?"

"No, not anything like that. That's not the way I

meant it. I just felt so close to you—like somebody I can really trust."

"Good old Johnny—is that it? Good old faithful Johnny?"

"Well, that's not—no, that isn't the way I meant it. I'm just trying to be honest."

"Well, you know, damnit, I've got feelings too," I said, moving in front of the fire. I'd about had enough. "And I'm getting a little tired of all your vaunted 'honesty,' Delia, which you seem to use as a shield to make yourself feel superior. You do that, you know—sort of like little Goody Two-Shoes. And by the way, Goody Two-Shoes was a fraud."

"I do what's right."

"No matter who it hurts?"

"No matter who it hurts. It's the best way, the only way. I learned that a long time ago."

"In boarding school?"

"Yes, that's one place. I suppose Frankie told you all about that too."

"He did."

"Well, it taught me a valuable lesson."

"Yeah, but the problem is that for you, Delia, the truth is whatever *you* say it is, but it never occurs to you that what's 'honesty' in your view might be bull-shit to somebody else."

"I don't care about the somebody elses. I've got my own sense of right and wrong. That's enough."

"Maybe so, but that doesn't mean that I've got the

morals of a ghoul either. I'm getting the impression that all you really want here is to just reconfirm to yourself that you're still an object of desire. And once you've verified that, you back away, 'keep your distance,' withdraw. You did it with me before, many times, and you're doing it again now. And how the hell do you think it makes *me* feel? I always wanted to be your hero, Delia—or at least a hero to you—but what I get in return is behavior that's best described by a high school phrase."

The conversation suddenly began to remind me of that unpleasant scene in *Little Women* between Lawrence and Jo. . . .

"That's not true."

"No, because you don't want to believe it. You know what I think this is all about, Delia? It's about control. That this is one way you can establish it over people—over men. Normally men are supposed to be the control freaks, but in your case, it's the opposite. Even the way you made love, you're always the one who had to be in control."

"You didn't seem to mind, if I remember correctly," she said coolly, straightening up.

"No, because it was new, and, sure, it was exciting, but the more I look back on it, it was a kind of trap too. Because you're a builder of traps, Delia. And a good one. Lately I've seen the wreckage. But in your self-righteousness, you always suspect trap-building from the men in your life, and always with *you* as their intended victim, and that's when you split."

"And mostly I've been correct," she said, rising, pulling her robe about her as though she was suddenly chilled. "It certainly appears that way about Brad. And what about you, Johnny? You've been laying a trap for me since we ran into each other that first night at the Peninsula Hotel. And even before that, in the old days back in New York, you were always scheming for some way to get me to fall in love with you. But I didn't. I even tried, but I couldn't."

"No, I guess not. Although I'll still be damned if I understand your notion of 'trying' to fall in love with somebody. And it wasn't just me—I've heard you 'tried' with other people too. What about good old Professor Vining? He couldn't get over it either, about how calculating it seemed."

"Well, it was honest, and that's the way it was, and that's the way it is," she said icily, making for the door.

"Horseshit, Delia. Have you ever walked around a movie lot? Stroll down one street and you're in Dickens's London, turn right and you're in Orwell's Calcutta, make a left and suddenly you're in Henry James's New York, or maybe there's Mel Gibson on the *Road Warrior* set, dressed in a bearskin and wearing a stockpot on his head. And it's all as phony as a three-dollar bill. . . ."

"Look, I'm—"

"No, let me finish!" I said. "Because then we turn down some side street and there *you* are, Delia—superior in your own little smug alley. But the fact is, you lie like everybody else when you have to, and you know it. And what you call 'honesty' is just something that saves you time."

"I'll see you in the morning," she said.

After she'd gone, I sat on the hearth by the dying embers of the fire, her words still ringing in my head with a terrible finality I'd refused to believe for way too long.

CHAPTER 29

WHAT SLEEP I had that night was restive and next morning at seven I got off for San Francisco, which, with the twisting roads, was about a three-hour drive. Delia wasn't awake, so I left a note under her door telling her where I was going.

The whole drive up, through Carmel and along the peninsula road, was some of the most spectacular scenery on earth, but I was in no mood for it. I felt like just driving back to L.A. and getting back to work, but I'd already resigned myself that, whatever else, I was in this now to the end, which didn't seem far away. I'd do the best I could to find out if Brad had access to the film of himself and Delia and if I could establish that, the rest was up to her and I'd be rid of the whole repulsive affair. I regretted in a way I'd ever got mixed up in it, but I guess I'd learned some things along the way, not only about her, but about myself. Toby Burr had probably pegged it right—I *did* have all the things I wanted, and the only things that mattered were those I couldn't have. It was childish and I felt disgusted with myself over it.

In San Francisco I checked into a suite at the Fairmont, big high-up corner rooms overlooking the cold blue water and the shining white city. Christmas was only a week away now and I called my travel agent to make arrangements to go back east and see my folks for the holidays. A different coast, a world apart, and I somehow wished I'd never have to see the Pacific Ocean again. I vowed that after I finished this script for Burr, I'd sit down and write another novel and this one would be damned good. I owed it to myself.

I had lunch at a place offering West Coast oysters and abalone and then went back to my room to take a nap. About five I showered and dressed and headed out for the Onion Dungeon. I figured the best time to find out something was before the crowd arrived. The Dungeon was in a kind of seedy warehouse district and faded lettering on its grimy brick facade told me it had once been a place for manufacturing sewing machines.

It was closed up tight for the moment, so I drove around awhile, stopping at a little pull-off where I could view Alcatraz Island out in the middle of the bay. If it'd been up to me, if Brad was in fact the culprit, that's where he would be spending time for putting her, *and* me, through all this, but my guess was that she'd just confront him with it, get a divorce, and have her lawyer read him the riot act about letting any of those pictures or tapes get out.

When I returned to the Dungeon, the door was unlocked, but nobody was inside that I could see. I heard noises in the back, so I waited at the bar and presently a good-looking brunette in red leather hot pants and a white shirt appeared. She was the bartender and seemed surprised to see anybody in there at this hour.

"Heard about this place through friends," I told her. "I'm just in town for a few days and thought I'd check it out."

"You're gonna have to do some waiting for anything much to check out," she said. "Nobody really starts getting here till about nine or ten."

"Well, I don't have anything better to do," I said. "Maybe I'll just have a drink or two and then come back later."

I ordered a beer and swiveled my stool to take a look around. It was pretty much what I'd expected, but I didn't see any door that looked like it led downstairs. There was a long, wide hallway, though, going someplace and that's probably where it was located.

"You from San Francisco?" I asked.

"Nope, Seattle," she said.

"Which do you like best?"

"I'm here, aren't I?"

"My friends tell me wild things go on here."

"Wild things go on everywhere," she said as she rearranged bottles of booze.

"I enjoy wild things sometimes."

"Yeah, what line of work are you in?"

"I'm a writer."

"What kind of writer?"

"Books, movies."

"Anything I've seen?"

I mentioned a few. She perked up at this news and it seemed to loosen her up. I thought she looked a little like Veronica Lake, with a straight lock of hair swept over one eye. We talked for a while about movies, what she liked and didn't. Typical American theatergoer. She said her name was Sunshine. San Francisco is about the only place left I can think of where people still call themselves names like "Sunshine."

"Say," I said, "you ever know a guy named Brad who comes here sometimes?"

"Brad, I don't think so—oh, wait a minute. A kind of cute guy? Forty-something? He's friends with Rick?"

"Yeah," I said, "that's him. He's a friend of mine too. So's Rick."

"Rick's a prince of a guy," she said. "His company's our security."

"What's that, bouncers and stuff?"

"Everything, bouncers, the cameras, alarm systems—all of it."

"Cameras?" I asked. "What cameras?"

"Oh, we have them in places," Sunshine said. "Need to make sure nobody goes too far, if you know what I mean. Occasionally we'll get some serious weirdos in here."

"Brad told me there's a room downstairs with cameras."

"Three or four rooms," she said.

"This room's private."

"They're all private—maybe he's talking about

Ray and Jeff's room—they're the owners. It's kind of their special thing for them and their friends."

"And there are cameras there? Just kind of recording the action, huh?"

"Look, it's their room. They own this place. If they got cameras in there, I suppose they have a right to, if they want."

"Rick or Brad come here often?" I asked.

"Not too much. I haven't seen Brad in a good while. He got married, you know? And Rick, he comes in when he's in town. He moved down to L.A., but he was in here about ten days ago, though."

"Yeah, I talked to him just before he left. Said he was on his way to San Francisco."

"It was too bad about his wife," Sunshine remarked. "I don't think Rick's really been the same since it happened. That's why he was here, you know? He visits her at the cemetery."

"She killed herself, I understand."

"That's putting it mildly. Do you know what she did?"

"No."

"Committed hara-kiri, right next to him in bed one night. Just took out a knife and twisted it through her stomach. She was Japanese, you know?"

"Good Lord."

"Didn't make a sound. He didn't even know she'd done it till he woke up next morning all covered with blood—kind of like that scene with the horse in *The Godfather,* you know?"

"Anybody know why she did it?" I asked.

Sunshine shook her head. "He never talked about it much."

"So I guess Rick comes here to inspect his work; I mean, the cameras and things?" I said.

"I don't know about that. I've never seen him do anything but have a few drinks and leave. But he's got keys to everything. I don't know what he does."

I thanked Sunshine and left her a twenty and went back to the Fairmont. By now it was dinnertime, but I wasn't really hungry. I sat in my living room in the dark and watched the twinkling of lights across the bay. What I'd found out pretty much cinched it. Rick provided the videotape that his good pal Brad had needed. They must have enjoyed sending me on a wild-goose chase all across America, the sons of bitches. Must have gotten a good laugh out of it all. And Brad, that warped bastard, doing that to his own wife just to bring her back into what he imagined was his fold. Any guy worth his salt would have gone ahead and had it out with her straight off, and if she wouldn't quit the L.A. job and come back, then you walk away. Of course, with Delia, that would have only made her more determined not to.

I didn't realize how exhausted I was from the lack of sleep the night before and the early drive, and at some point I dozed off in the chair. Dawn was breaking when I woke up. So I packed up and left the hotel, deciding I'd beat the morning traffic, and headed back to Big Sur.

*   *   *

THE BMW TOOK to the curvy road like it was on roller-coaster tracks. Out of San Francisco traffic I stopped, gassed up, put the convertible top down, and made a phone call from the service station to check my messages back in L.A. Burr had launched his usual blizzard of calls, Meredith had phoned once, and there was one or two from friends. But nothing from Brad or Rick, which surprised me. I'd have thought they would have at least tried to get in touch with me once it was discovered Delia had taken off. They probably had, and not left a message.

I wasn't feeling great and I realized I wasn't anxious to get back to Big Sur. In a way I wanted to get there and get it over with, but after the scene with Delia two nights ago, I knew this would also be the end of it between us, no matter what happened with Brad and her marriage. The past couple of days had been like watching a glass of exquisite champagne go flat. Despite everything, Delia was still an object of desire, but, in the long run, facts are better than dreams.

Since I hadn't had breakfast, I stopped off in Monterey, where I had a filleted slab of lemon-buttered sea bass with scrambled eggs and toast at a quaint place on Monterey Bay, which Steinbeck used as the setting for so many of his stories. By the time I got back to Ventana, it was nearly noon. When I passed by her room, I noticed her door was open. I looked in and a maid was cleaning up. I didn't see any of her things—the room was bare. I went immediately to the front desk.

"Did Miss Jamison check out?" I asked.

The clerk looked at a register. "Yes, sir, she did. I think it was a few hours ago. She left you a note." He handed me a sealed envelope of the inn's stationery.

"Dear Johnny," it said, "I'm going back to L.A. with Rick. Don't worry, everything's okay. Thanks for all. Delia."

"Were you here when she checked out?" I said.

"Yes, sir."

"Did she seem all right?"

"She didn't come in herself. A gentleman came in and said he was checking out for her. I saw another gentleman carrying luggage to a car."

"What did the guy who checked her out look like?"

"He was a tall guy. I'd say in his early forties, blond hair."

Jesus, I realized, it was Rick. "What about the one carrying her luggage? What'd he look like?"

"Older, sort of heavyset. Bald with gray hair on the sides," he said, puzzled.

That ruled out Brad, I thought. Probably somebody who worked with Rick.

"Look, when she went with them, did she seem okay? I know this is a strange question, but I need to know."

"I never saw her," he said. "I guess she was already in the car, because after the gentleman checked her out, he got in the back and they all drove off."

"When he checked her out, did he sign the bill or anything?"

"No, sir, but she'd left her credit card when she

checked in. I asked if she needed a receipt, but he said she didn't, to just go ahead and run the charges. I did because I thought they were in a hurry to get to the airport."

Damn, I thought, her credit card! They must have somehow been able to track her through her credit card!

"Why do you think they went to an airport?"

"Because they were driving in one of those kinds of cars they rent at the airport up in Carmel. It's a small strip and they only have two or three of them. But a lot of people who stay with us rent them to come down here."

"I'm checking out too," I said. "Just run my charges like you did hers, okay?" I rushed back to my room and threw my stuff in the suitcase, put the suitcase in the BMW, and headed for Carmel. I'd passed the Carmel airport on the way up to San Francisco; it was about an hour away.

If the clerk was right about where the car had come from, Carmel was the place to go. Certainly something was very wrong. Rick shows up at Ventana—coincidentally when I'm not there. Since she wasn't supposed to take any phone calls, what happened? Did she call him? Or Brad? Unlikely. So Rick arrives on his plane and suddenly she's gone in a big hurry. What did that mean? She didn't even come in to check out or go over her bill. Nobody even saw her get into the car. Was it that she was so put out by our conversation two nights ago that she just decided to up and leave? Knowing Delia, maybe—but why with Rick, since she still had the sticky situation with Brad to deal with? It didn't make sense.

I got to the Carmel airport about one-thirty. It wasn't a big place and there was a guy standing around a tiny glassed-in office who by his dress could have doubled for a maintenance man.

"Sometime this morning," I said, "I think a plane landed here and a couple of guys got off and rented a car. Am I right?"

"Yeah, we've had some planes, but the guys who rented the car, I remember them. We don't have but two cars we rent."

"Are they still here?"

"Nope. They came back and then took off an hour or so ago."

"Was there a woman with them?"

"If there was, I didn't see her."

"When they turned the car in, did they leave it off here, or go out to the plane first?"

"I don't know. I was having lunch when they came back."

"Was anybody here?"

"Jerry was. Hey, Jerry, those guys in the Gulf-stream II, was there a woman with them when they took off?"

"I didn't see one," said a voice from the back room.

I poked my head in the door. The voice belonged to a guy wearing shorts, with his feet propped up on a desk, reading a *Playboy* magazine. He reminded me of Moe, from The Three Stooges.

"They rented a car. Do you know if they went right to the plane with the car before they turned it in?"

"Nope, I wasn't watching. All I remember is one of them came up here and paid the landing fees and turned in the rental and then they left."

"Did they file a flight plan?"

"Don't have to, with us. But they signed the book; let's see." He went out to the main desk and opened a folder.

"Ajax Security, Inc., that's who the plane belongs to. Landed at eight-oh-seven from Los Angeles. Departed eleven fifty-four for San Francisco. Pilot's name is J. E. Dobbs."

"Does it say what airport in San Francisco?"

"Harrison—that's northeast of the city. Good little private field."

I thanked them and started back for my car. As I walked away, I heard one of them say, "Sounds like that guy might have wife troubles or something."

I pulled back on Route 1. Nothing added up. Delia's note said she was going back to Los Angeles, but the plane was headed to San Francisco. At least that's what the sign-out had said. On the other hand, once it got into the air, they could have decided to go anyplace. She must have been in the car when they left Ventana, but nobody saw her get in there or get out at the airport. Had Brad planned an abduction? And if so, to what purpose? They must have tracked us down by running a check on her credit card that she used at Ventana. Even though she hadn't made any charges on it yet, the inn would still have placed a hold with the company for the anticipated amount of her bill, and that would have been traceable. After all my careful planning about not using phones there and everything, I could have kicked myself for forgetting about that. It's the first thing Rick's people would have looked for. They must have followed us right up the coast, the shopping spree in Santa Barbara, the inn at Ventana, dinner at Nepenthe—why, they might even have been checking me out at the Fairmont in San Francisco for all I knew.

I took the car phone out of the glove compartment and dialed San Francisco information for Brad's company. When they put me through to his office, a secretary said he wasn't in at the moment. I asked if he would be, and she said yes, in an hour. I must have set a speed record, getting back to San Francisco.

CHAPTER 30

I'D DECIDED TO show up at Brad's office unannounced. Maybe he'd gone to meet Rick's plane, maybe he'd stashed Delia someplace, who knew? The company was out in a small industrial area not far from the heart of the city. His office was off the main reception area and when the lady behind the desk phoned back with my name, Brad fumed into the lobby, looking suspicious and angry and cold. He motioned me to come with him to what looked like a conference room.

"Do you know where Delia is?" I asked.

"No, do you?"

"I did."

"What's that supposed to mean?"

"It means what it says. Apparently she left Big Sur this morning on Rick's plane."

He's lying, I thought . . . there was something in his voice.

"What the hell was she doing in Big Sur?" he demanded. "I've been looking for her for four days. She was there, with you?"

"I took her there because she wanted me to. Do you want to know why?"

He glared at me with an expression of intense distaste and revulsion. Maybe it wasn't my business to say what I was about to, but Brad must have known exactly where his wife was and why she'd gone on the run in the first place. Anyway, it seemed time to get all this out into the open and if Delia hadn't done it, I would.

"I know all about the goddamn Onion Dungeon and the cameras in the little sex room, Brad. And that Rick got the pictures for you so you could play your shabby little trick on her. She knows it too, if you haven't found that out already."

He looked startled. "I don't know what in hell you're talking about," he spat, but a troubled look passed over his face at the mention of the Dungeon. "What's the Onion Dungeon got to do with anything? And why the hell are you here?"

"C'mon, Brad. It's over," I said. "You and Rick have had your goddamn joke on her and on me. And it's a lot less than funny."

I figured this was just an exercise in verbiage, but I recited to Brad the plot as I saw it: his jealousy over Delia's move to L.A., the notes and pictures and tape from the Onion Dungeon, his getting the satellite receiver so he could watch her, Rick's role in providing the videotape and getting letters sent from all over the country through his network of detective offices.

"This is crazy," Brad said, but he wasn't as hostile.

"I went on the wild-goose chase you people sent me on. But you forgot one thing in all this—that the tape in the video camera that was used to make the pictures, that tape is very rare. Not only that, but it's traceable—right to your doorstep."

"Listen, I don't know what you're talking about," he said. "But if you've been with my wife, I'll . . ."

"You won't do shit. You tormented her with all this extortion stuff and you ought to be in jail for it, though you probably won't be. Sure, I've been with her to get her away from you because she's scared out of her mind."

"Where is she!" he ordered.

"Don't play games with me, Brad. You know damned well she's either with you or your best buddy Rick. It looks like an abduction and I'm getting ready to call the police."

"I haven't spoken to Rick since last night. As a matter of fact, I haven't been able to reach him today. He's supposed to be looking for her."

"Well, he found her," I said. "And took her away in his airplane, presumably up here to San Francisco this afternoon."

He seemed bewildered. "Found her where? All we knew from the TV station is that she'd called in and asked to take vacation, and how did you know about the Onion Dungeon?" he asked, seeming to deflate.

"Delia figured it out, you dummy. It was the only place she could remember where she'd had sex with anybody in a situation like that, and the same type of one-of-a-kind videotape sort of proves it, doesn't it?"

"I don't understand," he said, shaking his head. "What video . . . ?"

I was suddenly beginning to feel a little uncomfortable in this confrontation. At first he'd been belligerent and I thought I had him, but now there was something believable in his protests and the look of bewilderment in his eyes told me he might just be telling the truth.

"You said she was with Rick," Brad said. "He must have found her."

"He did."

"And you said he's bringing her here?"

"His plane took off about noon from Carmel. It was flying to Harrison airport, which is just north of the city."

"So she should have been here hours ago then."

We stood looking at each other for a long moment and when it had ended, I think we both changed our minds about each other.

Brad walked to the far end of the conference room, where there was an intercom on a table. "I'm going to call over to Harrison and see if his plane's there. That's where he keeps it when he comes up here." He punched a button and told his secretary to ring up the airport. A few moments later she flashed that they were on the line and he had a conversation with somebody in operations.

"It got here like you said. About twelve-thirty."

"Was Delia on it?"

"Nobody saw her. The guy on the phone said a limo went out to get passengers."

"What about the pilot? Do you know him?"

"Not really, I've flown with him a few times."

"His name's J. E. Dobbs—does it ring a bell?"

"No. All I know is he's worked for Rick a long time. I think they were in Vietnam together."

I looked at my watch. "It's six forty-five," I said. "Why don't you try calling your house."

He did and nobody answered. Next he called a neighbor and asked him to look out and see if any lights were on. They weren't. He checked his answering service too, and there were no messages from her.

"Where does Rick stay when he's in town?"

"He keeps a suite at the Fairmont," Brad said. "He's got the security contract there."

"Nice place. I just stayed there last night," I remarked. "Maybe my room was next to his."

Brad tried it and nobody answered. Then he phoned the front desk and was told the suite was empty. He also tried Rick's offices in San Francisco and L.A. Nobody knew a thing, except he said he was going to San Francisco today.

"She have any friends in town that she might stay with?"

"A few. I'll call around to the ones I know, but I don't have her phone book." He spent the next half hour on the phone—but nothing doing. Brad hung up the receiver and sat heavily in a chair.

"Can you think of anyplace else they might be?" I asked.

"I don't know, but they've been here eight hours or so, if she's with him."

"Maybe they went somewhere to have an honest hour," I offered. "Maybe she opened up to him about you and her suspicions about all this."

"I doubt it," he said. "Delia doesn't really like Rick. Doesn't trust him. And I think he feels the same way about her."

"Why not?"

"He dated her before I met her. He was married, but he wasn't really clean with her about it. Just let her assume he wasn't. Then she ran into his wife and found out. It really set her off. She and the wife had words, I don't know exactly what, but it was unpleasant. A few weeks later the wife commits suicide. I think Rick blames Delia for some of that, and Delia blames him for it too. It's complicated."

"Was he really hurt by her?" I asked. "I mean, when Delia bugged out?"

"It's funny you ask that," Brad said. "He never told me that in so many words. After the breakup, and after Mishoki died, I asked him one time if he'd mind if I asked Delia out. I can't remember exactly what he said, but it was to the effect of 'sure, go ahead.' I think, deep down, he loved Mishoki, even if he did fool around a little. She was having some emotional problems and wasn't very easy to live with at times. Matter of fact, when I say 'fool around,' as far as I know, Delia was the only one Rick fooled around with in all the years I knew him. I still don't think either one really likes the other. Eventually, I guess, they made their peace because Rick and I are such good friends."

"Well, you're not going to like this either," I told him, "but if it wasn't you sending those letters and pictures to her, who else might it have been?"

"Who knows?" Brad said.

"Well, who had access to the video camera tape at that Dungeon place, where you and she got it on that night?"

"Rick—no—are you suggesting that Rick's involved in this?"

"His company runs the security for that hole," I said. "Certainly he'd have access to the tapes if he wanted. If it's true that's where they came from, who else could it be?"

"That's preposterous!" Brad exclaimed. "I've known Rick fifteen years."

The picture was formed now. Rick. He certainly had access to watching Delia on the tube. He didn't like her—she'd shafted him too. And there was his obvious ability to send letters from almost anyplace. And I remembered him telling me about those voice modulators that disguise you on the phone. And probably by hook or by crook his people had the capability of tracing her through her credit cards. When you thought about it, it made a lot of sense.

"Look," I told him, "whether you believe it or not, what's he doing with her right now—he's had her for seven or eight hours?"

"Doing what?"

"I don't know. But I'll tell you this, whoever is behind this has a twisted, sadistic, and probably vicious personality. If I'm right, Delia could be in actual danger right now."

"Good God," Brad said in almost a moan. "Good God." His face seemed to ashen.

"We aren't doing a whole lot of good sitting around here," I told him. "First, I think the police ought to be brought into this right now."

"Well, that . . . that's going to pose some complications," he said. "I mean, she told me time and again she didn't want the police involved. That if they were, she'd have to tell them everything and it would get leaked out and—"

"Better that than the possibility of having her hurt," I broke in.

"And what about Rick?" he asked. "He's my best friend. What if he's not involved in any of this?"

"What if he is?" I said.

CHAPTER 31

IT'S NOT ALWAYS a good thing to keep taking your pulse and asking yourself whether you're right or you're wrong; sometimes you've got to go by instinct. This was on my mind as I turned the BMW down Barrow Street toward the Onion Dungeon. Brad sat beside me, jumpy but somehow meditative. He'd digested a lot this evening and, like spectators in a Shakespearean drama, we were now rushing toward noises in another part of the forest.

Brad had agreed to call the police but, abiding by Delia's wishes, withheld particulars of the blackmail and also the ramifications to do with Rick. The cops sounded sympathetic enough, but as it happened, the detective said Delia's disappearance fell into the category of a 'missing person' and the department's policy was to do nothing for forty-eight hours because the so-called missing person almost invariably turned up during that period. They didn't guarantee in what shape. In any case, they suggested that Brad go home and wait.

I wasn't buying that and neither was he. There was only one connection in town we hadn't tried and that

was the Onion Dungeon. Brad phoned there looking
for Rick and was told he wasn't there. But I remembered Sunshine, the bartender, had mentioned to me
Rick had his own set of keys, and the Onion Dungeon
was a pretty big place, especially with a crowd of
degenerate turds hopping around and diddling with
each other on its various dance floors and in its dark
dens.

I pulled up in the parking lot and we went in
through the front door. Sunshine was behind the bar
and Brad greeted her, shouting over the din. He asked
if she'd seen Rick.

"Not tonight. Didn't know he's in town."

He asked if Ray or Jeff was there.

"They'll be in later," she said.

Brad led me downstairs to his old haunt. The door
was where I'd suspected it was when I'd been there
the night before—off the long, narrow foyer. Some of
the rooms had glass windows and even for an old
hand like me, the kind of grabass that was transpiring
behind them was close to shocking. A lot of people
were milling around in the hallway and a guy I took
for a bouncer paced up and down sort of like a guard
at Sing Sing, peering into the windows as he passed.
I supposed, as Sunshine had told me, it was to make
sure that "nobody goes too far."

We came to the end of the hall, where Ray and
Jeff's private room was. It had no window and the
door was locked. You couldn't tell if there were any
lights on inside either. Brad and I looked at each other
in consternation. Loud rock music vibrated every-

where. It seemed like another dead end. But just then I noticed a guy leaning up against the opposite wall, sort of eyeing us. He was a big heavyset man in his early fifties, bald on top but with gray hair on the sides, and he immediately reminded me of Peter Boyle in *The Brink's Job*. I remembered what the desk clerk at Ventana had said about the man who'd been with Rick when Delia left and, well, it was crazy, but I decided to give it a stab.

"You got any keys on you?" I asked Brad.

"Keys?"

"Yeah, if you do, take them out and act like you've got a key that fits this door here," I said.

He looked at me like I was nuts, but I just nodded and he got the message. Brad took out a set of keys from his pocket that looked like they opened everything in San Francisco. Must have been the keys to his plant. He selected one and played like he was trying to insert it in the door lock to Ray and Jeff's private room. He hadn't even gotten it to where it looked like it fit before the big bald fellow strode over and put an arm on his hand.

"Private party going on in there," he said.

"We're friends of the owners," I told him.

"Doesn't matter, pal," Baldy said. "There's people in there don't want to be disturbed."

"We were just going in for a look around," Brad said.

"No, you're not. Like I told you, pal, that's a private party. Why don't you try one of these other rooms? There's all sorts of good stuff going on in there."

"You one of Rick Olsen's people?" I said to him.

He gave me a look that would have frozen ice all over again.

"I think you guys have outstayed your welcome," he said. "Time to go someplace else."

Brad was staring at Baldy, but I tugged at his sleeve and led him back upstairs. The chances were that Delia was locked in that flesh bin with Rick, for whatever ungodly purposes. I told Brad to come with me to the bar. My stomach was churning, but I tried not to let it show. Sunshine was serving drinks at one end. I ordered two beers and then leaned over to her.

"You wouldn't by any chance have a set of keys to that private owners' room would you?"

"Honey, I don't even have a set of keys to the liquor closet," she said. "Ray or Jeff come in early and open it, and I get out my stuff, then they lock it up again and take off till playtime starts. Why, you and Brad got something going?"

I paid for the beer and motioned Brad to a corner.

"If they've got surveillance cameras in here, I expect there's a monitoring place in here somewhere," I said. "You have any ideas?"

"Well, the offices are upstairs," he said. "It's a pretty big floor, maybe it's there."

Brad knew the way and we took our beers and headed up a narrow flight to the second story. There were several long hallways with doors leading off them.

"That's Ray and Jeff's office," he said. "I never did it, but they have people they know come in and do dope and stuff."

It figured. "What about down here?" I asked.

We walked further down a dark hall lined with tables turned on their sides and chairs stacked to the ceiling. At the end was a door marked Private. You couldn't tell if anyone was inside, so I tried the knob. It was locked. I looked at Brad, then knocked three times on it rapidly, like you used to see in old detective films. A moment later a guy opened it up with an expectant look on his face. Behind him I saw a bank of little television-like screens glowing in the darkened room.

"We'd like to talk to you," I said.

"There's no admittance here," the guy said. "This is the security room." He was about thirty, with greasy hair, but wearing a white shirt and tie, and I also noticed he was wearing white sneakers. He moved to shut the door, but I lunged into it hard as I could, knocking him back into the room.

"What the goddamn hell—?" he croaked.

I grabbed him by the collar and shoved him down in an armless swivel chair.

"Where's the monitor for the private room?"

"What private room. Who are you?"

I pulled out the pistol from my waistband that had been my companion for most of the past week and pressed the muzzle hard against his temple.

"The owners' private room, downstairs. Don't tempt me."

"Please, mister. It's not in here," he said.

"Don't screw with me, damnit. Where is it?"

"You'd better tell him," Brad said, and sounded as mad as I was.

"It's in the other room," the guy said.

"What other room?"

"Across the hall—the owners' room."

"Is it open?"

"No."

"You got a key?"

"Me? No."

I cocked the pistol, slowly. It hadn't occurred to me when I bought it, but this was a good reason to have a revolver instead of an automatic. When you cock a revolver, you hear a big sinister *click* as the hammer draws back and the cylinder locks on a round. That sound was not lost on Mr. Security Monitor. Jesus, I thought, I'm really pointing a gun at a guy.

"There're some keys in that drawer," he said, pointing to a desk. "For God's sake, mister, take that gun away from my head, will you please."

"Just as soon as we get the keys and get into that room," I said.

Brad found a key ring in the desk's top drawer and brought it over.

"Which one is it?" I said.

"That silver-looking one."

"All right, let's all go over and see about what you

say." I stuck the pistol in my jacket side pocket like Jimmy Cagney did in *Angels with Dirty Faces,* and yanked Mr. Security to his feet, pushing him ahead of me. I stopped when we were near the door, and Brad put the key into the lock. It worked. The room was pitch-black and Brad reached inside fumbling for a light switch. He found one that lit some dim overhead can lights, which illuminated a scene of boundless infamy. I nudged Mr. Security in and closed the door. The walls, floor to ceiling and even the ceiling itself, were covered with explicit pornography that almost defied description. It would have been tailor-made for Justice Potter Stewart's declaration that while he couldn't define pornography in the law, he "knew it when he saw it." Around the room were scattered dingy old sofas and chairs, covered in a kind of black felt material. Even the windows on a far wall were painted black, and an air of carnality hung over everything.

On one wall was the biggest TV monitor I've ever seen. It must have been four or five feet square. So this was where Ray and Jeff and their friends got their jollies. I held the gun on the guy and told Brad to turn on the monitor. It took a few moments to warm up and then an image of degradation suddenly appeared before us.

Almost large as life, Delia's face was looking right at us. There was a device covering her nose and she had some kind of rubber ball strapped in her mouth. What looked like a red sweater was wrapped tightly around her neck, choking her, and the sleeves of it were being jerked back like they were reins on a horse. Naked, she was trussed up in stirrups that hung from a ceiling so that she was leaning forward with her feet hanging down, and there was a terrified, wild-eyed expression on her face. Hunched behind her was a figure I guessed was Rick, wearing form-fitting leather pants with the fly cut out. He had on a Batman mask and was flogging Delia with a cat-o'-nine-tails. Whenever she tried to scream, Rick would pull up on the sweater sleeves, obviously cutting off her air supply.

For a moment I was speechless. So was Brad, but I heard him gasp.

"Jesus," croaked the security man.

"Goddamn filthy whore murdering bitch!" Rick's voice came over the audio. "You killed her and you're gonna die a good, slow death tonight, you fucking asshole. You did this to me! You *did* it!" He yanked back on the sweater sleeves again so that her neck reared back, tightening the rubber ball, and you could actually watch Delia's face turning blue.

"Jesus," the security man repeated. The horror of what we were witnessing on the screen seemed to cascade past in slow motion, monstrously out of control.

"How do I get into that fucking room!" I yelled at the guy.

"I don't know. I really don't. I think the only keys are the owners' and Mr. Olsen's."

"Brad, go back to that security room. There's a phone on the desk. Call the police right now!" I said. "Then come downstairs."

As Brad rushed out, my mind was racing about what to do with the security man, but he solved that problem for me.

"Listen, mister, I don't know anything about this. This is . . . I don't want nothin' to do with this here. It's gotta be stopped."

I glanced again at the screen as Rick yanked Delia's head back with the red sweater so hard I thought he might have broken her neck.

"All right, goddamnit," I said. "Then if you want to stop it, you come with me, but I guarantee you, you're gonna get shot dead if you screw up."

I ran to the end of the hallway and down the stairs and heard the security guy's footsteps pounding behind me. We raced through the main room, knocking aside dancing people, and flew down the stairs to the basement. Baldy was still leaning against his wall outside the door to the room. Surprise was out of the question. I had the gun in my hand and when he saw me coming, he reached for his own gun from a shoulder holster. I tried to fire a shot but couldn't stop in time to aim and he fired first from some professional-looking two-handed crouch. The concussion was terrific and the bullet grazed my shoulder, spinning me against the wall and to my knees. I don't think any time in my life I've ever felt brave. I might have felt exhilaration or fear or even recklessness, but never brave, and yet this was something I needed to feel right now because my first impulse was to run and hide. Other people in the hallway were shouting and cursing and scattering in all directions.

"For chrissake, Mr. Molinari," the security man screamed, "he's murdering her in there!"

But Baldy simply raised his gun again and fired, hitting the security man in the chest, which knocked him about five feet backward. For all he was worth, the bouncer who we'd seen earlier looking through windows in the other rooms fled past me and disappeared up the steps. By that time I was able to raise my revolver again and cock it with my thumb. Baldy was headed over to finish me off when I squeezed the trigger. I knew it must have hit him someplace midsection, but he didn't seem fazed; he just lumbered on toward me. I didn't cock the gun again but used the double action to get off another shot, which I think missed because before I could fire again, all three hundred pounds of him was on me. His hands were wrapped around my neck and he was choking the wind out of me when all of a sudden he got a strange, glassy look in his eyes and collapsed onto my chest. I knew I'd hit him with that first shot. It took all my strength to roll him off and get to my feet. My shoulder was a little numb, but his bullet hadn't seemed to have entered anything. The hallway was deserted now and the ugly stench of gunpowder nitrate hovered in the air. I ran over to the door where Rick had

Delia and pounded hard as I could, shouting to open up. Just then Brad came dashing down the stairs.

"Look in that fat guy's clothes and see if he's got a key to this room!" I hollered. Brad began rummaging through Baldy's pants.

There isn't time for this, I thought. The door to the room where Delia was wasn't anything fancy and neither was the lock. For an instant I considered shooting it off, but then I realized I didn't know from the monitor picture just where Delia was in the room. Bullets go anywhere and I could have killed her accidentally.

I clamored down the hall to the first of the rooms with a window and saw that inside, the naked occupants were blissfully unaware of what was going on out in the hall. I threw open the door to confront the startled faces of about a dozen men and women engaged in sex acts it would take all day to describe.

"Listen!" I yelled. "I need your help. There's a man in the next room strangling a woman to death. You've got to help me get through the door." Consternation was the featured look on all their faces, but slowly several of the nude men began to stand up. One went toward a peg on the wall to fetch his pants.

"There's no time for that! She's dying!" I shouted.

Brad had seen me and ran to the other rooms himself and it wasn't half a minute before we had a mob of naked people seething through the hall. I put my arms around four or five guys and pressed them together sort of like a rugby scrum and we crashed into the door. It gave but didn't break. Another group saw what we were up to and formed their own scrum. When they hit it, it splintered and a tangle of naked men along with a woman or two burst inside.

By now, Rick had pulled off his Batman mask and taken Delia out of the sling he had her in and was bent over, choking her from behind with the sweater wrapped around her throat. I pointed the pistol at him, shouting, "Get away from her, get away!" but it was almost as though he couldn't hear me at all. He was still screaming hysterical curses at her, his face a grotesque contortion of fury and tears. Several of the naked men rushed over and pulled him off and held him down on the floor as he writhed and railed insanely.

Delia was alive but barely conscious and in shock. I took off my jacket to cover her, while Brad held her head in his hands and stroked her cheeks, trying to reassure her it was over.

"What the hell went on here?" one of the naked men asked. Later I reflected how strange it was that when they were all in the same pile together, they seemed to have no sense of their sexuality, but now, standing around in a different situation, both men and women tried to cover their private parts with their hands.

"The police are coming, you'd better get dressed," I said. "It's over. And thanks a lot."

I looked at Rick, who was still being restrained by four of the guys. He seemed to have come down from his madness. Brad was staring at him in absolute disbelief.

"She killed her, you know?" Rick said in a strange, measured monotone. "She didn't have to do it, but, no, she was just 'being honest.' "

"What are you talking about?" Brad said.

"Your precious wife, Brad—she killed Mishoki," he continued. "She killed Mishoki just as sure as if she'd driven the knife herself."

"You're crazy!" Brad yelled at him.

"Mishoki wouldn't have known a thing if Delia hadn't sent that goddamn Christmas card to me— with a picture of herself on the front of it, for chrissake—and wrote 'lots of love,' at the bottom, too. That was really brilliant, wasn't it? Sending it to my home!"

"Delia didn't know you were married," Brad spat. "You didn't tell her either, did you?"

Rick began to sob. "And then, when they met, she never had to say anything to Mishoki. Mishoki really didn't know what was going on. She could have just let it go when Mishoki told her she was my wife. All she had to do was say, 'Yes, I've met your husband.' She could have made up something—like that she was interviewing me for a television story— anything! But, no, what did she do? She told her everything! Actually talked to her about it! Said that she'd been seeing me for months. Said that I'd told her I wasn't married. My God—do you know what that means to a Japanese! And to think that I actually loved her, when I should have been loving Mishoki! So the week before Christmas, she kills herself!"

"For chrissake, Rick . . ." Brad said.

"Honesty!" he groaned. "That's what comes from Delia's *honesty*. At least Mishoki was honorable!"

Two policemen entered the room, wading through a sea of nudity.

"What's happened here?" they asked.

"It's a long story," I said.

CHAPTER 32

THE WEATHER IN L.A. is balmy and tomorrow is Christmas Eve. My flight leaves in the morning. The news shows pictures of snow-covered streets in New York and the storm has even blown as far south as my parents' town in North Carolina. Long time now since I've seen a white Christmas.

It's been almost a week since the affair between Delia and Rick reached its tawdry finale. I hadn't seen her since then, though she'd called me two days afterward and thanked me. I figured it would take a while for her to get over it, if she ever did. Naturally, as soon as the police got involved, the story leaked out to the press but just in pretty general terms. No photos or videotapes were published, but it was big news around the country. In L.A., naturally, the papers treated it like the greatest story since the Resurrection.

Rick posted bond and got out of jail on charges of extortion, abduction, assault, and attempted murder. His lawyer indicated they would put on an insanity defense.

This morning Delia called and asked me to lunch.

I met her at a cozy little place near her TV studio in between her midday and early evening broadcasts. She was wearing a prim blue suit with a white scarf and her hair pulled back and piled on top of her head, which, ever since I'd known her, was the way she wore it when something serious was on her mind. At least she wasn't wearing a red sweater.

"Well, Johnny, you can't say it hasn't been an interesting few months."

I looked at her across the table. She seemed a little worn and for the first time I perceived some slight wrinkles around her eyes and mouth and neck. I guess they were there all the time, I'd just never noticed them before. Still, to me, she seemed ageless.

"No, I can't say that," I said.

"I know I keep telling you, but I can't thank you enough. I wish there was something I could do."

"Well, you're buying me lunch," I told her. "How about that?"

"It all still seems so unreal."

"It isn't, but it's over."

She told me that she and Brad had separated and that she'd quit the station in L.A. and taken a job with a rival network down in San Diego. She'd be leaving the day after Christmas.

"Does the station have that satellite hookup around the country so I can still watch you if I wanted?"

"No, it's just local," she said.

She told me she'd known it was coming with Brad even before all this recent mess started, that she'd postponed it long enough. I told her I was sorry, because I thought Brad was a nice guy. In fact, I really did.

"I don't know who he's more broken up about, me or Rick," she said squeamishly.

"What are you doing for Christmas?" I asked.

"Broadcasting the news."

"Not going home?"

"I've used up my vacation." She hesitated for a moment and looked at me with her most solemn, earnest expression.

"Johnny, you're upset with me, right?"

I took a sip of coffee and slowly shook my head. "I don't think so, Delia."

"It's not because of what Rick said—that night—is it?" She took a deep breath of resignation and finished her martini.

"Not at all."

"Because I want you to understand that what I did—what he said I did—really didn't happen quite that way. When she came up to me to tell me they were married, I was utterly shocked. I might have thought of telling her it wasn't true, or made something else up, but I just couldn't think. I just blurted out the truth."

"Honesty was always your strong suit," I said.

"And a woman's dead because of it."

"You didn't kill her, Delia. If anyone did, it was Rick. She was *his* wife, not yours."

"Thank you, Johnny." I noticed a little tear in the corner of her eye. It was only the third time in all these years I had seen Delia cry, and never because of anything I'd done, one way or the other. She brushed it away and straightened up.

"Well, I guess I'd better be getting along. I'm trying to pack up my apartment between shows. I'm not very good at it, though."

"At what?"

"Packing," she said.

"I would have thought you'd be excellent," I observed. It was a dig I really didn't mean to say, but she seemed not to notice it.

I walked her out to her car and before she got in, we stood there looking at each other for an awkward moment.

"And you still won't tell me what it was you did with all those guys that let you narrow down your list?" I asked.

"Nope. Besides, it's not important anymore, is it?"

"No, just curiosity."

"Good, let it stay that way," she said.

Whatever it was, I expect it was going to the grave with her, like whoever Deep Throat was in Watergate.

"Well, let me ask you this," I said. "Was this something you did with Rick?"

"No, that's why it was so strange. But I think now he must have believed I had."

"How about with me?"

She glanced down, as though shocked that I'd asked the question, which made it all the more tantalizing, but I let it go. Perhaps life needs these little mysteries. When Delia looked back at me, there was an expectant glow in her sun-filled green eyes and I could see the little flecks of black inside them. Then, spontaneously, we both leaned toward each other at the same time, me to place a little good-bye kiss on her cheek and she turning her head ever so slightly to receive it. I think that was the most bitter-sweet moment I've ever experienced.

THAT EVENING I'D arranged drinks with Meredith at the Peninsula bar. She was lovely in gray slacks and a white silk blouse and we sat at Toby Burr's regular table by the fake gas-log fire. Bland Christmas music with no words still played over the sound system. Meredith's eyes blinked with excitement and she had the loveliest smile on her face. In a way it reminded me of the smile Delia had given me that first time in this same room when I'd seen her at the table with her friends. For some reason, just now, that seemed like a helluva long time ago.

"You've certainly had a cracking few weeks," she said. "You're a hero in all the newspapers."

"Well, I'm not."

"She's a beautiful woman. I can see why your business is unfinished."

"It's finished," I said.

Meredith was headed home in the morning to spend Christmas with her folks in the Valley.

"And you're going back east?" she asked.

"Sure am. Ten A.M. flight."

"New York?"

"Nope, to Carolina."

"I'd like to see it sometime," she said.

"Carolina?"

"New York too."

"Well, I'll be there after New Year's and probably for quite a while. I guess I've done about all the damage I can do out here—to myself, that is."

"Like me to come visit you there sometime?" she said.

"I'd be delighted," I told her, and I was surprised I really meant it. There was something solid there, not just some gauzy unattainable dream.

Just then Burr walked up to the table. I'd also arranged to see him tonight, later, for dinner. He'd demanded it after receiving the final version of my script.

After I introduced Meredith, she said she'd better leave to get ready for her trip.

"Got lots of presents to put together," she said. Then, reaching into her bag, she took out a little gift-wrapped package about the size of a book.

"I already did this one for you." She handed it to me with her blue eyes glowing.

I opened it and it was a lovely framed sketch of me, reclining in a beach chair, that she'd obviously drawn the day I took her to the ocean. Both Burr and I oohed and aahed over it. It was really excellent and I'd never even noticed she was doing it. I'd just thought she'd been drawing pictures of people walking up and down the beach.

"Well," she said, giving me a quick but inviting kiss on the lips, "see you next year."

"So, YOU SLY old bastard," Burr said with his usual charm, "you've done it again."

"Yes, she's nice, isn't she?"

"I'm not talking about her, you moron. It's the script—it's wonderful!"

"I'm glad you like it."

"Like it! I love it! It's got Academy Awards written all over it!"

"I told you to trust me."

"You'll still drive me to the grave with that line, but right now I don't care," Burr chortled.

"You just smell money," I told him.

"It's absolutely perfect, Johnny. I'd never imagined it in a thousand years, the way you ended it— 'the knight in shining armor slays the dragon, but *doesn't* get the *girl*!' There hasn't been a movie like this since *Shane*!"

"Shit happens," I said.

"How on earth with all that other going on you managed to get this screenplay finished, I'll never understand."

"Maybe I work better with a few distractions."

"That TV girl," he went on, "I told you she was trouble. Was I right?"

"She was *in* trouble."

"And dragged you into it with her. I still don't understand how you cracked the case. From what the papers said, there was some kind of list she gave you—was that what kept you busy back east all this time?"

"Just don't forget, that was also when I wrote your script," I reminded him.

"So how'd she come up with this list? The papers said they were all her former lovers."

"Not all of them. She'd narrowed it down."

"How?"

"It was something she did with some of them that she never did with the others."

"Like what? She was a hum-jobber or used ben-wa balls or something? Am I right?"

"She won't say."

"Christ," Burr groused, "what kinds of people are those, anyway—all tangled up in sexual blackmail and dirty movies and kinky leather and whips and stuff?"

"Who are you to talk, you old pornographer!"

AFTER DINNER I went alone up to the hotel's roof garden. A cool Pacific breeze had blown the smog eastward to irritate the people out in the canyons and valleys and for once in Los Angeles the skies were clear and black and brilliant with stars and the planet Venus outshined everything else in heaven. The sight gave me a lift from the deep, almost inexpressible melancholy I'd been feeling the past week or so. After all, I'd killed a man; even though the district attorney ruled it justifiable homicide, I had looked into the abyss and saw the abyss looking back at me. Not a comfortable feeling.

It was getting late and I thought about going down to my room to turn on the TV set. Most likely this would be the last time I'd ever see her, unless I wanted to go to San Diego someday and watch her show from a hotel room. Instead, I sat down in one of the pool lounges and lit up a smuggled Havana Monte Cristo while a single cloud drifted high overhead, backlit only by starlight.

Honesty—now *there* was a subject of magnitude. In a way it was a source of Delia's splendor; but in the instance of Rick's wife, she'd parlayed naked honesty almost into indecency. Yet her passion for honesty seemed to be the glue that held her psyche together, a sort of holy faith without which she'd be lost.

Overall I don't think I'd done much wrong, but I hadn't done much right, either. I'd sacrificed some of my own integrity by making a play for another man's wife, but there was more to it than animal instinct. I'd needed a kind of vindication from her but of course she couldn't give it, so I'd had to find it for myself. Sort of like a detective returning to the scene of a crime to reenact it in his search for clues—or, more likely, the criminal drawn back to re-live it. And what was this strange vindication? In the end, it finally boils down to this: peace of mind over piece of ass. It wasn't what I'd expected, but there it is, and all the rest only turned out to be like having a rock in your shoe for twenty years.

I got up and headed back to my room. There was more work to do tonight. I'd bought a bunch of Christmas cards I was going to send to all the guys I'd met during my quest for Delia's nemesis. I wanted to tell them I was sorry about any misunderstanding, that the affair was over and solved. Somehow I figured this would close things out from my end.

The big old cloud had sailed over the San Gabriel Mountains by now, on its way eastward. It might, I mused, even beat me back to Carolina. I stubbed out most of my eight-dollar cigar before getting on the elevator. Wouldn't want to violate the law. One day, maybe somebody will write a movie about all this, but it's not going to be me.

ABOUT THE AUTHOR

WINSTON GROOM is the author of ten books, including the bestselling *Forrest Gump, Gump & Company,* and *Gumpisms: The Wit and Wisdom of Forrest Gump.* He also wrote the acclaimed Vietnam War novel *Better Times Than These,* as well as the prize-winning novel *As Summers Die,* the prize-winning Civil War history, *Shrouds of Glory,* and the Pulitzer Prize nominee, *Conversations with the Enemy.*

He lives in Point Clear, Alabama, and in the mountains of North Carolina.

LARGE PRINT EDITIONS

SEE THE DIFFERENCE

Random House Large Print Editions are available in bookstores throughout the country. For a complete listing of our wide selection of current bestsellers and timeless favorites write:

Random House Large Print
201 East 50th Street, Dept. CK, 23-2
New York, NY 10022

For Customer Service or to place a direct order
call toll free: (800) 726-0600 or fax: (410) 857-1948

Our email address is audio@randomhouse.com

Visit our Random House Web Site at:
www.randomhouse.com

LARGE PRINT EDITIONS

Look for these at your local bookstore

American Heart Association, *American Heart Association Cookbook, 5th Edition Abridged*
Angelou, Maya, *Even the Stars Look Lonesome*
Ben Artzi-Pelossof, Noa, *In the Name of Sorrow and Hope*
Benchley, Peter, *White Shark*
Berendt, John, *Midnight in the Garden of Good and Evil*
Brando, Marlon with Robert Lindsey, *Brando: Songs My Mother Taught Me*
Bragg, Rick, *All Over but the Shoutin'*
Brinkley, David, *David Brinkley*
Brinkley, David, *Everyone Is Entitled to My Opinion*
Byatt, A. S., *Babel Tower*
Carr, Caleb, *The Angel of Darkness*
Carter, Jimmy, *Living Faith*
Carter, Jimmy, *Sources of Strength*
Chopra, Deepak, *The Path to Love*
Chopra, Deepak, *Ageless Body, Timeless Mind*
Ciaro, Joe, editor, *The Random House Large Print Book of Jokes and Anecdotes*
Crichton, Michael, *Disclosure*
Crichton, Michael, *The Lost World*
Crichton, Michael, *Airframe*
Cronkite, Walter, *A Reporter's Life*
Daley, Rosie, *In the Kitchen with Rosie*
Dunne, Dominick, *A Season in Purgatory*
Dunne, Dominick, *Another City, Not My Own*
Flagg, Fannie, *Daisy Fay and the Miracle Man*
Flagg, Fannie, *Fried Green Tomatoes at the Whistle Stop Cafe*
Fulghum, Robert, *Maybe (Maybe Not): Second Thoughts from a Secret Life*

(continued)

García Márquez, Gabriel, *Of Love and Other Demons*
Gilman, Dorothy, *Mrs. Pollifax and the Lion Killer*
Gilman, Dorothy, *Mrs. Pollifax, Innocent Tourist*
Guest, Judith, *Errands*
Hailey, Arthur, *Detective*
Hepburn, Katharine, *Me*
Hiaasen, Carl, *Lucky You*
James, P. D., *A Certain Justice*
Koontz, Dean, *Dark Rivers of the Heart*
Koontz, Dean, *Intensity*
Koontz, Dean, *Sole Survivor*
Koontz, Dean, *Ticktock*
Krantz, Judith, *Scruples Two*
Krantz, Judith, *Spring Collection*
Landers, Ann, *Wake Up and Smell the Coffee!*
le Carré, John, *Our Game*
le Carré, John, *The Tailor of Panama*
Lindbergh, Anne Morrow, *Gift from the Sea*
Ludlum, Robert, *The Road to Omaha*
Masson, Jeffrey Moussaieff, *Dogs Never Lie About Love*
Mayle, Peter, *Anything Considered*
Mayle, Peter, *Chasing Cézanne*
McCarthy, Cormac, *The Crossing*
Meadows, Audrey with Joe Daley, *Love, Alice*
Michaels, Judith, *Acts of Love*
Morrison, Toni, *Paradise*
Mother Teresa, *A Simple Path*
Patterson, Richard North, *Eyes of a Child*
Patterson, Richard North, *The Final Judgment*
Patterson, Richard North, *Silent Witness*
Peck, M. Scott, M.D., *Denial of the Soul*
Phillips, Louis, editor, *The Random House Large Print
        Treasury of Best-Loved Poems*
Pope John Paul II, *Crossing the Threshold of Hope*
Pope John Paul II, *The Gospel of Life*

(continued)

Powell, Colin with Joseph E. Persico, *My American Journey*
Preston, Richard, *The Cobra Event*
Puzo, Mario, *The Last Don*
Rampersad, Arnold, *Jackie Robinson*
Rendell, Ruth, *The Keys to the Street*
Rendell, Ruth, *Road Rage*
Rice, Anne, *Servant of the Bones*
Rice, Anne, *Violin*
Rice, Anne, *Pandora*
Salamon, Julie and Jill Weber, *The Christmas Tree*
Shaara, Jeff, *Gods and Generals*
Smith, Martin Cruz, *Rose*
Snead, Sam with Fran Pirozzolo, *The Game I Love*
Truman, Margaret, *Murder on the Potomac*
Truman, Margaret, *Murder at the National Gallery*
Truman, Margaret, *Murder in the House*
Tyler, Anne, *Ladder of Years*
Tyler, Anne, *Saint Maybe*
Updike, John, *Golf Dreams*
Weil, Andrew, M.D., *Eight Weeks to Optimum Health*
Whitney, Phyllis A., *Amethyst Dreams*